ANYONE BUT HIM

ANYONE BUT HIM

Sheila O'Flanagan

headline

First published in 2004
by HEADLINE BOOK PUBLISHING

10 9 8 7 6 5 4 3 2

Cataloguing in Publication Data is
available from the British Library

ISBN 0 7553 0752 6 (hardback)
ISBN 0 7553 0755 0 (trade paperback)

Typeset in Galliard by Palimpsest Book Production Limited,
Polmont, Stirlingshire
Printed and bound in Great Britain by
Clays Ltd St Ives plc

HEADLINE BOOK PUBLISHING
A division of Hodder Headline
338 Euston Road
LONDON NW1 3BH
www.headline.co.uk
www.hodderheadline.com

With much love to my mother who might go on a cruise herself one day . . .

Acknowledgements

Thanks as ever to the following people:

Agent and friend Carole Blake who looks after my career so well

My brilliant editor Marion Donaldson who gently but firmly keeps me on the right track

The Headline teams in Ireland and the UK who work so hard on my behalf

My family and friends who are always there for me

Colm for sharing the duvet at night

Finally, and as always, thank you to all of you who've supported me by buying my books over the past few years. I hope you enjoy some time out with Andie, Jin and Cora. If you'd like to contact me with your thoughts on *Anyone But Him* or my other books, please visit my website at www.sheilaoflanagan.net. I'd love to hear from you.

Chapter 1

The Four Seasons: No 3 in F Major (Autumn) – Vivaldi

Andie Corcoran walked out of the bedroom, shook her burnished copper hair back from her face and cleared her throat.

'OK,' she said. 'Not that I want to sound like a walking cliché or anything, but – does my bum look big in this?' She turned slowly so that Tom could see the back view of the figure-hugging electric-blue dress she was wearing.

He whistled slowly as she turned. 'Yes,' he said.

'Yes!' She whirled around and her eyes, soft grey with little flecks of the brightest green, stared at him in horror. 'Yes!?'

He laughed. 'Oh, come on, Andie. Of course your bum doesn't look big in it. You have a lovely bum. Neat but kind of voluptuous. And you look amazing. Stunning, even. It's so – so unlike you. And it's enough to make me want to rip that dress off you straight away.'

She tried to glare at him but couldn't quite keep the twinkle out of her eyes. 'Well you can't. Not yet. Just wait here a minute.' She disappeared back into the bedroom and reappeared a moment later, this time wearing a button-fronted dress in maroon silk. 'Is this better?' She turned around again.

Tom exhaled slowly. 'It's more what you usually wear.'

'More boring?'

He hesitated. 'More ordinary,' he said eventually. 'But honestly, love, you'll look great no matter what you wear. The clothes aren't important.'

'The clothes are vitally important,' she corrected him. 'And I don't want to look great – even though great is exaggerating just a fraction anyway, given that I weigh at least half a stone more than this time last year. Great isn't good enough, Tom. I have to look sensational.'

'I suppose it's pointless saying that you always look sensational to me?' He walked over to her and began to undo the tiny buttons at the front of the dress.

'Utterly pointless,' she agreed as she wriggled away from him. 'I know it doesn't usually matter very much to me what I wear, but this is the one day of the year that it does.'

'Another year, another wrinkle.' He grinned at her. 'And you're only thirty-two. Hardly pension territory yet.'

'Old enough to think I'd have more sense.' She pressed her fingers to her temples. 'I guess if I was really mature I'd just grab something out of the back of the wardrobe and fling it on, but I'm not quite ready for that yet. Besides, I don't want to be the one who looks as though she couldn't afford to be there.'

Tom grinned. 'I'll never quite get to grips with the whole designer oneupmanship that goes on among women,' he told her. 'Although I'm glad that you don't normally fret so much about what you're going to wear.'

'Most of the time it doesn't really matter,' commented Andie. 'But this is different.' She leaned against the wall and looked at him pleadingly. 'So what do you think?'

'If you want to look demurely sensational and more like your usual self then I'd wear the maroon,' said Tom. 'But if you want to make a statement about being an elegant sex-bomb, the blue's the one.'

Suddenly Andie started to giggle. 'Sex-bomb. If only.'

'You are to me.' Tom put his hands on her shoulders. 'You know you are.'

His lips found hers and this time she didn't stop him as he fumbled at the buttons.

'Hell's teeth,' he muttered. 'There's enough of them.'

'Designed to slow men like you down,' she murmured breath-lessly.

'Men like me!' He slid the dress off her shoulders so that it suddenly rippled to the floor. 'What d'you mean, men like me?'

2

'Sexy men.' She pushed her hands beneath his black T-shirt. 'Stamina men.'

'I'm glad you think I'm sexy. But stamina?'

'Oh, you've got that in spades.' She led him through the open door and into the bedroom. His eyebrows lifted as he couldn't help but notice the scene of devastation. Dresses, blouses, skirts, shirts plus shoes in a variety of heel heights were scattered in disarray so that it resembled a communal changing room during the January sales.

'How come you have so many clothes when you don't give a stuff about what you wear?' asked Tom.

'This is my entire wardrobe.' She pushed a rose-coloured top out of the way and lay on the bed. 'Some of these things are absolutely ancient.' Her teeth found the lobe of his ear and she bit gently on it. 'Like me.'

He laughed. 'You didn't obsess as much about it last year.'

'Last year was Jin's turn. She was the one who'd turned thirty. When it was me, I was devastated. Remember? I cried.'

'Well I think you improve every year.' He gathered her fiercely to him and rolled so that she was over him. 'You're on top,' he told her, and grinned delightedly as she slid on to him.

'This was supposed to happen after my bath.' She lay beside him on the crumpled duvet and picked up her discarded bra with her toes.

'What's wrong with now?' he asked.

'Because once I have a bath your closeness disappears,' she told him. 'I wanted you to be with me this evening.'

'I wish I could be,' he said. 'I really do.' He slid off the bed. 'How about I run the bath for you?'

'If you like.' She closed her eyes and listened to him walking barefoot to the bathroom.

'What would you like me to put in it?' he called. 'There's a nice-looking bottle of something purple on the shelf.'

'Not that!' she called back. 'In the cabinet. An Elizabeth Arden bath crème. It's the only expensive one I have and I want to be expensive the whole way through.'

'Whatever you say.'

She heard the sound of the water flooding into the bath and

sighed. It would be nice, she thought, not to have to go anywhere tonight. To stay in the flat with Tom and make love to him again, and then to send out for some Chinese food and eat it, half naked, on the bed while they watched something romantic on the TV. And then to sleep for a while, wrapped in each other's arms. So much more appealing than going out. Especially going out to Jin's triple birthday celebration, an event which Andie knew would be as stage-managed and over-the-top as everything her younger sister did.

'Come on then!' She felt him lift her into his arms and opened her eyes. 'Let's get you clean and scrubbed and ready to go.'

'Put me down!' But she laughed as he carried her into the bathroom and held her over the foaming tub.

'Gently or with a splash?' he asked.

'Oh, gently, please.' She kissed him on the nose. 'Otherwise the tidal wave – a result of the Archimedes principle of displacement and due to the fact that my bum is definitely big no matter what you say – will engulf the entire bathroom and possibly leak down on to poor old Tina below.'

'You're no fun.' But he lowered her slowly into the bath.

'I know,' she said. 'That's why you love me.' She closed her eyes and disappeared beneath the foamy water.

'Wrong,' he said as she emerged.

'Wrong?' She blew foam from her nose.

'I love you because you're the most fun I've ever had.'

'With my clothes off or on?' she asked.

'Either.'

'Fair enough.' She flicked some foam at him.

'Don't,' he said dangerously. 'Or I'll jump in there with you and Tina will definitely have to worry.'

'Promises, promises,' said Andie and disappeared beneath the water for a second time.

He was sitting in the pink tub chair beside the window when she emerged into the living room again.

'Oh.' His eyes widened and he looked at her in stunned appreciation. 'How come you don't bother getting done up like this for me?'

'Would you want me to?' She walked across the room, and the electric blue of her dress shimmered in the late afternoon sunlight. Her hair, partly pinned up and partly falling in studied carelessness, was a perfect counterfoil to the elegance of the dress. The narrow gold necklace which he'd given her for her birthday glittered at her throat.

'Well, maybe not all the time,' he said. 'But – Jeez, Andie, you look totally stunning.'

'I'll still be a fish out of water,' she told him.

'Stop putting yourself down.' He shook his head. 'An hour ago you were an ordinary, though admittedly desirable, female. Now, I'm telling you, you look good enough to eat.'

'Too late,' she told him. 'We did that earlier.'

'Actually, I'm afraid to touch you,' confessed Tom. 'In case I smudge some part of the perfection.'

'Then don't,' she said. 'It took me ages to create this look and I couldn't bear to do the make-up again.'

'Aren't you meant to tell me it's all to do with your bone structure or something?' he asked. 'I mean, you've got cheekbones this evening that I never even noticed before.'

'And the squashed nose bequeathed to me by some malevolent ancestor.' She shrugged helplessly. 'I might look good to you, Tom, but I've too many flaws to be beautiful. And I'm nothing, absolutely nothing compared to Jin. Or her crowd.'

'You're worth a million of her,' he said fiercely. 'More than a million. And there's nothing wrong with your nose.'

'You know it's awful, but thanks anyway.' She moistened her lips and then grimaced. 'Better try and remember not to lick off all my lipstick before getting there. I know there are women who can do the whole long-lasting lipstick thing but I'm not one of them. Two seconds of normal living and no matter what it is, it's gone.'

'When you get into the car you needn't say a word,' Tom told her. 'I won't ask you questions and you won't have to speak. If that doesn't keep your lips red and glossy nothing will.' He smiled at her. 'But, oh boy – they're very kissable like that.'

'Well don't even think about it,' she said warningly. 'I am now

5

officially a creation, Tom Hall, and I can't possibly have your slobbery kisses destroying my look.'

'Wouldn't dream of it,' he assured her as he picked up the car keys from the table. 'Wouldn't dream of it.'

They didn't speak as he turned on to the Malahide Road and drove through the Dublin suburbs until the road abruptly narrowed and detached homes surrounded by cultivated land replaced the serried rows of houses. The sky was milk white, an evening haze dampening the effect of the earlier summer sun. Andie removed the sunglasses she'd previously perched on her despised nose. She turned them over and over in her hands, tracing her index finger around the frame, and then, finally, dropped them into her lap. She picked at the cuticle of her little finger, pushing it back down the nail. Then she fiddled with her gold necklace as she looked out of the window at the high walls and electronic gates which guarded the privacy of the ever more impressive houses along the road.

Tom glanced at her, noticing the worry lines creasing the corners of her eyes, feeling the tension rising within her with every mile they travelled. He took his hand from the steering wheel and placed it on her thigh. The squeeze he gave her was comforting and companionable.

'You'll be fine,' he said.

'I know.' She stared straight ahead as the road turned and the trees on either side formed a green archway above them. They saw the double gates and she made him drive past as she turned to look at the driveway. About a dozen cars were lined up in the huge cobbled circle in front of the house itself, while more had been parked at one side of the driveway.

'Stop now,' she told Tom.

Immediately he pulled in to the left. She reached down and picked up her tiny blue bag from the footwell. Tom got out of the driver's seat, opened the rear passenger door and took out the bouquet of flowers and two gift-wrapped boxes.

'Sure you can manage?' he asked as he handed her the flowers and the boxes.

'Yes. It's not far.'

'But can you walk in those shoes?'

She glanced down at her spindly-heeled blue and gold Marks & Spencer sandals, which she'd managed to find the day before in their end-of-season sale and which looked much more expensive than the half-price she'd paid for them. 'Of course I can.'

'OK then.' He looked anxiously at her.

'I'm fine,' she said. 'I've been exaggerating the nervousness of it. When I'm there it never seems so bad. *She* never seems so bad either!'

He chuckled. 'Will you have a good time?' he asked.

'Not as good as earlier.'

'Will you think about me?'

'Not at all.' She smiled at him.

'I'll call you,' he said. He leaned towards her and, avoiding the flowers, kissed her on the cheek. 'Have fun.'

'I'll do my best.'

'And – happy birthday, Andie.'

'Thanks.' She touched the gold necklace before she turned to walk towards the house.

The driveway was long and gravelled. Despite her confidence of earlier, Andie was finding it difficult to keep her balance on the chipped stones. She stepped off the driveway and on to the lush green lawn which bordered it instead, but this time the spindly heels of her nearly-there sandals disappeared into the grass. With each step a clump of earth stuck to the heels. By the time she arrived at the house she was wearing a large portion of the garden.

Briarlawns was the house of a self-made man, thought Andie, as she approached the steps up to the front door. Built ten years earlier, it was a collection of design features from homes that the owner had seen in other places. Red-brick, because it was in a semi-rural setting. A Dutch-style roof. Wrought-iron balconies outside the upstairs windows. A Georgian-inspired front door. It wasn't ugly but it wasn't beautiful. It was the house of someone who wanted to say that he could afford to build it. Having built it, though, the owner had never actually lived in it and according to Jin had been glad to make a profit on the sale.

'Hello.' The tuxedo-wearing Adonis at the open front door had a list in his hand. 'Do you have an invitation?'

'I'm Andie Corcoran.' Andie moved the bouquet of flowers so that she could see him more clearly. 'I'm Jin's sister.'

'Mrs Dixon's sister.' He scanned his list and then looked at her again. 'Andrea?'

'Yes,' said Andie.

'They're at the back,' said the man. 'Through the hallway and down—'

'I know,' said Andie. She walked past him and into the white and black tiled hallway with its wide staircase. 'Oh,' she added, turning back. 'Has my mother arrived yet?'

He nodded. 'Mrs Corcoran arrived an hour ago,' he said.

Andie smiled to herself. She could just imagine the panic on Jin's face when her mother arrived at the house half an hour before she was supposed to. No doubt Cora would've said that the time on the invitation was for guests, not family. That she'd arrived before then in case they needed a hand with anything, knowing deep down that of course they didn't need a hand with anything, that they'd paid a fortune to the caterers not to need a hand with anything. Which would have left Cora with plenty of time to wander through the house on her own. Andie knew that her mother was fascinated by its three reception rooms, dining room, billiards room (honestly, thought Andie, billiards!), Kevin's study, the huge country-style kitchen and seven bedrooms (she sometimes wondered whether they slept in a different one each night of the week). When Andie had first come to visit, she'd been given the whole tour, the one that also included the eye-popping master bedroom with its walk-in wardrobes and en-suite bathroom with separate bath (including water jets), shower and sauna. It had overwhelmed her at first and then she'd felt dismissive of it all, telling herself that money wasn't everything and that happiness was more important.

Afterwards she'd gone back to her one-bedroom first-floor flat (which didn't have a balcony because it had been built in the sixties when things like that were far too fancy for what was considered a place for people who couldn't afford an actual house) and told herself that everything she had, she'd worked for herself.

And that she should feel satisfied and proud as well as being happy.

Which she did, of course. After all, she wasn't the kind of girl who got a kick out of having a walk-in wardrobe because she wasn't the kind of girl who bothered buying the amount of clothes she'd need to fill it! But whenever she came to one of Jin's parties she couldn't help feeling a little inadequate, as though somehow by not wanting the wardrobes and the clothes and all of the things that Jin thought were important, she'd managed to fail at being a twenty-first-century woman.

She shook her head to dismiss the negative thoughts as she crossed the hallway and walked down the short flight of stairs which led to the open door at the back of the house. She was fine. Jin was fine. Different didn't matter.

The garden had been dotted with enormous green sunshades. Andie wondered at what point the organisers had decided that the Irish summer evening was exactly that – summer, without the threat of a potential cloudburst – which meant that they could actually use the sunshades for their true purpose. The milk-white haze still hung in the sky but hadn't built up into grey banks of cloud as it so often did, the air was warm and still and heavy with the scent of the multicoloured flowers which spilled out of the carefully cultivated flowerbeds and the cobalt-blue Italian glazed pots.

Groups of people strolled round the vast lawn and sipped champagne, the occasional burst of laughter breaking through the hum of conversation. The women were all dressed for an occasion, the men wore suits. Andie remembered this time the previous year when she'd been the one hosting the triple birthday celebration – the three of them, herself, Jin and Cora, had ended up having an indoor barbecue in her flat while the rain bucketed down ferociously outside.

'Andie! Over here.'

She turned at the sound of Jin's voice and smiled at her sister. I will *not* be intimidated, she told herself, as Jin approached and kissed her on both cheeks. And I won't let her occasional comments about how I could do better annoy me.

'Hi there,' she said. 'You're looking well.'

9

'And you.' Jin smiled at her sister and Andie felt guilty at her thoughts of earlier. Yes, Jin was stunningly beautiful; yes, she was rolling in money; yes, it had all come so easily to her. But she was still her sister and they shared a lot of childhood memories. They'd seen each other naked in the bath and crying after a dressing-down from Cora. They'd gone on wet-weather summer holidays in the west of Ireland together and they'd shared the trauma of falling out of the apple tree in the tiny back garden of the house in Marino, Andie spraining her wrist and Jin (dramatic as always) breaking her arm. They had a lot of things in common. She shouldn't always focus on the things that were different.

'Happy birthday,' said Andie and handed Jin the bouquet of flowers. 'This is for you too.' She also gave her sister one of the gift-wrapped boxes.

'Thanks.' Jin kissed Andie again and waved at a nearby waiter to take the bouquet. She looked at the box. 'Will I open it now?'

'If you like,' said Andie.

Jin unwrapped the matt-black paper and lifted the lid from the velvet box. The narrow-handled silver spoon nestled on purple silk. She ran her finger lightly over the inscription – her name and the date.

'It's lovely,' she said.

'I didn't know which one to give you and which to give Ma,' said Andie. 'Hers is a sugar spoon this year.'

'This is great,' said Jin. 'And yours is in the house. I'll give it to you later.'

'Whatever you do, don't forget.' Andie grinned. 'I only have about a million spoons in the flat.'

'Kevin thinks that giving each other spoons is a great idea,' said Jin.

'So do I,' said Andie. 'And I love them all.'

Jin raised an eyebrow.

'I do,' Andie told her. 'They're cute. They all have a story to tell.'

'More importantly, as Kevin says, they're a good investment.'

'That was the original idea. Investments for us all.' Andie looked round wryly. 'Not that you needed it in the end.'

'You never know.' But Jin laughed. 'Anyway, I think it's nice that the three of us buy each other the same thing. And it's always interesting to see who picked what.'

Andie nodded, then looked round the garden. 'Where *is* Ma?'

A frown creased Jin's brow. 'Somewhere,' she said vaguely. 'Probably telling Genevieve Boyd all about my wonderful sauna or something while Genevieve is thinking that she could buy and sell me and my saunas.'

'Could she?' asked Andie.

'Look, honey, you might think that there's a bit of wealth on display here. But what me and Kevin have is buttons, just buttons, compared to some of them. Lily and Conor O'Shea have just bought a damn island.'

'An island? Off Ireland?'

'Are you mad? Who'd want an Irish island where it'd piss rain on them three hundred and sixty-four days a year. No, in the Caribbean.'

'Like Richard Branson. Anywhere near him?'

'I don't know,' said Jin. 'They haven't invited us out yet.'

'Well, you do already have the house in Antigua, don't you?'

'Yes, but it's not the same as an island!'

Andie giggled.

'What?' demanded Jin.

'It's just so ridiculous,' said Andie. 'You grew up in a house that originally had an outside toilet!'

'Andie, that toilet was never outside. You say things like that to make yourself seem more earthy and grounded than me.'

'It was so outside!' Andie made a face at her sister. 'OK, not when we were kids. But before that.'

'Yes, well it doesn't give you permission to think that you come from an impoverished background and that wealth is a disgusting ploy of the middle classes.'

'I don't think that at all,' said Andie mildly. 'I just can't quite see the point of island oneupmanship.'

'It's exactly the same as musical oneupmanship,' returned Jin. 'You know, where you tell someone that the latest top-selling single is all very well but it's not actually music. And you refer them instead to something obscure by Prokofiev.'

11

Andie's eyes narrowed. 'I do not.' Then her expression softened. 'Well, maybe. But in that case it's true, isn't it? After all, you can hardly compare Stock, Aitken and Waterman to Dvorak or Tchaikovsky, now can you?'

'As you once, bitingly, told me – Strauss would've been the number one of his time.'

'At least he'd have deserved it,' muttered Andie.

'Same old Andie.' Jin accepted a glass of champagne from the tray which a waiter had proffered. 'Are you having one?'

'Sure.' Andie took a glass and sipped at it. 'Nice,' she said.

'Veuve Clicquot,' said Jin.

'Nice outfit too.' Andie decided that revisiting the past wasn't a good idea, and she knew that Jin always loved talking about clothes.

'D'you like it?' Jin beamed at her. 'It's Chlöe. Hopefully not too young for me today.'

'It looks great on you,' said Andie. 'And I like the colours.'

'Kevin prefers plain,' Jin told her, 'but I wanted to look cheerful.'

'Well, you're outdoing us all by a mile,' Andie said.

'I'd be disappointed if I didn't,' Jin told her, 'with the amount that he gave me to spend for today!' She looked at Andie speculatively. 'Mind you, you're looking particularly well. That's not a chain-store ensemble, is it?'

'The sandals are M&S,' Andie told her.

'But the dress . . .'

'I bought it in Pia Bang,' said Andie.

'Well, well.' Jin looked at her appraisingly. 'Taking it all seriously, are you? For my benefit? Or is there – finally – a man?'

'I dress for myself and not for men, as you very well know,' said Andie spiritedly.

'All the same.' Jin sipped her champagne. 'You need a man, Andie. Otherwise you're in danger of turning into one of those tweed-wearing old dears whose only interest is their work.'

'There are no tweed-wearing old dears in the Academy,' said Andie.

'Tweed-wearing young dears?' suggested Jin.

'Have you ever actually seen me in tweed?'

'So – no man?'

'It's absolutely none of your business.'

'I know it's none of my business, but I care about you.'

'Really?' said Andie drily.

'Really,' said Jin. 'And it's such a waste that you're all glammed up and there's no one to enjoy it.'

Andie thought of Tom's appreciative looks earlier, and his desire to rip the dress from her body, and said nothing. She wished that he was with her now.

'No one at all?' Jin spoke again.

'Why should it matter?' asked Andie. 'I've told you before, there are people in my life. Not as glamorous and interesting as the people in yours, obviously. But I'm OK.'

'Is there a man only you won't bring him because you're embarrassed?' asked Jin. 'Do you think that I'd look down on another music teacher?'

'Would you?' asked Andie wryly. 'Do you think that only important business magnates qualify as potential husbands?'

'Of course not!' Jin shook her head and the sun glinted off her copper curls. 'But they're a good start! Anyway, I'd love to meet whoever you were going out with.'

'Well, there's no one you need to meet,' said Andie dismissively.

'Andie!' Jin's emerald-green eyes widened suddenly. 'Is it – is it a woman?'

'What?'

'A woman,' said Jin. 'I never thought . . . but it's possible, of course . . .'

'You think I'm a lesbian?' Andie looked at her sister in amused horror. 'Is that what you think?'

'Well, let's face it, honey, there hasn't been a man that I know about since Michael Kennedy. And that was years ago.'

'Just because you don't know about them doesn't mean they don't exist,' Andie pointed out. 'And no, there isn't a woman. I'm not a lesbian.'

'Pity,' mused Jin.

'Pity?'

'Well, it's terribly chic these days.'

'I don't indulge in my sexual preferences to be chic,' Andie told her.

'You rarely indulge in anything to be chic.'

'Are you making the point that despite everything I'm still your frumpy older sister?'

Jin sighed. 'Not really. But—'

'I don't want to have this conversation.' Andie drained her glass of champagne. 'And Kevin's waving at you.' She nodded towards her brother-in-law and walked away, while Jin's eyes followed her in frustration.

Andie was standing under one of the enormous parasols when Cora walked up to her and handed her a packet.

'Happy birthday,' she said.

'Oh, Ma, thanks.' Andie took the box.

'I wish you wouldn't call me that,' said Cora.

'What?'

'Ma. It sounds so—'

'Irish?' suggested Andie with a grin.

'A little,' admitted Cora. 'In this sort of company . . .'

'You know you love it really,' said Andie. 'It's a term of affection.'

'Maybe.' Cora smiled.

'Anyway, here's yours.' Andie handed over her gift-wrapped box.

'You know,' said Cora as she unwrapped it, 'it'd be easier if we all bought our own spoons.'

'But not half as much fun. Oh, this is really lovely!' Andie slid the tiny egg spoon from the box.

'Victorian,' said Cora. 'I liked it myself.' She opened her own box and looked at the decorated sugar spoon inside. 'And this is lovely too.' She smiled at her elder daughter and kissed her fondly on the cheek.

'It's awkward,' said Andie. 'All of us sharing birthdays.'

'Unusual, certainly,' said Cora. 'But you were the best birthday presents I ever had.'

'You say that every year.'

'I mean it.'

'Thanks.' Andie returned her mother's kiss and they stood side by side for a moment. Andie wondered whether, at fifty-eight, she'd look as good as her mother did now. Though not possessing the delicate bone structure which both daughters had actually inherited from their father, Cora Corcoran was an attractive woman. The fine lines which she possessed added character to a face whose most arresting feature was her emerald-green eyes, which sparkled with pleasure as she looked around her. Her hair, once copper like Andie and Jin's, was a silver-grey which she no longer bothered to dye but which wasn't unduly ageing. And her lips still retained a fullness which Andie would have associated with a much younger woman. In fact, she thought as she observed her mother covertly, Cora was beginning to look more like her old self again. Which was a huge relief, because both Andie and Jin had worried about her over the last nine months.

A metallic whine filled the garden, and mother and daughter looked towards the house. Andie shifted uncomfortably as she saw her brother-in-law, with a microphone in his hand, step up on to a low bench. She didn't want a fuss, but there was going to be one anyway. She'd known that all along. Kevin liked a fuss.

'Ladies and gentlemen.' As always, she was impressed by the richness and authority in his voice, though it simply matched the authority of his personality, if not his figure. Kevin was a man of medium height who just about managed to keep middle-age spread at bay. His face was square and solid, his dark hair now thinning, though perfectly groomed. He didn't look at all like Tom, Andie thought wistfully, suddenly wishing he was beside her again. He looked much older, much more serious. Well, of course, he *was* older. And he carried around his neck the responsibilities of a company that employed almost a thousand people, so she could understand his seriousness.

'Ladies and gentlemen,' said Kevin again. 'You're very welcome here this afternoon. I'm not going to keep you long . . .'

Andie didn't bother to listen as Kevin rattled on. She was thinking of Tom again and how wonderful it had all been earlier. How he'd

15

brought her to the brink and back again so many times. How he knew just where to touch her, to kiss her, to caress her. He was a superb lover, thoughtful and considerate. She wondered whether Kevin and Jin had as great a sex-life as she did. Somehow she doubted that anyone else did.

'. . . my lovely wife, Jin.' Kevin's voice broke into her thoughts again as Jin stood beside him, smiling happily and looking, thought Andie, not a day over twenty-one, even though it was her thirty-first birthday. Exactly a year younger than her, almost to the hour, Cora had told them.

'. . . her equally lovely sister, Andie.' His eyes locked on to hers and he gestured for her to join them at the front of the crowd. She pushed her way forward and stood uneasily beside them, feeling underdressed despite the electric-blue creation and the gold necklace which lay on her throat.

'And of course their absolutely wonderful mother, Cora, who could easily be mistaken for Jin's younger sister!'

There was an amused and appreciative murmur from the crowd as Cora followed Andie to stand beside the rest of the family.

'So can I ask you all to raise your glasses and join with me in wishing these three fantastic women a very happy birthday.' He raised his glass. 'Happy birthday!' he cried.

'Happy birthday!' echoed the crowd, and then the DJ put on a recording of the Stevie Wonder song and the guests sung along.

After they'd finished singing, Kevin held up his hand. 'One more thing,' he said. The assembled group looked at him. 'An extra gift this year.'

Andie frowned. There were never extra gifts. That was the arrangement. A spoon each. From each of them.

'I know that Cora hasn't been away for a while, and although Jin and I asked her to stay with us in Antigua earlier this year she didn't feel able to come.' His voice was suddenly softer, more caring. They'd all been worried about Cora. Worried that, since Des's death, she hadn't wanted to go out, hadn't socialised. Had been a much, much quieter woman than she'd been before. Andie felt hot tears scorch her eyes. It had been hard for her too. She missed her father more than she'd imagined possible.

'Anyway,' continued Kevin, 'knowing how much Cora loved to travel in the past, we felt that the time had come perhaps for her to take a trip again. So Jin and I would like to present her with a small gift.' He took a gold-coloured envelope out of his top pocket. 'For you, Cora.'

Cora stared at him, her eyes wide in surprise. She took the envelope and ran her fingernail along the edge. The letter inside confirmed that Mrs Cora Corcoran and Mrs Doireann O'Doherty were booked on the *Seascape Spray* for six nights, outside cabin, upper deck, departing Florida in a week's time on a cruise to Mexico.

'You're joking,' said Cora.

'Not at all.' Jin smiled. 'It's something we wanted to do. We spoke to Doireann about it. She can't wait.'

Cora stared at the piece of paper as Kevin told the crowd what had been arranged. They burst into a round of applause, while Cora continued to look stunned.

'It's – really too good of you,' she said slowly. 'I don't know if . . .'

'You have to go,' said Jin. 'We can't cancel it. And Doireann's really looking forward to it.'

'She never said.'

'We told her not to say a word,' Jin explained. 'We knew that you'd find excuses not to go and we didn't want you to find excuses.'

'Well . . .'

'Hi, Cora.' Doireann, her sister-in-law, pushed her way into the family group. 'What d'you think?'

'I think you should have told me.' Cora looked at Des's youngest sister, the one she'd got on with the best.

'But Jin told me that you'd only object. And I agreed with her. I didn't want anything putting a spanner in the works. I've always wanted to go on a cruise.'

'Well, me too,' murmured Cora. 'Des and I had planned . . .' She bit her lip.

'Des would've wanted you to go,' said Doireann firmly. 'I know he would.'

'Yes.' Cora nodded slowly. 'Yes, I suppose he would.'

'So it's settled then.' Doireann grinned. 'I was a bit worried you'd freak out and say no.'

'How can I freak out and say no,' asked Cora, 'when all of you are looking at me like that?'

People had broken into little groups again. Cora and Doireann were sitting beneath one of the parasols, although by now the sun had slipped gently below the horizon and they didn't need to be shaded. Kevin Dixon was talking to three men, their seemingly serious conversation suddenly ruptured by a loud belly-laugh from one of them. Andie stood near the house, half hidden from the rest of the group by a russet Japanese maple tree.

'All on your own?' asked Jin as she approached her.

'Tired of talking to people,' said Andie.

'It gets a bit wearing after a while,' agreed Jin.

'You should've told me.' Andie's voice was suddenly hard. 'You should've asked me before springing the cruise thing on her.'

'Oh, for heaven's sake, Andie. It was a gift from me and Kevin.'

'Our agreement was spoons,' said Andie. 'It's worked for the last eight years. It saves trouble.'

'Look—'

'And when you didn't have any money, before you married into it, spoons were perfectly adequate.'

'I was making enough myself,' snapped Jin. 'I didn't just marry into money. My modelling career was lucrative.'

Andie bit her lip. She knew that she was being unfair and irrational but she couldn't help herself.

'Andie, you know that Mum needs a break,' said Jin. 'You know it's been difficult for her. Why shouldn't Kevin and I do this?'

Because it makes me feel jealous, thought Andie uncomfortably. And because it makes you seem like some kind of fairy godmother. But she said nothing.

'Mum will have a great time and she'll come back looking better than ever,' said Jin.

'Maybe she'll even find a rich Texan.' Andie was annoyed at herself for even momentarily begrudging the gift to her mother.

18

'Exactly.' Jin looked pleased.

Andie sighed. Sometimes she felt that Jin brought out the worst in her even when her sister was acting with the best motives.

'I'm sure she'll have a really great time,' she said.

'Of course she will,' Jin agreed. 'And hopefully she'll come back more like her old self. I know she's looking good today, but it's the first time in a long time.'

Andie nodded. 'You're right.'

'So we're OK with all this now?'

'Of course.' Andie wished she could sound totally convincing. 'I need the loo,' she told Jin abruptly. 'I'll see you later.'

She walked back to the house on her own. It was cool and quiet inside and her high heels clacked across the marble tiles. The thin straps of her sandals were cutting into her ankles and toes. She slipped them off and held them in her left hand as she walked across the hallway to the elegant downstairs bathroom. She washed her hands and then yawned deeply, stretching her arms above her head. She lowered them again as she felt the blue dress strain across her back. It might look sensationally sexy, but after a few drinks and too much finger food it was a bit on the tight side. Andie hated the feeling of her clothes being too tight. She looked at her watch. The party would start to break up soon, wouldn't it? She didn't really feel like going back and having any more idle conversations with people she didn't know while feeling as though she might pop out of the dress. She wanted to go home, pull on a comfortable sweatshirt and bottoms and curl up in front of the TV on her own.

Kevin's study was at the end of the hallway. Andie decided to look up the number of a local cab company in his phone book and order a taxi to take her home. She'd done her duty by turning up, but there was nothing that said she had to stay till the bitter end. She pushed open the study door and walked inside. The room was almost as big as her entire flat. It was lined with bookshelves packed with books. They were business books, not novels, Andie noticed, and they looked as though they'd actually been read. She sat down in Kevin's high-backed black leather swivel chair and rested her feet beside the computer keyboard on his walnut desk. The desk itself was neat and tidy. A blotter (did anyone actually use ink any more?

she wondered) sat in the middle, there was a stack of folders to the left and a few glossy brochures about Kevin's bar and restaurant chains to the right. On the desk too was a small silver double frame which contained photographs of Cian and Clarissa, Kevin's children from his previous marriage. They were quite like him, she thought as she picked up the frame and studied the photos more closely. Determined-looking. She wondered whether, if Jin and Kevin had kids, they'd looked equally determined. Or whether they'd inherit Jin's more fragile beauty instead.

She replaced the frame and began to take the pins out of her hair so that gelled sections of it tumbled around her face again. Parents and kids and the relationships between them were horrendously difficult, even when everyone was grown up. She was a horrible, horrible person to have felt that spurt of annoyance when Kevin had told everyone about sending Cora on the cruise. She wished that she didn't get so wound up when he and Jin made extravagant gestures. They couldn't help it. It was their nature, after all. Besides, she conceded, Cora deserved a fabulous holiday. Andie closed her eyes and leaned back in the chair. She wondered if it was actually possible to be the sort of person you knew you should be, or whether everyone's efforts were doomed to failure.

'Are you all right?'

Her eyes snapped open and she jerked her feet abruptly from the desk. Kevin was standing in the doorway, looking at her.

'Fine, fine.' She stood up and pulled at her dress to tidy it. 'Sorry. I came to call a cab.'

'Leaving already?' asked Kevin.

'Yes. Sorry. Class tomorrow morning,' she said.

'You should've just asked me,' said Kevin. 'I'd have called a cab for you.'

'You were talking to people,' said Andie. 'I didn't want to disturb you.'

He walked into the room and picked up the phone. 'Let me get it for you,' he said. 'I can put it on my account.'

She said nothing as she listened to him order the taxi. She was embarrassed at having been caught in his study, even though she'd only looked at the photos, not rifled through folders on his desk or opened the drawers or any of the things she could've been guilty of doing. She rubbed her eyes and smudged mascara over her cheeks.

Kevin looked at his sister-in-law and wondered, as he had done so often before, how it was that she was so different from his wife. Jin would never have allowed herself to be caught with her hair in such a state and mascara streaks on her face. Some men might have found Andie's bed-head look attractive. He preferred sophistication in his women.

'The cab will be here in a few minutes,' he told her.

'Great, thanks. I'll walk down to the gate and wait for it.'

'Aren't you going to say goodbye to Jin and Cora?'

'You do it for me.' Andie ran her fingers through her hair, wishing that she hadn't used so much gel to keep it in place. She was sure that she looked a fright. 'I don't want to go back out there given that I've destroyed my look.'

'Best take your shoes with you then,' said Kevin. He picked them up from the window ledge where she'd left them.

'Oh, yes. Thanks.'

'I'll tell Jin you had a good time, will I?'

'Of course.'

She slipped the sandals on to her feet. This time it was her little toes that chafed. She wondered if Jin's excruciatingly expensive Marc Jacobs gave her blisters too.

'We did think about sending you on the cruise with Cora,' remarked Kevin as she reached the study door. 'But Jin thought you'd resent it.'

Andie turned to look at him. 'I wouldn't have had the time to go anyway,' she said.

'Don't you ever take holidays?' He looked at her with amusement. 'I'd have thought that even teachers at the Academy took holidays from time to time.'

'The summer holidays are over,' she told him. 'I'm busy.'

He nodded. 'Pity, though. I'm sure you would've enjoyed Mexico.'

'I'm sure I would.' She smiled briefly at him and then walked out of the house, refusing to slow down even though her feet were now on fire. Once she reached the lawn she slipped the sandals off again and allowed the dew-laden grass to cool her burning soles. By the time she reached the gate, the cab had arrived. She waved at it, got in and settled back for the journey home.

Chapter 2

Canon in D Major – Pachelbel

Kevin flopped on to the deep, biscuit-coloured sofa and stretched his full length out on it.

'Shoes,' said Jin automatically.

Kevin said nothing, but slid his Italian leather loafers from his feet and allowed them to drop to the floor with a soft thud.

'Tired?' asked Jin, who was curled up in the armchair opposite.

'I thought the Campbells would never bloody leave.' He yawned. 'He's such a bore and she's the social climber from hell. Lost a few pounds, though. Looks the better for it.'

'She wore that outfit to the charity lunch last month,' remarked Jin. 'Times must be tough in the world of bathroom fittings.'

'Actually, one of his clients went bust,' Kevin told her. 'Owed him quite a bit. Maybe that explains the fashion economy.'

'Maybe,' said Jin thoughtfully. 'Poor old Celeste.' She perked up again. 'Lily O'Shea was on top form as usual, though, wasn't she?'

'She's some woman,' agreed Kevin admiringly. 'Perfect corporate wife.'

'And I'm not?'

'You do your best.' Kevin smiled. 'But Lily has it all down to a fine art. She was especially good when Jennifer Halpin made the comment about the tax enquiry.'

'Tax enquiry?'

'Conor's having some problems with the tax man. He's supposed to be resident in Monaco but he may have spent too many days in Ireland last year. Now they're after him for tax.'

'He can afford it, surely?'

'Jin!' Kevin looked at her in horror. 'It's not that he can't afford it, but why should he have to pay it?'

'Why not?' Jin shrugged. 'What difference would it make to him?'

'Like all of us, Conor wouldn't mind paying the money if it wasn't frittered away by incompetent politicians who wouldn't, in a mad fit, be employed in any real job.'

Jin giggled. 'You think?'

'Of course,' said Kevin. 'And you shouldn't be so liberal, my love. If I didn't have a really good accountant you'd never be able to buy dresses like that.'

'I'm sorry.' She kissed him. 'I didn't really mean to be liberal. Just fair.'

'We donate money to charity,' said Kevin. 'It's more worthwhile than donating it to the government.'

'You're probably right,' agreed Jin. 'Though I was accosted by some mad Sandal-ista-type woman last week who was trying to get rid of technology in the world on the basis that the magnetic fields were being distorted or something. Apparently it's why all of our chakras are messed up.'

Kevin shook his head. 'She'd be better off getting a job.'

'That's what I said.'

'That's my girl.'

'Thank you,' said Jin as she stood up. 'D'you want a drink? I'm sure there's some wine left if you'd like it.'

'They took away the unopened bottles,' said Kevin.

'Were there unopened bottles?' She was surprised. 'I thought our guests demolished the lot.'

'Water will do me anyway,' said Kevin. 'I want to go through some papers.'

'It's nearly midnight,' Jin objected. 'It's too late to be looking through papers.'

'I have to,' said Kevin.

'Oh come on, darling.' She leaned over the back of the sofa so that her long, shining hair brushed his face. 'Forget about work at least for a few minutes!'

'Don't,' he said irritably.

'You used to like it.'

'Not when I'm trying to think,' he said.

Jin sighed. 'OK then. I'll get a bottle of water. I think I've had enough to drink today too.'

The kitchen was at the end of the corridor. It was a big, west-facing room which overlooked part of the garden. When they'd first moved into the house Jin had liked the rustic feel of it, with its honey-pine units, pots hanging from the ceiling and huge red Aga along the far wall. But even then the country look was growing passé. Jin just hadn't been sure what she wanted in its place. She felt that kitchens were going through a transition period and decided to wait before making radical changes. She'd done the bedrooms instead. But the kitchen was now in dire need of a facelift. She'd let it drift, she thought as she opened the heavy door of the American-style fridge, and it was unlike her to let things drift. Especially for the guts of three years! Next week she'd start looking at designs again. Come up with something really stunning. Unless, she mused as she took a bottle of sparkling water out of the fridge, unless they moved house. Moving house would be fun. This place was lovely, no question, but it lacked atmosphere. That was probably why she'd originally liked the rustic kitchen. It gave a sense of home and stability. But there was nothing special about the house itself, nothing that made her feel as though it was part of her, as though it was a privilege to live in it.

She picked up a couple of glasses and brought them and the bottle back to the room which they'd designated as the chill-out area.

What would be really nice, she thought, would be a genuinely old house near the city – along the canal perhaps – which she'd be able to painstakingly restore to its former glory. Lots of people did it; in fact, now that she thought about it, most people in their position lived in restored houses. Not cheap, of course, she realised that. But elegant.

'Water,' she said as she walked into the chill-out room.

'Thanks.' Kevin swung upright on the sofa and took the glass from her. She filled his glass, then her own.

'I'm a bit dehydrated,' she admitted as she took a sip. 'Too much champagne earlier.'

'Never let it be said I don't do a good garden party,' he said.

She smiled fleetingly at him but she knew what he was coming next. He was going to reminisce about how he'd started in business. How, working in a pub during his holidays from college, he was sent to be the barman at a similar garden party. And how he'd got talking to the owner of the house about his ideas for developing bars and restaurants. And how Martin Murphy had listened and liked what he heard and had offered the young Kevin Dixon some capital to get started. And how, between them, they'd built up the chain that owned some of the trendiest night spots in the city. She nodded attentively as he spoke but let his words slide past her. She'd heard the story so many times she could have recited it word for word herself.

'. . . and then, of course, I met you.' She smiled at him at that point. She never minded recalling the first time she'd met him, his look of surprise as she walked into the office of the advertising agency wearing her highest heels so that she towered over everyone there, even Kevin. Especially Kevin. In her bare feet she was still two inches taller than him.

It had been a day like today, haze in the afternoon sky but with a silky warmth which made walking up Mount Street to the agency's office pleasant and relaxing, except for the pain from the blister on her toe which had started to form a few minutes before she reached her destination. But it was part of her job to cope with blisters and she knew that the fanciful shoes she was wearing made her legs look even longer than usual. Her agent had called her about the job. Kevin's chain were about to run a poster campaign advertising their bars. They wanted a picture of a modern woman sitting at the bar looking confident and sexy. They had, Felicity Bryant told Jin, specifically requested her.

'Why?' she asked Kevin directly when she met him. 'Why are you particularly interested in me?'

Kevin smiled and pushed a brochure towards her. Jin recognised it as a catalogue she'd done a couple of years earlier. In it she was wearing a frumpy dress in eggshell blue. But she was peeping out at the camera from beneath her copper fringe, and her smile was friendly, beguiling and very, very sexy.

'One of the women in the office was looking through this,' he said. 'I saw you. I thought you would do.'

'This catalogue is two years old,' she told him. 'She's way out of fashion. And I've changed.'

'For the better,' he said. 'Definitely for the better.'

She'd got the job, and a short time later billboards across Dublin were plastered with shots of her showing that same smile. One, said Kevin, that welcomed both men and women. One that would bring the punters into their bars.

It did.

At the same time, it brought Kevin and Jin together. He'd been attracted to her from the moment he'd seen her picture in the catalogue and had wanted to meet her. As he told her months later, he always got what he wanted. She was overwhelmed by his sophistication and generosity. He enjoyed her warmth and appreciativeness. They married a year later.

Of course, Jin remembered, there'd been the hassle of his former wife and their two children to contend with – not that Monica caused any trouble, but suddenly there were a rash of interviews in the paper with her, comparing her low-profile domestic situation and her apparently endless charity work unfavourably with Jin's celebrity lifestyle. As if, Jin muttered when she read one of the most cutting pieces, as if any celebrity worth her salt would consider going for a meal and to a nightclub on a Friday night as a lifestyle worth the celebrity tag. All of the pieces carried a description of her as a 'former model', which, she thought, made it sound as though she'd just flashed her boobs at Kevin and shown him her single brain cell. It hadn't been like that at all. She'd fallen in love with him as hard as she'd fallen in love with anyone in her life before. And the best part about falling for Kevin Dixon was the fact that she knew he'd be able to love her and protect her and cherish her like no one else. He gave her the beach-front property in Antigua as a wedding present. His former wife, she discovered, had been given a much bigger and more impressive property in the south of France, but Kevin told her that the Antiguan island was far nicer than the south of France and that he'd always loved Zoë's Place.

'Who was Zoë?' she asked as he led her up the wooden steps.

'Nobody to do with me,' he replied. 'It's just the name that goes with the house.'

She loved Zoë's Place too, so close to the fine white sand of the west-coast beach. She couldn't believe how lucky she was to have found Kevin and the life she'd always wanted to lead. And she didn't care if Monica Dixon-Smith, as she now called herself, gave a hundred newspaper interviews saying that Kevin was a cold-hearted bastard. Jin knew that he wasn't. He'd left Monica before Jin had met him, and had made a very generous settlement to her and the children. His first wife was pissed off at the fact that he'd found someone else. Especially, Jin thought viciously, someone younger and more attractive.

Their honeymoon had been perfect, romantic in a way that she hadn't believed possible, a languid fortnight of frangipani blossoms falling on to the wooden deck, chilled cocktails overlooking the setting sun and lovemaking beneath the gentle swish of the ceiling fan as it moved the warm air over their glistening bodies. She'd never experienced anything as idyllic. Before or since.

'What's going on in Andie's life?' Kevin's words broke into her thoughts.

'Huh?'

'I just wondered. She looked great earlier,' said Kevin. 'But then she decided to push off early. Your mother was annoyed that she went without saying goodbye.'

'Oh, you know Andie.' Jin snorted. 'She's in a snit because of the cruise.'

Kevin sighed. 'I did warn you.'

'I knew she'd get pissed off about it. But honestly, Kevin, she's so juvenile sometimes. I feel like I'm the older sister, not her.'

'She doesn't like me, does she?'

'That's just her general bolshiness,' said Jin. 'She hasn't a bean so she resents anyone who has. And, of course, she tells herself that teaching is so much more noble than pure commerce.'

Kevin shrugged. 'Foolish girl. Though a bit refreshing, I suppose.'

'How?'

'I'm so used to having women falling at my feet because of

my bank balance that it's quite a surprise to find that Andie doesn't.'

'I didn't fall at your feet because of your bank balance.' Jin grinned at him. 'I fell at your feet because I was wearing those high heels.'

Kevin laughed. 'True. And you haven't worn anything with heels ever since.'

'I'm used to flatter shoes now,' said Jin. 'Much more comfortable.'

He laughed again. 'Those are comfortable?' He nodded at the pair of flat but very narrow and pointed Marc Jacobs that Andie had noticed earlier.

'Mostly much more comfortable,' she amended. She got up and sat beside him on the sofa. 'You sure you have to do paperwork tonight?'

'Yes,' he said. 'I'm going to Oslo on Monday. I need to have gone through them before then, let Shaun throw his solicitor's eye over them once more.'

'But you've got all weekend to worry about papers.' She leaned up against him. 'And even the best tycoons need time out to play.'

'I've been playing all day,' he told her.

'No you haven't,' she said. 'You were talking to Robert and Austin and Martin and Shaun . . . it was like having a mini board meeting on the lawn.'

He smiled. 'Wasn't I attentive enough for you?'

'Not entirely.' She pouted at him.

'Come here then.' He pulled her closer to him and slid her multi-coloured dress over her head. She kneeled over him, her generous breasts rounded by the Agent Provocateur bra she was wearing.

'That bra doesn't go with that dress!' He smiled.

'Why?'

'Wrong colour.'

'This dress has about fifty colours in it,' she told him. 'One of them is bound to be right.'

He shook his head. 'None of them match the shade exactly.'

'Then you'd better get rid of the bra,' said Jin suggestively.

He reached up and undid the clasp with one hand, then dropped the bra on the floor.

'You know, I'm not sure I approve of the ease with which you can do that,' she said.

'Years of practice,' he told her.

'I know.' Her eyes glittered green over him. 'But years of practice on who?'

'Mostly you,' he assured her as he drew her closer to him until her nipple was grazing his lips. 'Mostly you.'

She hadn't realised that she'd fallen asleep on top of him until he shook her shoulder.

'Oh.' Her eyes opened slowly and she blinked a couple of times to focus on him.

'I have to look at those papers now,' he said.

'Now?' She yawned. 'What about coming to bed?'

'Were you planning more of the same?' he asked. 'Or just sleeping?'

She smiled sleepily. 'Whichever.'

'Attractive though both propositions are, I do need to work,' he said.

'But it's so late.' She swung her legs off the sofa and picked up her discarded clothing. 'I can never understand why you work in the middle of the night.'

'I get my best ideas in the middle of the night,' he told her. 'I can't help it.'

'It drives me mad,' she muttered.

'Monica used to say that,' he said casually.

Jin stiffened and looked at him. 'Are you saying that I've become like Monica?'

He smiled. 'No. Only that you once told me to tell you if you ever said or did anything like her. So that you could avoid it in the future.'

'So I did.' Jin slipped into her dress. 'I'm sorry.'

'Don't be.' He stood up to face her. 'You're nothing like Monica.'

'Good,' she said.

'And I won't let you become like her either. Now I absolutely must get to work.'

'I know.' She yawned again. 'I'll see you in the morning.'

'Yes,' he said.

'It must be great being able to get by on four hours' sleep.'

'Actually it's a curse,' he said. 'I'd rather conk out for the full eight like you. But I can't. So I might as well use the time productively. Earn more money. Keep you in the style et cetera.'

'OK.' She grinned suddenly. 'So why are you nattering to me about it instead of getting on with it?'

'Goodnight.' He kissed her lightly on the lips.

'Goodnight.' She smiled at him and then went upstairs to bed.

Andie could hear the steady beat of the rain outside her window. It had started around two in the morning, a gentle hiss which had penetrated her half-sleep so that she opened her eyes, suddenly alert. And then she realised that it was only rain, not the sounds of a maniac who'd broken into the flat to murder her in her bed.

She didn't normally think like that. Only she'd sat up and watched TV when she'd arrived home from Jin's party. They'd been showing the psychological thriller *Sea of Love*, with Ellen Barkin and Gabriel Byrne. Andie fancied Gabriel Byrne. She like those smouldering dark looks and his Americanised accent. But it wasn't the kind of film that a girl living on her own should watch before going to bed alone. It had left her tense and unable to sleep. She'd looked at her watch and wondered whether or not she could ring Tom. But it was too late. Tom would be in bed too, with Elizabeth, his wife of ten years, beside him. Perhaps her arm would be resting across him, like Andie's own did on the rare occasions when they fell asleep together. Perhaps Elizabeth was spooned into Tom's back, the way she did too sometimes. Perhaps Tom and Elizabeth were making love . . . She'd clamped down on the thoughts of Tom and Elizabeth making love and willed herself to fall asleep, but it wasn't a deep sleep and now she was awake again, thanks to the persistent drum of the rain.

She threw off the quilt and got out of bed. She peered through the gap in the curtains and watched the drops running down the window pane, distorting the yellow glow from the streetlight outside. She heard footsteps but they were from the flat above. She recognised the heavy tread of Dominic Lyster, the divorced father of two who owned the flat. She wondered if he couldn't sleep either. And then she heard a high-pitched giggle and realised that sleep was probably the furthest thing from his mind.

She walked barefoot into the kitchen and filled the kettle. She knew that if she wanted to sleep she should really be heating up hot milk, but she thought that hot milk and any of the drinks made with it were totally disgusting. As a sop, however, to the fact that coffee in the early hours would make it even harder to get back to sleep, she spooned decaffeinated blend into her yellow mug.

While she waited for the kettle to boil she went into the bathroom and grabbed some paracetamol from the cabinet. She had a nagging headache and didn't know whether to blame it on champagne or stress. She hadn't really had enough champagne to have an alcohol-induced headache. And, she thought ruefully, if she was stressed out then it was entirely her own fault.

But still. She swallowed the tablets and then poured hot water over the coffee granules. Jin should've told her about the cruise for Cora. The only reason she hadn't, Andie knew, was that she was well aware that she was breaking their birthday law. The law that had been decided eight years earlier when they'd been debating the whole birthday thing. Des had organised a big bash for Cora's fiftieth, and Jin and Andie had decided not to buy each other presents so that they could club together and buy something extravagant for their mother. Cora had learned about this and argued that she wasn't an extravagant woman and hated extravagant gifts, and that the three of them having birthdays on the same day had caused all sorts of problems when they were younger and she didn't want it to happen now they were older too. And then she'd said that her collection of silver spoons, which she'd started years ago, hadn't had an addition in ages and that what she'd really like was a spoon from each of her daughters. Andie couldn't remember now whether it was herself or Jin who had suggested that spoons all round would be a good idea, but suddenly it had taken off and that was what they had done. And at no time over the intervening years had any of them wavered from it.

Andie gulped some coffee and swore as she scalded her tongue. It didn't really matter what Jin and Kevin did. She had her own life to lead. And she had Tom. Tom, who loved her. Tom, who made her feel cherished and wanted. Tom, who'd do anything for her. Except, of course, leave his wife. Andie added more milk to her coffee and took the mug back into the bedroom. She got into the double bed and pulled the covers over her knees to protect them from the heat of the mug.

Of course Tom wanted to leave Elizabeth. He'd explained it to Andie when he'd first met her, four years ago. At Jin and Kevin's wedding. All the managers of Kevin's chain of bars had been invited. Tom managed one of the city-centre bars. He'd been accompanied to the reception by Elizabeth. He'd even introduced her to Andie, a slender, pale-faced woman who possessed huge pinot noir eyes and soft bee-stung lips. Andie had sat down beside her at one point, exhausted by the whirl of dancing, wanting to catch her breath. Tom – tall and muscular, overshadowing Elizabeth completely – had arrived back at the table carrying a glass of wine and a pint of lager. Andie had been sitting in his seat. She'd apologised to him, explained that she'd simply collapsed, and smiled at both him and Elizabeth, which was when he introduced them.

'Are you having fun?' Andie had asked.

'Tom would like to dance.' Elizabeth's smile was hardly there, her voice little more than a whisper. 'He likes dancing.'

'Why don't you dance then?' Andie's own smile was stronger.

'I don't want to,' said Elizabeth. 'But you feel free if you like.'

Andie had looked at them in puzzlement, and then Tom had grabbed her by the hand and whirled her on to the floor.

'Look, I'm sure your wife would rather be dancing with you,' said Andie.

'My wife would rather be at home,' Tom replied.

'To be honest, so would I.'

'Why would you rather be at home?' he asked.

'A pathetic reason,' said Andie.

'Try me.'

'I don't like my brother-in-law.'

'Oh. Why not?'

'Too much of a suit-type for me,' said Andie. Then she looked at Tom and winced. 'You're not a relative, are you? I've had too much to drink and my mouth kind of runs away with me.'

33

'An employee,' he said.

'Of Kevin's?'

He explained about the bars.

'Shit,' said Andie. 'Forget I even said that.'

'Well I would.' Tom grinned and twirled her around. 'But he can be a bit overwhelming at times.'

She laughed. 'And so why would your wife rather be at home?' she asked when she'd caught her breath.

Tom looked at her seriously. 'She hasn't been well,' he said. 'She had a miscarriage.'

Andie stopped dancing and stared at him. 'I'm so, so sorry.'

'It was a year ago,' Tom explained. 'She hasn't really recovered yet.'

'Christ.' Andie looked uncomfortable. 'I'll leave you. I don't want—'

'No,' said Tom. 'Dance. I do want – a bit of fun. We haven't had fun, Elizabeth and me, in ages. It was her second miscarriage.'

'Oh Lord.'

'I don't want to think about it right now.'

'Yes, but . . .'

'She doesn't mind. Really.'

So Andie danced with him for a little longer and then made her excuses. A pity, she'd thought in the Ladies afterwards, that the good-looking ones were always married. And a tragedy for Tom and Elizabeth that they were having such trouble in starting a family.

It was a few months later before she saw him again. This time at a summer barbecue organised by Kevin's company. Jin had insisted that Andie come along to the barbecue. Now that she was married herself she seemed to think that it was her duty to find Andie a husband too.

This time Tom was on his own. He'd walked up to her as she stood awkwardly trying to balance a paper plate and her glass of wine. He'd taken the wine from her while she sat down on a low stone wall.

'Hello again,' he said. 'Remember me? Tom Hall.'

'Of course I remember.' She smiled. 'The John Travolta of the Dixon–Corcoran wedding. How could I forget?'

He laughed. 'Somehow I don't think John Travolta has anything to worry about. How're you?'

'I'm fine,' said Andie. 'How's Elizabeth?'

A shadow of pain crossed his face. 'We thought she was pregnant again but . . .' He shrugged. 'It's not officially a miscarriage until after three months.'

'Oh hell.' Andie exhaled slowly. 'You're having a really awful time.'

'And I'm never there.' His tone was light but she could hear the tension behind it all the same.

'Difficult when you're managing a bar,' she agreed.

'Difficult full stop,' he said. 'She's obsessed about it. Part of me can't blame her. We tried for so long before she got pregnant the first time . . . we thought there was something wrong, you know. And then – well, I suppose there was something wrong. She blames herself, though it's not her fault.'

Andie bit her lip. She felt terribly sorry for him and for Elizabeth. But she felt worse over the fact that she found him so incredibly attractive. She couldn't believe that she was listening to him telling her about his personal tragedy while she was actually thinking of what he might be like in bed.

'I'm boring you,' he said. 'I'm sorry.'

'God, no,' she told him. 'It's just – well, I don't know what to say. I've never been in the situation and it must be so awful for you.'

'You know what's awful?' He half smiled. 'It's awful going out to places where you should be having fun and feeling guilty about it. It's awful knowing that the person you loved can't cope with what's happened. That's what's awful.'

'You have each other,' said Andie. 'It must give you strength.'

'You'd think,' agreed Tom. 'But it's made us worse. Because maybe we both blame each other.'

'Oh.'

Suddenly he shook his head. 'That's not true. I don't blame her. Not for what's happened. But I blame her for not being able to deal with it. I'm having to deal with it. I have to go out to work every day. I can't sit at home and mope.'

35

'Maybe she shouldn't be sitting at home moping,' said Andie. 'Maybe she should be out working too.'

'Of course she should,' said Tom. 'But she doesn't want to. She doesn't really want to do anything.'

'I am sorry,' said Andie. 'I truly am.'

'And I'm sorry for sounding off at you.' Tom smiled suddenly. 'You're the only one I've ever said all that to. I wonder why.'

'Right place, right time,' she said.

'Not really,' Tom told her. 'This is supposed to be a fun event and I'm sure I've ruined it for you.'

'You haven't,' said Andie.

'Can we talk about something else?' asked Tom. 'You're easy to talk to.'

'Thanks.' She grinned.

'No, really.' He looked round. 'Unless, sorry, unless you're with someone, of course.'

'Nope.' She shifted on the wall to make herself more comfortable. 'I'm here because my sister is hoping I'll find a nice rich bloke to marry among the throng.'

'Really?' He opened his eyes wide.

She laughed. 'Maybe I'm exaggerating. But Jin's forever dropping hints about my single state.'

'I like your single state,' said Tom.

After that they hadn't been able to stop talking. About everything. Until Tom saw Kevin Dixon walking towards them and told Andie abruptly that he had to leave. She said nothing, but watched him walk away.

Kevin sat down in the spot which Tom had left.

'Nice bloke,' he said. 'Tom Hall.'

Andie nodded. 'Had a bit of a rough time, though.'

'Yes,' said Kevin. 'Hasn't let it interfere with his work. I told him that maybe it should. He said not. I agree really. Better to get on with things rather than brood.'

'Yes.' Andie nodded again.

'I know his wife,' said Kevin. 'Known her for a long time. Lovely girl.'

'I met her,' said Andie. 'At your wedding.'

'Lovely girl,' said Kevin again. 'They'll work it out.'

'I'm sure they will.' Andie smiled at Kevin as he got up. But she didn't feel like smiling. She felt as though Kevin had given her a warning. A warning she'd better heed.

But if it had been a warning, she hadn't heeded it. The next day she'd received a phone call from Tom.

'How'd you find me?' she asked.

'Phone book,' he said. 'Not difficult.'

'I guess not,' she said. 'I keep saying that I should go ex-directory so that strange men can't call me up whenever they feel like it.'

'Too late,' he said.

'You think?'

'I need to see you.'

She held the phone and stared out of the window. This wasn't what she wanted from life. This wasn't the kind of relationship she needed.

'When?' she asked.

'Tonight?'

She knew that it was physical. She'd expected that it would run its course, that after a while she'd stop fancying Tom Hall and that he'd stop fancying her. After all, she reasoned, for him it was probably just sex. She couldn't imagine that sex with Elizabeth was much fun any more. But then she realised that it was more than sex. That she'd fallen in love with him. That she wanted to be with him more and more. That she missed him when he wasn't around.

She couldn't believe they'd been having an affair for nearly four years. That this was what her life had become – waiting for Tom, waiting for him to call her, waiting for the right time to call him. Wondering how she could get through the hours and sometimes days before she would see him again. She couldn't believe that she'd accepted the fact that he wasn't going to leave Elizabeth, because to leave Elizabeth would be to leave a vulnerable woman in a vulnerable state. But that was OK with her, because it was the way things were if she wanted to love Tom.

And she couldn't help loving Tom.

Only right now, she wished he wasn't with Elizabeth. She wished he was with her.

Chapter 3

Piano Concerto No 2 in G Minor – Saint-Saëns

Jin lay in her big bed, the Egyptian cotton sheets cool beneath her hot body. She knew that she should get up but she was too tired. It had been another late night – the third that week – and she was running out of steam. She was also sure that she was positively destroying her liver, because she'd chugged back cocktails at the reception in the Four Seasons hotel, thinking that they'd be light on the alcohol – but had suddenly realised that whatever alcohol they contained had kicked in radically and she was walking round in a little world of her own. Then she'd decided that she was entitled to be in a world of her own that night because she wasn't really enjoying herself, there were too many people there that she didn't feel like talking to. You could, she thought, overdose on corporate dinners and receptions.

She slid out of the bed and walked slowly into the marble en-suite bathroom. She ran the cold tap and soaked her white flannel under the icy stream before pressing it to her forehead. She looked at her face in the mirror and groaned. There were lines and wrinkles everywhere! That was what being entertained did for you.

It hadn't all been bad last night of course. Kevin had been amused rather than annoyed (as sometimes he could be) by her giggly, drunken state and had jokingly called her his Margarita Moll. Because he knew he'd be drinking at the reception too, he'd requested a company driver to bring them home. He didn't use the driver very often when he was with her, but it had been fun last night because the partition between the driver and the passengers had been firmly closed and Kevin had made love to her on the back seat of the car, pulling her on to his lap almost as soon as they'd begun to drive and entering her quickly so that she gasped with surprise and then squirmed with excitement.

'You get better with every passing day,' he had murmured into her ear as he thrust deep inside her. And she'd pushed herself closer to him, turned on by the fact that they were having sex while driving through the streets of Dublin. When she looked out of the Merc's tinted windows she could see other people strolling hand in hand or hurrying along the pavements, and she laughed out loud to know that none of them had any idea that she, Jin Dixon, was making love to her husband as they sped past.

Later, at home, they'd made love again, this time on the pillow-strewn bed, and it had been slower, less exciting but still wonderful. The thing about her husband, Jin thought, was that nobody knew how bloody good he was at sex. Powerful, intuitive, interesting – just as he was at business. She wondered which drove which – good at business meant being good in bed, or good in bed led to him being a whizz in the boardroom? Not that it mattered once he was good with her!

She examined her wrinkles more closely. Being in her damn thirties wasn't helping. She wondered if her body knew the moment she'd hit the milestone birthday and had begun to go into terminal decline. She walked into the shower, turned the taps on full and allowed hot water to cascade over her. Then she pulled on her white robe, dried her mane of hair, dressed in a pair of faded jeans and a grey Calvin Klein T-shirt and went downstairs.

It was ten o'clock. Kevin had long since departed for the office – no matter how late they were out, he was nearly always at his desk by eight. She really didn't know how he managed it. In her previous life, when she'd had to go to early-morning photographic shoots, she'd been totally out of it before midday. Her brain, she'd often told them, didn't kick in until after twelve. And even then it was a bit of a struggle. They'd always believed her about that and it was certainly true that she wasn't at her best early in the morning. But it irritated her mildly at how quickly they were prepared to believe that she didn't have a brain at all!

Even Kevin would sometimes refer to her as his itsy-bitsy-ditsy model wife.

She was none of those things really, thought Jin as she filled the kettle. Given that she was taller than him, itsy and bitsy were singularly inappropriate adjectives, and just because she enjoyed shopping it didn't make her terminally stupid. After all, she'd looked after her own accounts when her modelling career had been at its peak and had never allowed her affairs to get into a state of chaos like some of the other girls. In fact she'd helped some of them with their record-keeping. At one time she'd thought that this was something she could develop further when the modelling work dried up. But, of course, she'd met Kevin and that had changed everything. When she'd married him he told her that she'd never need to worry about anything again, that she could concentrate on simply enjoying life. And there was no doubt but that life with Kevin was very enjoyable! All the same . . . She took a mug out of the cupboard and ladled two large spoonfuls of dark coffee into it. All the same, she wasn't using her brain very much these days. She needed something to keep her occupied. It wasn't as though she had a family . . .

She exhaled sharply and pulled the *Irish Times* across the table. Kevin always read the paper before going into the office – he didn't approve of managers sitting at their desks turning the pages. She flipped to the crossword page and frowned. He'd done both of them already, the simple and the cryptic. What was worse, he'd completed both of them. Every box was filled in in his neat print. Overachiever, she thought irritably, as she pushed it away again.

Andie listened in despair as one of her supposedly talented students butchered Saint-Saëns' Piano Concerto No 2 in G Minor. Well, she conceded, butchered might be too strong a word for it, but really and truly, Daniel Jones was managing to turn a light and airy piece of music into something heavy-handed and leaden. Instead of skipping along the keys, his fingers thudded against each one, as though he could force the music out of the piano by sheer strength.

'OK,' she said when he'd finished. 'Needs a bit more work, though.'

Daniel looked at her. 'A lot more work.'

She grinned suddenly. 'Well, Daniel, if you could get out of the habit of trying to beat the damn instrument into submission it might help.'

He sighed deeply. 'I'm never going to make it, am I?' he asked.

'What d'you mean?'

'I'm never going to be a concert pianist.'

'Maybe not,' she said. 'But you're very talented.'

'You're more talented than me,' protested Daniel. 'And you're only a teacher. What hope have I got?'

'Nobody goes into music for the money.' She sighed. 'Yet less talented people than either of us have made successful careers out of it.'

'Didn't you ever want to?' Daniel took the sheaf of music from the stand and bundled it together.

'I have made a career of it.' She smiled at him. 'I teach it.'

'You know what I mean,' said Daniel.

She shook her head. 'I'm not a performer. I play best when I'm on my own.'

'I heard you earlier,' he told her. 'You were playing this piece. It sounded wonderful.'

'One of my favourites,' she told him. 'And the bloody composer knocked it off in two weeks. Bastard.'

He laughed. 'You're a good teacher, Andie.'

'And you're a good student, Daniel. But you try too hard.'

'Yeah, I know.' He shrugged. 'I wanted to be great. But sometimes hard work isn't enough, is it? You need the talent.'

'Hell, Daniel, sometimes the talent isn't enough either,' Andie told him. 'You need talent, hard work and lots and lots of luck. And it all has to fall into place at the same time.'

'I guess,' said Daniel. He shoved the music into his case. 'See you Friday.'

She nodded. 'See you Friday.'

He walked out of the room and left her sitting beside the piano. She flexed her fingers. Long, long fingers. Artistic, her father had once told her, and she'd believed him. And he'd sent her to music lessons because he thought that she might have the talent for it. Andie closed her eyes. She'd loved her music lessons. From the

41

first day that she'd walked into Mrs Bowen's slightly dusty living room. Mrs Bowen was the sort of person that Jin thought Andie would one day become. Salt-and-pepper hair pulled into a rigid bun on the back of her head. Dove-grey skirts and pink blouses with ruffles at the neck. And half-moon glasses perched on the tip of her beaky nose. Andie hadn't believe that women like Mrs Bowen existed outside the world of period TV shows. But her Mrs Bowen certainly did. And she was a bloody good music teacher.

Before she knew where she was, Andie was sitting and passing an exam a year, not even thinking of it as work, never minding the time she spent at the piano, practising. Of course, because she played only classical pieces, because her focus was so much in the past rather than the future, she occasionally felt disconnected from the music she heard around her. So that sometimes when she listened to pop music she was offended by its triteness. But not always, she reminded herself. After all, she loved Queen, over the top and all though Freddie Mercury had been, and she enjoyed watching MTV. She knew that the classical composers would've used every possible electronic device to make music if they'd been available to them then. But she was glad they hadn't been. She loved the mechanics of music. The vibration of the strings, the actual beat of a drum, the rush of air from a wind instrument. She was out of date really. Maybe Jin was right. Maybe in another few years she'd end up like Mrs Bowen after all.

She played a few scales and then began a Chopin waltz. She closed her eyes as she played, opening them only occasionally to glance at the black and white keys which she was caressing. As always when she played, she lost herself completely in the music, caught up in the tones and cadences of the piece and proud of the fact that she was bringing the composer's ideas to life. She knew that she moved on to a different plane when she played the piano, totally distanced from everything else around her. She heard the door open but ignored it. It was lunch time. The visitor was either a student who just wanted to listen or another teacher with a request to take a class or – more likely – an administrative problem.

The last notes of the piece faded and she lifted her hands from the piano.

'Wonderful,' said Tom.

She spun round at the sound of his voice, a strand of her copper hair tumbling across her face. 'What are you doing here?'

'Lunch?'

'I didn't think you were working today. And how did you get in?'

'I wasn't. But I decided to come in anyway. I got in by asking at reception. Simple really.' He grinned at her.

'Where's Elizabeth?'

'Getting her hair done,' said Tom.

'In town?' Andie's voice was anxious.

'No.' He laughed. 'Near home. Don't worry, we won't bump into her.'

'I'm not really worried.'

'You always are,' said Tom. 'We've been seeing each other for nearly four years and you're still worried that someone will find out. If they haven't now, they never will.'

'They haven't found out because we're careful,' said Andie. 'Coming here wasn't careful.'

'I'm tired of being careful,' said Tom petulantly. 'I want to bring you for lunch. Come on, Andie, it's not as though we're likely to meet anyone we know.'

'Tom, I work here. I know lots of people.'

'But none of them know me.' He smiled brightly. 'Stop being so repressed, sweetheart.'

'Right.' She got up from the piano stool.

'Sorry.' He saw her purse her lips and knew he'd upset her. 'You're not repressed. You know you're not.'

'Maybe sometimes.' She shut the piano lid gently.

'It's like another world in here, isn't it?' He looked around him. 'So genteel. I can even smell lavender wood-polish.'

'It's not really genteel.' Andie smiled as she picked up her bag. 'Music is as cut-throat as anything else. People wanting to be famous. People settling for not. Students getting places elsewhere, joining the right orchestra . . . there's all sorts of stuff going on that you don't know about.'

'I like to think of evil-doing among the violins,' said Tom. 'Makes it much more interesting.'

43

'Fool.' She jabbed him in the ribs with her elbow and they left the red-brick Academy building and walked towards St Stephen's Green.

'What d'you fancy for lunch?' he asked.

She shrugged. 'Don't mind. It's just so nice to be with you.'

'You're easily pleased.' He put his arm around her shoulders and she stiffened. 'Darling, nobody is going to see us,' he said in exasperation. 'None of Kevin's bars are anywhere near here, nobody knows me, you're being paranoid.'

'Tom, Dublin is a bloody village for all that we like to pretend it's a modern, vibrant city. It's almost impossible not to bump into someone you know. And if we do I want us to appear as friends. Nothing more.'

'If you think that anybody we meet would possibly think that we're nothing more than friends then you're sadly mistaken,' said Tom. 'But OK then. Let's just walk side by side.'

She glanced at him. His jaw was set, she could see his facial muscle twitch. She said nothing as she fell into step beside him, knowing that she'd annoyed him and sorry that she'd been so uptight. But it was important for both of them to keep their relationship under wraps, and she was always terrified of someone finding out. Normally Tom was equally concerned, but every so often he would do something mad and crazy, like bringing her to a city-centre restaurant where there was a chance of their being seen together. Those times he told her that they could pretend they were talking business. That he was investigating the provision of live music in the bar. Which always made her laugh, because Tom's hip-hop bar was certainly not a place where anyone would be found listening to Vivaldi or Mozart.

They walked along the Green, then turned into Ely Place, where he ushered her into a wine bar. They were shown a seat near the window.

'Why are we here?' asked Andie. 'Why did you come to see me?'

A waiter handed them laminated cards with food and wine choices.

'Duck salad,' said Andie after a momentary glance.

44

'The same for me.' Tom handed back the menus. 'And a bottle of sauvignon blanc.'

'Tom!' She stared at him. 'I can't drink wine during the day. I have students this afternoon.'

'A glass won't kill you,' he said.

'What's going on?' she asked. 'You've never done this before. Never called in to the Academy. You've never been so careless.'

'I'm tired of being careful,' he said, and his voice echoed the weariness of his words. 'I'm tired of caring whether or not anyone sees me with you. I'm tired of caring about Elizabeth's feelings all the time.'

'I thought you were happy the way things were,' said Andie evenly. 'I thought you wanted to stay with Elizabeth.'

'Jesus, Andie, how could you possibly think that?' asked Tom. 'My life in that house is miserable. She's miserable. It would've been different if we'd had the children, I know. But we didn't and it's not.'

'So what do you want?' she asked.

'I want to be with you,' he said. 'Since the first day we met I've only wanted to be with you.'

The waiter set their food and drink in front of them. Andie picked up her fork and poked at the nest of rocket salad.

'You can't be with me,' she said calmly. 'You know you can't. We've talked about it.'

'I know,' said Tom. 'But Andie – it's getting harder and harder for me to live like this.'

Andie pushed at her salad some more. More than anything in the world she wanted Tom to be with her. She didn't want him to be a secret part of her life. She wanted everyone to know that she loved Tom Hall and that he loved her. She hated knowing that her own feelings had to take second place to Elizabeth's. And it was difficult to always be the perfect partner for Tom, never pressuring him, never begging him to leave.

'I think of leaving her all the time,' Tom continued. 'You know I do. But I'm afraid of what might happen. Of what she might do.'

'D'you think she'd – kill herself?' Andie couldn't believe that she was saying something like this. Not at lunch time in Dublin

45

while office workers strolled the streets in light tops and rolled-up sleeves because the sun was still, even at the end of September, astonishingly warm.

'That's the thing.' Tom's voice was toneless. 'Maybe she would. And then I'd've killed her.'

'You're being silly,' said Andie. She put down her fork, the salad untasted. '*We'd* have killed her.'

'I'm glad you can joke about it.'

'I'm not joking,' she said. She looked up from the plate. 'If you came to live with me, and Elizabeth . . . it'd be my fault as much as yours. Is she really so unstable, Tom?'

'I don't know.' Tom looked despairingly at her. 'Sometimes everything's fine. Sometimes we have a normal life and I remember why I loved her. Then she goes into these black, black depressions and nothing I can do or say gets through to her.'

'She needs help, Tom.'

'She's had help,' he told her. 'You know that. But she has to want to get better. Sometimes I don't think she does. Sometimes I think she feels it's better to be a tragic figure. You know how everyone feels about her. Kevin adores her.'

At the mention of her brother-in-law's name, Andie bristled. 'It's nothing to do with Kevin.'

'I know,' said Tom. 'And he's a great one to talk anyway, given that he dumped his wife for a selection box of dolly-mixture arm candy before he married Jin. But he takes an interest in Elizabeth's welfare. God knows why. And if I left her . . .'

'Oh, so what?' demanded Andie. 'What could he do? Fire you?'

'Make my life uncomfortable,' said Tom.

'If you left Elizabeth for me it would throw him completely,' said Andie. 'After all, you'd be living with his wife's sister. He couldn't really make your life uncomfortable.'

'He could,' said Tom. 'Only you wouldn't know it.'

'Maybe,' said Andie impatiently. 'But Kevin isn't really the issue here, is he? The issue is Elizabeth.'

'It's awful when you stop loving someone,' said Tom. 'It really is. We used to have fun together, Andie. It used to be great.'

Andie wasn't sure that she wanted to hear how great things had

46

been for Tom and Elizabeth. What she wanted to hear was that he no longer loved her, could no longer live with her and was going to move out.

'So what do you want to do?' she asked.

'One day I'll leave,' said Tom. 'But I need to do it at the right time.'

'There'll never be a right time,' said Andie. 'You know that.'

'There are times that will be better than others,' Tom said.

'It's a long while since we've had this sort of discussion.' Andie pushed her uneaten food away. She couldn't, in fact, remember the last time they'd talked about Tom leaving Elizabeth. It was a topic that she was always very careful to steer clear of. She didn't want him to think that it mattered to her, that she felt somehow second-rate because their relationship was a secret. She never wanted him to know how much she longed to bring his name into conversation, how she would love to say 'me and Tom' when talking with Jin. As far as she was concerned, being with her was supposed to be a break for Tom. She was the person who never got upset about anything. Who was always ready to make him laugh, who followed the fortunes of his beloved Aston Villa so that she could talk about the team's performances with him (though she really wished he supported a decent team like Liverpool instead). She was the one who never said no when he wanted to make love . . . but maybe that was because she always wanted to make love with him too. She wondered if living with Tom would make her love him or desire him less. She didn't think so.

'So do you plan to raise the subject with her?' she asked briskly, realising that Tom himself had gone into a dream world.

'I have to,' said Tom. He reached out and took Andie's hand. She almost drew it away but instead she wrapped her fingers around his.

'When?'

'Soon,' he said. 'In the next few weeks.'

'Are you sure?'

'I think so.' He looked at Andie miserably. 'I'm thirty-eight years old, Andie. I need to get a life. I married Elizabeth and I thought we would be happy together, but how can we be? We try not to blame each other for our misery, but underneath it all we do. Maybe she thinks a better man would've given her stronger sperm or something. And a better man would be with her all the time. I can't be that man for her. I just can't.'

'And what about us?' Andie asked.

He stared at her, his eyes suddenly fearful. 'I thought we'd be together. That's what we want, isn't it?'

'Are you sure?'

'Of course I'm sure,' said Tom fiercely. 'I've never been more sure of anything.'

'And you think you'd have the life you want with me?'

'How can you even ask?' He held her hand tighter. 'I love you, Andie. You're the other part of me. You make me laugh. You make it all worthwhile.'

'And I'm good in the sack,' she said lightly.

'Don't joke about this,' he begged. 'I'm really serious. I've got to make a choice. And I've made it.'

'I've got used to joking,' she said. 'Whenever we talk seriously. So that you don't see how much it matters to me.'

'Oh, Andie – I do love you.'

'I love you too. And I want to be with you all the time.'

'That's what I want too,' he said.

It was weird, she thought, how she wanted to laugh and cry at the same time. For so long their declarations of love had been peppered with phrases like 'if only things were different' and 'I wish I'd met you sooner', but now Tom was finally talking about taking the step that was so difficult. She couldn't help feeling sorry for Elizabeth. But maybe the other woman would actually do better if Tom wasn't around any more. Maybe her misery was feeding off his.

'So you want to move in with me?' she said.

He looked into her clear, grey-green eyes. 'Of course. Providing you'll have me.'

She smiled suddenly. 'Oh, I'll have you all right,' she promised. 'It's just how many different ways that's the question.'

Jin checked Teletext to see whether the flight from London was on time. She'd promised to pick up Cora and Doireann from the airport and was looking forward to hearing about their experiences on the cruise. Cora had sent a few e-mails from the ship saying that they were having the most wonderful time, but Jin wanted to hear from her mother's lips that it had been the holiday of a lifetime. She loved the pleasure Cora got out of the gifts and treats that she and Kevin provided, even if she had to keep them quiet in front of Andie, who, Jin felt, was far too sensitive about the fact that she herself couldn't afford to spoil Cora too. Money was money, Jin thought; it surely didn't matter who was able to give you something, once you received a gift that gave you pleasure. She knew that Andie couldn't see it quite that way, and she thought that her sister was very foolish about it all. Jin snorted as she perched her Carolina Herrera sunglasses on her pert little nose. A nose which was probably the difference between her beauty and Andie's merely quirky good looks. Andie needed to lighten up a bit, Jin thought. Sniff the roses, smell the coffee, whatever – only stop taking it all so damn seriously!

Jin eased the car along the gravelled driveway, pointed the remote control at the electric gates and waited for them to open. She hadn't spoken to Andie since the party, but that was nothing unusual. She didn't speak to her sister very much at the best of times.

She was almost at the airport when her mobile phone, resting in its hands-free cradle, chirped at her.

'Hi, Jin.'

'Livia!' she exclaimed with pleasure. Livia Harper was one of Jin's oldest friends. Previously also a model, she too was now married – although, as she jokingly told Jin, she hadn't quite managed to snare someone like Kevin Dixon. Livia's husband ran a wine-importing business and they'd spent the last three weeks travelling through Spain and Portugal.

'How was the holiday?' asked Jin.

'Oh, well, you know how it is with Spence,' Livia said philosophically. 'I want to lie on a beach in the Algarve but he wants to wander around the vineyards, so we compromise. My part was great, but I was bored with the rest.'

'Why didn't you stay on the beach and let him do the wine thing?' asked Jin as she turned on to the main road.

'Because I might complain about it but I prefer to be with him,' said Livia simply. 'And even though it gets a bit boring, it can be a lot of fun too.'

'Softie.' Jin laughed.

'Maybe,' agreed Livia. 'Anyway, now that I'm back, how about lunch?'

'Love to,' replied Jin promptly. 'Where?'

'It's your turn to visit me.'

One of the disadvantages of Livia's marriage had been her move to Dalkey, on the other side of the city, which meant that they didn't have as much opportunity to meet as they did when Jin was living in Marino and Livia renting a studio apartment off Fitzwilliam Street.

'How about town instead?' suggested Jin.

'It's just that there's a lovely new restaurant opened on the main street that I'd like to try,' said Livia. 'Perfect lunching territory.'

'Oh, all right. Because it's you.'

Livia laughed. 'Take the Dart so that we can have a few drinks.'

'Maybe.' Jin knew that she was very snobbish about public transport, but she couldn't help herself. When she was a child a car had been a status symbol, but the Corcorans had been the only family on their road who didn't own one and it had rankled. Now that she had a Mercedes of her own she liked driving it wherever she wanted to go.

'Or get a taxi,' suggested Livia, 'if mixing with the hoi polloi upsets you.'

'Don't be silly,' said Jin. 'I'll take the Dart.'

'OK,' said Livia. 'Ring me when you get on and I'll meet you at the station. The restaurant is only a couple of minutes away.'

'Sure,' agreed Jin. 'When suits?'

'Later in the week?' asked Livia. 'Friday would be good for me. Or else Tuesday next.'

'I think I'm OK for either,' said Jin. 'But I'm in the car at the moment so I can't check. I'll give you a shout later or tomorrow to confirm.'

'Great,' Livia said. 'I'll bring my Portuguese holiday snaps and bore the pants off you.'

'I'll bring my Antigua ones,' said Jin.

'Quit with the oneupmanship!'

'Sorry.'

'See you then.'

'Yes. Great.' Jin stopped at the barrier to the car park and took a ticket. Honestly, she thought as she looked at the tariff, parking fees were totally outrageous at the airport. She might be a millionaire's wife but that didn't mean she didn't know a rip-off when she saw it.

Chapter 4

Impromptu in A Flat Major – Schubert

S he parked the car and walked to the arrivals area, wishing that she'd been a little less fashion conscious and more practical when she'd slid on her summer mules that day, because they were really too high for anything other than standing around in an elegant pose, and elegance and the mêlée that was usually the arrivals area didn't quite go together. Still, she told herself, it was always important to look good. She studied the monitor for information on Cora's flight. It had already landed and so, if they weren't delayed for too long in the baggage hall, they'd be through soon. She strolled over to the bookshop and bought a bundle of magazines as well as a bottle of Volvic. She glugged back the water appreciatively because she was still a bit thirsty from her overindulgence the night before. Then she leaned against a pillar and idly flicked through the pages of *Heat* while keeping an eye on the emerging passengers.

A sudden flurry of people came through the opaque glass doors, dragging their suitcases behind them and scanning the crowd for familiar faces. Just as she was beginning to think she'd have to wait a bit longer for them, she saw her mother. Her eyes opened wide at Cora's honey-brown tan, subtly coloured hair and new outfit of white top and indigo jeans. Cora hadn't worn jeans in years! But, thought Jin as she moved towards them, they were fabulous on her and she looked totally revitalised. Just as she managed to skirt around a reunited family of six or seven, a tall man, dressed in olive-green T-shirt and faded black denims, detached himself from the edge of the crowd and strode purposefully towards Cora and

Doireann. Jin stood stock still in amazement as she saw him throw his arms round her mother in a warm embrace, peck Doireann on each cheek and then hug Cora again before kissing her lightly on the lips. Much to her astonishment, she saw Cora hug him back while Doireann smiled at him. He kept his arm round Cora, who leaned closer to him and smiled up at him, an intimate smile which shocked Jin even more.

She pushed herself abruptly past the two children in her way and called out to Cora. Her mother saw her and her eyes lit up.

'Jin!' Cora beamed at her. 'Oh, darling, thanks for meeting us. What a bloody crush, though.'

'Yes,' murmured Jin. Her eyes flickered from the two women to the tall man whose arm was still around Cora's shoulders. He was impossibly handsome, she realised, with dark cropped hair and almost navy-blue eyes in a lightly suntanned face. He smiled, showing two rows of impeccably white teeth.

'This is Jack,' said Cora. 'We met him on the cruise. He got an earlier flight than us.'

'Hi.' Jack released his hold on Cora and thrust his hand towards Jin. She grasped it automatically. His handshake was firm and dry, his accent vaguely American. She looked at him again. He was in his thirties, she guessed, but which end of his thirties was uncertain. The lines on his face were faint except when he smiled, and those blue eyes were young and sparkling. As far as she could see there wasn't a speck of grey in his hair.

'Hello,' she said.

'Jack was wonderful to us on the boat,' said Cora.

'That's good,' said Jin cautiously.

'He made the whole cruise so much more enjoyable,' Cora continued.

'Oh, I think you girls would've had just as good a time without me.' Jack put his arms round both of them.

'No way,' said Cora. 'You know that.'

'Are you here on holiday?' Jin frowned at him. She was uneasy with all this hugging and embracing and concerned by the way Cora was looking at him in that besotted fashion.

'Sort of,' said Cora. 'He's staying with me for a while.'

53

Jin stared at her mother. 'He's what?'

'Staying with me.'

Jin looked from Cora to Doireann and then to Jack, who gave her the full force of his Tom Cruise-like smile. She realised that he too had a suitcase – or at least a huge carry-all which looked as though it had seen a lot of travelling.

'Your mom asked me to stay,' said Jack. 'Which I really appreciate. And which I want to do, of course.'

'For how long?' asked Jin. 'Are you on your way somewhere else?'

'Not exactly,' said Jack. 'I was part of the entertainment on the ship. I guess I'm taking a little time out and then researching my next project.'

'The entertainment?' Jin was startled. 'What sort of entertainment?'

'Really, Jin, you don't have to interrogate Jack here and now,' Cora said.

'I'm sorry,' said Jin helplessly. 'When you said Jack was on the cruise I thought he was a passenger.'

'Why don't we get the car.' Doireann broke in. 'It's far too crowded here for a decent conversation. And I'm knackered. I want to sit down again.'

'Yes. Of course. I'm sorry, Doireann.' Jin took the car park ticket out of her bag and walked out of the arrivals hall, the others following in her wake. She could sense Jack looking around with interest as they stepped out into the mild September sunshine.

'You said it always rained, Cora,' she heard him say to her mother.

'Nearly always,' Cora replied. 'Don't worry, you won't be disappointed.'

Jin paid the parking fee and led them through the car park and up to Level 6.

'Nice wheels,' observed Jack as she opened the boot of the Mercedes.

'Thanks.'

They loaded the luggage into the boot, then got into the car, Doireann and Jack in the back seat, Cora in the front passenger

54

seat beside Jin, who slid her mules thankfully off her feet and put on a pair of flat shoes instead.

'So.' Jin started the car. 'Tell me about it.'

'So we had the best holiday ever,' Cora told her. 'Thank you very much, Jin. And Kevin too, of course.'

'It was wonderful,' Doireann piped up from the back. 'Those islands were fabulous, the boat was magnificent, the food . . .' She laughed. 'There was so much food that I spent my time in an agony of indecision about what to eat. And then felt guilty because I couldn't be bothered to go to the gym to work it off.'

Would you shut up talking about things that don't matter and tell me what the hell the Hollywood Hunk is doing in my car? demanded Jin silently. But she didn't say anything as she eased the Merc out of the parking space.

'We used to walk round the boat,' Cora said. 'It's a mile the whole way round.'

'Of course Cora and Jack did a lot more walking than me,' Doireann added. 'But it was very pleasant. It didn't feel like a mile and you could always cut through the lounges if you got fed up anyway.'

'Really,' said Jin faintly.

'Well, we tried not to cut through too much. You could get far too tempted by the cocktails being touted around the place. Oh, Jin, it was a truly wonderful experience.'

'And where does Jack fit into the wonderful experiences?' She glanced in the rear-view mirror and caught the amused glint in his eye. Was he laughing at her?

'Like I said, he was great to us. Made us feel so welcome.'

'So you invited him back to stay?' Jin knew that her voice was sharp and edgy but honestly, she thought, this bloke – this *young* bloke – had apparently tagged on to Cora and Doireann and foisted himself on them to get some kind of free Irish holiday. And worse – she swung the Merc round the airport roundabout – his behaviour was totally suspect, hugging Cora, kissing her, for God's sake, and keeping his arm around her proprietorially.

'I'm a writer,' said Jack.

Jin groaned. Conor and Lily O'Shea had suffered at the hands of a

55

writer one year when they'd allowed some friend of a friend to spend the summer in their hillside retreat on the east coast of Spain. As far as she could remember, the so-called artiste had used the house as a real home from home, run up exorbitant bills and drunk Conor's wine cellar almost dry. As for the book (in which a dedication had been promised to Conor and Lily for their hospitality), that had never even appeared; in fact Lily had doubts that it had ever been started.

'Let's face it,' she'd confided to Jin over lunch. 'I do sweet f-all when I'm there. Why should anyone else be any different?'

And what, Jin wondered, did Jack expect to do at Cora's?

'What sort of book?' Jin asked him as she glided to a halt at traffic lights.

'I'm a travel writer,' Jack explained.

'Like Bill Bryson?' enquired Jin.

'My books are a bit more prosaic than Bill's, I think,' said Jack. 'Huh?'

'Well they're not rambling sort of discussions. They're more – well, they're . . .'

'It's a series,' interrupted Cora. 'They were on board the ship. *Twenty Things To Do In . . .*'

'In where?' asked Jin.

'New York. Las Vegas. California.'

'Oh, I see.' Jin glanced in the rear-view mirror again. 'More like travel guides.'

'Yes,' he said. 'The company commissions them and I write them and that's that.'

'So what were you working on?' she asked. '*Twenty Things To Do On a Cruise Liner*?'

Jack laughed. A rich, warm laugh. 'Nope,' he said. 'I was giving lectures on places to go. I know a lot about Mexico, lived there for a year. So I got this opportunity to give talks on the ship and I took it.'

'An opportunity not to be missed, I suppose,' said Jin drily.

'Would you turn it down?' he asked.

She shrugged and glanced in the mirror again. He was still smiling.

56

'And you got plenty of time to holiday with the passengers too?'

'Why not,' said Cora. 'He was wonderful, I said so.'

'So what are you planning to do here?' asked Jin.

'He's writing a novel,' Cora told her proudly.

'What sort of novel?' Jin looked back at him for a second. 'A novel about Ireland? Is that why you've come here? To research it?'

'No,' said Jack. 'My travel publisher has been considering doing some European guides for a time now. I told them I'd do them a draft *Twenty Things To Do In a European City*, see what they thought. When your mom suggested Dublin I thought, why not?'

'But wouldn't they rather use someone who knows the city?' Feeling herself grow more hot and bothered, Jin turned the air-conditioning up to max. 'After all, what can you tell them about things to do in Dublin?'

'You're right, of course,' said Jack. 'But they're looking for an outsider's view.'

'I said I'd help him,' Cora told her.

Jin turned down the tree-lined Griffith Avenue towards her mother's house. Well, she thought, as she indicated at the next junction, if Jack whatever-his-name-was had thought he was going to stay in a luxurious family home in Dublin city to research any kind of book he was in for a rude awakening. She eased the car along the narrow roads and finally stopped outside Cora's house. Then she looked round at Doireann in contrition.

'I'm so sorry,' she said. 'I should've dropped you off first.'

'No bother,' said Doireann. 'I'll ring Frank to pick me up. He wanted to come to the airport anyway but I said not to because you'd be there. I think the poor old dear misses me. At least, he'd better be missing me.'

'Sure I can't drive you back?' Jin opened the car door.

'Certain,' said Doireann.

'Wow.' Jack stood, hands in the pockets of his jeans, and looked at Cora's house. 'How utterly cute this is.'

'I wouldn't exactly call it cute,' said Jin.

'Oh, but the character!'

Jin made a face. Their family house wasn't cute at all. It was small. Neat, tidy, well maintained. But just a small house. With overgrown

57

grass in the front garden because it had shot up in the last week even though Cora had trimmed it before going away. But the roses which grew either side of the front door were still a pretty mass of pink and the flowerbeds a mosaic of bright colours.

'We don't have anything like this at home,' said Jack.

'What about white-painted clapboard houses?' asked Jin. 'With picket fences. Whatever the hell picket fences actually are.'

Jack grinned at her. 'Not the same.' He put his arm round Cora's shoulders and hugged her yet again. 'I'm so pleased you asked me to stay.'

Jin's eyes flickered towards Doireann. Her aunt was being remarkably cool about the whole thing instead of freaking out like Jin would've expected. For God's sake, she exploded mentally, I let my mother off for one bloody week on her own and she comes back with some kind of toy-boy, and Doireann seems to have done nothing to stop her.

Cora took her keys out of her bag and opened the door to the house. Jack carried her suitcase inside. Doireann began to lift her own but Jin stopped her and picked it up instead.

'What the hell's going on?' she demanded fiercely. 'What's with Mum and the hanger-on?'

Doireann shook her head. 'I don't really know,' she said uncomfortably. 'Nothing really.'

'Nothing?' Jin was incredulous. 'Nothing? Come on, Doireann. He's mauling her in front of me!'

'He's certainly tactile,' Doireann agreed. 'But it's just his way, Jin. You're overreacting.'

'Doireann, I'm certainly not overreacting!' Jin looked towards the house, where Jack and Cora had gone inside. 'He's here and he's staying with her and she hardly knows him and what the hell does she think she's doing? How did she get to know him?'

'Like he said, he was talking about travel, particularly the Aztec ruins at Tulum which we were going to see. And he was really interesting. Afterwards your mum asked him a question and next thing I know they're going for a drink together in the bar.'

'God Almighty!'

'And they saw each other every night.'

58

'But Doireann, he's young enough to be my brother,' hissed Jin. 'Surely there's not anything really . . .' Her voice trailed off at the thought of what might be going on between her mother and the handsome hunk. She wondered whether or not Cora had forgotten that she was, in fact, a fifty-eight-year-old widow and not a mad teenager.

'I don't think so,' said Doireann uncertainly.

'You don't *think* so.' Jin looked at her aunt in horror. 'You mean there might be?'

Doireann looked uncomfortable again. 'It's not something I got involved in,' she said.

'But surely you could have done something about it?' said Jin.

'Like what?' asked Doireann. 'Your mother's a grown woman. What did you want me to do?'

'Stop her making a fool of herself would've been a good start.'

'She didn't make a fool of herself on the boat,' said Doireann.

Jin still looked worried. 'OK, Doireann, maybe I *am* overreacting. But it's not often a girl's mother comes home with a bloke young enough to be her son in tow and casually announces he's staying for a while. I don't think it's wrong of me to wonder exactly what his motivation is.'

'It's mostly just friendship,' said Doireann. 'And it's nice for Cora to have a man interested in her again.'

'But why is *he* interested in *her*?' asked Jin. 'She's older than him!'

'Just because she's older doesn't mean she's ready to be put out to pasture,' said Doireann waspishly.

'I'm sorry. That sounded all wrong,' admitted Jin. 'I'm – I suppose I'm in shock.'

'He probably won't stay long,' Doireann comforted her. 'And he is quite a nice guy. Really.'

'I just don't want him to take advantage of her.'

'Of course you don't,' said Doireann. 'But she's an adult. She can look after herself. What advantage can he actually take?'

'How the hell do I know?' demanded Jin. 'But he's got to be after something. For God's sake, he could be a murderer for all we know.'

'Hopefully not,' said Doireann. 'I have some faith in Cora's ability to judge characters.'

'Lot of good realising he's a murderer will do her when he's standing over her with a butcher's knife,' said Jin gloomily.

Doireann laughed. 'It'll probably all blow over in a week,' she said. 'Meeting people on a cruise is one thing. Having them in your home is something else entirely.'

'I hope you're right,' said Jin. 'What on earth was she thinking by inviting him in the first place?'

'Yes, well, I wasn't entirely happy about that,' Doireann confessed. 'But it wasn't up to me to stop her.' She sighed. 'I did try, Jin. Honestly. I asked her if she thought it was a good idea to extend this invitation. And she said she didn't care, she liked Jack and why not?'

'There are all sorts of reasons why not!' cried Jin.

'Look, this is a fad of your mum's,' said Doireann. 'It'll blow over.' She shrugged. 'I hope.'

Jin rubbed the tip of her nose. 'Her fads are usually more domesticated,' she said. 'Like going through a phase of only eating Indian food or drinking Spanish wine or something. And she has fashion fads too, or at least she used to. Remember when she insisted on wearing those ridiculous pedal-pusher trousers all the time? But this is different, Doireann . . .'

Cora reappeared at the doorway. 'Aren't you coming in?' she asked them. 'I thought you said you wanted to phone Frank to pick you up, Doireann.'

'Yes,' said Doireann. 'I do.' She walked into the house, followed by Jin.

Jack was standing in the tiny kitchen.

'Cute enough for you?' asked Jin.

'It's all so perfect,' said Jack.

'So what will you be saying in your book? That one of the twenty things to do is to visit Marino and see a little house?'

'I think you've kinda got the wrong idea about me and the books,' said Jack.

'Have I?'

'Anyone want a cup of tea?' asked Cora.

60

'Love one,' said Doireann.

Cora filled the shiny chrome kettle and plugged it in.

'Jin, will you show Jack where to leave his stuff upstairs?' she asked.

Jin's eyes flickered between her mother and the younger man. Where upstairs, she wondered, did Cora expect her to bring him? There were two bedrooms in the house. The one that Cora and Des had shared for their entire married life. And the one that she and Andie had shared until they'd left home and which was now somewhat euphemistically called the guest room despite the fact that Cora rarely had people to stay.

'This way,' said Jin.

Jack followed her up the narrow wooden staircase. She didn't hesitate but flung open the door to the guest room, which, she realised suddenly, was far too pretty and chintzy for a bloke to stay in. The walls were painted in blueberry white, the furniture was distressed white and the duvet cover also white but covered in tiny blue and pink flowers. The room was totally inappropriate for him, thought Jin, but there was no way in hell that she was showing him into her mother's room. Besides, she hadn't been in that bedroom in ages. For all she knew it could be even girlier.

'Cool.' Jack dumped his bag on the flowery duvet.

'I hope you enjoy your stay here,' said Jin. 'I don't expect it'll be for too long, will it?'

'I don't know.' Jack looked out of the window and then turned to her. 'I haven't really decided yet. It depends on Cora, I guess.'

Jin could feel her heart thudding in her chest.

'But if it depended on you?' she asked.

He shrugged. 'I like travelling. I like staying in new places.'

'But here? With my mother?'

'Why not?' asked Jack easily. 'We've a lot in common. She invited me here. It's no big deal, you know.'

But it was a big deal, thought Jin. Really it was. And she was struggling with the fact that Jack talked about Cora as though he already knew her better than Jin herself did. As though they had a private relationship that Jin couldn't possibly understand . . . And

61

what could a thirty-something travel writer and a fifty-eight-year-old widow possibly have in common?

She had a sudden image of her mother and this man making love and almost threw up on the carpet. They couldn't be. They just couldn't. She closed her eyes. She was totally unable to deal with this right now.

'I'm going to get some tea,' she told him.

She walked down the stairs again. Doireann and Cora were sitting at the kitchen table while they waited for the kettle to boil.

'What's with this writer bloke, Mum?' Jin tried to keep her tone casual but her words ended in a squeak. 'Are you out of your mind inviting him here? I put him in the spare room. I get the feeling that he thinks he should be in your room.' Her voice wobbled. 'I can't believe you could possibly . . .'

The kettle clicked itself off and Cora stood up. She poured boiling water over the tea bags in the dark brown ceramic pot. 'We've already explained to you,' she said. 'He's a nice man and he gave me a good time on the ship. And I felt I could return his hospitality.'

'Return his hospitality!' Jin stared at Cora in disbelief. 'He worked on the bloody ship, he wasn't being hospitable. And you were paying for him to be nice!'

'Well, *you* were actually paying for it.' Cora poured tea into china mugs. 'But who cares? He wanted to come to Ireland and I invited him. Why shouldn't I?'

'Because—' Jin broke off as Jack walked into the room. She felt as though she was in a comedy sketch where everyone else was getting the point except her. It looked as if her mother was having some kind of relationship with a bloke half her age, a bloke she hardly even knew. Cora had obviously lost the run of herself completely! And Doireann – her aunt, her father's sister, for God's sake – didn't seem to care. Surely Doireann would want to protect her brother's memory, thought Jin in bewilderment; surely Doireann didn't want to see Cora betray Des. She sat at the table and took the mug of tea from her mother. She splashed milk into it and pushed the jug across the table towards Cora.

'I don't bother any more,' said Cora. 'I drink it black. Actually

I prefer it with lemon now but I don't have any lemons in the house.'

There was an awkward silence, broken, thankfully as far as Jin was concerned, by the ringing of the doorbell which meant that Doireann's husband, Frank, had arrived to collect her. Both Jin and Doireann drained their cups while Cora got up to let Frank in.

'Jin, thank you for the holiday,' said Doireann. 'We really had a great time.'

'Did you?' Jin looked anxiously at her aunt. 'I wanted you to enjoy yourselves, but . . .'

'Of course we enjoyed ourselves,' said Doireann heartily. 'We really did. The cruise was wonderful and so was Mexico.'

'I'm glad you enjoyed it, but—'

'I made sure they enjoyed themselves,' said Jack unexpectedly, butting into the conversation.

Jin said nothing. She was completely lost for words.

Doireann walked out into the small hallway and greeted her husband. Suddenly Jin knew that she couldn't stay here any more. Her head ached, her exhaustion of earlier had returned and she didn't know what to make of her mother's totally unexpected and irrational behaviour.

She picked up her soft leather handbag and stood up.

'I've got to go,' she said.

'Nice meeting you,' said Jack.

'I'm sure you'll have moved on before I get the chance to see you again,' she said.

'Maybe. Maybe not.'

She walked out of the room. Frank and Doireann were already getting into their car. Cora followed Jin out to the garden and waved at them.

'I'm heading off too,' said Jin.

'Are you all right?' asked Cora. 'You look quite pale.'

'Anyone would be pale when their mother arrives back from the States with a strange man in tow,' said Jin. 'Especially a strange man who's far too young for her.'

Cora laughed. 'He's not in the slightest bit strange.'

'You know what I mean.'

'He's very nice,' said Cora. 'You were a bit rude, Jin. And who cares how old he is?'

'For goodness' sake!' Jin looked at her in exasperation. 'You should care. You brought him here and he's totally out of place.'

'I don't think so.' Cora's tone was amused.

'Mum, this is a Dublin suburb, not flipping Los Angeles,' said Jin abruptly. 'Middle-aged women don't have gorgeous men hanging round them.'

'Why not?' asked Cora.

'Why not?' Jin stared at her. 'Because – because – they just don't. It's not real life, Mum. It's some kind of fantasy.'

'Maybe.' Cora grinned. 'But I'm living it.'

'With a gigolo.'

Cora chuckled. 'That's such an old-fashioned term. I'd hardly expect you to even know it.'

'Well what would you call him?' demanded Jin. 'Your toy-boy?'

'Perhaps.' Cora winked at her.

Jin felt her mouth drop open. She'd been her mother's favourite daughter in the past, the one to go shopping with her, to try on make-up with her, to do the girlie things with her that Andie clearly couldn't be bothered to do. She'd thought she understood Cora. But right now she felt as though her mother was a complete stranger.

'Look, I'm exhausted,' said Cora. 'I haven't slept in ages and I really just want to go in, finish my tea and go to bed. How about I give you a ring tomorrow or the next day?'

'Sure,' said Jin. 'Sure. I send you on a cruise and you come back and dismiss me.'

'I wasn't aware I had to be grateful for ever,' said Cora.

Jin looked at her, afraid that suddenly she was about to cry.

'Go home,' said Cora gently. 'I'll call you.'

'OK,' said Jin. She took out the keys to the Merc. 'But if not, I'll call you.'

'And Jin?'

'Yes?'

'I am grateful,' said Cora. 'You gave me a truly wonderful birthday present.'

'But Andie was right,' muttered Jin as she got into her car. 'I should've stuck with the damn spoons.'

Chapter 5

Waltz in A Flat Major – Brahms

T he house was empty when she got home. Not that she was
expecting anyone to be there, of course. Kevin would be at
work for hours yet and Lara, the Romanian woman who came to
clean three times a week, wasn't due until the next day. But Jin
wished there was someone around for her to talk to. Someone to
share the totally unbelievable situation with. Because whatever it
was that her mother was doing was unbelievable. Whether she really
had just invited Jack to stay for a couple of weeks while he worked
on his stupid travel guide, or whether there was something more to
it – either way it was silly and childish and not the sort of behaviour
Jin would have expected from a fifty-eight-year-old mother of two
grown-up daughters!

Cora couldn't really be sleeping with Jack, could she? Like most
offspring, Jin had rarely thought of her parents as people who
indulged in sex. The idea that her mother might have slept with
someone as young and handsome as Jack – bloody hell, Jin thought
inconsequentially, she didn't even tell me his surname!; anyway the
idea of Cora and Jack in bed together was so impossibly nauseating
that it made her shiver. She shoved the truly awful image to the
furthest recesses of her mind.

It wasn't as though she didn't want Cora to form new relationships. Not really. Although, she admitted to herself as she poured
some cold water from the filter jug into a glass, she was still
uncomfortable about the idea of a serious relationship between
her mother and any new man because the gap left by the death of

her father couldn't be filled by just anyone. But lately both herself and Andie had tried to encourage Cora to get out and about a bit more. She was a member of the local book club and involved in a number of different activities in the community, but none of them was geared towards meeting eligible men. Jin felt that Cora was of a generation where a man was important. In fact, she acknowledged, she felt as though a man in any woman's life was important. She couldn't understand Andie's apparent indifference to her seemingly permanently boyfriend-less state despite her best efforts at inviting her sister to any event at which she might meet someone suitable. But Andie's love life was of much less concern to her now than Cora's! She couldn't quite believe that she was worrying about her mother's association with someone entirely unsuitable. This was not something she'd ever expected to have to worry about. And what the hell would Kevin say? Her husband hated gossip about himself or his family, and if people got wind of Cora's latest escapade they'd gossip themselves silly.

She picked up the phone and tried to ring Andie to let her know about this sudden and unexpected turn of events. But her sister's mobile was switched off and Jin supposed that she was in a lesson which couldn't be disturbed by the discordant electronic sounds of a mobile phone. She didn't bother leaving a message. Andie would laugh at her, she thought. She'd probably take some moral high ground about the fact that Kevin and Jin had organised the cruise in the first place. Maybe, thought Jin, she'd wait a day or so before phoning Andie. Give herself a chance to get to grips with the situation. The effects of being out late the night before and the shock she'd received when she'd met Jack were beginning to take hold. She needed to lie down. She drained the glass of water and walked upstairs.

It was nearly eight before Kevin came home, surprised that, though Jin's car was parked outside, the internal lights of the house were off and the curtains still open. He frowned as he put his key in the door and walked into the silent hallway. Usually, when he came home, he was greeted by the sound of the TV or the phenomenally expensive sound system he'd had installed so that there were speakers in every room of the house, including the hall. He went into the kitchen, saw the empty water jug and glass on the table and frowned. He left his briefcase beside the door, closed the slatted window-blinds, and went upstairs.

She was lying on her back, her copper hair fanned out around her face, a tiny wisp falling gently across her cheek. Her arms were outstretched, one hanging over the edge of the bed. She was still wearing her crisp white blouse but she'd taken off her figure-hugging Sass & Bide jeans, which lay in a crumpled heap on the floor. She looked exquisitely beautiful, thought Kevin.

'Jin!' He put his mouth close to her ear and she jumped awake, eyes wide in confusion.

'God Almighty, Kevin, you scared the living daylights out of me.' She sat up and pushed her hair out of her eyes.

'Why are you in here?' he asked. 'Have you been here all day?'

She flinched at the icy tone in his voice. If there was one thing she didn't like about Kevin (and she was reluctant to think that there might be anything about him that wasn't perfect), it was his sudden coolness in the face of something he disapproved of. She knew immediately that he suspected her of being so hungover this morning that she hadn't managed to make it out of bed. He'd told her once that hungover women were totally unattractive. That Monica, hungover, had been grounds for divorce without question. Kevin rarely got drunk himself. He did drink, of course, it was almost impossible to be in business and not to, but he usually drank sparingly, on the basis that he liked to know what everyone else was doing.

Jin rubbed her eyes and looked at her husband. 'Of course I haven't been here all day,' she told him. 'I've been picking Mum and Doireann up from the airport.'

'And that tired you out so much you had to go to bed?' As well as not drinking very much, Kevin rarely seemed to be tired either. But he'd grown used to Jin's desire for a full eight hours (preferably more) every night.

'No,' said Jin slowly. 'I was utterly exhausted when I got home because—'

68

'You really shouldn't have knocked back so many cocktails last night,' Kevin interrupted her.

'It had nothing at all to do with the cocktails,' returned Jin. 'Besides, you liked me last night. You called me your Margarita Moll.'

'There were a few other names that sprang to mind,' remarked Kevin.

'Oh for God's sake!' She glared at him. 'It didn't bother you when you were shagging me in the back seat of the limo, did it?'

'Jin!' He looked at her coldly.

'Look, I'm sorry,' she said hastily. 'I really am.' She hated arguing with him. She never won, for starters; he was capable of staying frosty for so much longer than she was, and he always managed to find the right riposte to whatever she said, making her feel like a silly schoolgirl. 'I admit I was a bit under the weather this morning and I didn't really mean to knock so many back last night. But I was fine later. It was picking up Mum and Doireann that . . . because Mum has come back . . .' She shook her head in disbelief at the image again. 'Mum arrived back in Dublin with a toy-boy in tow.'

Kevin stared at her. 'You're joking.'

'I wish I was,' she said. 'But I'm deadly serious.'

'A toy-boy? How toy? How boy? Are they lovers?'

Jin sighed. 'She hasn't exactly admitted the lover bit,' she said. 'But he's staying in the house with her.'

'Well then, perhaps he's just a friend.'

'No,' said Jin firmly. 'They might not have slept together yet but he's definitely not just a friend.'

'How can you be sure?'

'I saw them together.'

'How old is this toy-boy?' asked Kevin. 'Who exactly is he?'

'His name's Jack.' She rubbed the back of her neck. 'He's in his thirties, I guess. He's American. He was a guest lecturer on the ship talking about travel destinations. And it seems that Mum was rather taken by him.'

'You can't be serious.'

'Well he's installed in her house right now,' said Jin. 'So that's serious enough.'

'And why is he here? Just to be with her?' Kevin's voice was utterly incredulous.

'Apparently he does some travel writing and he's supposedly doing research,' said Jin drily. 'But I've never heard of him; besides, he only writes travel guides, not real books.'

'And he's staying in your mother's house while he researches Ireland?'

'The guides are called *Twenty Things To Do In* . . . whatever,' Jin explained. 'Presumably he's thinking of twenty things to do in Dublin. Or twenty things to do with my mother,' she added gloomily. 'Of course it's not just travel writing. He's supposed to be working on a novel as well.'

Kevin exchanged a knowing look with her. He was remembering Conor and Lily and the so-called writer who'd borrowed their Spanish villa.

'It's quite unbelievable that Cora would do something this silly,' he told Jin. 'She's having you on.'

'Kevin, he's in the damned house!' cried Jin. 'He's staying there with her. He's a gorgeous-looking thirty-something bloke and he's having some kind of relationship with my mother. And I don't approve of it.'

'Neither do I,' said Kevin. 'Because she's going to make a fool of herself and of us too. Can you imagine what people will say!'

'I know, I know.' Jin looked at him anxiously. 'But Doireann said that there was nothing I could do about it.'

'There's plenty we can do about it if we need to,' said Kevin grimly. 'But hopefully we won't have to.'

'The thing is,' Jin pushed her hair out of her eyes, 'I want Mum to be happy. You know I do. But this won't make her happy. He's using her. And she'll get hurt.'

'What d'you think he's using her for?'

Sex was the first thought that came into Jin's mind, but it was so utterly preposterous that she couldn't even say it. And it seemed impossible to believe that the Cora who hadn't even gone out with a man since Des had died would bring back a hunky bloke for sex! Besides, young men didn't use older women for sex. It was the other way round, wasn't it?

'Maybe he's not a travel writer at all,' said Jin eventually. 'Maybe he's simply conning a free holiday out of her.'

'Did he know what he was talking about on the ship?' asked Kevin.

Jin shrugged. 'I've no idea. But anyone could bluff their way through a travel talk, couldn't they? And if he makes a living by blagging people into giving him free holidays . . .' She looked at Kevin aghast. 'Maybe this is what he does for a living! You do see this sort of thing on TV shows, don't you? Where some smarmy bloke worms his way into the affections of gullible women and cons them out of their life savings or something.'

'Cora isn't wealthy enough,' Kevin pointed out.

'But maybe he thinks she is!' cried Jin. 'After all, she was staying in a great cabin. Maybe he thinks Mum and Doireann are rich widows.'

Kevin pursed his lips. 'It's not entirely outside the bounds of possibility,' he admitted. 'But surely your mother would already have told him that it was you and I who paid for her holiday.'

'Why would she tell him that?'

'I'm sure she would have mentioned at some point that the trip was a birthday gift,' said Kevin.

'Perhaps he didn't believe her!' Jin wriggled into her jeans and looked at Kevin despairingly. 'He could be in the house now, trying to wheedle information out of her about her investments, and she'll be saying she has nothing and he'll be thinking that she's just extra smart or something and—'

'There's no point in getting into a state about it now,' Kevin interrupted her. 'We'll go and see her and check the whole thing out.'

Jin bit her lip. The idea of Kevin striding into Cora's house and demanding to talk to her about Jack wasn't a pleasant one. Subtlety had never been one of his strongest points. If he barged in and started telling Cora that she was a silly old fool they'd get nowhere.

'You've got to be nice to her,' she told him.

'Of course I'll be nice to her,' he said. 'It's not her fault she's being taken for a ride.'

'She doesn't think she is.'

'That's exactly what being taken for a ride is all about,' said Kevin. 'You're made to think that you're doing what you want. We'll sort it out. Don't worry.'

'I hope so.' Suddenly Jin's eyes filled with tears. 'Oh Kevin, I know she's had a hard time since Dad died and I've often wished that she could find someone to go out with. Maybe have some male friends her own age to socialise with, but nobody so serious that they could usurp Dad.' She smiled shakily. 'That's selfish, I know. But that's how I felt. Now, though.' She shuddered. 'It's like she's a different woman! She's had her hair coloured, she has a great tan, she's wearing new clothes which knock about ten years off her age, and she's acting totally out of character.'

'I really don't think she can be serious,' said Kevin. 'She's not a fool, your mother.'

'Well, no.' Jin hesitated. 'But she used to be quite frivolous, Kevin. When we were younger. She enjoyed going out. You never really got to know her as that sort of person because Dad was already ill when you met her first, and that was a strain. So she changed a lot. But now she's gone completely in the opposite direction.'

'OK, then,' said Kevin. 'We'll drop in tomorrow at lunch time and see how she is.'

'Tomorrow at lunch time!' Jin's eyes opened wide in surprise. 'But it's a weekday. You're at work.'

'I can spare an hour,' said Kevin grimly. 'If my mother-in-law is making a complete fool of herself I can spare an hour to sort it out.'

'Kevin, please don't give out to her or lecture her or anything,' begged Jin.

'Of course I won't,' said Kevin. 'I just want to assess the situation myself.'

'All right.' Jin sounded doubtful, but she knew she'd have to give in. Besides, it wasn't a bad idea for Kevin to see this Jack bloke. Might put the frighteners on him if he had some mad designs on Cora.

'Now why don't you make me something to eat,' said Kevin. 'I've had a long day, no lunch and I'm absolutely starving.'

'No lunch!' Jin smiled at him. 'You poor thing. What would you like for dinner?'

'Steak,' he told her. 'If I'm going to confront Cora tomorrow I want to do it with some iron in my blood.'

As if you ever needed it, thought Jin as she went downstairs to do what he asked.

Andie was sitting in her deepest armchair listening to Ravel's Bolero. She found it almost impossible to hear the piece of music and not recall fragments of the wonderful ice-dance created by Torvill and Dean years earlier. She'd watched them perform the routine as she sat on the living-room floor leaning against her father's legs. Des Corcoran had loved ice-dancing. Andie hadn't been quite so keen on the skating, but she loved the music. And that particular piece always reminded her of a peaceful evening with her father, a time when everything had seemed perfect and wonderful.

She closed her eyes. She missed him. She missed his wit and humour, his pleasure in simple things. She was, she thought, much more like her father than her mother. Much more like him than Jin was too. Cora and Jin loved glitz and glamour, shopping and spending. She and Des had been different. They'd enjoyed music together. And fixing things simply for the fun of the work rather than throwing them out and getting the newer version. Jin used to laugh at her. Cora too, although to a lesser extent. Cora saw the fun in what they were doing, but to Jin it was simply a waste of time. Of course, thought Andie, Cora had changed since Des's long illness and his death. She was less fun, less frantic. After he'd finally given up the battle with the cancer that had eventually ravaged his body, she'd retreated into herself. Shocked, Andie believed, that Des had gone and left her behind. As far as she could see, Cora didn't get the same pleasure out of buying a frivolous dress or a totally unnecessary pair of shoes if Des wasn't there to look at her with fond amusement and tell her that she'd bankrupt him one day.

The music grew louder. Andie reached for her glass and took a slow sip of the ruby-red Rioja. It must be hard, she thought, when the person you love leaves you after a lifetime together. Suddenly all of the things that you did as a couple had to be faced on your own. Cora was an intelligent woman who'd held an interesting secretarial job until she'd had Jin and found it too difficult to manage running

73

the house and looking after two children. She'd been ahead of her time in many ways, surprising her friends by not immediately giving up work when she married Des. So, mused Andie, it wasn't as though her mother didn't have experience of the world and a life outside her marriage. It was just that after thirty-three years with one man it must be very difficult to adjust to being on your own. Andie wasn't certain that she'd be able to do it herself.

If there was ever a realistic chance of it happening in the first place. She took a larger gulp of her wine. After her lunch with Tom today she'd begun to think about it again, even though she normally tried to put thoughts of Tom and permanence out of her mind. They'd agreed at the start that their relationship was built around an attraction to each other and a desire for fun that would one day run its course and fizzle out. They'd told each other that when it happened they'd acknowledge it was over and that there'd be no regrets. Only it hadn't fizzled out; the attraction had grown stronger, their feelings for each other deeper. And even though she'd known it was wrong, she hadn't been able to stop it. She'd reminded herself about it supposedly being a bit of fun. She'd told herself that it wasn't meant to be serious. She'd said over and over again that nobody was supposed to get hurt. But someone was going to get hurt. And no matter how she and Tom felt about each other, it was Elizabeth who had the prior claim to Tom and a very effective hold over him. If only Elizabeth had been an ordinary woman, thought Andie as she refilled her now empty glass. But everyone saw her as a tragic figure, and if Tom did leave her then her tragedy would be even greater. He couldn't walk out. No matter what he said. She couldn't let herself believe that he ever would.

The music stopped and Andie removed the CD from the player. She remembered suddenly that Cora was due home today and picked up the phone to ring her. But then it occurred to her that Cora would probably be jet-lagged and might be asleep and she thought it wouldn't be fair to wake her. She'd call in the morning instead and listen to her stories about the cruise and Mexico and how great it had been. She felt guilty and a little silly about how she'd reacted when Kevin had given the present to Cora, and she knew that Jin was probably annoyed with her about it. She really and truly wished that the Dixons didn't bring out a side of her that she didn't like very much, but she always felt overwhelmed by Jin's insistence on splashing money around like she had a bottomless pit of the stuff. Thing was, thought Andie ruefully, Jin was hugely generous. She'd even offered to buy Andie a car once and had been insulted by Andie's insistence that she could manage by herself. She doesn't realise that I want to do it on my own, thought Andie. And sometimes I think that I badly want to do it all myself simply to prove a point!

That was the difficult bit, she mused, as she walked over to her piano and lifted the lid. These days so many people seemed to think that everyone wanted a celebrity lifestyle, with sudden wealth, designer clothes and the latest in everything. And if you didn't want it you were seen as not playing the game. When she listened to people gasping and wondering about Jin's latest car or holiday or whatever it was Kevin had just spent a fortune on, Andie couldn't help feeling that they thought she should be like Jin too. And, of course, Cora would sometimes unthinkingly say that it would be great if Andie could find herself a husband like Kevin so that she never had to worry about money again.

She ran her fingers over the keys. Having listened to Ravel earlier, she slid into some of his waltzes. She supposed that they'd have been considered easy listening in the early part of the last century. At least I wasn't born then, she thought. When not being rich would be bad enough, but not having a man in my life would have been a complete disaster! She laughed at herself. Because she wasn't a woman without a man; she was a woman with the wrong man. With someone else's man. And she couldn't help but think that she really should have lost her heart to somebody else.

Chapter 6

Sabre Dance – Khachaturian

Kevin didn't go into the office the following morning but worked from home, barking down the phone and sending e-mails at a furious rate. The company was trying to buy another chain of pubs to add to their own but there was intense haggling over the price. Kevin desperately wanted the deal to go through but he was determined that he would just walk away from the deal if he didn't get what he wanted – or as close to what he wanted as made no difference. Kevin believed that you should always hold out for what you wanted and never pay over the odds for anything. It was a maxim he applied to both his business life and his personal life, although, as he'd admitted to Jin shortly after he'd met her, he hadn't quite kept his eye on the ball when he married Monica Smith without a decent pre-nup. He'd thought about it, but at the time it seemed ludicrous because he hadn't any money, the pub and restaurant business still a dream for the future. He should have gone with his gut instinct despite the fact that he hadn't yet made it big. These days he factored everything into the equation. So he went through the papers for the umpteenth time, pestered his legal advisers for instant opinions and continued to hold out for what he wanted while Jin stayed out of his way.

She'd taken to heart the things he'd told her about Monica – Kevin's first wife had been involved in the businesses at the start and had continued to dish out unwanted advice to Kevin even after she'd lost touch with what was going on because Cian and Clarissa had become her main focus. And she pestered him about stupid

76

domestic details that he didn't need to know about, distracting him from his main focus. It had, Kevin told Jin, driven him demented.

It seemed to Jin that Monica hadn't been able to cope with Kevin's obsessiveness about his work. She'd been clingy and needy and, Jin thought, used the children as a way of making him feel permanently guilty that he wasn't at home. It was a tactic that had ultimately backfired on her. Kevin had told her that as she was clearly unhappy with things the way they were she had a choice. To live with it and be permanently miserable, making everyone else permanently miserable in the process, or to divorce him and live the kind of life she really wanted to live. Monica had opted for the divorce and the money. It didn't really surprise Jin; she reckoned that Monica was as hard as Kevin in her own way. But although he could be a stubborn bastard when he wanted, essentially he was a decent man. It was just that he'd grown used to getting his own way in business and found it difficult to accept that things didn't always work out the way he expected at home.

Like with the chain they were trying to buy now. Jin winced as she heard him bang down the phone and mutter loudly that those fuckers needed to cop on to themselves and that neither he nor his partner would wait for ever. She glanced at her watch. Nearly twelve. She'd phoned Cora earlier and told her that they were going into town for lunch and that they'd call in to see her on the way.

Cora had sounded faintly amused at that, but she couldn't say anything because, very occasionally, Jin and Kevin had done that before. So it wasn't simply a pathetic excuse dragged up so that Kevin could see Jack and figure out what was going on. Or at least it was, but one with some basis in previous events.

Jin hurried up the stairs and into the bedroom, where she changed out of the Adidas sports gear which she normally wore for uninterrupted pottering around the house and into a floating summer dress by Matthew Williamson. She left her hair loose, wore less jewellery than usual and sprayed herself rather too generously with Cacharel to complete the laid-back, innocent look. Nobody could be certain how long the Indian summer would last and she wanted to make the most of it. In a few weeks the Matthew Williamson dress, along with the rest of the season's wardrobe, would be brought into Stock Xchange or one of the other second-hand designer boutiques where the office staff who couldn't or wouldn't pay full price for brand-new clothes could pick them up at a deep discount. Of course, Jin mused, they'd be a season out of date by the time they got to wear them, but that was the price you paid for not paying the price in the first place.

She went back downstairs and rapped on the door to Kevin's study.

'I'm almost ready,' he said in response to her knock. 'Two minutes.'

She strolled out to the car and he joined her exactly two minutes later. Kevin's Mercedes was a saloon model, in contrast to her slightly sportier version. She got into the passenger seat beside him.

'So what are you going to say to Mum?' she asked as they pulled away.

'Nothing very much,' said Kevin. 'I'm going to see how the land lies.'

'Business wisdom?' asked Jin.

'Common sense,' replied Kevin.

Cora was cutting the front lawn when they arrived. She was dressed in a T-shirt with the ship's logo and a pair of loose cotton trousers, and looked quite carefree as she swung the light hover-mower across the tiny patch of grass. She looked up and waved at them as they got out of the car.

'It was a forest,' she explained to Kevin, nodding at the lawn. 'The fine weather sure made it shoot up while I was away.'

'I believe you had a good time?' Kevin kissed her on both cheeks.

'Oh absolutely,' said Cora. 'I can't thank you enough. It was the most rejuvenating thing I've done in years.' She unplugged the mower. 'Jin said you two were going into town for lunch. Would you like a cup of tea beforehand?' Her eyes twinkled suddenly. 'Or maybe a sandwich? Are you going to one of those places where the portions look ever so pretty on the plate but wouldn't feed a starving sparrow?'

'Don't be silly, Mum,' said Jin. 'We won't have anything to eat but tea would be lovely.'

'I'd have thought that your new lodger would be doing the grass,' remarked Kevin as they walked inside. Jin shot a glance at him. Straight to the point, she thought. No small talk. Typical Kevin.

'No.' Cora filled the kettle and switched it on while they sat at the kitchen table. 'He's gone into town himself. Researching.'

'The travel guide,' Jin said to Kevin.

'Yes, I believe you're harbouring an artiste under your roof.' Kevin looked at Cora enquiringly.

Cora chuckled. 'Nope. An artisan,' she corrected him. 'At least that's what he tells me. Travel guides are hard work. Not artistic at all.'

'But he's trying to do something creative,' said Kevin. 'A novel. Or so Jin said.'

Cora nodded. 'He said that the cruise would give him some good material.'

'So what's the novel about?'

'I've no idea,' said Cora. 'I didn't ask.'

'And he didn't say?'

'No.' Cora shook her head. 'I didn't want to pry either. Some novelists might like talking about their books and others might not. I'd have been interested if he'd told me but he didn't so I kept quiet.'

'What do you know about him?' asked Kevin.

'Enough.'

The phone rang and Cora went to answer it while Jin made the tea.

'That was Jack,' said Cora as she returned to the kitchen. 'He got the Dart to Clontarf but he wasn't sure what way to come to get here.'

'So as a travel writer his sense of direction isn't much good,' remarked Kevin.

'I told him that the Dart was an alternative if he was near a station,' said Cora easily. 'But he has no idea where it is relative to here. Obviously.'

'But like a true boy scout he'll find his way?'

'I think so,' said Cora. 'He's well travelled.'

'Well travelled in America,' said Jin. 'It's hardly global, no matter what the Yanks think themselves.'

'I suppose you're right.' Cora smiled at her daughter. 'But let's give him a chance. Do you plan to stay long enough to be here when he gets back? It won't take him that long to walk from Clontarf.'

Kevin looked at his watch. 'We'll wait,' he said.

'Fine.'

Jin glanced at her mother. Cora seemed so relaxed, so – so self-satisfied. Smug even. As though she had everything she wanted. If this guy was helping her to get over Des wasn't that a good thing? But if he was only stringing her along then surely he was making matters worse? Because if Cora thought that it meant something to him and it didn't wouldn't she lose all confidence in herself? Jin nibbled at the tip of her finger and then immediately sat on her hand. Nail-biting was a habit she'd long since grown out of!

She listened while Cora told them about the cruise itself, the elegance of the dining area on board, the extravagance of the late-night buffets and the absolute wonder of the clear blue seas. She talked about the beauty salon on board – she'd spent most of her money there, she admitted, and winked at Kevin, who looked at his mother-in-law in amazement. He'd never seen Cora in a skittish mood before and she was very definitely skittish now. It wasn't a good sign, he thought. Middle-aged women could become so very stubborn. He didn't want a stubborn mother-in-law. And he didn't want a mother-in-law who could leave him open to gossip.

Fifteen minutes later they heard the creak of the front gate and the sound of a key in the door. Jack strode into the tiny conservatory where they'd taken their tea and dumped a backpack on the floor. He kissed Cora on the cheek and smiled at Jin before turning to Kevin, eyebrows raised.

'Kevin Dixon.' Kevin stood up and held out his hand. Jack towered over him.

'Jack Ferguson. Pleased to meet you.'

'Would you like some tea, Jack?' asked Cora.

He shook his head. 'Thanks, no. I had coffee in Grafton Street,' he told her. 'In the place you told me about. Bewley's. It was good. Different to Starbucks.'

Cora smiled. 'Old fashioned,' she said.

'But nice.' Jack nodded. 'Definitely one of the Twenty Things To Do In Dublin.'

'This is the famous travel guide Cora's been telling us about,' said Kevin.

'Yes,' replied Jack easily as he lowered his tall frame into one of Cora's wicker chairs. 'There's lots to see in the city. It should be interesting.'

'Tell me about the ones you've already done. And the novel you're supposed to be writing.'

Jin glanced anxiously at both Jack and her mother. Kevin's tone was brisk and businesslike, as though he was interviewing Jack for a job. Quite honestly, she thought suddenly, if he spoke to me like that I'd tell him to sod off.

But Jack Ferguson simply smiled his beaming American smile and ran his fingers through his tar-black hair before launching into his CV for Kevin.

'So you write travel guides and you've never had a novel published before and you've no real idea what the one you're writing is actually about.' Kevin looked at Jack sceptically.

'Nope,' said Jack. Then his blue eyes sparkled. 'Well, I've had some ideas. Since I met Cora.'

Jin looked at him in horror. What sort of ideas? she wondered wildly. Was it an erotic novel? Would Jack describe some of the things he and Cora were getting up to? Jesus Christ, she thought, she'd never be able to set foot outside the house again!

Cora smiled. 'I was telling him about growing up in Ireland,' she said.

'The publishing world is awash with books about people growing up in Ireland,' said Kevin dismissively. 'It would have to be pretty special to stand out from the crowd.'

'I think with Cora's help I could do something very special,' said Jack easily. 'Anyway, it's marginally on the back boiler while I consider the travel thing. That's what pays my wages after all.'

81

'Have they paid you?' asked Kevin. 'For *Twenty Things To Do In Dublin*?'

'Not yet,' said Jack. 'I'll pitch it to them later.'

'Are you broke?' asked Jin anxiously.

'Nope.' Jack grinned. He looked even younger when he grinned, she thought uneasily. 'I was paid for my stint on the ship, you know.'

'And of course he's hardly pushing the boat out by staying with me,' added Cora.

There was an awkward silence. Jin wondered whether Kevin would ask him his intentions towards Cora. It was impossible not to see that there was a spark between them, but Jin didn't know whether or not it was a sexual thing or simply a wicked amusement at the situation they were in. She wondered whether her mother was just teasing them, but that had never been Cora's style and it didn't make sense for her to start now. All the same, her mother was doing lots of things she'd never done before.

'When d'you plan to go back to the States?' asked Kevin.

'I really have no idea.' Jack smiled at Cora. 'I'm having a great time here and I enjoy being with Cora, so . . .' He shrugged. 'No hurry.'

Jin couldn't help her sharp intake of breath. He was flaunting it now, she thought. He had slept with her mother and he was flaunting it. She felt perspiration tickle the back of her neck.

'How old are you?' The words were out before she could stop them.

'Why do you want to know?' asked Jack.

'I – wondered, that's all,' she said feebly.

'Thirty-three,' he replied. 'A little older than you, I gather.'

'Yes.' She glanced at Kevin and saw that his jaw was set. He wasn't happy about this either. She was suddenly afraid that he would bring everything to a head, ask the difficult questions and find out exactly what was going on between her mother and the travel-writing freeloader. Right now, she realised, she didn't want to know. Not for certain.

'We'd better go.' She stood up abruptly, the hem of her floating dress snagging on a piece of wicker from the chair. She swore softly.

'Let me.' Jack Ferguson gently disentangled it and then stood in front of her so that he was looking down at her. There were very few men who, when Jin was wearing her highest heels, could look her straight in the eye let alone stand taller than her. Jack's navy-blue eyes sparkled with promise, hinted at a passion within that Jin found difficult to ignore. She turned away from him.

'Come on, Kevin,' she said. 'We'll be late.'

Both Kevin and Cora stood up too. Jack stretched out his hand to Kevin again. 'Nice meeting you,' he said.

'Yes.' Kevin shook the other man's hand briefly then turned to Cora. 'We'll be in touch,' he said. 'Let me know if you need anything, Cora.'

'I don't need anything.' Cora's green eyes sparkled too. 'You've given me so much already.'

Kevin called the office from the car and spent the entire journey to the city talking to his PA and issuing instructions about the deal they were currently working on. Meanwhile Jin leaned back into the leather seats and allowed herself to think that it didn't really matter what Cora did with her life. That the important thing was that she was happy. After all, she mused as she revisited some of her previous thoughts, if young women had affairs with older men all the time, why should it be different for Cora?

Because, she reasoned as Kevin turned into the St Stephen's Green car park, most younger women married older men for the security. What bloody security would Cora have with Jack? Not security of mind, surely, because with a body like his, which was clearly designed for as much steamy sex as possible, he wasn't going to stay faithful to a fifty-eight-year-old mother of two for very long. It just wouldn't happen. There was no sense in pretending otherwise. And not financial security either, because Jack Ferguson clearly didn't have a bean to his name, and if anyone had a few bob it was Cora, with the proceeds of the insurance policy that had paid out after Des had died, and with the backing of a filthy-rich son-in-law.

Kevin still didn't say anything as he escorted her out of the car park and through St Stephen's Green itself to the restaurant. Jin knew that he was mulling things over in his mind and that there was no point in bringing up the Cora and Jack situation until he was ready. Kevin wasn't a man who chatted for the sake of it. He thought things through before he spoke. So Jin remained silent too and allowed herself to enjoy the feeling of the sun on her shoulders and the smell of the multicoloured flowers neatly arranged in the centre of the manicured grass. She smiled as a sudden gust of the warm southerly wind caused the water from the fountain to splash passers-by. Warm weather made you feel different, she thought as she linked her arm with Kevin's. Made you feel more at peace with the world in general, more open to new things, more like falling in love. And she wondered whether it was the warmth of the Caribbean sea-air that had caused her mother to make a complete fool of herself with Jack Ferguson.

The maître d' welcomed Kevin to the restaurant as an old friend, smiled at Jin and showed them to a secluded window table which looked out on to the rambling gardens at the back of the Georgian house in which it was located. He brought them menus and a wine list and a large bottle of mineral water.

Jin frowned. 'You didn't order that,' she said.

'I didn't need to,' said Kevin. 'I'm a regular. He knew to bring it.'

'Oh.' Jin looked around her. She rarely ate here because it was located on the side of the Green away from the shops. Even when she was in her 'lady who lunched' persona she and her friends usually ate in one of the smaller restaurants off Dawson Street or Nassau Street. This was a business restaurant, she decided. Even the women were wearing suits.

'Well?' She looked at Kevin after they'd both ordered (panned beef fillet with braised oxtail for him, crab and herb tagliolini for her). 'What d'you think?'

He pursed his lips. 'I think your mother's out of her bloody mind.'

'I think so too,' said Jin gloomily.

'It's not that I'm a prude,' continued Kevin, 'and if she wants to have a bit of fun with someone that's entirely her own business. Whatever she got up to on the cruise was her own affair as far as I'm concerned. But honestly, Jin, bringing him into her house!'

'I know.' Jin bit her lip. 'But what can we do about it?'

Kevin shrugged. 'There are ways of dealing with men like Jack Ferguson,' he said. 'Usually financial.'

'Buy him off?' Jin's voice was a disbelieving squeak.

'It's possible.'

'D'you think that's what he wants?' asked Jin.

'Why else would he be with her?'

'Oh, but Kevin!' Jin fiddled with her linen napkin. 'That's kind of ridiculous, isn't it? I mean, how does he know we'd buy him off? It's not as though we're actually in a Hollywood movie, despite his movie-star looks!'

'If he's trying to con her somehow and I just offer him a few bob then we've got to the nub of the matter,' said Kevin.

'I still don't think it's a very good idea.'

'Think about it yourself,' said Kevin. 'Let's say you were going out with someone totally unsuitable. And the guy's father came along and offered you a hundred thousand dollars to get out of his life.'

'A hundred thousand dollars!' Jin nearly fell off the chair. 'Kevin, you can't be serious. You wouldn't give him that sort of money to leave Mum, would you?'

'Of course I bloody wouldn't!' said Kevin. 'It's a hypothetical situation and it's about you. So you're going out with a guy and nobody approves and they offer you money. What would you do?'

Jin fiddled with her napkin again. 'It'd depend,' she said finally.

'On what?'

'On whether I really loved him.'

'Oh for heaven's sake, Jin. I thought I knew you better than this.'

'It's true,' she protested. 'If I really loved him then I wouldn't care how much money they offered me.'

'Well, we're working on the assumption that Jack doesn't really love your mother,' Kevin told her.

'But maybe *she* really loves *him*,' said Jin miserably.

'Jin, she's not a fool even if she's behaving foolishly at the moment,' said Kevin. 'This man is leading her on. I could see that straight away. But money is just an option; I'm not saying it's something we should do immediately.'

'What should we do right now?' asked Jin.

'I'll check up on him,' said Kevin. 'I can do a bit of searching about him and his books. Let's see if even that bit is true.'

'You think he's lying about all of it?'

'It wouldn't surprise me in the slightest,' said Kevin. 'And I didn't get to the top of my business without recognising a con artist when I see one.'

'Oh, Kevin.' Jin's face crumpled. 'Why did I ever ask you to arrange the cruise? Andie was right after all!'

'Don't be so silly,' said Kevin. 'Cora had a great holiday, she's just lost the run of herself at the moment. We'll sort her out again. It's a problem, but I'll fix it.'

Jin nodded and took a slug of her sparkling water. The waiter arrived with a bread basket and asked if they wanted to order wine. Kevin took some bread but refused the wine. Jin murmured that she needed to use the Ladies.

She stood in front of the mirror and wondered how she'd looked to Jack Ferguson. A younger, more attractive version of Cora? Not really. Her bone structure had been inherited from her father. Her eyes – which had made such direct contact with him as they'd faced each other – her almond-shaped green eyes were the only real inheritance from her mother. So when Jack had looked at her had he seen someone completely different to Cora? Or had he imagined that somehow Cora might have had those same cheekbones, that same smooth skin twenty-five years earlier? She took out her creamy pink lipstick and applied it to her rosebud lips. She knew why Cora had allowed him to stay. She'd felt it herself today. Jack Ferguson was a desirable, sexy man who simply oozed charm and a certain magnetism, and Cora would've had to be a dried-out old prune not to notice. He'd oozed the charm and the magnetism at Jin today and it had left her almost breathless.

She snapped the top back on the lipstick. It was OK for her to be left breathless by him, it wasn't as though anything was going to happen. She was a happily married woman, for God's sake. And even if there was the remotest chance that she was a likely candidate to fall under his spell, well, it wouldn't be such a disaster, because she was young and able to take care of herself. Cora was a vulnerable woman who'd recently lost her husband. It was damn different.

There was no way she could allow him to upset Cora, even though she knew that her mother would freak out if she thought Kevin was considering offering Jack money to leave. She grimaced. They'd have to work out something else before Kevin decided to go for the jugular.

She smoothed back her hair and walked out into the restaurant again. She spotted Ivor McDermott, a business friend of Kevin's, sitting at a table on the far side of the room and almost waved at him, but he was deep in conversation with his dinner companion and she didn't want to disturb them.

She pointed him out to Kevin as she sat down at the table again. He frowned.

'Hardly discreet of Ivor,' he remarked.

'Huh?'

'It's all very well having an affair,' said Kevin, 'but the least he could do is take her to quieter restaurants.'

'Ivor's having an affair!' Jin was shocked. 'With that girl?'

Kevin looked at her with amusement. 'You didn't know? I'm surprised. I thought there was a corporate wife bush telegraph that knew everything.'

'Well, sometimes, but . . . I must have missed it. He and Bettina always seemed such a good partnership.' Jin looked across to Ivor and the woman again. She was extraordinarily beautiful, with straight blonde hair and smooth creamy skin. 'How long?'

'A year. Maybe more.'

'No.' Jin's eyes widened. 'Weren't Ivor and Bettina in *Hello!* or *VIP* only a couple of months ago showing off their house in Howth? And talking about how happy they were?'

'Ivor's PR people set that up,' said Kevin. 'Remember they launched that new gin mixer drink back then?'

Jin nodded.

'Great publicity,' Kevin told her. 'There was a photo of Bettina pouring the drink in her garden.'

'I remember.' Jin nodded and then her brow creased. 'But I can't believe I didn't know. It's hard to keep secrets in Dublin.'

Kevin laughed. 'That's why Ivor should be discreet. So you girls can't dissect it all over your coffee mornings or shopping lunches. Which is what you usually do, I suppose.'

'Not always,' said Jin. 'Sometimes we talk about running the house and going on holiday and the latest fashions.' Her eyes twinkled. 'At least, that's what you want us to talk about, isn't it?'

'I couldn't care less.' Kevin buttered a warm bread roll. 'What you do is entirely your own business.'

'But we do normally know if someone's being cheated on,' said Jin.

'How?' asked Kevin.

'There are ways,' she said airily. 'Husbands bringing home unexpected bouquets of flowers, lots of calls to the mobile, sudden late meetings or dinners with clients, that sort of thing.'

'I'll bear it in mind,' said Kevin.

'Oh, I'd be the last to find out,' Jin said wryly. 'Wouldn't I?'

'If I was having an affair, you'd never know,' said Kevin calmly.

'Just like Bettina then.' Suddenly Jin's voice was serious.

'She knows,' said Kevin.

'Does she?'

'Of course she does. You're never really the last one to know,' said Kevin. 'But she's relying on him not flaunting it around the place.'

'He's been very discreet so far,' said Jin, 'because I never would have guessed.'

'But not this time.' Kevin's glance flickered over to the other table again.

'Bettina must think it'll fizzle out,' said Jin.

Kevin shrugged. 'I don't know what she thinks.'

'I can't believe she's never said anything.' Jin tried hard not to look at the couple on the other side of the room.

'Presumably discretion means hers too,' said Kevin.

'Who is she?' asked Jin, glancing across the room.

'Ivor's woman?' Kevin smiled. 'Lucky, if you ask me. She's an air hostess. Swedish. Anthea, Adrienne – something like that.'

Jin groaned. 'You're joking. I thought bonking air hostesses had gone out with the last century.'

'Not yet,' said Kevin.

'She's certainly stunning,' said Jin.

'And good in bed,' added Kevin.

'He hasn't told you that!' Jin was shocked.

'At the start,' said Kevin.

'Poor Bettina.'

'Why?'

'I bet she isn't happy about it for all that she's taking it on the chin and telling him to be discreet.'

'Why?'

'Kevin, her husband's having an affair! Of course she won't be happy about it.'

Kevin shrugged. 'Bettina's living in a gorgeous house on Howth Hill with a couple of acres around her. She has a new car every year, a variety of people to help her round the house, unlimited holidays, unlimited new clothes . . . Why should she be unhappy because her husband is having a meaningless affair?'

'Is it meaningless?' asked Jin.

'Sure.'

'But presumably it means something to the air hostess,' said Jin. 'And Bettina.'

'You're showing your suburban upbringing,' said Kevin. 'I'm telling you it doesn't mean anything at all.'

Jin was silent for a moment. She took a sip from her glass of wine and looked at Kevin. 'You were brought up in the suburbs too,' she reminded him. 'So keep that in mind if you're ever tempted.'

Chapter 7

Arabesque No 1 – Debussy

Andie was half sitting, half lying on the grass in St Stephen's Green when she saw Jin and Kevin on their way back to the car park after lunch. Once again Jin had linked her arm through Kevin's, and she looked strikingly beautiful as she walked beside him, her back ramrod straight, shoulders back, her gleaming hair caught by the gentle breeze and her skin glowing with the biscuit-coloured tan which was a still-present legacy of her month in Antigua earlier in the year. Kevin was an equally commanding presence, though in his case due to the force of his personality rather than his looks. Andie had never found her brother-in-law attractive, but he was always a difficult man to ignore, and with Jin beside him they were undoubtedly an arresting couple.

She was surprised to see them here in the early afternoon, a time when she would've expected Kevin to be behind a desk and Jin at the hairdresser or the beautician or doing whatever it was that kept her occupied all day. Maybe Kevin had been buying something for her, she thought, a new ring or necklace or bauble of some sort to hang on his trophy wife. She flinched at the thought. She knew that she was being totally disloyal in allowing herself to believe, even for a moment, that Kevin Dixon had married Jin Corcoran simply because she looked good. But sometimes she couldn't help thinking that if Jin had been anything less than as beautiful as she was, Kevin wouldn't even have noticed her.

They were walking past her now, caught up in their own deep conversation and oblivious to her presence. Andie thought about getting up and talking to them but she didn't. She was still embarrassed about her reaction to the cruise and not yet ready to discuss it rationally with her sister. Anyway, she didn't want to talk to either of them. Right now, as well as resenting their gift to Cora, she was resenting the fact that they were strolling through the park, happy to be with each other, parading their togetherness for everyone to see. They were doing what she would have given anything to do herself with Tom Hall. Simply walking side by side, not worried about anyone seeing them, knowing that they were going home together, that they would sleep together, that they would wake up together . . . She gritted her teeth as she clamped down on the waves of jealousy that threatened to engulf her.

She'd chosen the life she was leading with Tom. She'd chosen to be with him in a different way. She'd known from the first moment she'd met him that he was attached to another woman, and she'd discovered very quickly that nothing would change. But when he'd called to the Academy and taken her to lunch earlier in the week and had spoken about leaving Elizabeth, she'd suddenly wanted him to do it with such ferocity that it scared her. Despite staying calm and unruffled outside, she'd felt her stomach churn and her heart race at the thought. And now it was something that, having allowed to bubble to the surface, she couldn't forget. Ever since that day, everything she'd done had been touched with the idea that maybe one day soon she'd be doing it with Tom, who would be a recognisable, permanent feature in her life. When she'd got up each morning she'd imagined how it would be getting up with Tom still in the bed, the top sheet wrapped around him as it always seemed to be when he was sleeping. Sitting on the bus as she travelled home from work, she'd allowed herself to pretend that Tom was waiting for her back at the flat, and she held imaginary conversations with him, asking him what he'd like for dinner or wondering if he'd managed to fix the leak from the shower head yet. They were silly domestic fantasies and she was ashamed of them while at the same time revelling in them.

She wished he hadn't said anything. She'd schooled herself over the past four years not to think of themselves as a conventional couple. She'd tried to take delight in the fact that he didn't stay

91

the night with her, that the very brevity of some of their encounters was exciting and passionate in a way that people who really did live together could never experience. But now – now she was longing for the stability of that togetherness and feeling unsettled at the thought that he'd spoken about it for the first time in so long.

Kevin and Jin disappeared over the little humpbacked bridge across the duck pond and out of her sight. There was a part of her that wished she'd gone up to them and said hello – surely, she thought, it was very odd to watch your own sister walk by and say nothing, even if you were mad at her about something? It was no wonder Jin thought she was weird. She actually was. Possibly even getting weirder. That was what happened to spinster music teachers after all, wasn't it?

She glanced at her watch. She was on a two-class break at the moment and she'd wanted to spend it listening to the sounds of the birds chattering in the trees, the rustle of the leaves in the light breeze, the hum of conversation punctuated by sudden bursts of laughter from Dubliners strolling through the park, and all of it underlaid by the steady drone of traffic as it circled outside. Sometimes when she sat in the park she thought of the myriad of noises as a symphony in themselves. Something by Dvorak perhaps. Or Grieg. Anyway, as far as she was concerned, sitting in the Green on a sunny day was one of life's great experiences, and nothing ever bothered her so much that she didn't enjoy being here.

She got up and brushed the grass from her lavender skirt. There was a green stain on the hip which she couldn't remove. Gives it character, she thought as she picked up her big floral bag. Then she walked to the top of Grafton Street and bought herself a double scoop of rum and raisin ice cream from the vendor before walking back to the Academy and a session with her star pupil, Mia Moriarty. The eighteen-year-old had great potential, but a regrettably pushy mother who felt that not enough was being done to foster her daughter's future career. God preserve me from pushy mothers, thought Andie, as she licked the melting ice cream from her fingers and pushed open the heavy wooden doors that led into the cool corridor beyond. And from pushy sisters too.

*   *   *

92

'She's actually quite brilliant,' Andie told Tom later that night. 'But you sometimes wonder if it's worth all the effort.'

'When she wins some award and gratefully thanks you amid floods of tears then you'll feel differently.' Tom grinned and kissed Andie very softly on the side of her breast.

'Maybe.' Andie sighed.

'You're a bit down this evening,' said Tom as he propped himself up on one arm and looked at her, concern in his eyes.

'Just a fit of the blues,' she told him. 'I got hot and bad-tempered and haven't snapped out of it yet.'

'I know how to fix that.' He rolled off the big double bed and went out to the kitchen, returning with a bowl of ice cubes. She smiled as she saw them.

'So,' he said. 'What first?'

'Up to you.'

He took an ice cube from the bowl and placed it on her forehead. She closed her eyes and felt a trickle of water slide down her temple. Then he caressed the cube towards her eyes, along her nose and rested it on her lips. He slid it gently along her chin, down her neck and stopped when it was between her breasts. He reached out for another ice cube and placed one on each of her nipples, which immediately stood to attention.

'OK?' he murmured.

She nodded wordlessly. He slid the ice cubes across her body until he could see goosebumps appear. Then he held them between her legs until she opened her eyes and looked at him with a fierce hunger that made him bring his lips down on hers and pull her to him. He thrust inside of her, and she held him ever tighter so that she felt as though their bodies had fused together as they rocked and writhed on the bed.

'Oh God!' She bit her lip. 'Oh, Tom!'

'I love you.' He panted the words. 'I love you. I always have.' He thrust even harder. 'I always will.'

Later, they sat beside each other on the worn and battered but comfortable sofa.

'I've been cranky for ages, haven't I?'

'A little,' Tom agreed.

'I'm sorry.' She smiled at him in contrition. 'You know how it is when you let things get on top of you. But I was in the Green at lunch time today, and suddenly everything seemed OK again.'

'I'm glad,' said Tom. 'I hate to think of you being miserable.'

'I'm hardly ever miserable,' Andie told him. 'And I've got over my bad mood now, so don't you dare say anything to change it.'

'I won't.' Tom grinned and kissed her on the lips. 'I'd be afraid!'

'Come on then,' she said. 'I want to know if you can do that trick without the ice cubes.'

'What trick?' he asked.

'The one where you make me feel as though I'm melting too.'

'Demanding little thing, aren't you?'

'Very.' She laughed.

He began kissing her, his lips hot on hers. She slid her arm around his neck.

The phone rang and she swore.

'Leave it,' said Tom.

'I can't.' She leaned over and reached for the receiver. 'Hello?'

'Hi, it's me.'

'Oh, Jin.' She made a face at the receiver and grinned when Tom mouthed, 'Shouldn't have answered' at her.

'I'm not interrupting you, am I?' asked Jin. 'You're not composing a major symphony or making blackberry jam, are you?'

'Me – blackberry jam? As if.'

'I have to talk to you.'

'What about?' Andie slid out of Tom's embrace and sat up straight.

'Mum,' replied Jin scathingly. 'You obviously haven't been too worried about her, but I am.'

'Why are you worried?' asked Andie. 'You picked her up didn't you? I didn't ring her because I thought she'd be getting over the jet-lag.'

'She'd be well over it by now,' said Jin. 'I take it you still haven't spoken to her?'

'No.' Andie was suddenly anxious. 'I was going to call later. Why? What's wrong?'

'Get ready for this,' said Jin. 'Mum has a boyfriend.'

'A boyfriend?' Andie sounded sceptical. 'Who? Anyone we know?'

'If only,' said Jin. 'It's a complete disaster.'

'What d'you mean?' asked Andie as she frowned at Tom, who was making enquiring expressions at her. 'Tell me about this boyfriend.'

'Boyfriend?' mouthed Tom, eyes wide. 'Has Jin a new boy-friend?'

Andie flapped at him to butt out.

'Boy is the operative word,' replied Jin.

'Huh?'

Jin, sitting on her leather sofa, shook her copper tresses out of her eyes and proceeded to bring Andie up to speed on Cora's relationship with Jack Ferguson.

'It's a complete disaster,' she said. 'This bloke – well, Andie, you only have to see him. Kevin thinks he wants money, but I really don't know . . .'

'Ma doesn't have any money,' Andie pointed out. 'So that's a bit stupid.'

'You know Kevin,' said Jin. 'He thinks everyone wants money. Not that there's anything wrong with that,' she added hastily. 'Only I'm really not certain . . . Oh, Andie, I don't know what to do.'

'Why do anything?' asked Andie.

'Because if we don't, her heart will be broken and she's only just getting over Dad.'

'Maybe this is her way of getting over him completely,' said Andie.

'No way!' cried Jin. 'Not with this bloke. Absolutely no way.'

'What the hell is going on?' whispered Tom as he slid his hand beneath Andie's sweatshirt and caught her nipple between his fingers. She shook her head and squirmed out of his hold.

'Why not?' Andie turned her back on Tom and spoke to her sister.

'I've met him,' snapped Jin. 'He's not a decent bloke. He's sex on legs and he – well, he flirted with me.'

'Flirted with you!'

'My dress got caught in one of the conservatory chairs and he freed it up and looked at me, and I swear to you there was a come-to-bed look in his eyes.'

'Well, if he's really a complete shit I'm sure Ma will cop on soon enough,' said Andie.

'You still haven't got the picture, have you?' demanded Jin. 'This isn't your ordinary bloke, Andie. Jack is a real hunk. And God knows why, but he's probably sleeping with our mother. It's a totally impossible set-up.'

'Hardly impossible if it's actually happening.' Andie was amused at how wound up Jin was getting, and found it hard to take the whole thing seriously.

'You don't have a clue,' said Jin, 'because you haven't seen him yet. You've got to go there and tell her how stupid she's being.'

'I might not have a clue,' said Andie mildly, 'but I do know that if I was going out with someone totally unsuitable and everybody kept telling me how unsuitable he was I'd make damn sure I kept going out with him just to piss them off.'

'Very helpful,' Jin snorted. 'But you might have a point. The question is, are you going to help with Mum or not?'

'Well, I'll call round if you think it'll do any good,' said Andie. 'But I bet you anything the whole thing fizzles out in a week. Romance on board a cruise ship is one thing, romance in Marino is something else entirely.'

'You do that,' said Jin. 'Because your attitude will change when you imagine them sleeping together.'

'You think they're sleeping together?' Despite trying to take Cora's side, Andie suddenly realised that this was something she couldn't quite get her head around. The idea of her mother and a smoulderingly attractive hunk writhing around in passion was just a little too difficult to accept.

'I'm trying very hard not to think about it,' admitted Jin. 'It'd be one thing if she'd met some bloke her own age; at least it'd seem a bit more, well, normal and maybe they wouldn't be doing it as much anyway. But this guy – Andie, this guy is flipping walking sex!'

'What does Doireann think?'

96

'I phoned her last night,' said Jin. 'Obviously she couldn't say much when I picked them up. She's trying to be open-minded, but she thinks Mum has lost her head completely. And of course she feels bad for Dad's memory.'

'She'd feel that regardless of who Ma might meet,' Andie observed.

'I guess so,' Jin agreed reluctantly. 'But oh, Andie . . .'

'He's really got under your skin, hasn't he?' Andie realised that Jin was genuinely upset.

'I'm telling you, he's bad news.'

Andie sighed. 'Like I said, I'll call round.'

'Tomorrow?' asked Jin.

'I'm not sure if—'

'Because I get the feeling you think it's all a bit of a joke. It's not. I swear it's not. You'll have to see him to realise it.'

'OK, OK. I'll do my best,' said Andie.

'You might think I'm being over-the-top about it, but honestly, I'm trying to think of Mum's welfare. That's all.'

Andie bit her lip. There was no mistaking the sincerity in her sister's voice.

'It's probably just a holiday fling,' she told Jin comfortingly. 'After all, don't a lot of people go a bit crazy on holiday? And cruises are probably hotbeds of lust and passion.'

'Maybe there's lust and passion on the cruise, but not afterwards,' said Jin. 'And you do hear about gold-digging lotharios going after older women.'

'Only if they're rich,' Andie told her. 'And if he's with her in Marino, he's established by now that she isn't.'

Jin groaned. 'It's such a mess. And all I wanted was for her to have a good time.'

Andie said nothing.

'Go on,' said Jin. 'Put in the dig about the whole cruise thing backfiring on me. I don't care.'

'I wasn't going to,' said Andie. 'And look, Jin – I'm sorry I was so ungracious about it.'

'Oh.' Jin was surprised. Andie's apologies were rare. 'It's OK.'

'Anyway, what's done is done,' said Andie. 'I'll call round. But she probably thinks it's hilarious, all of us rushing to the house to see the new man.'

'If he was closer to her own age,' said Jin, 'if he was even remotely suitable . . .'

Andie laughed shortly. 'You sound like Dad when he was talking to you about Terry Dunne.'

'Dad had a point,' said Jin, 'even though I didn't see it at the time. And it's the same with Mum now.'

'I'm not going to lecture her,' warned Andie.

'That's OK. Just go. See them. Report back.'

'All right,' said Andie. 'I'll visit. And call you.'

'Do,' said Jin ominously. 'And I bet you'll see exactly what I'm talking about for yourself.'

'What was all that about?' asked Tom when Andie replaced the receiver and turned back to him again.

As she told him, Tom's face broke into a wide grin. 'Good for your mum,' he said.

'Yes, well, Jin doesn't think so.' Andie made a face.

'And you?'

She looked uncomfortable. 'If Ma has found someone, that's good, I suppose. I'd kind of prefer it if it was someone more suitable, though, because to be honest, Tom, this guy doesn't sound suitable at all. And I can see why Jin is worried. I'm a bit worried myself. But I think she has the wrong end of the stick completely about him thinking Ma's some rich widow. Anyone would realise once they got back to the house. It's not exactly Beverly Hills.'

She exhaled slowly.

'You all right?' asked Tom.

'I never thought me and Jin would be worrying about Ma's love life.'

Tom grinned. 'Now you know how she felt when you went out with some totally useless boy as a teenager.'

'I never went out with useless boys,' Andie told him. 'They were always wonderful.' She giggled. 'Actually, that was the problem. I went out with blokes both my parents approved of. No wonder I got so messed up in later life.'

'Am I messing you up?' Tom looked at her seriously.

'No,' said Andie. 'I have you exactly where I want you.'

'How old did she say he was?' he asked as he located his shoes under the sofa.

'Thirty-three,' said Andie. 'I bet he isn't. He probably just looks like that. You know the Yanks and their health freakiness. He's probably at least forty-three.'

Tom laughed. 'So you're going to go and suss it out yourself?'

'I have to,' said Andie. 'I promised. Besides, she has me intrigued now. I've got to see him for myself.'

'Don't go falling for him,' said Tom sternly, 'if he's a hunky Yank who looks half his age.'

'I don't have time to fall for other men,' she told him. 'You're more than enough for me.'

'Good.' Tom pulled her to him and kissed her on the lips. 'And you're everything I ever wanted.' He held her close for a moment then let her go. 'I'm sorry, Andie, it's getting late. I have to head off.'

'Oh yes, of course you do.' She looked at her watch. 'You'd better hurry.'

'I'll call you soon,' said Tom as he stood up and put on the leather jacket she'd bought him the previous Christmas – he hadn't worn it until the New Year, had told Elizabeth he'd bought it himself in the January sales.

'Bye, Tom.'

'Bye, love of my life.' He blew her a kiss as he let himself out of the door.

Chapter 8

Prelude in D Flat Major (Raindrop) – Chopin

The Indian summer was suddenly over. Rain sluiced down the red paving slabs of Grafton Street as Andie hurried towards the bus stop, holding her sturdy umbrella in front of her face to protect her from the sheeting water. She swore softly as she stepped into a puddle and felt the cold spray squelch inside her shoe. And she swore even louder when she saw the length of the queue waiting for the bus.

There wasn't enough room for her on the first single-decker that arrived, and despite the promised schedule of a bus every seven minutes it was nearly a quarter of an hour later before the next one pulled up. It was hardly surprising that it was late, she thought as she slid her multi-journey ticket into the machine; the rain had caused Dublin's traffic to turn into a snarling, slow-moving snake.

Andie got a seat near the back and rubbed her fingers over the steamy windows. Sometimes she wished she'd accepted Jin's offer of a car, especially on days like today when the bus was crowded and her feet were wet. But a car just didn't make sense for her. They were expensive to run and it wasn't as though she needed one for work because she lived on a really good bus route. Nor did she need one for leisure because, well, where did she ever go?

She bit her lip. That was the worst of her relationship with Tom. They never went anywhere together. And because of that she felt that people had the perception of her as a sad loser with a boring life. Only thing was, that was hard to deny. Her social life shouldn't be boring at all, of course. She was having a clandestine affair after

100

all, and many people would consider that a kind of exciting thing to do. There was the frisson of their secret meetings, the special thrill of sleeping with someone who couldn't stay the night, the romance that would never die beneath the weight of dirty laundry or scuzzy tide marks around the bath. Shouldn't that mean her life was more interesting than other people's? And yet, when she considered it, it wasn't. Because of the secrecy, she usually met Tom in her flat. They never went anywhere together as a couple, and last week's unexpected lunch in Ely Place had made her realise how rarely she saw him in any setting other than sprawled across her squashy sofa or lying beside her in bed. Not that these were bad things, she told herself, not that she didn't want him to be there. It was just that it might be nice to do something else. A late-night movie. Dinner in a swanky restaurant. Drinks in a new club. It was impossible for them to do any of those things. As a social life, a life outside the four walls of her flat, it wasn't much to write home about, even though what went on inside those walls was sensational.

But nobody knew about the sensational stuff, and so they all saw her as Jin probably did. A dry old music teacher. A young woman leading an old woman's life. Work, home, work, home, and nothing else to occupy her. Yet it wasn't as though the perception of music teachers being dry and uninteresting was accurate in the first place. Andie knew that Cathryn Marriott, one of the violin teachers, was having a sizzling long-distance relationship with an Italian singer. Donald Smith, a voice coach, was notorious for bonking any woman under the age of fifty. And Johann Aregbesola, the Academy's artistically attractive piano teacher, who made both men and women go weak at the knees, was conducting relationships with two equally gorgeous male pianists who were totally unaware of the other's existence. In fact, thought Andie a little miserably, the Academy was a hotbed of other people's sensational relationships. She should be part of that. But she wasn't. Because she didn't want anyone to know about Tom. Because he didn't want anyone to know about her.

She swallowed the lump that had suddenly appeared in her throat. A further reason her life wasn't really as boring as it appeared was that it was always touched by the fact that there was another woman on

101

the edge of it – an unstable, unhappy woman, and she didn't know what to do about it. Catholic guilt, she muttered under her breath as the bus rattled along the bus lane towards Marino. No matter how miserable his relationship is, I still feel guilty about my part in it. And I'll feel just as bad if he ever does pluck up the courage to leave her. If only their relationship had broken down like Kevin and Monica Dixon's. Jin hadn't had to worry about Monica's feelings. Jin hadn't had to worry about anything at all.

Suddenly the bus juddered to a halt. The driver revved the engine, which was now making a distinctly unhealthy noise. The passengers looked at each other doubtfully. The driver revved the engine again and there was a loud bang. The woman in the seat beside Andie shrieked and dropped her mesh bag so that the assorted fruits that it had carried now careered along the aisle while she chased after them.

'Sorry!' called the driver. 'You'll have to get off.'

'As if we couldn't have guessed that,' muttered the woman, who was now pursuing a rosy red apple under the seat.

It was typical, thought Andie, as she started to walk, that the day the bus broke down would be the day that the skies had opened for the first time in ages. The only rain that had fallen in the past month had been at night. She opened her umbrella again and began to walk in the direction of her mother's house. She felt tired and miserable and she wanted to be at home. Tonight wasn't the night for confronting her mother and her sexy boyfriend. Andie wasn't sure that she had the strength to cope with this potentially cataclysmic relationship right now. She wondered whether Jin would phone later to see if she'd kept her promise and called in to see Cora. She probably would. Once Jin got a bee in her bonnet about something she couldn't let it go. She'd pester Andie until she did call to see Cora and she'd probably throw in a few more insults about her sister's boring, spinsterish lifestyle for good measure.

Cora's house – the house they'd grown up in – was a ten-minute walk from Andie's own flat off Griffith Avenue. She briefly toyed with the idea of going home before going to see her mother, but she knew that if she got in and dried off she wouldn't feel like coming out again. So she resolutely turned to the right into

Cora's neighbourhood instead of continuing towards the main road.

She walked up the small pathway and knocked at the door. There wasn't a sound from inside the house and Andie wondered whether her mother was even in. Out sightseeing with the toy-boy, perhaps. The thought made her smile. She waited for another few seconds and was just about to leave when the door opened and Cora stood there.

'Andie!' Her mother smiled at her. 'It's lovely to see you.'

'You too.' Andie dropped a kiss on Cora's cheek. 'You're looking well.'

'Thanks,' said Cora. 'Come in out of the rain, for heaven's sake. Leave the umbrella in the porch.'

Andie shook the folds of her sedate mauve brolly and leaned it against the brick wall of the porch before following her mother into the house. She realised then why it had taken Cora so long to answer the door. The CD player was on – she recognised the London Symphony Orchestra's playing of Strauss's Radetsky March – and the music filled the room, which now had two orange walls thanks to Cora's efforts with a tin of paint.

'Redecorating?' asked Andie.

'Time for a change,' said Cora as she lowered the volume on the CD player.

'Strong colour.' Andie's eyes flickered from the orange to the original magnolia and back again.

'I wanted something definite,' said Cora.

'You've certainly got that.' Andie looked at it critically. 'It's nice.'

Cora laughed. 'It's a bit more orangey than I expected. But if it turns out really awful I'll paint over it again.' She picked up the kettle. 'Tea? Coffee?'

'Tea would be lovely.' Andie shrugged off her damp coat and took it out to the tiny hallway to hang on the hook. She slipped out of her wet shoes too. 'I'm cold,' she added as she came back into the kitchen-dining room.

'It's turned a bit miserable all right,' agreed Cora. 'And it's chilly in here because the windows are open for the paint. I know it says that it's virtually odourless but I want to be sure.'

103

'The weather's a bit of a change for you after Mexico,' observed Andie.

Cora smiled. 'A bit of a change, yes.'

Andie said nothing but sat down in the deep armchair that had once been her father's favourite. She looked at the gas-effect fire, which was switched off.

'Light it if you like,' said Cora, who'd followed her gaze.

Andie shook her head. 'It's not really that cold. The tea will warm me up.'

Neither of them spoke while they waited for the kettle to boil. Cora closed the windows, then made a pot of tea. She waited for it to brew and poured a mug for Andie.

'Thanks.' She took the red mug from her mother. 'You'll have to get new crockery. The red will clash with the walls.'

'It'll have to clash,' said Cora. 'I like these mugs.' She sipped her tea.

'Having it black now?' Andie's look held the hint of a challenge. She'd always drunk her tea black, had hated the taste of milk in it, but Cora usually poured milk in unthinkingly.

'Got a taste for it on the cruise,' said Cora equably.

'Not the only thing you got a taste for, I hear,' said Andie.

'Oh?'

'Come on, Ma.' Andie put the mug on a side table. 'What's the story about the lodger?'

'Jin's been in touch with you, then?'

'What do you think?'

'Oh, I knew she'd be round to you before I could say anything.' Cora shrugged. 'She thinks I'm having some kind of affair with a lovely guy I met on the ship.'

'And are you?' asked Andie.

Cora said nothing, but gazed into her mug of golden tea.

Andie shivered abruptly. When Jin had freaked out about Cora's possible relationship it had seemed silly and possessive. Now Andie was beginning to sense a little of how Jin felt. It was all very well being adult and mature about her mother having a younger boyfriend, but she suddenly realised that she wasn't quite as comfortable about the idea as she'd thought.

104

'He's a very nice man,' said Cora slowly, breaking the silence.

'And?'

'He's fun,' said Cora. 'He treats me well. He's definitely a dish.'

'A dish!' Andie laughed.

'Well, he is,' said Cora defensively. 'That's why Jin is so upset, I suppose. She can't imagine that a gorgeous young man could see anything in an old fogey like me.'

'You're not an old fogey,' said Andie. 'You're only fifty-eight.'

'An old fogey to someone of thirty-three,' said Cora.

'I'm thirty-three,' Andie reminded her. 'And I might have considered fifty-eight a top candidate for fogey-hood when I was thirteen, but not any more.'

Cora smiled. 'But it's different when it's the man who's thirty-three.'

'It shouldn't be,' said Andie. 'Yet it is, yes.'

'So what do you want?' asked Cora.

'Only to be sure you're OK,' said Andie. 'Jin is worried, and when she phoned me . . . well, I said I'd come round and see how things are for myself.'

'I suppose I should be pleased that my daughters are worried about me,' said Cora. 'Or should I be insulted that you think I'm an old fool?'

'If one of us was in a dodgy relationship you'd want to know about it.'

'So you do think it's a dodgy relationship?'

'Tell me about him.' Andie didn't answer her mother's question. 'Where is he now?'

'Gone to the off-licence in Fairview to buy wine,' said Cora. 'He's making dinner tonight.'

Andie said nothing.

'He's a good cook, apparently,' continued Cora. 'He's got a lot of recipes from the ship. He's doing some kind of chicken dish.'

Andie looked at her watch. 'Nothing that takes too long, I hope,' she remarked. 'Otherwise you won't get to eat until very late.'

'I've got used to eating a bit later since the cruise,' said Cora. 'Of course I know it's really bad for my metabolism or whatever, but a few late dinners won't do me any harm.'

'I guess not.'

'He'll be back soon,' said Cora.

'He really matters to you, doesn't he?'

'Right now, yes,' replied Cora.

'Are you . . . you know, are you . . . do you . . . sleep with him?' She looked uncomfortably at her mother and blushed.

'Andie, I've never asked you that question about anyone in your life,' said Cora sharply. 'And I really don't think I'm going to answer it.'

'I'm sorry,' said Andie hastily. 'I shouldn't have . . . It's just – well, it's a bit weird. You know it is. And neither of us can help being concerned about you.'

'Why?' asked Cora.

'Jin's worried that he's after you for money,' said Andie. 'And I'm just worried he's after you!'

Cora's green eyes gleamed with a spark of mischief. 'He knows I don't have any money. And if he's after me – well, it's flattering, Andie.'

'Yes,' said Andie slowly. 'But . . . I suppose we're afraid that you'll get hurt.'

'I was hurt when your father died,' said Cora. 'I was more hurt then than I've ever been in my life before. I know what real hurt is. I can cope with it.'

'I know,' said Andie. 'It's just – why put yourself through it if you don't have to?'

Cora lifted an eyebrow as she looked at her daughter. 'If we all took that attitude we'd never do anything,' she said. 'We'd never meet other people, never go out with them, never fall in love. Love hurts. Life hurts. That's the way it is.'

Andie said nothing.

'It's something you should think about,' continued Cora. 'I've never interfered in your life, Andie. But as much as you're saying that you worry about me, I worry about you. Why haven't you got anyone who matters to you? Why do you never have anyone?'

'I have people,' said Andie. 'I have some very close friends, as well you know. Unfortunately, Kajsa is in Denmark until the new

106

year and Ashley's touring at the moment, so that's why you haven't heard me talking about them.'

'I really meant boyfriends,' said her mother. 'There hasn't been anyone in your life since that Kennedy boy, and that was ages ago.' She looked at Andie sympathetically. 'You should be over that by now, sweetheart.'

Andie grimaced. 'Of course I'm over it. I was upset at the time. Anyone would've been. I thought he cared about me, but it was his career, his place in the orchestra . . .' Her voice trailed off. 'Anyway, just because there hasn't been anyone you know about doesn't mean I haven't had plenty of boyfriends since him.'

'But not the right person,' said Cora. 'I'd like you to find the right person, Andie. It makes such a difference to your life. I was happy with your dad. Really happy. And everyone deserves that sort of happiness.'

'When I find the person who'll make me that happy I'll tell you about him.' Andie found it difficult to say the words as though they didn't mean anything.

'You're so fussy,' said Cora. 'Always were, of course. Even as a child. Wanted perfection. You don't find perfection in relationships, Andie. There's give and take, you know.'

'Of course I know,' said Andie. 'And I really don't want you to be concerned about me. I'm very happy.'

'You don't look it,' said Cora bluntly. 'At Jin's birthday party you looked bloody miserable. And you left early.'

'I'm not good at those kind of things,' said Andie. 'You know I'm not.'

Cora picked up the teapot and refilled Andie's mug. 'You have to make an effort,' she said. 'Or you'll never find anybody.'

Both women looked up at the sound of the key in the door. Andie slowly placed the red mug on the side table again.

'Hi, honey,' called Jack. 'I'm back.'

Andie glanced surreptitiously at her mother. Cora was smiling. Her eyes sparkled with anticipation and at that moment Andie knew that her mother had fallen for Jack Ferguson. She bit her lip.

'In here,' Cora called. 'Andie's come to visit.'

'Andie?' Jack opened the door and walked into the room.

And now I know why Jin is so worried, thought Andie as she looked at him, his black hair plastered to his forehead from the rain, his blue eyes dazzling in his tanned face. I'm worried too.

Jack put a bottle of Sangre de Torro wine on the table and advanced towards them, hand extended. Andie stood up and grasped it. It was cold and a little wet.

'Sorry,' he said. 'It's bucketing rain outside. Nice, though.'

'I hate the rain,' she said.

'I spent three months floating around the Caribbean,' Jack said. 'Rain is a welcome change.'

Andie looked at him appraisingly while he continued to hold her hand. He was every bit as smoulderingly attractive as Jin had suggested. She wasn't in the slightest bit surprised that her mother had fallen for him. It would've been more surprising if she hadn't. He was the kind of man that anyone would fall for. They probably couldn't help themselves. Hell, she thought, if I wasn't already spoken for I could fancy him myself. And she smiled very slightly as she remembered that Tom had jokingly warned her against him the previous night.

'Did you get what you were looking for?' asked Cora easily.

'Sure did,' said Jack. 'That's quite a good liquor store you have there.'

'Great,' said Cora.

'Looks like you need it after all the painting.'

'You did your share.'

'I know!' He laughed. 'My hands are covered in Orange Slice.' He held out his palms for her inspection.

They were acting like a married couple, thought Andie. The easy conversation. The banter between them. She shivered.

'Are you OK, Andie?' asked Cora.

'Suddenly cold,' she said. She looked at her mother. 'I'd better be off.'

'You've only just got here,' said Cora. 'Stay a little longer. You've hardly spoken to Jack.'

'I'm sure you two have things to talk about,' she said.

'I'd like to exchange more than a word with you,' said Jack. 'Cora tells me you're a music teacher, that right?'

'Yes,' she said.

'But not kids. Adults.'

Andie glanced at Cora. 'Not exactly,' she said. 'Not beginners, that's all. I have some young kids working with me as well as older people.'

'And you're into classical stuff?'

'Not just,' she said.

'You teach at an academy?'

She nodded. 'And you write travel books?'

He smiled. 'Yes. Though I'm also working on the Great American Novel.'

'I doubt you'll get much inspiration for it here,' she said.

'People are people,' said Jack. 'Doesn't much matter whether I observe them in the US or Europe.'

'Are you observing us?' asked Andie.

Jack laughed. It was a nice laugh, she thought. A sincere laugh. And it was warm and friendly. 'I guess so. I like the family dynamic, you see. And it's not true that people are the same. Europeans are a bit more tight-assed than Americans.'

'You think?' Andie smiled.

'I think.' He nodded. 'Mind you, your mom, she's a really laid-back lady and I was pleased when she asked me to come here.'

'It's surprised us,' said Andie.

'I know,' said Jack. 'Your sister doesn't like me much.'

There was a challenge in his voice as well as his eyes. Andie met his gaze as steadily as she could. 'She's concerned about my mother,' she told him as though Cora wasn't in the room with her.

'She's no need to be,' said Jack.

'I'm concerned too,' said Andie.

'You've no need to be either.' Jack kept his eyes locked on hers. 'I won't do anything to hurt your mom.'

'Sometimes people hurt other people without meaning to,' said Andie.

'I can look after myself,' Cora interrupted them.

Andie tore her eyes away from Jack and looked at her mother.

'I know you can,' she said. 'You've already forced Jack into helping you do up this room. Not a bad move on your part. It hasn't seen a lick of paint in years.'

'But why did she have to pick such a bright colour?' asked Jack. 'I thought a nice muted taupe would've looked good.'

'I've been living in neutral for the last few months,' said Cora. 'I wanted to brighten things up a bit.'

'It's certainly doing that.' Andie smiled. 'Look, I'd better go.'

'It's still raining,' Jack told her. 'Why don't you stay, have dinner with us?'

It was odd, thought Andie, hearing Jack suggest that she stay in her own house. Because that was the one thing Jin was right about. The Marino house was theirs. Cora's and Jin's and Andie's. In fact Jack had a nerve talking to her like that. She shivered again.

'Do stay,' said Cora. 'I don't remember the last time you were here for a meal.'

'I've lots to do,' Andie protested.

'Like what?' asked Jack.

'I've scores to look at, lessons to prepare,' said Andie.

'And I've a wonderful Mexican chicken meal to get ready,' said Jack. 'You can do your lesson thing after dinner, surely?'

'Well . . .'

'Oh, sit down, Andie,' said Cora. 'It's not as though there's anyone waiting for you, is there?'

Not tonight, Andie thought, Tom was working tonight. He'd phoned her at lunch time and told her he wished he could be with her this evening, but that he'd be thinking of her. That he was always thinking of her.

'I'm expecting a call,' she said feebly.

'Well if you're not home they'll ring your mobile, surely?' asked Cora briskly.

'I suppose so.'

'Then you'll stay.' Jack grinned at her. 'Excellent.'

She helped Cora tidy away the paint and the old sheets.

'You're lucky,' she told her mother. 'It *is* virtually odourless paint. You can't really smell it at all. I must use it myself next time I'm decorating.'

110

'A nice bit of orange would brighten up your place no end,' remarked Cora.

'I couldn't live in orange,' said Andie.

'I don't see why not.'

Cora changed the CD so that the music was easy listening. Andie sat in the armchair and read the paper while half watching Jack Ferguson sizzle strips of chicken in his ship's recipe hot sauce. She cooked for Tom occasionally. In fact they were her favourite times, while he sat and watched her as she was watching Jack now. She would pretend that they were married, pretend that he wasn't going to go home to fragile Elizabeth, and she'd load up his plate with food so that he could barely move afterwards. Sometimes she'd set the square table in the corner of the room, bringing out her napkins and best glassware, but usually they'd eat sitting side by side on the sofa, plates propped on their knees, a bottle of wine on the floor between them. She wished she was back in the flat now, knowing that Tom was coming to see her, wondering what she could cook for him.

'Grub's up,' said Jack, bringing the Teflon pan to the table so that the food was still sizzling as he spooned it on to their plates.

'Looks fantastic,' said Cora. 'Very like Mexican night on board.'

'The difficulty with the recipes from the liner is that they give you the ingredients for hundreds.' Jack grinned as he took a flour tortilla from the bowl in front of him. 'So it's a bit of pot luck with the sauce. Hope it's OK.'

'A bit spicy.' Andie coughed as she swallowed a piece of chicken.

'Oh, gee, is it too hot? I'm sorry.' He poured water into her glass. 'Here.'

'I'm OK,' she gasped. 'Took me by surprise, that's all.'

'Cora?' He looked at Andie's mother anxiously. 'It's not inedible, is it?'

'It's definitely on the hot side,' agreed Cora. 'But very tasty.'

Cora had always liked spicy food. She dug in quite happily, while Andie was rather more cautious about her next mouthful.

'Tell me about the travel guides,' she said suddenly, turning to look at Jack.

'Poor Jack, you'll be so fed up talking about them,' Cora sympathised.

'I don't mind,' said Jack. 'They're my one achievement to date.'

He started to talk about the guides, telling Andie about the *Twenty Things To Do* in various US cities, including getting liposuction in Los Angeles and married in Las Vegas. She laughed.

'So what about Dublin?' she asked.

'Haven't decided yet,' he told her. 'As you can see, I try to mix culture and klutz.'

'Actually they sound quite fun, your guides.'

'They're meant to be.' He smiled at her. She felt her stomach flip. No man on earth could be that attractive and still be single. Not unless there was something very, very wrong with him. Maybe he was gay, she thought. Maybe Jin was getting into a tizzy about nothing. She smiled to herself – maybe she should introduce him to Johann and that would be the end of all their problems.

'What's your favourite US city?' she asked.

'Oh, New York,' he replied quickly. 'Has to be, doesn't it? It has it all. Culture, klutz and everything in between.'

'So what are your Twenty Things to Do there?'

'Breakfast in Central Park,' he said, 'on a frosty morning when everything is tipped white and there's a crackling of ice on the lake. You buy a coffee and a bagel and watch your breath steam up in front of you. And sometimes a NYPD guy will go past on a horse. You think you're in the middle of the country and then you look up and you know that there are millions of people around you.'

'A little bit like St Stephen's Green,' she said. 'Though without the NYPD.'

'I haven't been there yet.'

'Haven't you?' She smiled. 'I work nearby. And at lunch time I sometimes bring my sandwich into the park and sit down by the lake and throw bits of bread to the ducks.'

'I must meet you for lunch one day,' said Jack, 'and engage in a bit of duck feeding myself.'

Andie was shocked at how enticing the thought was. She could sense a warmth in the pit of her stomach as she envisaged sitting

112

beside Jack Ferguson throwing bread to the ducks. Then she glanced at her mother to see how she was taking the fact that her toy-boy was talking about lunching with her daughter. But Cora was absorbed in her sizzling chicken and didn't even seem to have heard Jack's remark.

'It's probably turned too wet to consider lunching in the Green any more,' said Andie after a pause.

'If we get a good day,' said Jack.

'Perhaps.' Andie tried to sound dismissive.

'Taking the Staten Island ferry,' he said.

'Huh?'

'That's another one of my Twenty Things. And it's free.' He grinned. 'Give me a Dublin thing.'

'Oh, I don't know,' said Andie.

'Taking the Dart to Killiney,' said Cora, who'd now finished her chicken. 'When it comes around the bay and the water is always such a sparkling blue.'

'Sounds good,' said Jack.

'Standing on O'Connell Bridge and looking upriver,' suggested Andie. 'In the evening, when the sun is setting.'

'You see!' Jack laughed. 'Plenty of things.'

'Looking at the bullet holes in the GPO,' said Cora. 'From the Rising.'

'That's the post office, isn't it?' asked Jack.

Both Cora and Andie nodded.

'Sitting in Merrion Square,' Andie suggested, 'and then going to the National Gallery opposite. Very cultural.'

'Shopping in Grafton Street,' said Cora. 'Very everything!'

They laughed, and Jack refilled their glasses with the ruby-red wine.

'So, Andie, who's your favourite composer?' he asked, changing the subject.

She shrugged. 'I don't really have one. I have favourite pieces of music, but that's different.'

'What's your favourite piece of music then?' asked Jack.

'I don't have one. It depends on my mood. I always like *Carmina Burana*, though,' she added.

'What about that Chopin thing you used to play all the time?' remarked Cora.

'The Prelude in D Flat?' asked Andie. 'The raindrop thing?'

Cora nodded.

'Raindrop?' asked Jack.

'It's supposed to represent the sound of a raindrop dripping from the roof of his house in Majorca,' explained Andie.

'Though it might be more suitable for here right now,' said Cora.

'I don't know the piece,' said Jack.

'You might if you heard it,' Andie told him. 'Most people don't think they know any classical music and then they hear something and realise it's been used on a TV ad. *Carmina Burana* was used for an aftershave lotion.'

'What about Chopin's raindrop?' asked Jack.

'I don't know,' confessed Andie. 'Horrible to think that someone might associate it with washing powder!'

Jack laughed. 'Perhaps you could play it for me?'

'There isn't a piano here any more,' said Andie. 'Besides, I'm not that good a performer. I'll lend you the CD sometime.'

'It'd be nicer to hear it live.'

'Trust me,' she said. 'You'd prefer the CD.'

'You're a good pianist, Andie,' said Cora. 'You shouldn't knock your talent.'

'I don't,' said Andie. 'I'm realistic about it.'

'Sometimes being realistic is limiting,' Jack said. 'Realistically I know that I'm good at the travel guides but I still want to write my book.'

'Yes, well, I had to accept the truth about my performances a long time ago,' said Andie briskly.

'But they're still good,' Cora insisted. 'Just because you're not a concert pianist . . .'

'I'll lend Jack the CD,' said Andie. She looked at her watch and frowned, then abruptly stood up. 'Sorry, but I really have to go. I do have things to prepare for tomorrow.' She smiled at Jack. 'Thanks for the food. It was wonderful.'

'My pleasure,' he said.

'And it was nice to have you here for more than five minutes,' said Cora.

'I'm sorry I haven't been round in so long,' Andie said. 'I'll try and be a more dutiful daughter in future.'

'I'm not looking for you to be dutiful!'

Andie grinned. 'I know. If you keep Jack cooking, though, I'll find myself duty bound to be here more often.'

Jack laughed. 'I think that's a compliment.'

'Of course it is.' Andie went into the hallway and retrieved her coat, which had dried out, and her shoes, which were still slightly damp. She kissed her mother on the cheek. 'I'll be in touch.'

'Jack won't be cooking every evening,' Cora told her. 'But you can call by anyway.'

'Will do.' Andie walked to the hallway again and Cora followed her.

'It's still raining,' said Cora.

'Not as heavily,' Andie assured her. 'And it's not far.'

'I meant it about calling round more,' said Cora.

'I know,' said Andie. She picked up her umbrella from its place in the porch. 'Look, I'm not trying to interfere or anything, but, well, if you need . . . if something goes wrong . . .'

'Let me worry about my life,' said Cora. 'And you worry about your own.'

'The trouble is, we all worry about each other,' said Andie.

'That's what families are for.'

Andie walked down the pathway and waved at Cora before closing the gate behind her. She turned towards Griffith Avenue. The wind buffeted her umbrella and she struggled to keep it from blowing inside out. Somehow, she thought, I don't think I'd give up cruising on the Caribbean to do 'research' in Dublin. She bit her lip.

Jack was such a damn charmer, she could see why her mother had fallen for him. And there was no doubt that was what had happened. Cora had looked and behaved like a teenager this evening. And it wasn't at all surprising, because Andie knew that, given the right circumstances, she'd have fallen for Jack Ferguson herself. He was certainly attractive enough! And he was nice to talk to. Interested. And interesting.

Andie wondered if he'd made much money out of the travel guides. She didn't think so, but maybe things were different in America. Maybe a person writing a travel guide could make lots of money. Maybe he was richer than Jin thought. Although in that case he'd hardly be staying in a two-bedroom house in Marino. He'd have booked himself in to the Morrison or the Clarence instead.

Cora was happy with him, though. Andie could see it in her mother's eyes, the brightness that hadn't been there since Des died, the enthusiasm for being part of the conversation. And she responded to Jack like a flower to water, perking up every time he spoke to her. That was hardly surprising, thought Andie. He'd made her feel the same way too, as though he was interested in everything about her. Suddenly she felt wanted and appreciated and – well – cared for by Jack Ferguson. It was easy to imagine herself sitting on her sofa with his arms around her and— She stopped abruptly. What the hell was she thinking? Jack was her mother's boyfriend. Toy-boy. Whatever. She shouldn't be thinking about him like this. She should be thinking about Tom. She began to walk faster. If she was lucky, she'd get home before he phoned.

Chapter 9

Art of the Fugue – Bach

A ndie's apartment was cold and dark. Outside the window the brown-edged leaves of the chestnut tree rustled in the wind, which was getting stronger with every passing minute. She switched on the lights and the heat before pulling the curtains and removing her wet-again coat and shoes. Then she went into the bedroom and changed from her working clothes into dark tracksuit bottoms, a grey sweatshirt and a pair of thick sports socks. She pulled her hair back into a ponytail, which made her look younger than most of her students, and then sat down on the sofa with her legs curled up beneath her. She looked at her watch. It was nearly nine o'clock. She wondered whether Tom had phoned. It was impossible to tell, because he never left messages for her. If she didn't pick up the phone he always disconnected before the answering machine had finished her 'I can't come to the phone now' recording so it didn't register the call. He usually rang before nine whenever he was working late. But not always. Of course, she could never call him, even though sometimes, when she was missing him badly, she actually picked up the receiver and allowed his number to ring once before hanging up. She rarely did this in case the calls were traced back to her. It seemed a melodramatic sort of thing to have to worry about, but she was very well aware that her relationship with Tom was still a secret because both of them were so careful. Making obsessive phone calls wasn't careful. It was stupid, and neither of them was stupid. At least, not in that way.

She switched on the TV and watched the news without really

117

listening to what was going on. By the time it was over he still hadn't phoned. She looked sternly at the receiver and picked it up to check that the line was working. Then she took her mobile out of her bag and put it on the table in front of her so that she'd hear it if he called it instead. Sometimes she missed calls to her mobile if it was in the bottom of her bag. She simply didn't hear it, despite its irritating jingle. Tom often told her that she managed to block it out because the electronic twang was so offensive to her.

Then the land-line rang and she jolted out of the seat to pick it up.

'Well?' demanded Jin.

'Oh, it's you.' Andie hadn't thought that the caller could be anyone but Tom. Hearing her sister's voice startled her.

'Who were you expecting?' asked Jin.

'Nobody,' said Andie.

'You sounded disappointed,' Jin said.

'It's nothing,' said Andie dismissively. 'What d'you want?'

'What d'you think?' demanded Jin. 'Did you do what you said? Did you call in to see Mum?'

Andie felt a sudden rush of relief that she had in fact visited Cora when she hadn't wanted to. 'Yes,' she replied.

'And? Did you meet him? Prince Charming?' asked Jin.

'Prince Charming is right,' agreed Andie.

'What did you think?'

Andie was silent. Her mind was still in turmoil regarding her mother and the hunk. Without expecting to, she'd liked Jack Ferguson, and had felt herself warm to his easy charm and hundred-watt smile. Plus he was a damn good cook; she hadn't eaten as well in months! But an enjoyable dinner with Cora and Jack was only enjoyable as a one-off experience, she thought. She couldn't quite accept the idea of him being a more permanent fixture around the place. And despite his undoubted charisma, Andie felt as though he was holding something back. She didn't think that Jack Ferguson had told her everything she wanted to know about him. Which wasn't a crime, she knew, but it made her a little more suspicious of him than she would otherwise have been. But then it was hard not to be in some way sceptical of the

118

relationship between her mother and a man young enough to be her son.

Cora had looked positively radiant beside him, making it almost impossible to believe that she was the mother of two grown-up daughters as well as a committee member of the local residents' association and a founder member of a sixteen-year-old book club. All these things were suitable for Cora as a fifty-eight-year-old woman. Andie didn't want her mother feeling old before her time or drifting (as she had seemed to do ever since Des had died) into a kind of late-middle-age apathy. But laughing and giggling with Jack Ferguson like some love-struck teenager – these were things that Andie found it far from easy to accept. Watching Cora flirt with Jack had been very unsettling and left Andie feeling extremely uncomfortable. The problem, she'd thought as she'd walked home after dinner, was that Cora was behaving in a totally uncharacteristic way with this man and none of her actions was grounded in what Andie knew about her mother at all. It was one thing, she thought, remembering Cora as a fun-loving person before Des's death; it was quite another to see her as someone who was capable of forming a new, flirtatious relationship with someone twenty-five years her junior.

'Well?' repeated Jin impatiently.

'He seemed very nice,' said Andie eventually. 'And he and Ma got on well together.'

'You're joking!' Jin sounded tense. 'He's not nice at all. He thinks he's some kind of love god and she's worshipping at his feet.'

Andie stifled a giggle. 'Not quite,' she said. 'She was painting when I arrived and he'd gone to the shops.'

'He's suckering her in with the domestic scene,' said Jin. 'You can't possibly think that this is natural.'

'I've absolutely no idea,' Andie told her. She sighed. 'I asked Ma was she sleeping with him.'

'You didn't!' Jin was both shocked and intrigued.

'I did,' said Andie. 'And she wouldn't answer. She was right, I suppose. She said she'd never asked me that question so why should I ask her.'

'It's different,' said Jin.

'Not really,' Andie replied. 'And, oh – Jin, I don't know. I think you're right in that whatever sort of relationship it is, it isn't long term. Even if he *is* the nicest bloke in the world he's hardly going to settle down in Marino with her, is he? He writes travel guides, for heaven's sake! It's hardly the life of someone who stays in the same spot for very long.'

'That's a good point,' said Jin thoughtfully. 'So maybe he'll just up and go.'

'Maybe.' Andie sounded uncertain.

'How long were you there?' asked Jin.

'I stayed for dinner,' said Andie.

'You what?' cried Jin.

'He was cooking and asked me to stay.'

'*He* asked you! Not Mum?'

Andie grimaced. 'Yeah, well, that bothered me too. But I couldn't say no and I thought it would be a good idea. Actually it was – he's a great cook.'

'Andie!'

'Well, he is,' said Andie defensively. 'He did Mexican chicken—'

'Andie, I didn't ring up to get the low-down on his cooking prowess,' snapped Jin. She frowned, forgetting that Andie couldn't see her. 'This makes it a bit awkward,' she said.

'What does?'

'Him being a good cook,' said Jin. 'Kevin suggested that we ask them over for lunch.'

'Why?'

'To get more low-down,' Jin said. 'To suss him out a bit more.'

'And why would his being a good cook be a problem?'

'Andie!' Jin sounded aggrieved. 'You know it's not my thing. Kevin doesn't realise how much of his food is ready-made from good old M&S or the local deli.'

'I guess existing on bean sprouts and celery for so long wouldn't have exposed you to the delights of beef tornados or raspberry pavlovas,' Andie agreed. 'If you're ordering in, get something good. His Mexican chicken was gorgeous. Very, very spicy but very, very tasty.'

Jin groaned. 'Is there no end to this guy's talents?'

'He's bound to be crap at something,' Andie said. 'Though as yet I don't know what it would be. He was so slick, Jin. Part of me was sure it was an act and yet . . .'

'When he bloody well gazed into my eyes it was an act,' snapped Jin. 'And probably the same one he pulled on Mum. What freaks me out is that she doesn't seem to see how ridiculous the whole situation is.'

'I know. I know.'

'Do you want to come to lunch too?' asked Jin suddenly. 'It might be a good idea.'

Andie hesitated.

'What's your problem?' demanded Jin. 'You never want to come to my house. Never.'

'It's not that,' said Andie hastily, although Jin was perfectly right. 'It's . . . well, it'll all seem like we're vetting him again. We did it individually and this is like doing it together, and I can't see myself enjoying it somehow.'

'You're not meant to enjoy it!' cried Jin.

'I suppose not,' acknowledged Andie ruefully.

'I could ask Doireann and Frank too,' Jin said slowly. 'Make it like a coming-home party for Mum.'

'She was only away for a week,' commented Andie. 'A coming-home party is a bit extreme.'

'Oh, so what,' said Jin dismissively. 'Any excuse.'

'Maybe.'

'So you'll come then?'

'I – I'll try.'

'Don't tell me you'll have something else on?' Jin's tone was close to scathing. 'It's not as though your life is a hotbed of social activity, now is it?'

'It could be,' said Andie defensively.

Jin laughed. 'Come on, darling sister. You make the nuns at St Brigid's seem racy.'

'I'll do my best,' said Andie shortly. 'Ring me when you've decided the exact day and time for this additional inquisition.'

'All right,' said Jin. 'But no pathetic excuses. I just won't believe them.' She sighed again. 'It's our duty to stop her making a fool of herself, Andie.'

'It's a question of how, though, isn't it?' Andie asked. 'I mean, short of shooting the bloke there's nothing we can do. We can't run him out of town like it was the Wild West. And really, Jin, why would we do it? Unless we find out some dark secret about him it's kind of unlikely he'll just go just because that's what we'd like, isn't it?'

'D'you think there's a dark secret?' Jin sounded hopeful.

Andie sighed. 'I felt he was doing his best to be ultra-nice to Ma and make a good impression with me. But I also thought there was something else . . . Thing is, I've no idea what that might be.'

'Kevin thinks he's a con artist.'

'Kevin thinks everyone is a con artist.'

'No he doesn't!' Jin sounded annoyed. 'Kevin deals with loads of important business people every day. He's intuitive about these things.'

'Intuitive about business and intuitive about potential boyfriends for our mother are two very different things,' said Andie drily.

'Don't even say the word boyfriend,' said Jin. 'It makes me want to throw up.'

Andie giggled. 'Listen to us. We're like two hens clucking about their chicks. Ma is a grown woman!'

'Who says that being grown up gives you any sense?' demanded Jin. 'Sometimes I think I get worse as I get older.'

'You might have a point there,' agreed Andie. 'I often feel that way too.'

'But Kevin is a mine of sense,' Jin told her. 'So I do think we should listen to any suggestions he might have. Besides, he's a bit more detached about it than us.'

'Possibly.'

'He's going to do a bit of checking into Jack's background.'

'Now *that*'s not a bad idea,' Andie acknowledged. 'After all, if we find out that he's some kind of bum from the West Coast . . . though I have to say, Jin, if he is they make them extraordinarily good-looking over there!'

'I might call to see her again tomorrow,' said Jin.

'If you keep calling round you'll drive her mad,' warned Andie.

'Plus, if there is anything dodgy about Jack you'll put him on his guard. Leave it be for a few days.'

'I don't like waiting,' said Jin.

'I know,' replied Andie. 'But try.'

'I won't call round but maybe I'll phone up about lunch.'

'Well, if I get any other great ideas I'll call you,' Andie told her.

'OK,' said Jin. 'Are you going out or anything tonight?'

Andie glanced at her watch. 'It's nearly ten,' she said. 'Where would I be going?'

'The best nights out start late.'

'Not mine,' said Andie shortly.

'I'll phone you again,' said Jin. 'You have to come to lunch.'

'Maybe.'

'Definitely.'

'We'll see,' said Andie and then hung up.

'She's hopeless.' Jin stuck the cordless receiver back on its stand and looked despairingly at Kevin.

'What did she say?'

Jin recounted Andie's comments and Kevin raised his eyebrows when she told him that Andie believed there was something suspicious about Jack.

'In what way?' he asked.

'She didn't know. She thought he was holding something back.'

Kevin pursed his lips. 'I think she's right. We'll see what my investigations throw up.'

'God Almighty.' Jin ran her fingers through her hair. 'I can't believe I'm sitting here talking to you about carrying out an investigation into my mother's lover.'

'Not exactly what I would've expected either,' said Kevin. 'And I'll tell you something, Jin, I really don't want her to be at the centre of a whole gossipy scandal that'll have all my business colleagues laughing at me.'

'She won't be,' said Jin forcefully. 'We won't let her.'

'She probably already is.' Kevin's tone was grim. He frowned and then looked at his wife quizzically. 'What if we find her someone else?'

123

'Like who?' asked Jin.

'I don't know yet,' admitted Kevin. 'But I'm sure there must be someone I know . . . Trevor McAllister, maybe . . . he's a widower . . .'

Jin's eyes lit up. 'That'd be the thing to do. Especially if this Trevor bloke is rolling in it like you.'

Kevin laughed. 'I wouldn't say rolling in it. But he's comfortable. Of course, I don't know whether or not he's seeing anyone. I could find out, though.'

'Perfect,' said Jin with satisfaction. 'Let's face it, Jack must seem very immature to Mum. If you give her a better alternative she's sure to jump at it.'

'And in the meantime we might lure Jack away with someone else too,' said Kevin pensively.

Jin laughed and put her arms around him. 'Now I know why you're so good in business,' she said. 'You think of all the options.'

'Of course I do,' said Kevin.

It was nearly midnight before Tom phoned. Andie had been half asleep on the sofa, made drowsy by the steaming mug of extra-rich hot chocolate she'd drunk at eleven. She jolted into wakefulness as the phone rang.

'Hello.'

'Hi, darling.' Tom's voice was as soft as he could make it but she could hear the din of the crowded pub behind him and the beat of the music it pumped out.

'I thought you'd phone earlier,' she said.

'I did,' said Tom. 'But I got your machine. Where were you?'

'With Ma,' said Andie. 'Meeting the boyfriend.'

'So did you fall for him?'

Andie giggled. 'Not quite. But I can see his charm.'

'I feel threatened,' said Tom jokingly.

'No need to be,' said Andie.

'Don't tell me it's serious with your mother?'

'I can't truly believe it is,' said Andie. 'But Jin is in a complete flap about it and she's making me flap too. I need a break. Can you call round tonight when you're finished at the bar?'

'I don't think so.' His voice was doubtful. 'It'll be another hour before I'm out of here.'

'Will Elizabeth be awake and waiting for you?'

'No,' said Tom. 'You know she takes sleeping tablets when I work late.'

'So come round.'

He hesitated.

'I need you,' said Andie.

'You never say that.'

'I'm saying it this time.'

'I'll phone you when I'm finished,' Tom said. 'See what I can do.'

'Come to bed.' Jin perched on the edge of the king-sized bed later that night and rubbed at her nails with varnish remover, while Kevin sat in the comfortable armchair and flicked through a sheaf of papers.

'In a minute,' he said absently. 'Just doing a final check on this stuff.'

'Is it more garbage about the Oslo deal?' she demanded.

'Yes.'

'The sooner all that's finished the better,' she snapped. 'It's the only thing you care about these days.'

'Hardly.' He bundled the papers together and looked at her. 'Despite the pressures of this particular deal I've found the time to organise your birthday party, visit your mother *and* think of strategies to get rid of the unwanted boyfriend.'

'All right, all right,' Jin conceded. 'Oslo isn't the only thing you care about.'

'I'm glad you realise it.' Kevin shoved the folder into his briefcase.

'This Trevor bloke you mentioned earlier,' said Jin. 'D'you really think Mum would like him?'

'I don't know,' replied Kevin. 'But he's sure as hell preferable to the bloke she's got at the moment.'

Jin nodded and replaced the cap on the bottle of nail varnish remover before throwing the cotton wool she'd been using into the wastepaper bin. 'You know, I can't help wondering if she has an ulterior motive herself.'

'Your mother?' asked Kevin. 'What kind of ulterior motive can she have?'

'I'm not sure,' said Jin. 'But maybe there's a bloke in the book club or the bridge club or one of her other associations that she fancies, only he's been slow to act. Perhaps she thinks Jack might galvanise him into action.'

'Talk about getting a sledgehammer to crack a nut,' said Kevin drily.

'Well I know, only I can't get my head around the fact that Mum might just be with him for – for sex.' Jin sounded so disgusted that Kevin couldn't help laughing.

'I agree that a lot of women might find him a just-for-sex-type bloke.' He looked at Jin thoughtfully. 'What about Andie? You said you thought she fancied him.'

'Oh, well, hard to say with Andie,' said Jin dismissively. 'But she did go on and on about how gorgeous he was.'

'Do you really think she's interested in him?'

'Maybe she doesn't realise it herself,' Jin said. 'But it really wouldn't surprise me.'

'Interesting.' Kevin looked thoughtful. 'That might be something we can use to our advantage. It just needs a bit of thinking through.'

Although she was now very tired Andie didn't want to go to bed in case she fell asleep. She knew that Tom's call would wake her but she hated being woken up soon after dropping off and always found it impossible to get to sleep again. So she sat on the sofa and for the second time that night watched a report on Sky News about drugs problems in inner cities. Right now she wished that she hadn't asked Tom to come round, but when he'd phoned she'd felt the misery of not being with him so deeply that she'd wanted him to come to her straight away. Maybe he would. She shivered with anticipation.

The phone rang.

'You still awake?' he asked.

'Yes.'

'You still want me?'

'Yes.'

'I'll be there in fifteen minutes.'

She was wide awake again. She changed out of the baggy sweatshirt and tracksuit bottoms into a pair of her tightest jeans. She pulled on a figure-hugging T-shirt, then squeezed eye drops into her eyes to give them sparkle before dusting her face with bronzer. She dropped the sports socks into her laundry basket and then put Kenzo behind her ears. The doorbell buzzed as she was dabbing it between her breasts.

Tom looked as tired as she'd felt earlier. His hair was tousled, his eyes were red from a night in the crowded bar. He looked shattered. But she didn't care. She kissed him as he stepped inside, surprised by the ferocity of her own desire. He was surprised too. He cupped her face in his hands and asked her was everything all right.

'I just missed you,' she said. 'I don't know why.'

'I'm sorry,' he told her. 'I really am.'

'I love you.' She undid the buttons of his white shirt. 'I love you and I want you to be with me and I hate knowing that you're not.'

'I love you too.' He followed her into the bedroom. 'I've never loved anyone the way I love you.'

Her teeth worried at his lower lip. 'I need you,' she whispered.

'I need you.'

She smiled suddenly. 'No talk. Just action.'

She held him tightly as he entered her, not allowing him to move at first, just wanting to feel him there. Then she rocked with him so that the pleasure inside her built up with every move he made. And when she cried out she gripped him hard by the shoulders, digging her fingers into his skin below the shoulder blade itself. He cried out too, calling her name and holding on to her wrists as she lay beneath him.

'That was incredible,' he said breathlessly.

'I know.'

'I can't get enough of you.'

'I love you,' she repeated.

127

They lay side by side, their chests still heaving with the exertion. Andie closed her eyes. She felt herself drifting towards sleep.

'I have to go.'

She opened her eyes again and looked at him.

'I'm sorry,' he said.

She looked at the alarm clock. 'You've only been here twenty minutes.'

'Twenty mind-blowing minutes,' he told her as he reached for his shirt.

'Stay a little longer.'

'I can't, Andie.' He grimaced. 'I want to, you know I do. But . . .'

'But she's asleep,' protested Andie. 'Drugged to the eyeballs.'

'Even so.' He pulled on his trousers.

'Sometimes I wonder . . .' Andie's voice wobbled.

'Don't,' said Tom. 'I'll never leave you, Andie. I promise.'

He kissed her gently on the lips and let himself out of the flat.

Chapter 10

Jin sat at the tiny table while Myrtelle, the manicurist, rubbed conditioner into her nails. She glanced at her watch, wanting to make sure that she had plenty of time to catch the Dart and meet Livia for lunch as she'd arranged a few days earlier (and subsequently almost forgotten about). She'd been lucky to get an early-morning appointment at the beauty salon; they were usually booked up days in advance, but as she was a very good customer, they'd managed to fit her in.

'What colour would you like?' asked Myrtelle.

Jin looked at her fingers consideringly. 'Something autumnal,' she said. 'It feels very autumnal this morning.'

'Dry, though,' said Myrtelle as she rummaged through her box of colours. 'Which is a relief after all the rain yesterday.'

'Ugh, yes,' agreed Jin. She pointed at one of the bottles Myrtelle had put on the table. 'That looks nice,' she said.

'Golden Glow,' said the manicurist. 'I like it myself.'

'Excellent.' Jin flexed her fingers.

She enjoyed having her nails done. It was like having her hair done, totally relaxing. It hadn't been like that in her modelling days, of course, when stylists rushed to change her look from one outfit to the next and when her hair was permanently style-damaged and her nails usually acrylic. Life was better now, she thought. Marrying Kevin had been the best thing that ever happened to her. She was lucky to have him. Lucky, too, that he didn't care how much she spent on herself as long as she looked good. She knew that he liked

129

her to be at her best all of the time. That was one of the mistakes Monica had made. Monica hadn't considered being Kevin's wife as a job in itself. She had constantly nagged him about 'doing her own thing' and 'being her own person'. And, according to Kevin, she never really much cared how she looked. Jin didn't think that looks were everything, but she knew that they made a difference. Interestingly, though, Monica had revamped her image since the divorce as she threw herself into her charity work, so that she was a regular feature in glossy magazines and gossip columns in the newspapers. There'd been a colour photograph of her in *VIP* magazine the previous month, at a gala ball, looking extravagant in a red silk dress. Kevin's lip had curled as he looked at the picture of her standing beside her escort for the night, a divorced bank manager who both of them had known for a long time. He'd thrown the magazine to one side and muttered to Jin that she shouldn't bring that kind of rubbish into the house. Jin hadn't said anything but resolved to keep her gossip magazines out of his sight in future.

'Hi, Jin.' Áine O'Brien, a member of the same tennis club as Jin, strolled into the salon.

'Oh, hi, Áine.'

'Did you hear the latest?' Áine sat on the black leather chair beside her.

'No, what?'

'Bettina McDermott has thrown Ivor out.'

'No.' Jin's eyes widened.

'Yes,' said Áine. 'Apparently he was spotted in town with his latest girlfriend and Bettina flipped over it.'

'Did everyone know about Ivor's girlfriends except me?' demanded Jin. 'I thought I was friendly with Bettina but she never said anything and nobody was gossiping about it.'

'Didn't you know that they've had problems for years?' asked Áine.

'No,' said Jin irritably. 'I thought they were OK. As it turns out, I saw Ivor and blonde bombshell myself earlier in the week.'

'Did you? Where?'

Jin told her about her lunch with Kevin, and spotting Ivor at the restaurant on the Green.

'You know, you're the really lucky one,' said Áine idly.

'Why?'

'You've been married to Kevin for – what – four years now? And you still meet each other for lunch. That's romantic.'

Jin decided not to tell her that the lunch had been a pretence so that she and Kevin could call in to see Cora. She certainly wasn't about to inform Malahide's biggest gossip that her mother was carrying on with an American beach-bum. It'd be all round the town in seconds. Jin felt herself flush at the thought.

'You're done,' said Myrtelle, saving her the bother of having to say anything at all. 'Let me spray some fast-dry on them for you.'

'So what was she like?' asked Áine, who wasn't going to be diverted from the really interesting issue of Bettina and Ivor's split.

'The girlfriend?' Jin shrugged. 'Young, blonde, pretty.'

'Poor Bettina.'

'That's what I said,' Jin agreed. 'Kevin believed she'd never divorce Ivor because she has everything she wants.'

'Men are such fools about things like this,' said Áine.

'I know.'

'Anyway, if you saw him with the girl and other people did too, Bettina obviously felt enough was enough.'

'I don't blame her,' said Jin. 'And Kevin says it's been going on for ages. He said she was tolerant as long as Ivor was discreet.'

'Maybe he wanted to get caught this time,' Áine suggested. 'Maybe this time it's serious.'

'I'd kill him if it was me,' said Jin.

'Kevin's never been a great one for playing away,' Áine told her. 'As far as I know, there was only one indiscretion when he was with Monica. Two at the most. And, of course, you didn't come along till much later.'

'That's cheering.'

'Another little nugget for you . . .' Áine smiled conspiratorially.

'Oh?' Jin held her hands in front of her and examined them. They looked really great, she thought.

'The Campbells are selling their house.'

'Really?' Jin frowned. 'Why? They only bought it a year ago. Where are they moving to now?'

131

'Somewhere a lot cheaper,' said Áine. 'He needs the money.'

'He won't get much from selling a house,' remarked Jin. 'Even if it is worth a few million. Because I presume if he needs money he needs it for the business, and that's surely far more than he'd get from the profit on the house.'

'Business and personal both, I believe,' said Áine.

'How's Celeste?' Jin blew on her nails to help the drying process.

'I haven't spoken to her. Marilisa told me.'

'You can't believe everything that woman tells you,' said Jin.

'There's a grain of truth in all of it,' said Áine. 'I know.'

'Remind me never to do anything you might gossip about,' said Jin.

Áine laughed. 'Sooner or later everyone does.'

Jin was pleased that she managed to get to the Dart and pay for her ticket without smudging her Golden Glow nails. Even with the drying spray it took ages for them to be truly smudge-proof, but she'd managed to extract the money and hand it over without making a mess of them. Now she gazed out of the window as the train sped along the coast towards Dalkey. Even though she didn't like public transport she liked this journey once it was south of the river. The views of the coast and the bay were spectacular, and today, with another late burst of sun, the sea was glittering blue topped with frothy white waves.

Livia sometimes complained that her pretty villa-style house near the village itself didn't have any views of the sea, and then she'd laugh and say that Spence would have to sell a lot more crates of plonk to manage a glimpse of the bay. Jin would agree with her that sea views were nice and sigh that despite Malahide being a coastal town, she and Kevin didn't have decent views either. But it didn't really bother her too much. After all, they had a house on the beach in Antigua.

The train slid into Dalkey station and Jin got up. Livia was waiting for her outside the station building, looking as tanned and healthy as Jin had imagined, her wheaten hair bleached by the sun and falling loosely around her shoulders.

'Hi!' Livia walked over to her and kissed her on each cheek. 'Made it all right then? Weren't attacked by the natives?'

'Sod off, Harper,' said Jin amiably.

'Well, I know how you love that car.' Livia led her down the main street towards the restaurant. 'But this way at least you can have a drink.'

'I parked the car in Malahide station,' Jin told her. 'So I can't get completely hammered. Besides, I've had a few social events with too much wine lately. One glass will do.'

'Whatever you like,' said Livia as they walked along the winding main street. 'Here we are, told you it wasn't far.'

The restaurant was small, with room for only half a dozen tables, but it was bright and airy. A huge mirror which took up the whole of one wall reflected back into the dining area and a narrow glass vase with a single marigold stood on each table.

'Nice,' said Jin appreciatively.

'I haven't eaten here yet,' said Livia, 'so it might be all show with crappy food.'

A waitress waved them to the window table, where they sat down happily.

'Did you bring the Portuguese photos?' asked Jin.

'Yes,' said Livia.

'I didn't bring any.'

'Good,' said Livia. 'I get jealous when I see that beach house of yours.'

'More of a beach hut really,' Jin told her. 'It only has four rooms.'

Livia giggled. 'I bet you never thought you'd see the day when you'd be complaining that your house in the Caribbean only has four rooms.'

'I know. That sounded awful, didn't it?' Jin picked up the wine list and scanned it. 'What are you having?'

'Well, just water for me. But you go ahead.'

'Water!' Jin looked at her. 'Just because I'm being moderate you don't have to hold back! We need a glass so that we can sip away and complain about our lot and then remind ourselves that actually we aren't that badly off.'

133

'I didn't realise you had the whole conversation planned,' said Livia in amusement.

'That's the way our conversations always are,' said Jin. 'And I don't care. I like them. So have a glass of wine. You're not on some stupid detox, are you?'

Livia shook her head. 'A bit more radical than that, I'm afraid.'

'What?'

'Haven't you guessed?' Livia looked at her friend. 'Come on, Jin. I'm wearing a pair of loose cotton trousers and a long T-shirt.'

'I don't – oh!' Jin's eyes widened. 'Are you pregnant?'

'Got it in one,' confirmed Livia.

'How long?' asked Jin.

'Five months,' Livia told her.

'You don't look it!'

'I'm starting to expand,' said Livia. 'You'll be able to tell soon enough.'

'Did you know when you were going to Portugal?' asked Jin.

Livia nodded. 'Which is why I definitely would've preferred the lying on the beach part.'

'How are you feeling?'

'Fine, to be honest,' admitted Livia. 'Very excited, actually.'

'I didn't know you and Spence were trying for a baby.'

'We've been married three years,' Livia said. 'It seemed like a good idea.'

'I guess so.'

A waitress came over and they ordered water for Livia and a glass of white wine for Jin, as well as pasta for both of them.

'In fact I've been really broody the last few months,' Livia confided. 'I kept looking at babies in prams and thinking, I want one of those. I never felt that way before. But lately I couldn't help thinking of how much I wanted a baby and how much I even wanted to do the whole pregnancy thing. I actually started to go gooey over maternity dresses!'

'A bit of a departure for the woman who once thought being seven stone was a lifetime tragedy,' said Jin wryly. 'Though you're surely not in maternity stuff yet. You've hardly put on any weight at all.'

'I have,' said Livia. 'I'm just good at hiding it.'

'Well, I wish you all the luck in the world,' said Jin.

'Thanks.' Livia took a sip of the water which the waitress had just put in front of her. 'You haven't changed your mind about having kids yourself, have you?'

Jin shook her head. 'It's not on our agenda.'

'It wasn't on my agenda either,' Livia pointed out. 'Or Spence's. But it hits you one day. I can't explain it.'

'It better not hit me,' said Jin. 'Kevin would freak out altogether.'

'Why?'

Jin shrugged. 'He has two kids already. He believes that they shouldn't lose out because he remarried. He also thinks that he's done the baby thing and doesn't want to do it again.'

'That's hardly fair on you,' Livia pointed out.

'I knew what I was getting into,' said Jin.

'Sure. But things change.' Livia looked earnestly at her friend. 'Look, when we were younger the most important thing was not to put on an extra pound or not to get spots or to be perfectly exfoliated. I've gone past that.'

'So have I,' said Jin. 'I just haven't moved into the gooey stage yet.'

'But you're telling me that you won't let yourself go there at all,' said Livia. 'What if you want to?'

'I won't want to,' said Jin briskly. 'So it's not a problem.'

'But what if you do?' demanded Livia. 'What then?'

The waitress returned and placed a basket of bread with flavoured oils on the table, which prevented Jin from replying.

'I'm going to eat the bread and I'll probably have a dessert too.' Livia was distracted by the food. 'I'm going mad on sweet things.'

'Oh my God!' Jin grinned. 'You've gone over to the Dark Side completely.'

Livia laughed. 'I know, I know. I can't help myself.' She dipped tomato bread into the oil. After she'd eaten it and licked the crumbs from her fingers, she took a folder out of her bag. 'Here's the Portuguese snaps.'

Jin looked through them, admiring the long beaches and the blue skies and even the shots of vineyards which Livia said were in different locations though they all looked identical to her.

'The worst part of it all was not being able to drink the wine,' said Livia.

'I thought you taster types just swilled it around and spat it out,' commented Jin. 'That'd hardly cause you any problems, would it?'

'Couldn't bear the taste,' Livia admitted. 'Did you ever think you'd see the day when I wouldn't like wine and I'd want to eat desserts?'

'To be honest – no.'

The waitress reappeared with their pasta and Livia sighed in appreciation.

'I do get a bit scared from time to time though.' She couldn't help talking about her pregnancy again.

'Why are you scared?'

'Why d'you think?' demanded Livia. 'Because now it's happened it's a force of nature all of its own. There's nothing I can do to stop it. That's a bit scary.'

'Oh.'

'D'you blame me?'

'Not at all,' said Jin. 'It'd scare the life out of me too. Mother Nature's been remarkably lax about our evolution that way. Still, I'm reliably informed that once you have it you forget all about the pain.'

'That's because you're far too knackered to remember,' said Livia. She grinned. 'I'm looking forward to having the baby in my arms, not to her getting there.'

'Is she a her?' asked Jin.

Livia nodded. 'We think so. They asked if I wanted to know and I thought, well, why should they know and me not.'

'And is Spence looking forward to it all?'

'Thrilled,' said Livia. 'You'd swear he was the first man to impregnate a woman in the history of the universe.'

Jin laughed.

'I'm glad for you,' she told Livia. 'Even if I don't really envy you. All those years of getting totally stressed out about your offspring.'

'Are you sure Kevin wouldn't change his mind?'

'Kevin never changes his mind,' said Jin firmly.

'And you?'

Jin shrugged. 'It's not for me.'

'But don't you sometimes—'

'No,' Jin interrupted her. 'As I said, he already has Cian and Clarissa.'

'But they're not yours,' said Livia. She looked at Jin curiously. 'Do you see them much?'

'Not really.' Jin shook her head. 'Occasionally Clarissa calls to the house, but that's rare. Usually after she's had a row with Monica about something or other and she's trying to put her point of view to Kevin! You know what sixteen-year-olds are like, trying to play one off the other. He gives in to her, of course, which drives Monica mad. With Cian, he plays golf every so often. They won a father and son competition earlier in the summer and Kevin was thrilled. Cian's not a bad kid actually. Well, hardly a kid. Young adult, I suppose. Very studious and not at all rebellious. They get on.'

'Do you resent them?' asked Livia.

'Why on earth should I?' Jin shook her head. 'They're part of his life and that's fine by me.'

'I think you're being remarkably mature about it all,' said Livia.

Jin laughed. 'I'm not always mature. I don't especially like Monica and I'm terrified of ending up like her even though she's nothing like me. But we agreed on the child thing before we got married and that's that as far as I'm concerned.'

'Fair enough.' Livia chased the last of her pasta around her plate.

'Anyway, are you going to get a personal trainer for the day after you give birth so that you can regain your gorgeous figure?' asked Jin.

'To be honest I'm having a great time being too lazy to do any exercise and justifying eating all sorts of rubbish by telling myself that my body is crying out for it,' Livia told her. 'Which is probably all wrong, but I can't help it.'

Jin laughed. 'Come on, Harper. I expect to see you kitted out in PVC à la Elizabeth Hurley, proving that you can still do it.'

'Not a bloody chance,' said Livia. 'I've consigned that part of me to the past. If I put on weight I put on weight.'

'But you'll want to tone up, surely?'

'Oh, eventually,' agreed Livia. 'But I haven't even had the baby yet, Jin. Give me a break.'

'Sorry.' Jin smiled at her. 'I find it hard to take in. You're the first of my friends to get pregnant.'

'Am I?' Livia looked surprised.

'If you don't count Shirley Munroe, who wasn't a close friend,' said Jin. 'Remember her? She used to do a lot of catalogue work.'

Livia frowned.

'Baby doll kind of look,' Jin reminded her.

'Oh yes! And she has a kid?'

'Three,' said Jin.

'Good for her,' said Livia. 'Though how anyone gets up the nerve to do it again is beyond me.'

'It mightn't be that bad,' Jin comforted her.

'It probably will,' said Livia glumly.

It was nearly two hours later before they left the restaurant. Jin had refused the desserts and had simply drunk black coffee while she watched her friend tuck into the biggest slice of blackberry pie topped with whipped cream she'd ever seen.

'The worst of all this is that I'll be hungry again in a few hours,' said Livia mournfully as she wiped the crumbs from her lips. 'I'm like a manic eating machine. I'm just hoping that my famed metabolism deals with it.'

'I'm sure it will,' said Jin reassuringly as they walked out of the restaurant and into the street again.

'You're right about the personal trainer too,' said Livia. 'I probably should book one now.'

'Oh, don't mind me, I was being facetious,' said Jin. 'Revel in your cream cakes and laziness. It actually sounds quite comforting.'

'It is,' admitted Livia. 'But sorry, Jin, I know I went on and on about baby stuff. I just can't help it right now.'

Jin smiled 'Don't worry about it.' She kissed her friend on the cheek. 'Keep in touch. Let me know how things are going.'

'Sure will,' said Livia.

'And give my love to Spence.'

'Yes.'

The green train pulled into the station.

'See you soon,' said Jin.

'See you.' Livia waved at her as she got into the carriage. Jin waved too, until the train moved off again. Then she sat back in her seat and mulled over Livia's news. It wasn't surprising, she supposed. All of her friends were getting to the broody stage, their body clocks telling them that if they didn't get pregnant now they might never manage it. And she understood how Livia might feel. After all, if it was that important to you, you had to act. You couldn't take the risk of waiting. She chewed at the inside of her lip. Livia had been so happy, so lit up by it all. Her eyes were brighter, her skin was as flawless as ever, but the incandescence came from within. She was happier than Jin had ever seen her. But that, Jin thought, was because both she and Spence wanted the baby. Jin knew that if she came home and told Kevin she was pregnant she certainly wouldn't get the kind of reception that Livia had got. Kevin would be furious. And he'd be furious because he'd know that the baby wasn't his.

Jin had never told a soul that Kevin had had a vasectomy when Clarissa was a baby. It was nobody's business but their own. He'd been perfectly upfront with her about it, telling her the first night they'd slept together that she didn't have to worry about getting pregnant. She'd been surprised at his candour and appreciated it. She didn't know whether it was because of the fact that she didn't have to worry about birth control (even though Kevin himself had insisted on wearing condoms until both of them had been to the doctor and been given clean bills of sexual health), or whether it was simply that he was very skilled at making love, but that night had been sensational. Their lovemaking had remained sensational ever since.

When he asked her to marry him he told her to think long and hard about the issue of children. He reminded her that vasectomies were to all intents and purposes irreversible and that if she had the slightest doubt at all she should refuse him. But of course she hadn't refused him. She loved him far too much for that. And, she told him, she was marrying him because she loved him, not as a potential father for children she didn't even want.

Since then she'd hardly given it a second thought. She loved her life with him. She loved her house and her car and her clothes and the social life that surrounded them as a couple. Even if there had been the possibility of children she wouldn't have wanted them because they would have interfered everything. There were occasions, of course, when she wondered what it might be like to have a baby of her own. But those times passed quickly and she pushed the thoughts to the back of her mind. Besides, they were hormonal thoughts, not rational, and certainly not needed.

The train pulled into Blackrock station and a crowd of people piled in. Jin realised, with a sense of complete shock, that Cora and Jack were among them. Jack had his arm around Cora's waist, and as Jin watched them, she saw her mother whisper something into Jack's ear. He laughed and kissed her on the lips. Jin thought she was going to be sick. She couldn't quite believe that on practically the only day of the year that she got the train it had to be the same one as her mother and her toy-boy. The odds were surely longer than those of winning the lottery. It was amazing how sometimes life seemed to cram in coincidences and bizarre meetings just when you didn't want it to. Although maybe this was an opportunity too. Jin hadn't phoned her mother to issue the lunch invitation yet because, on consideration, she thought that maybe Andie had a point about rushing things. So she'd decided to wait a couple of days before saying anything, even though it was driving her crazy. Now that they were here, on the train, she could invite them casually, as though the idea had just occurred to her. The only problem was that she wasn't sure she could be as pleasant as she should. She wished that there was even a small part of her that didn't think her mother was behaving like a menopausal old fool, but there wasn't. She took a deep breath and looked towards them at exactly the same moment Jack noticed her and waved.

Her smile in return was forced, but Jack took Cora's hand and led her along the carriage to where Jin was sitting.

'This is a surprise,' said Cora. 'I didn't think you ever took the Dart.'

'Occasionally,' said Jin. 'I was meeting Livia.'

'How is she?' asked Cora.

'She's well,' said Jin. She decided against telling her mother about Livia's pregnancy. Cora herself had dropped some heavy hints about Jin's childless state in the last few months and it wasn't a discussion that she wanted to have now. Certainly not in front of the toy-boy.

'Is she a lady who lunches, like you?' asked Jack.

'I'm not a lady who lunches,' retorted Jin.

'Yes you are.' Cora grinned at her. 'Lucky thing.'

'I do go out to lunch occasionally,' said Jin irritably. 'But you make it sound so mindless and shallow.'

'I don't mean to,' said Cora. 'I know you're not mindless and shallow.'

'Thank you.'

'I don't think you're mindless and shallow either.' Jack flashed his brilliant blue eyes at her.

'Well, look, why don't you two be mindless and shallow with Kevin and me and come to lunch on Sunday.' She blurted the words so that they came out in a rush. 'This Sunday,' she added. 'It would be nice.' Even to her own ears she sounded unconvincing.

'That's very kind of you,' said Jack. 'Cora's told me all about your lovely home.'

'Has she?'

'Of course I have,' said Cora. 'Why wouldn't I, and it so great! I like boasting about my children.'

Jin looked uncomfortable. 'It's Kevin you should be boasting about really,' she said.

'Nonsense.' Cora's voice was brisk. 'He wouldn't have half of what he has if it wasn't for you.'

Actually, thought Jin, it was Monica who'd been the one to help him on his dizzy rise to success. It had nothing at all to do with her, no matter what Cora might like to think.

'Well, I can't wait to see it,' declared Jack. 'What d'you think, honey?' He looked at Cora while Jin tried to hide her distaste at his use of a pet name for Cora which Kevin sometimes used for her.

141

'You know me, I love visiting.' Cora smiled at her daughter. 'Sounds good.'

'Excellent, then,' said Jin. 'About one?'

'Sure.'

They all smiled at each other. Jin felt as though her cheeks would crack with the strain.

'So what have you two been doing?' she asked eventually.

'Sightseeing,' replied Jack. 'I really like this city.'

The train pulled into the next station and a gaggle of schoolgirls pushed their way into the carriage. Jin watched Jack's glance flicker over them. More his type, she thought, more his age group. More his thing, surely, than my mother. She wondered if Kevin had found out whether Trevor McAllister was out there in the marketplace for a new woman in his life. Now there was a man who sounded eminently more suitable!

'Andie came for dinner recently,' said Cora.

'I know.'

'Really?' Cora's eyes widened. 'You were talking to her?'

'Yes.'

'Have you two been comparing notes?' asked Cora.

'Notes?'

'About me,' said Jack.

'Of course not,' Jin lied.

'Is Andie coming to lunch too?' Cora looked enquiringly at Jin.

'I don't know.' Jin suddenly recovered her composure. 'I haven't asked her. But I will if you like.'

'Whatever,' said Cora.

'It should be fun,' said Jack. 'Research for me, of course.'

'What do you mean?' asked Jin sharply.

'Families. Always interesting to see them together. It's something I want to explore in my novel. My idea was an all-American family but each person with a secret they keep hidden from the others.'

'We're a perfectly normal family,' said Jin. 'We don't have secrets.'

Jack laughed. 'Then you can't possibly be a normal family. Everyone has secrets.'

Jin shook her head obstinately. 'Not us.'

'Maybe I'll make up a secret for you.'

'If I see myself in your bloody book, I'll sue,' Jin told him acidly.

'You probably would.' He grinned at her and his blue eyes sparkled. How does he do that? Jin wondered. How does he look so – so gorgeous and handsome and carefree? And so damn sexy too.

'When are you thinking of going home?' Jin's question was abrupt.

'I haven't decided yet,' he replied.

'There's no rush,' said Cora comfortably. 'I like having him in the house.'

'But you will go back?' said Jin questioningly.

'Who knows?' Jack grinned at her. 'I might like it here so much that I'll want to stay.'

Jin's smile was barely there. She looked at her mother, who was simply ignoring the chilly atmosphere between them. Why, thought Jin, didn't Cora simply come out and say that she was being shagged senseless by Jack every night and that she didn't want him to go because he was so brilliant in the sack? But she shuddered mentally at the thought of Cora even uttering the words.

When the train slid into Pearse Street Jin got up.

'Where are you off to?' asked Cora.

'Shopping,' she said shortly.

'It's getting late,' objected Cora. 'You won't have much time for shopping.'

'I know what I want,' Jin said. 'No problem. See you Sunday.'

'OK,' said Cora. 'Have a good time.'

'See you,' said Jack. 'Don't break the bank.'

Jin nodded at them and got off. She walked towards the exit until the train had pulled out of the station, then she walked back and sat on one of the green-painted steel benches to wait for the next one. She couldn't have stayed in the company of Jack and Cora for much longer.

I should've driven after all, she thought glumly, as she discovered that there was a twenty-minute wait for the next train. I'd probably be home by now. And I wouldn't have met Mum and the toy-boy and I wouldn't now be feeling upset again. As if, she told herself, I

143

wasn't feeling upset enough after lunching with Livia. She frowned. She hadn't been aware that lunch with Livia had been upsetting. And yet, she realised suddenly, Livia's pregnancy news had disturbed her in a way that hearing about anyone else's expected babies had never done. It was, she recognised, because Livia had been so happy about it all.

It wasn't until she got on to the next train that Jin realised she hadn't told Livia about Cora and the American playboy. The baby talk had pushed him right out of her mind. Maybe just as well, she thought, as she settled back for the rest of the journey to Malahide. Some things were better off not being talked about at all.

Chapter 11

Symphony No 5 (Death in Venice) – Mahler

On Sunday morning, Cora sat in the armchair that had once been Des's and looked at her orange walls while she waited for Jack to come downstairs. Now that the painting was completely finished she was beginning to wonder whether orange had been a good choice. Maybe it was too strong and vibrant to look at every single day. And yet she'd wanted a cheerful colour, something that caught her and smiled at her and brightened up everything around her.

Her bottom lip trembled and she nibbled furiously on it. It was ridiculous to want to cry now, nearly a year after Des had died. She was over it, wasn't she? Over the shock of his initial diagnosis and over the months of his illness during which she saw him change into another person before her very eyes. She was over the nights where she would wake up suddenly, her eyes snapping open; nights when she would sit up in bed and turn to him and worry whether he was actually breathing or whether he had slipped away from her as she slept.

And surely, by now, she was over that terrible morning when she'd received a phone call from the hospital telling her that it would be a good idea to come in now. She'd been in his room for hours the previous night, first with Andie and then with Jin, but the kindly nurse had told them to go home and get some sleep. Everyone had thought, that night, that Des still had a few weeks left, but it hadn't happened like that. And so they'd called her the next morning and she knew that time was running out, and she'd

145

phoned Andie, who'd called Jin, and the two of them had hurried to the hospital together.

A tear spilled over and rolled slowly down Cora's cheek. She hadn't had time to say goodbye. For all the hours of sitting with him and waiting with him, he'd gone by the time they hurried into the room. And it had seemed so unfair to her not to be able to talk to him one more time, not to be able to send him on his way with a last word from her – anything, just for him to know that she was there and that she still loved him.

Andie, beside her, had been shocked too. She'd put her arm around her mother and Cora had allowed her daughter to hug her and hold her close even though right then she hadn't wanted to be held. She'd wanted to slap Des across the face and tell him that he couldn't die on her, that she was too young to be a widow and that he was too young to leave. And then Jin had hurried into the hospital too, her face pale and her eyes wide. Jin had provided the cathartic release for Cora, sobbing loudly in a way that Cora had wanted to do herself but had somehow not been able to.

The following hours were a jumble of mixed emotions – relief that Des wasn't suffering any more, guilt that a part of her was glad that he'd died, guilt that she hadn't been there, sorrow for herself and her inevitable loneliness, and anxiety about the funeral arrangements and what should be done.

It was Kevin who'd looked after that in his efficient way so that Cora didn't really have to do anything at all. Kevin had asked her to stay the night at their house in Malahide and she'd agreed, although not before going home and sitting in this self-same armchair, trying to feel something of Des still there but failing miserably. She'd been angry and envious of people who said that they could feel the presence of their loved ones by being in a certain room or touching a certain object. Cora could feel nothing of Des at all. He was gone as completely as if he'd never been there at all. Then the neighbours had called round and she'd made cups of tea while they all told her how great Des had been and how lucky she was to have had him, and she'd been grateful to them and glad that she lived in such a close-knit community in a time when more and more people didn't even know the name of the people who lived next door.

146

When she'd been younger Cora had never understood how people could say that a funeral was 'lovely'. And yet in many ways Des's funeral had been. Andie had been the one who had taken charge of the ceremony itself, turning it into a celebration of Des's life and playing the electronic keyboard at it so that the music was a selection of pieces that both she and Des had loved. She'd begun by playing the heavy and funereal Toccata and Fugue by Bach before moving on to lighter pieces including some of Des's favourites by Chopin and Mendelssohn, and ending with Mahler's fifth symphony, which had been moving and beautiful and very appropriate.

Cora wiped the tears from her face. It had been harder than she'd imagined afterwards. She'd expected to be lonely, but what she hadn't expected was to feel so completely alone. She'd expected grief, but she hadn't expected to be taken so completely by it sometimes so that she'd almost double over with the pain of missing him. The silence in the house now that he'd gone for ever was somehow a deeper, more profound silence than the quietness that had existed when he'd been in hospital. And it took her a very long time to get used to the fact that, when she went out, everything would be in exactly the same place as she'd left it when she came back. She was used to shouting things like 'What have you done with the remote control?' or 'Where are the front door keys?' but now she was the only one who needed either the remote or the keys. It was things like that, she thought, things like the fact that a tub of dairy spread seemed to last for ever or that buying a big bag of apples was a waste because Des wasn't there to eat half of them, it was those sort of things that hurt more than anything else.

It had taken so long to get over all that, and she knew that she hadn't really got over it yet at all. She'd managed to pick up the pieces of her life because she'd always known, from the moment the doctor had told them of her husband's disease, that she'd be left on her own and that she'd have to cope. And coping became easier with every passing day. It just didn't become something she wanted. She'd wanted to grow old with Des. There hadn't ever been anyone in her life whom she'd loved in the way that she loved him. She'd known, from the day that she'd first met him, that he'd be the man she married. He'd often told her that he'd known that too.

'Damn it.' She took a tissue from the pocket of her heavy cardigan and blew her nose. It had been weeks since she'd cried.

'Are you all right, Cora?'

She turned around. She hadn't heard the door open and hadn't been aware of Jack Ferguson standing in the room behind her.

'Yes, of course.' She blew her nose again, less noisily this time.

'Can I help?' he asked.

'No.' She shook her head. 'I'm sorry. I was being silly.'

'Silly?'

'Remembering,' she told him.

'There's nothing silly about that,' said Jack gently.

'No, but crying about it is,' she said. 'It's been a year.'

'Not quite, from what you told me,' said Jack.

'Nearly a year,' she amended.

'Things get better after the first year goes by,' Jack said. 'You can't say "this time last year" any more.'

Cora smiled faintly. 'I know.'

He took her hand. 'Don't stop crying if you don't want to.'

'I don't know why,' said Cora. 'I haven't cried in a while. I thought that was a good sign, but maybe I needed it.'

'Of course you did.'

Her smile was a little stronger this time. 'Is this homespun Mid-West wisdom?'

'Nope.' He grinned back at her. 'A year's therapy with New York's finest.'

She laughed shakily. 'I'm all right, Jack. Honestly.'

'Are you certain you want to go out today?' he asked. 'You can always phone Jin and tell her that you're not feeling well.'

'God, no.' Cora looked horrified. 'She'd think you'd put me up to it and she'd probably come tearing down here in the car to see what we were up to.'

Jack laughed. 'Surely not.'

'Oh, definitely,' said Cora firmly. 'I know you think that it's a bit of a joke but Jin takes it very seriously.'

'Funny, that,' observed Jack. 'I kinda thought Andie was the more serious one.'

'Only in some situations,' said Cora.

'Fair enough,' said Jack. He looked at his watch. 'The cab should be here soon.'

'I'd better nip upstairs and repair my face,' said Cora.

'It's fine.'

'Thanks. But I'll repair it all the same,' she told him.

It was weird, thought Jin as she polished wine glasses before setting them on the table, how once something had been put in your mind you kept being unexpectedly reminded of it. Ever since she'd met up with Livia and learned of her friend's pregnancy, she'd been confronted by baby things on an almost hourly basis. When she'd arrived back at Malahide station that afternoon she'd walked over to her gleaming car only to find that a woman parked beside her was using the roof of the Mercedes as a temporary home for a bright blue blanket and a golden teddy while she struggled with a folding pram, a tiny baby and a couple of toddlers. The woman had apologised profusely as Jin had approached and had grabbed the blanket and the teddy. The younger of the two toddlers had roared that she wanted the teddy and suddenly a cry-fest had begun among the three children while the harassed mother tried to ignore them. If Livia had been there then, Jin thought, she'd have rapidly changed her mind about babies and children!

Later that night there'd been a television programme about fertility problems which Kevin had immediately switched off (somewhat to Jin's relief, as she really didn't want to watch it either); and the following morning Marian Finucane had devoted her radio show to the problems of working mothers. Since then it seemed to Jin that every time she went out of the house she was confronted by women who were pregnant or women who were pushing prams or women who were dragging reluctant children along the streets of Malahide. And the trouble with all of these encounters, she thought ruefully as another part of her brain checked to see whether she'd forgotten anything, was that they kept making her think about babies and children although she'd never really thought about them before. Even her favourite magazine, which she'd bought that morning with the Sunday papers, had devoted a whole section to maternity fashion – Jin had sent a text message to Livia to buy it too so that

149

she could look stylishly gorgeous when her bump became more obvious. She'd flicked past the maternity pictures so that she could concentrate instead on the latest offerings from Joseph and Dolce & Gabbana, but it was the shots of big-bellied women, their bumps proudly showing over cut-low trousers, that stayed in her mind as she got things ready for lunch.

She wasn't becoming broody. She knew she wasn't. She didn't have a biological clock or any other mother-and-baby type issue burning away in the back of her mind. She couldn't afford to have them anyway. But the thought had suddenly come to her that, though vasectomies might be almost a hundred per cent effective, they did sometimes go wrong. She'd read about couples suing hospitals because wives had got pregnant after their husbands' tubes had somehow rejoined. Very rare, she knew. But sometimes . . . And once the thought had planted itself in her head, she couldn't help but wonder if something like that could ever happen to Kevin. And if it did, she thought, would he be as virulently anti-baby then as he was now? He was a good father, although sometimes she thought that he deliberately tried hard with his children simply to annoy Monica. Or, perhaps, that he regarded his relationship with them in the same way as he regarded his work. Something at which he had to succeed. Nevertheless, they seemed to get on with each other. Cian was very like Kevin in many ways. Single-minded and determined, even if his determination led him to engineering rather than business as a career. He'd argued with Kevin about it. It was the one occasion when Jin had seen her husband back down. Cian was always unfailingly polite to her too, even though her contact with him was very limited.

Clarissa was a different type of person to her brother but she also got on well with her father. Kevin indulged her shamelessly whenever he met her and the two of them often talked to each other on the phone. Less often, perhaps, in the last year or so as Clarissa had grown older and – according to Kevin – surrounded herself with a gang of air-headed female friends, not to mention some highly suspect boyfriends – but when they did talk they actually seemed to communicate. Something Jin thought that she and her own father had never really done. Of course, she mused as she rearranged the roses in the John Rocha vase, Des and Andie had been the father–daughter mix in their family, enjoying many of the same kind of things – mechanical, music, reading – which Jin had found boring. What often surprised her was that Cora found them boring too, but Cora had married Des all the same and it had been a good, strong marriage. Perhaps she and Kevin were like Cora and Des. They had lots of very separate interests but they enjoyed the time they spent together. She wondered whether his relationship with Clarissa was like her own father's relationship with Andie. She'd often felt excluded from the partnership the two of them had when they shared in-jokes about rawl plugs or hammer-action drills. Maybe Clarissa and Kevin talked about – well, heaven knows what really. Kevin's interests didn't lie in mending and fixing unless it had something to do with mending and fixing companies. She shrugged. Maybe Clarissa would be the one to follow Kevin into his business. Dixon and Daughter sounded quite good! The only thing about Dixon and Daughter, or even Dixon and Son, was that it was something Kevin shared with his children and not with her. From her point of view there wasn't another Dixon offspring to bond with.

She stopped her thoughts in their tracks. There weren't going to be any more Dixon offspring and she already knew that. There wasn't any point in thinking about it or wondering what it would be like because it simply wasn't going to happen. And even if Livia's pregnancy had made her think baby thoughts for a while, she was perfectly content with things the way they were. Day-dreaming was all very well, but if she was going to day-dream she should do it constructively. She could devote her time to deciding on which plates the duck in plum sauce which had been delivered by the deli the night before would look the most home-cooked.

Until the last minute Andie had been undecided about whether or not to go to lunch at Jin and Kevin's. But Jin had been on the phone to her at least a dozen times the night before (twice interrupting her lovemaking with Tom, so that in the end he'd suggested they watch the TV instead), totally freaking out about the fact that Cora and Jack had been kissing and cuddling on the Dart.

151

'On the Dart!' she had exploded. 'In public! Kevin and I don't carry on like that in public.'

In the end Andie felt she no option but to turn up. All the same she was dreading it with almost the same level of trepidation that she felt before the triple birthday celebration party. She really didn't know why it was that going to her sister's should intimidate her so much. As she invariably pointed out to Tom whenever the topic of the Dixons came up, and occasionally mentioned to Cora, she wasn't in the slightest bit interested in living in a house which was far too big for just two people and from which it was impossible to walk into town if that was what you felt like doing. In fact, she'd say, she'd be a bit uneasy about living in a detached house with a huge garden all around – despite the high walls and electronic gates, how would you know that someone hadn't broken in and wasn't ready to attack you? Whenever she said things like this, Cora would remind her that Jin and Kevin had a state-of-the-art security system with video cameras and God only knew what else and that if a stray ant wandered into their garden all sorts of alarms went off. But Andie would protest that being in the apartment block was much safer for a single person and that she kind of liked the occasional seepage of noise from one of the other flats so that she knew she wasn't the only person around. Tom would nod in understanding at that point and then mutter that having your own billiards room would be nice all the same; Cora would nod in understanding too but would remark that it'd be a bit difficult to have your own jacuzzi in a one-bedroom flat. And Andie would wonder whether they really believed her when she said that she was happy. Sometimes she wondered whether she believed it herself; whether in a world obsessed with wealth and celebrity and spending it like Posh and Becks it was still OK just to be content with what you had.

She blinked as she smudged mascara on to her lashes and swore softly as more ended up on her cheeks than on the lashes themselves. When they'd both lived at home with Cora she'd often watched Jin apply her make-up and had always been fascinated by the amount of time her younger sister took in putting on mascara – curling her eyelashes with that lethal-looking chrome curler before using a special undercoat and finally the glossy top coat itself. Andie couldn't be bothered with messing around like that, although, she admitted as she rubbed her mascara-ed cheek vigorously, maybe sometime she should make the effort.

She made a final check of her appearance in the mirror on the back of her bedroom door. She'd decided to go casual by wearing jeans and a jumper (though nice jeans, she muttered, Stella McCartney jeans which had been knocked down dramatically in the sale because the zip was broken. And although Andie herself hadn't a clue about fixing zips, Chandra Tilling – the violin teacher at the Academy – was brilliant at it. Most of Andie's more expensive items of clothing had been bought for very little and rendered wearable thanks to Chandra's skills, and that included the electric blue dress she'd worn to the birthday bash; Chandra had reattached the shoulder straps, the reason it had been marked down to a mere €25). She looked in the mirror again. The zip was perfect and the jeans looked good on her. Andie wondered whether Jin would notice the Stella label or whether she'd be more aware that the cranberry jumper was from Dunnes. She shook her head resignedly. It didn't matter. Clothes didn't matter. Really they didn't. It was what was inside that counted. Although, she thought, she really wasn't sure what she was like inside. After all, wasn't she having an affair with a married man? That hardly made her a good person, did it?

Chapter 12

Peer Gynt Suite: Hall of the Mountain King – Grieg

'Nice pad,' said Jack as the cab pulled up outside Briarlawns. '*Very* nice pad.'

'It cost them a fortune,' confided Cora, 'and then they completely redecorated so that it cost them almost the same again. The only thing they haven't done up is the kitchen. Apparently it was what Jin liked best about the place when they moved in.'

'I like kitchens too,' said Jack.

'Kevin has a billiards room.'

'I know. You told me. Twice.'

Cora smiled at him. 'Sorry. It's just that I can't quite get my head round the fact that my daughter is married to a man who can devote a whole room to billiards.'

'He probably doesn't even play.'

'Actually,' said Cora as she pressed the button on the intercom at the gate, 'I believe he plays very well. But that's Kevin for you. Everything he does he does to perfection.'

'Hi, Mum. I'm opening the gates now.' Jin's voice echoed through the speaker. Jack looked round in surprise, because Cora hadn't said a word.

'Video cameras,' she explained, nodding at the top of the wall.

'Christ,' muttered Jack.

Cora looked at him in puzzlement. 'What?'

He shook his head. 'Nothing. Big homes. Video cameras on gates. It's so . . .'

He didn't finish the sentence. Cora slid her hand into his. He squeezed it gently as they walked up the driveway together. The front door opened just as they arrived at the steps.

'Hi.' Jin's smile was tacked on to her face. 'You're very welcome.'

'It's nice to be here,' said Cora and kissed her.

'Thank you for the invitation.' Jack smiled too, his usual megawatt grin totally unlike Jin's ghostly one.

'Kevin's in the conservatory,' said Jin. 'It's lovely and warm in there. We thought you'd like a drink first.'

'Perfect,' said Cora.

They followed Jin across the hallway, Cora pointing out to Jack features like Kevin's Bose speakers and the original Knuttel paintings on the wall.

'The billiards room is that way,' she whispered, pointing to the left as they turned right towards the conservatory.

'Andie said she'd come too.' Jin was struggling to know what to say to them.

'Nice,' said Jack. 'I like Andie.'

But you don't like me, thought Jin, because you know I see straight through you. Andie's such an innocent even if she is my older sister.

'Hello, Cora.' Kevin greeted his mother-in-law by kissing her on the cheek. 'Hello, Jack.'

'Nice to meet you again,' said Jack.

'What would anyone like to drink?' asked Jin brightly. 'Mum, would you like a glass of wine? Or something soft?'

'When we were on the cruise my favourite aperitif was rum punch,' confessed Cora. 'I've kind of gone off wine before my meals since then.'

'I'm sure I could do a rum punch if that's what you want, Cora,' said Kevin. 'But I have a bottle of that champagne you liked so much at Christmas, which you'd probably prefer.'

'Cora really enjoys rum punch now,' said Jack. 'And I'll make it up if you want. I know exactly how she likes it.'

'Cora?' Kevin smiled at her.

Her glance flickered between her son-in-law and Jack.

'I did like the champagne,' she admitted, 'but the rum punch is lovely and fruity.'

155

'Then by all means have it,' said Kevin.

'D'you want me to mix it?' asked Jack.

'He's very good at it,' Cora said.

'Be my guest.' Kevin's tone was relaxed but his eyes were like flint.

Jack stood behind the custom-made bar in the corner of the conservatory and looked enquiringly at Kevin. 'D'you have cinnamon?'

Kevin glanced at Jin. 'Do we?'

'I'm sure we do.' Jin knew that there was a spice rack in the kitchen which was simply laden with spices she'd never used. There was bound to be cinnamon in one of them. 'I'll go check.'

The gate buzzer sounded as she returned with a jar of cinnamon which still had a plastic seal around the lid.

'It's Andie,' said Jin as she put the jar on the bar counter. 'I'll let her in.'

She opened the front door while Andie was still only halfway along the drive.

'He's making bloody cocktails,' she hissed as her sister walked up the steps. 'Kevin's going to have a coronary. Nobody mixes drinks in our house, only Kevin.'

'Why?' asked Andie as she handed Jin a brown paper bag and slipped off her coat.

'What's this?' asked Jin.

'A bottle of wine,' said Andie. 'What d'you think?'

'I know it's a bottle but why on earth did you bring it?'

'Because I always do when people ask me to lunch or dinner,' said Andie.

'This is different,' said Jin. 'For heaven's sake, Andie, you didn't need to bring anything from the local off-licence.'

'Why?' asked Andie tartly. 'Not good enough for Kevin?'

'Oh for heaven's sake!' Jin's voice was ragged. She looked at Andie wearily. 'OK, maybe. Kevin's picky about his drink and – oh.' She looked at the label and saw that it was a very respectable pinot noir. 'He actually quite likes this.'

'I know,' said Andie.

'Do you? Did he tell you?'

156

'I have my ways.' Andie had no intention of telling Jin that she'd asked Tom if he knew what Kevin's favourite wine was, and that Tom had actually brought it round to the flat the night before.

'Well, thanks,' said Jin. 'I guess it might take Kevin's mind off the fact that Jack is doing some kind of Calypso King routine in the conservatory.'

Andie laughed and Jin looked at her tautly. 'It's not a joke.'

'I know,' said Andie contritely. 'I'm just surprised that Kevin's getting into a state about it. I thought you were the only one who freaked out in your relationship.'

'And what's that supposed to mean?' demanded Jin.

'Nothing, nothing,' said Andie hastily. 'I'm sorry. I'm blathering. Maybe I'm nervous too.'

Her words seemed to have a soothing effect on Jin, who spoke quite normally as she led her into the conservatory and announced that it was great to have them all together.

'Isn't Doireann coming?' asked Andie.

'Doireann?' Cora looked surprised. 'Did you ask Doireann and Frank?'

'No, of course not,' said Jin hastily as Andie raised an eyebrow at her. 'I thought it'd be nice to have us all together.'

'Very thoughtful of you,' said Jack as he handed a burnt-orange-coloured drink to Cora and kept another for himself. 'Can I get you anything from the cocktail menu, Andie?' he asked. 'Kevin's on wine and spirits duty but I'm doing the exotic drinks. Oh, but I believe there's champagne on offer too.'

Andie glanced at her brother-in-law. Kevin's face was impassive.

'No cocktails for me,' she told Jack. 'No champagne either. I'll stick with Kevin's wine, if that's OK.'

'Certainly,' said Kevin. He went behind the bar and took a bottle of sauvignon blanc from the chiller. 'This OK for you?'

'Fine, fine,' said Andie quickly.

'It's a particularly good one,' Kevin told her as he handed her the glass. 'I ordered half a dozen cases from Spence Harper.'

Andie frowned.

'Livia's husband,' said Jin, and closed her eyes suddenly as images

157

of Livia, twice as pregnant as when she'd actually seen her, flooded her mind. She shivered.

'Oh, right, her.' Andie nodded as she recalled the stunning blonde. 'How's she keeping?'

'Great.' Jin wished she could stop thinking about Livia and her bump.

'Kevin, I'd just like to say thanks again for sending me and Doireann on the cruise,' said Cora. 'It truly was the holiday of a lifetime.'

Andie half expected for Jack to add a quip about it, but he gazed into his rum punch and said nothing.

'What did you like best, Ma?' she asked, wondering why Jin looked so wretched all of a sudden. It was difficult for her, she knew, but there was no point in getting into a state about Cora and Jack. She needed to take it all less seriously. And then Andie laughed to herself, because she was supposed to be the one who took things seriously, Jin was the happy-go-lucky one.

'It's hard to know,' said Cora. 'On the boat, everything was superb. On shore, I guess it had to have been the Aztec ruins. They were so impressive.'

'How about you, Jack?' Andie turned to him. 'What did you like best?'

'Jack was supposed to be working, not enjoying himself,' said Jin shortly.

'Fortunately I enjoy my work.' Jack's tone was mild. 'And of course I had plenty of leisure time to enjoy too. On board – leaving aside the pleasure of Cora's company – it had to be the food. You haven't lived till you've gone on a cruise and stuffed yourself at the midnight buffet even though you've only just finished dinner.'

'How much of your time was taken up with work?' asked Kevin.

'A couple of lectures about Mexican culture now and the culture of the Mayans at the time the temples were built,' replied Jack.

'That's all?' Kevin sounded incredulous.

'Well, I did it for three months,' Jack told him. 'I don't think I'd hack it as a full-time lecturer, though. I kept thinking that I'd said all this before and it was true, I had, but to a whole different heap of people. It's hard to keep yourself focused each time.'

'I know what you mean,' said Andie feelingly. 'When I've told the twentieth pupil that *andante* is not a bloody gallop I can't understand why the twenty-first doesn't know it too.'

Jack laughed.

'He was very patient,' Cora told them. 'Even when we asked the same questions he'd probably been asked a million times before.'

Jin looked at her watch and cleared her throat. 'I'm sure the food is almost ready,' she said. 'Kevin, will you lead the way to the dining room?'

'Can I help?' asked Andie.

'Yes,' said Jin.

The two of them walked to the kitchen. Jin put her empty wine glass on the counter. 'Kevin hates him,' she said. 'And so do I. This was a mistake.'

'You asked him to come,' Andie pointed out. 'You wanted to get to know him. And Jin, really, how can you hate him? He's cute.'

'Cute!' Jin snorted. 'Mum doesn't need cute. Mum needs someone to support her.'

'Maybe he will,' said Andie.

'No chance,' snapped Jin. 'I loathe that man, Andie. I really do. And it disgusts me to think that he's staying with our mother and sleeping in the very same bed as her and Dad—' Jin broke off and Andie looked at her thoughtfully, then put her arm round her sister's shoulders.

'I didn't realise that was what was upsetting you so much.'

'I'd have thought it would upset you,' cried Jin. 'You were supposed to be Dad's favourite after all.'

'Now you're being silly,' said Andie.

The two of them were silent for a moment and then Jin yelped in dismay. 'The duck!' She pushed Andie out of the way and turned down the oven heat. 'I nearly forgot. I've probably burnt it to a damn cinder!'

'Did you make it yourself in the end?' asked Andie.

'Oh, don't be stupid,' replied Jin. 'I got it sent over yesterday.' She opened the oven door and a blast of heat filled the room. 'I suppose it's not too bad.' She looked at the five individual foil containers in which their portions of duck nestled. The

159

plum sauce was slightly caramelised but otherwise they looked OK.

'Are we going straight to this or did you do starters?' asked Andie.

'Shit,' said Jin. 'Smoked salmon. It's in the fridge. And the vegetables to go with the duck are in that serving dish.'

'Have you heated them up?'

'The girl at the deli said I could bung them in the microwave,' said Jin.

'Are you really this hopeless all the time?' asked Andie as she opened the door of the fridge and slid out the plates of smoked salmon.

'I'm not hopeless at all,' said Jin. 'I'm just distracted.'

The last time she'd been here, Andie remembered as she sat down at the glass-topped table with marble and wrought-iron supports, was on Christmas Day the previous year. Jin and Kevin had invited her and Cora to dinner, but the atmosphere was strained because less than two months had passed since Des had died and none of them was feeling in a celebratory mood. Jin had gone to vast trouble to turn the day into something that could have been found in a lifestyle magazine – the table had been laid artistically with that year's favourite colour scheme of purple and gold, a huge tree which took up the corner of the room was also draped in the same colours, while in the living room, the huge log fire burned brightly amid the scented candles and spray-painted pine cones which littered every available surface. Kevin had arranged a selection of seasonal CDs on the player, which reached every corner of the house, making the festive sounds inescapable (Andie had been a bit put out to hear 'Rudolph the Red-Nosed Reindeer' booming through the ceiling speaker as she used the loo). They'd done their best, she knew, but Cora's pain was still raw and nobody truly felt in the humour to pull crackers or put on silly hats or do all the things they felt they should do at Christmas. Later in the evening Cora had fallen asleep in front of the fire while Kevin retreated to his study for some peace and quiet – according to Jin, he liked to be on his own for a couple of hours every day. Andie and Jin had drunk

160

another bottle of wine between them and had spoken in low voices about how Cora was coping, and it was then, Andie remembered, that they first wondered whether she'd ever meet anyone else.

Only they hadn't thought of anyone like Jack Ferguson.

'You OK, Andie?' Jack's voice broke into her thoughts.

'Fine,' she said. 'Fine.'

'You were lost in thought.'

'I know.' Actually, she realised, she'd been so lost in the past that it was hard to drag herself back to the present.

'She was thinking about last year, weren't you?' Jin looked at her enquiringly.

'Actually, yes.'

'Last year?' asked Jack.

'Christmas,' supplied Cora. 'We had a lovely day with Jin and Kevin.'

Jin looked pleased at Cora's comment, and Kevin nodded.

'It was very pleasant,' he said. 'A family day.'

'Of course, it was still very soon after your husband died, wasn't it, Cora?' asked Jack.

Jin and Andie stiffened and Kevin's eyes opened wide. They never talked about Des when they were all together with Cora. They didn't want to upset her. But she smiled at them and at Jack and nodded.

'It was difficult,' she admitted, 'but I got through it. We all got through it.'

'He was a wonderful man,' said Kevin. 'Very considerate. He's still a great loss.'

Andie's eyes flickered to Kevin. She knew perfectly well that although Des had been impressed by Kevin's business acumen and wealth, he wasn't that keen on him as a man. 'A bit one-dimensional,' he'd told Andie one Saturday afternoon when she'd dropped by. 'Though I suppose Jin is too, in a way.' And they'd shared a guilty laugh together at finding the Dixons less than perfect.

'But he would have wanted me to move on,' said Cora into the sudden silence. 'I know that people often say that about their partner, but I know that Des . . .' She looked down at the table

161

and fiddled with her napkin. 'I know that Des wouldn't want me to mourn him for ever.'

'And just because you stop mourning doesn't mean you ever forget.' Jack squeezed her hand. Andie realised that she was holding her breath.

'Yes, well, absolutely right that you should enjoy life, Cora,' said Kevin. 'Of course some things are just short-term flights of fancy.'

'I don't mind being Cora's flight of fancy,' Jack said. 'She's a wonderful woman and I love her dearly.'

Jin dropped her fork and scrabbled under the table to retrieve it. Her face was red when she sat up again.

'When you say love, you don't mean in love, I suppose?' she said breathlessly.

'Jin!' Cora looked at her younger daughter with a mixture of amusement and irritation.

'Well, Mum, you know . . . it's a bit . . . I'm not convinced . . .'

'How's the research going, Jack?' Andie blundered into the developing silence with an abrupt change of subject.

'Oh, not too badly,' he said easily. 'Got quite a bit of work done on the travel guide but I'm not achieving much on the novel front yet.'

'He's doing it about family secrets,' said Jin.

'We don't have any of those,' said Andie quickly.

'Why is it that everyone thinks that?' asked Jack. 'I bet you do.'

She felt her face flame red and took a quick slug of wine.

'I hope you don't think you're going to unearth some and then write about them,' said Kevin.

'Jin more or less suggested the same thing.' Jack grinned. 'But why would I write about people's secrets when I can make up much, much better ones?'

'What d'you mean?' asked Andie.

'Well, let's see. What kind of secret could you have?' He looked at her enquiringly and she felt the colour stain her cheeks all over again. 'Maybe you never really qualified as a music teacher at all.'

'But she did,' said Jin.

'So she tells you,' Jack said. 'But maybe she was lying.'

'Oh, don't be stupid,' snapped Jin.

'All I'm saying is that it could be a secret. But not a very exciting one. Now if I was making up her secret I'd say that she was – oh, I don't know, having an affair with Kevin.'

'Jack!' Andie spluttered on her wine.

'Really, Ferguson!' Kevin's impassive demeanour finally cracked.

'I'm not saying she *is* having an affair with you,' said Jack equably. 'Only that if I was making something up that's what I'd do.'

'I told you that I'd sue,' Jin said sharply, 'if you write anything, anything at all . . .'

'I'll sue too,' said Kevin.

Jack smiled at them. 'But I've no intention of writing about you,' he said. 'That's what I'm trying to say. It's much more fun to make it all up.'

'Well, you might make it up, but if you use anything about me or my wife . . .'

'Relax, Kevin,' said Jack. 'I don't need to.'

'I'll get the main courses,' said Jin. 'Andie, can you come too.'

Andie pushed back her chair and helped Jin carry the empty plates to the kitchen.

'You see!' hissed Jin. 'Manipulative, dangerous . . . God knows what he's up to. And Mum is at the receiving end. He loves her dearly! Oh really. As for that shit about the book . . .'

'He was having you on,' said Andie, although not as convincingly as she would have liked. She'd been made uncomfortable by Jack's suggestion that she could be having an affair with Kevin. Right secret, wrong husband had been the thought that had flashed through her mind, and she'd found it difficult to keep her face expressionless.

Jin grunted as she opened the oven door again and then frowned. 'You know, I think I should've left the duck portions out. They're looking a bit overdone now but I wanted to keep them warm.'

'They're fine.' Andie had pressed the button on the microwave to cook the vegetables. 'Have you done potatoes or anything?'

Jin slid another, larger foil tray out of the oven and Andie grinned. 'Catering as it should be,' she said. 'Done entirely by someone else.'

'There's nothing wrong with that,' snapped Jin.

163

'I never said there was,' protested Andie. 'God knows where I'd be without the microwaveable dinner for one.'

Jin looked at her. 'Why don't you have someone in your life?'

'Let's not go there again.' Andie groaned.

'But Andie, you're not getting any younger. And what happens when you want kids?'

'Maybe I just find some bloke and use him for procreative purposes,' said Andie lightly.

'You wouldn't!'

'Right now I wouldn't,' agreed Andie. 'But who knows? Maybe if I stay on the shelf as you suspect I might suddenly decide to do something about it.'

'But could you?' asked Jin. 'Could you just use a bloke for sex and hope to get pregnant?'

'Why not?' asked Andie. 'Blokes use women for sex and hope they don't.'

Jin closed her eyes as the images of Livia returned. And she wondered whether or not she could do what Andie was suggesting. Sleep with someone, anyone, simply in the hope that she could have a child.

'Jin?'

'What?' She opened her eyes again.

'Are you OK?'

'Sure I am.' Jin frowned at her sister. Honestly, she thought, I'm going a bit demented here if I could even think of having sex with someone other than Kevin. And I don't want a baby. I don't. I want to move house. I can't do both.

The microwave pinged and broke the silence.

'Come on then,' said Andie, who was still looking at Jin curiously. 'Let's get these plates loaded up.'

'Yes, right.'

'Did you do this at Christmas?' asked Andie as she slid duck on to a plate.

'What?'

'Buy it in. I remember dinner being pretty good.'

'I was less stressed then,' said Jin. 'I didn't forget things or burn things. But, well, yes. I bought most of it ready done.'

'Brilliant idea,' said Andie.

'Really?'

'Absolutely.'

'I thought you'd laugh at me.'

'Why?' asked Andie. 'I believe that people should do what they're good at and get someone else to do what they can't.'

Jin made a face as she looked at the duck portions again. 'I suppose there aren't too many people who fake being bad at cooking,' she said.

Andie laughed. 'Burnt sauce gives the authentic look. Come on. Let's get back.'

It seemed to both women that Kevin, Cora and Jack had been sitting in absolute silence, because they looked up in relief as Jin and Andie entered the room.

'A little overdone maybe,' said Jin as she put a plate in front of her mother.

'Looks great,' said Cora.

And actually, thought Jin, as she tasted it herself, it wasn't at all bad. She supposed that the people at the deli knew what they were doing and had infused the duck with flavours so that even an undomesticated person like herself could burn it without worrying too much.

'So, Jack.' Kevin stuck his fork into a piece of potato as he spoke. 'How lucrative is the travel-writing industry for you?'

'Well, Kevin,' said Jack slowly, 'it kinda depends.'

'On what?'

'On my participation in the books. On the contracts that I sign. On a whole heap of things really.'

'Let's say you've got the best possible deal,' said Kevin. 'How lucrative?'

'Don't think it'd be enough to buy a place like this,' said Jack.

'What would it buy?'

'You know, I don't look at my deals that way,' said Jack carelessly. 'I look on them as how much satisfaction they bring me.'

'No point in being self-satisfied if you can't pay the bills,' said Kevin.

Jack grinned at him. 'I get by. I've done things that were more lucrative than the guides and some things less.'

'What would have been less lucrative?' asked Kevin.

'The time I ran a soda-pop shop from my parents' garage,' said Jack, his navy-blue eyes twinkling. 'Although I suppose as a percentage increase in my income at the time it was pretty good. I doubled what I'd been getting as pocket money.'

Andie stifled a smile. Jin looked grim.

'And more lucrative . . .' Jack gazed at the ceiling. 'Well, Kevin, I've done lots of things that could be classified as more lucrative. But not as much fun.' He brought his eyes back to the other man. 'Do you have fun?'

'Pardon?'

'Doing whatever it is you do. Is it fun?'

'I enjoy what I do,' said Kevin. 'I get great satisfaction from it.'

'Yeah,' said Jack. 'But is it fun too? That's my other barometer of whether or not something is worthwhile.'

'I suppose you think that spending the night on a flea-infested blanket in some hick town is fun?' said Jin acidly.

'Actually, no,' replied Jack. 'Painful, I'd think. But I've never spent a flea-infested night anywhere. I like my comforts too much.'

Kevin, Jin and Andie exchanged glances. It was Jack's comforts and how he was getting them that they were worried about now.

'How's your own business going, Kevin?' asked Cora into the short silence.

'Very well.' Kevin took on the slightly lecturing tone he always used when talking about his restaurant and bar empire. 'We're expanding into Scandinavia, you know.'

'Really?' asked Jack. 'Now that'd be an interesting guide. *Twenty Things To Do In Norway and Sweden* . . . both in winter and in summer.'

'One of them would be to come to our bars,' said Kevin. 'Of course alcohol is outrageously expensive in Nordic countries so we have to offer a whole experience.'

'And what's that?' asked Jack.

'It depends on the location,' said Kevin. 'The thing about our bars and restaurants is that they're not identikit places like Burger

166

King or Taco Bell or whatever franchise you like to pick. There are certain similarities but each is developed with an appreciation of the surrounding area.'

'Sounds very laudable,' Jack said.

'The flagship bar in Dublin is called Bar Tender,' said Jin. 'It's fantastic.'

'I must visit,' said Jack. 'Maybe one of the Twenty Things To Do.'

'Visiting bars shouldn't be on the top of anyone's list,' said Andie. 'I mean, yes, you visit them, but they shouldn't be the same as looking at castles or sitting in the park.'

'You can be such a drip,' said Jin. 'Everyone wants to see Bar Tender.'

'Why?' asked Jack.

'It's three storeys high,' Kevin told him. 'Circular, round a central core. You can look right down. There are TV screens on the core and they zoom in and out on the clientele.'

'Sounds futuristic,' said Jack.

'It is,' said Kevin and Jin simultaneously. 'A radical departure from previous bars,' Kevin told him.

'I'm not sure it's my thing, to be honest,' said Jack.

'Oh, it's worth a visit,' said Cora. 'I haven't been since it opened but it's unbelievable.'

'We must go in that case.' Jack smiled.

Jin and Kevin exchanged glances. Bar Tender wasn't aimed at fifty-eight-year-old mothers of adult daughters. Andie could almost feel Jin shudder beside her. 'Will I make coffee?' she asked.

'Go ahead,' said Jin, not bothering to get up. 'You know where everything is.'

'I don't,' said Andie. 'But I'll find it.'

It was a relief to be on her own in the kitchen and out of the uneasy atmosphere of the dining room. Although the tension had eased a little when Kevin started talking about his businesses, Andie had noticed. It was as though he couldn't help himself when he got on to the subject of the bars and restaurants – they were the most important things in the world to him and he'd go on about them for as long as he could, even if that meant talking to Jack Ferguson.

167

Andie spooned coffee into the jug. She had no interest in listening to stories about Bar Tender and the rest of them. And she'd had enough of the tension-filled gathering to last a lifetime. She wished she was somewhere else. At home alone in the flat would be fine, she thought. Tom rarely came to see her on Sundays so they were usually her designated chill-out days.

She shivered suddenly at the thought of Tom. She hadn't been able to think of anyone other than him while they'd talked about Bar Tender because, at the beginning of the summer, Tom had taken over as the manager there. He'd been excited about it, and nervous too, because it was a huge step up for him. Andie had hugged him and wished him well and been totally supportive. A few weeks later, when she'd bumped into Jin at Cora's one evening, she'd had to appear completely unaware of who Tom was when Jin was explaining to Cora about the new manager of the bar. 'Oh for heaven's sake!' she'd snapped at Andie. 'You must remember him. You talked to him at that barbecue a few years ago.' Andie had simply shrugged and said that she had a terrible memory for faces and names.

She leaned back against the kitchen wall and closed her eyes. She conjured up her mental keyboard and began to play one of her favourite relaxation pieces, Chopin's Nocturne in E Flat Major, which she'd learned early on in her music career and which many people recognised when they heard it. She loved the way the music seemed to fall easily from the keyboard, gently soothing her no matter how tense or upset she was feeling. Andie thought that Chopin was one of the best composers for the piano who'd ever lived and it was a tragedy that he'd died from tuberculosis at only thirty-nine.

'Need a hand?' The sound of Jack Ferguson's voice made her break off the final mental chords and she opened her eyes. 'In fact,' he asked, 'are you all right?'

'Fine, fine,' she said. 'I'm waiting for the coffee to brew. What are you doing here?'

'Thought I'd escape the inquisition room for a breather,' he explained. 'Found my way here.'

'They don't mean to be rude,' said Andie. 'It's just that none of us can quite fathom what's going on between you and Ma.'

'None of your business,' said Jack.

'You said you loved her.'

'I do.'

'How much?'

He laughed. 'Enough to be with her today.'

Andie said nothing but picked up the coffee pot. The problem was, she mused as she led the way back to the dining room, none of them knew whether Jack loved himself more than Cora. And none of them could feel confident about the answer to that particular question.

Chapter 13

Piano Concerto No 1 in C Major: Rondo – Beethoven

A few days later Andie sat at the table in her apartment and read through the score of a piece that one of her students had composed. She had no lessons that afternoon and had decided to work from home instead of staying on at the Academy. She enjoyed working from the flat occasionally because nobody ever interrupted her. The only problem about today was that it was extremely difficult to concentrate on what she was doing and not let her mind wander on to thoughts of Cora and Jack instead. She kept seeing them as she'd last seen them on Sunday, sitting side by side in the cab the three of them had shared from Jin and Kevin's, Cora's hand resting lightly on Jack's thigh. And it was that moment that stuck with her and bothered her so much more than anything else. It was such an intimate yet public gesture from her mother. And the thing was, thought Andie, as she looked at the jumble of notes dancing in front of her eyes, Des and Cora hadn't ever shown their love or affection for each other in public in quite the way Cora was showing it for Jack. No matter how much she didn't want to interfere in her mother's life, Andie was becoming more and more uncomfortable with Jack's presence in it.

Using a technique she'd learned years ago to block out distractions, she resolutely pushed the thoughts of her mother and Jack into an imaginary room in her brain and locked the door. She was not going to spend any more time thinking about their situation. She had work to do. Firmly she turned her attention back to the job in hand and listened to the music in her head as her eyes raced across the score. A little bland, perhaps, though she wasn't a fan herself of the school of thought that believed music had to be consistently challenging and that listeners had to work hard to find the harmonies that the composer had in mind. Andie felt that music should be pleasurable from the start, that it shouldn't be difficult for anyone to lose themselves in the joy of the composition. All the same, Karin could have put one or two surprises into her work. As it was, it was very predictable; Andie was almost able to guess what note would follow the previous one.

She brought the score over to the ancient upright piano at the other end of the room and played the music straight through. It was as sweet and undemanding as it had sounded in her head. She played the closing bars slowly, as Karin had instructed, and then jumped in shock as her doorbell buzzed loudly and interrupted her. Not quite the surprise she'd wanted from the music, she thought as she walked over to the intercom, but it had jolted her all the same.

'Andie? It's me. Dominic from upstairs.'

'Hi, Dominic, what's the problem?'

'I don't have my keys. Could you buzz me in?'

'Sure.' She hit the buzzer and heard the front door unlock. She opened the door to her flat and waited until Dominic had reached her landing. 'Have you got the key to your flat or are you missing that as well?'

'Ah, well . . .' Dominic made a face at her. 'I was rather hoping I could use your phone and ring a locksmith.' He ran his hands through light brown hair sprinkled very sparingly with grey.

'Are you sure you need to do the locksmith palaver?' asked Andie. 'You've probably left the keys in your office or something.' She knew that Dominic worked for a north-city branch of a nationwide estate agency.

'Unfortunately not,' said Dominic. 'I don't have my keys because I was mugged on my way home and the muggers are now the proud possessors of them.'

'Dominic!' Andie was horrified. 'Are you all right?'

'Perfectly,' he said. 'It wasn't a beat-you-up kind of mugging. They just grabbed my briefcase and my keys were in it.'

'Have you reported it?' asked Andie.

'What's the point?' He smiled wryly. 'There was absolutely nothing else in the case. Well, one slightly battered cheese sandwich which I'd bought earlier but hadn't time to eat. So if they were hungry muggers they'd be happy. Otherwise all they've got is the briefcase, my keys, and a selection of brochures about commercial property in Dublin 12. Oh, and my mobile, but at least it was switched off and you need a password to activate it.'

'You should report it,' said Andie sternly.

'Waste of my time and the cops' time too,' said Dominic. 'The keys are useless to them, there's no indication of what they're for. I'm a bit miffed about the briefcase because it was a present. But I'll get over it. So all I want to do is give the locksmith a shout and see if they can't let me in.'

Andie frowned. 'Feel free,' she said. 'You know, we should have spare keys to each other's apartments in case of emergencies like this.'

'You're right,' he said. 'I thought about it before, but you know how it is, you just don't bother because you don't think you'll be stupid enough to lose your keys in the first place.'

'I'm glad these things happen to people other than me,' she told him. 'Though obviously I wouldn't have wished a mugging on you! Still, it makes me feel as though I'm not the only person in the world that gets trashed by life on a regular basis. Would you like a cup of coffee or anything while you're waiting?'

'Love one,' he said.

She filled the kettle while he skimmed through the Golden Pages and, on the second attempt, found someone who was in the area and could call out to the flat almost immediately.

'Make yourself at home.' Andie heaved a pile of clothes which she hadn't yet got round to ironing off the armchair and dumped them on the table instead.

'Have I come at a bad time?' asked Dominic as he looked around the untidy flat. 'Were you in the middle of something?'

She shook her head. 'Work.'

'What kind of work do you do at home?' he asked interestedly. 'I thought you were a music teacher.'

172

'Yes,' she said. 'But there's more to it than sitting at the piano watching the little darlings get their fingers in a knot.'

'My parents wanted me to learn the piano as a kid,' said Dominic, 'but I was utterly useless. Stubby digits, you see.' He extended his hands to show her fingers which were definitely shorter than average.

'Oh well.' She handed him a mug of coffee. 'Music's loss is the property market's gain.'

'Play something for me,' he asked.

'I don't,' said Andie.

'Huh?'

'I don't play for people,' she said. 'I don't like performing in public.'

'Hardly in public,' Dominic pointed out. 'We're in your flat.'

'You know what I mean,' she told him.

'Not really.'

'Sorry.' She shrugged. 'I just can't.'

'Oh, OK.' He smiled. 'No big deal. I often hear you anyway.'

'What?'

'In the evenings. When you play.'

'I'm sorry,' she said. 'I didn't think—'

'It's nice,' he interrupted her. 'Don't be sorry. I enjoy it. That's why I asked you to play now.'

She looked uncomfortable. 'It's different.'

'Sure. No problem,' he said easily. 'Don't worry about it.'

'I'll try and keep it down in future,' she promised.

'No, don't,' said Dominic. 'I meant it when I said I enjoyed it.'

She shrugged again. 'Let me know if it becomes a nuisance.'

'You've been living in the flat below me ever since I moved in,' he said. 'It's never been a nuisance.'

'Thanks.'

'Do you like it here?' he asked casually.

'It suits me,' she told him. 'Close to my mother's – not that I call to see her often enough, but still. Handy for the bus and for town . . . Yes, I like it here.' She looked at him enquiringly. 'How about you? I'd have thought that as an estate agent you'd probably have your pick of properties.'

'I had,' he said ruefully. 'Unfortunately my ex-wife kept it.'

'Ouch.' She winced. 'Sorry, I forgot.'

'Oh well, could be worse. At least we're civil to each other.'

'Are you?'

'It took time,' said Dominic. 'But we've finally reached the stage where we've stopped snarling every time we meet.'

'Good,' said Andie.

'What about you?' asked Dominic.

'What about me?'

'Your bloke? Is he ever going to leave his wife?'

She felt the colour drain from her face and grasped her mug more tightly between her fingers. 'What d'you mean?'

'Well, you've been going out with him for years, haven't you? Don't you think it's time he made a choice?'

'How – how did you know he was married?' asked Andie.

'If he wasn't he'd have moved in with you by now,' said Dominic. 'Or you'd have moved in with him.'

'Not necessarily,' she said sharply. 'I could just be a very independent woman.'

'You could,' he agreed. 'But he wears a wedding ring.'

Andie bit her lip. The wedding ring was a bone of contention between Tom and herself. She hated him wearing it in her flat, always begged him to take it off. But he would point out (reasonably, she hated to admit) that if he took it off it would only be a matter of time before he forgot to put it back on again. And if he went home without his wedding ring the game would be up.

'Touchy subject?' asked Dominic.

'I guess.'

'Didn't mean to bring it up,' he said.

'You asked about him,' Andie pointed out.

'Well, didn't mean to upset you,' he amended. 'I thought you must be OK about it.'

'I am. More or less,' she said.

'Don't waste yourself on him,' said Dominic.

'You're a fine one to talk!' she retorted. 'You've got a different girl up there every week.'

'Not every week.' He laughed. 'Occasionally. And I *am* actually divorced, so I can have as many women as I like.'

'I guess so,' said Andie.

'You're right, though.' He sighed. 'I'm probably the last person in the world to give advice about relationships. So forget about me, Andie, and do your own thing with the married man.'

'Don't worry, I will.'

The buzzer sounded and she was relieved to realise that it was the locksmith. Dominic thanked her for the coffee and went upstairs to deal with his locks while Andie closed her door and went back to Karin Dahnhardt's score. But she couldn't help thinking about Dominic's casual words, his easy assumption that Tom wouldn't leave Elizabeth for her. She stared at the forest of notes on the stand in front of her, not really seeing them, as she wondered whether Tom really had taken her for a fool these past few years. Whether she wasn't being the biggest idiot in the history of the state by believing that his marriage was over and the only reason he hadn't left Elizabeth was because he was so concerned about her. Maybe it was a complete load of cobblers and he loved Elizabeth as much as he'd said that he loved her, Andie. So now she was worried that perhaps the reason she'd kept her relationship with him so secret wasn't that she was afraid of anyone getting to know about it in itself, but that she was afraid of people talking about her behind her back, secretly feeling sorry for a girl who was wasting her life on a man who would never leave his wife. They were feeling sorry for her anyway, she reminded herself. Since everyone thought she was totally alone, they sympathised. She wondered whether they would be as sympathetic about her true situation.

She leaned her head against the piano. She wished she didn't feel so discontented all of a sudden. She'd been happy before. Why on earth wasn't she happy now? She hadn't expected Tom to leave Elizabeth when she'd first started seeing him so why had it become so important? Why couldn't she simply get on with things the way they were, the way they'd been for the past four years? She loved Tom and she knew, she really did, that he loved her too. These were facts. And nothing would ever change them.

*   *   *

175

Tom dropped by at six o'clock. He was due in Bar Tender at half seven. Andie wondered if Dominic had noticed him parking outside the apartment block and if he was silently sympathising with her again for losing her heart to such an unsuitable man. It was none of Dominic's business, she thought angrily. And he shouldn't have said anything at all about it.

'I think I'm getting a cold.' Tom flopped on to the sofa and closed his eyes.

'Better not give it to me then,' said Andie as she sat beside him.

'I'll do my best not to,' he promised. 'It's Elizabeth's fault. She was snuffling yesterday.'

Andie stiffened at the other woman's name, but Tom didn't notice and reached out for her. She'd thought, very briefly as he arrived, that maybe she'd be cool and standoffish with him tonight, just to let him know that she wasn't always available and in a good mood just because he expected her to be. But when he stretched out towards her she simply curled up beside him, content to be held in the circle of his arms. She snuggled up to him so that his chin was resting on her head. They lay together for a few minutes and then she felt his fingers begin to unfasten the buttons on her faded green cardigan.

'I thought you weren't feeling well,' she murmured as he eased it from her.

'You have this therapeutic effect on me,' he whispered back. 'No matter how bad I'm feeling, no matter how tired or miserable, when I'm with you I perk up.'

'That's what you call it, is it?' she chuckled as she reached for him.

'As good a name as any!'

She wondered whether or not sex could ever be as good with any other man. How could anyone else possibly know how to touch her, where to touch her in the way that Tom did? Was there anyone else in the world who could match his desire so closely to her own that invariably they came together in a roller-coaster of mutual passion? She stopped thinking and lost herself in the physical pleasure of being with him again. And when they lay together side by side afterwards, she wasn't plagued with doubts any more.

'So how was Sunday?' he asked languidly.

She shuddered beside him. 'Awkward and horrible.'

'Did Kevin try and clock Jack? Was there a major bust-up?'

'No,' said Andie. 'Maybe it would have been better if there was. Jack said that he loved Ma and that had us all in a tizzy even though we didn't really believe him. He was driving Kevin crazy, Jin wasn't much better, and I was in shreds by the time I got home. I wanted to ring you and dump on you.'

'Sorry you couldn't,' said Tom.

'Oh, probably better not,' said Andie lightly. 'You don't want to hear about our family problems.'

'I like hearing anything about you,' he told her.

She laughed.

'I do,' said Tom. 'And I want to be there for you.'

'I know. But you can't. So let's not get into a fuss about it.'

She didn't want this discussion again. They'd had it in the Ely Place wine bar and she couldn't bear to hear him say yet another time how miserable he was and how much he wanted to change things, only to realise that he couldn't.

'I can't go on like this,' he said abruptly. '*We* can't go on like this.'

She looked at him silently.

'It's not fair on you or me or Elizabeth,' continued Tom.

'As if I didn't know,' said Andie. 'Oh, Tom, we've talked about it so many times. But every time it's the same conclusion. You can't leave her.' She bit her lip as a sudden chill gripped her heart. 'Perhaps you think it's better not to see me any more?' Although her voice was even, she could hardly get the words past her lips.

He tightened his hold on her. 'No,' he said.

'Well then, there's nothing you can do.' She tried to keep the relief out of her voice.

He shook his head. 'This time it's different,' he said.

'Oh?'

'Last night . . .' He was silent for a moment and Andie realised that her heart was thudding against her chest with nervous antici-pation about what he was going to say. 'Last night I was home late and she was asleep and I realised that if she's ever going to get better then we have to change things.' He cleared his throat.

'I mean, maybe the way I've gone about things hasn't helped at all. Pandering to her. Giving in all the time. I know I keep saying I'm going to leave and not actually leaving because then I panic about it, but this time, Andie, this time I have to.'

'So what do you want to do?' Andie spoke carefully. She didn't want Tom to see how much it meant to her.

'Tell her.'

Andie swallowed and stared wordlessly at him.

'I must, Andie. For all our sakes I have to. I can't back out of making decisions simply because they're hard to make.'

'When?' Andie tried to keep the tremble out of her voice.

'The weekend. Friday, I think. I'll be home early on Friday and I'm off on Saturday. I'll tell her that staying together isn't working. Hell, Andie, she knows that already. Sometimes I think she's waiting for me to go. Maybe she wants me to make the first move.'

'And will you, this time?'

'Yes,' he said. 'I'll tell her that I do still care about her – because I do. I just don't love her any more. And that I've got to leave. I know I was uncertain about it before but now I think it's the right thing to do. I have to leave her, sweetheart. I have to be with you.'

Andie stared at him. 'You're sure about this?'

'Absolutely,' said Tom.

'But what about her mental state?' asked Andie.

'That's the thing,' said Tom. 'It's always been the reason we don't talk. But maybe we should. Maybe she'll just be glad to see the back of me.'

'You plan to leave her there and then?'

'Yes,' said Tom.

'Oh my God.' Andie's eyes brimmed with tears. 'Oh my God.'

'Hey, hey.' He pulled her to him again. 'I thought you'd be happy about this.'

'I am,' she sniffed. 'These are tears of joy, you moron.'

The buzzer sounded and she frowned. Tom looked at her questioningly as it sounded again, and she got up to answer it, pulling on the loose cargo pants she'd been wearing earlier.

'It's me,' Jin's voice crackled impatiently. 'Were you asleep or something?'

'Jin!' Andie was shocked. Jin never called to her flat, something was wrong. Could it be – the thought rushed into her head, taking her by surprise – could it be that Jin was right about Jack Ferguson being an axe murderer? Had the unthinkable actually happened? Was that why her sister was here? She dismissed the thoughts, annoyed at herself for even allowing them into her head. 'What's the matter?' she added anxiously.

'Nothing's the matter,' said Jin. 'I need to talk to you.'

Andie looked over at Tom, who was frantically getting dressed.

'It's not – I'm kind of busy right now,' she said helplessly.

'Oh don't be ridiculous,' snapped Jin. 'I've driven all the way from Malahide. The least you can do is let me in.'

'I'm – uh – I'm going out shortly,' said Andie as she pulled on her cardigan.

'Fine, it won't take long. Now press the damn door release. It's cold out here.'

Andie pressed the button while Tom looked at his watch.

'You'd better go into the bedroom,' she told him. 'I'll get rid of her as quickly as I can.' Then she looked at him quizzically. 'Unless you want Jin to know in advance?'

'No,' he said sharply, and then his voice softened. 'No. Not yet. I'll wait. But do your best to shift her. I've got to be in work in less than an hour and I don't expect her husband would be too pleased if I was late.'

Andie opened her door as Tom disappeared into the bedroom. She wondered if Jin would guess that she'd been making love to someone. If she would sense it by looking at her, by the indolent way she was moving or even by the scent of Tom in the room. She laughed shortly. Jin might guess that Andie had been making love, but she'd never guess to whom.

But her sister simply strode into the flat and plopped down on the sofa. Andie whipped her bra from the floor where Tom had discarded it and put it with the pile of unironed clothes on the table.

'This place is a tip,' observed Jin.

179

'Thanks.'

'Well, it is. I don't know how you can live in the mess.'

'It's my mess,' said Andie. 'What d'you want? What's happened?'

Jin tipped the contents of the bag she'd been carrying out on to the table.

'What are these? Oh, I see.' Andie picked up one of the brightly jacketed books. *Twenty Things To Do In Seattle*. She looked at Jin. 'His books.'

'Well, if you could call them that.' Jin snorted. 'His name isn't even mentioned on them.'

'Isn't it?' Andie flicked through the pages. There were four of the books, and no author name inside any of them.

'Contributors,' said Jin. 'Editorial and all sorts of things. See – here's a list of names, Todd Hunter, Jerzey Higgs, Tallulah Baker, Amy Smith, Michael Adams . . . but no Jack Ferguson.'

'Um.' Andie wrinkled her nose.

'Kevin ordered them from Amazon,' Jin told her. 'You can't get them in Europe, only the States.'

'Um,' said Andie again.

'So he lied to us,' Jin told her. 'He doesn't write these books at all.'

'Shit.'

'Now can't you see that I was right?' demanded her sister. 'Now can't you understand how worried I am?'

Andie bit her lip. 'Maybe he's using a pseudonym,' she suggested.

'Maybe he's just a complete faker,' snapped Jin. 'Come on, Andie! Who d'you think he is, Amy Smith?'

Andie heaved a monumental sigh. 'I didn't want this to happen.'

'None of us wanted him to be a blagger,' said Jin. 'But he is.'

'You did,' Andie pointed out. 'You didn't like him from the start. And Kevin made his feelings perfectly obvious on Sunday.'

'At least Kevin's feelings are genuine,' retorted Jin. 'God knows what that con artist really feels about anything.'

'Con artist?'

'What else?' said Jin scornfully. 'Did he really think we wouldn't find out?' She threw *Twenty Things To Do In Chicago* back on the table. 'Let's face it, Andie, he was never a likely partner for Mum.'

'So what now?' asked Andie. 'Are you and Kevin going to confront him? Shake his true intentions out of him? Torture him?'

Jin shot her sister a withering look. 'We're not sure that confronting him is the best way to go about it,' she said. 'Because it's getting more serious between them and confronting them might make her dig her heels in. You know how she gets sometimes, Andie. She'll just go into denial about it.'

'How could it be *more* serious?' asked Andie incredulously. 'He's living with her!'

'I phoned Doireann this morning to tell her about lunch. And she said that she'd been round to the house and that Mum had answered the door wearing her dressing gown. In the middle of the afternoon! A new dressing gown, by the way. Silk. When did she ever go round in a silk dressing gown before? She was wearing mules as well. For God's sake, Andie, she's turning into some kind of caricature. And apparently she spent yesterday at some bloody beauty place in Drumcondra getting God knows what done. Maybe even booking in for face lifts for all we know. So tonight I decided to drop in unannounced. She didn't answer the bell.'

Andie giggled. She couldn't help it.

'Take it seriously!' cried Jin.

'I am,' said Andie. 'I don't ever remember Ma being in her dressing gown in the afternoon before.'

'Exactly.' Jin looked at her accusingly. 'They were at it, Andie. In our house. In the afternoon. And tonight too, obviously.'

'Well, we have to assume—'

'In our house in the middle of the afternoon! And ten minutes ago when I was standing on the doorstep! How d'you think I felt standing outside knowing that Mum and that man were – were . . .' Jin shuddered.

'I know, I know,' said Andie. 'And to be honest, even though I'm trying to be really cool about it I can see why you freaked. I can't get my head round the idea of Ma swanning round the house in

181

silk dressing gowns and mules, for heaven's sake. But I still don't know what we can do about it.'

'I do,' said Jin triumphantly.

'What?'

'I talked about it with Kevin after lunch last Sunday – which was a nightmare, as you damn well know. And he thinks that we should put this plan into action. *You* can put the plan into action.'

'What plan?'

'It's simple.'

'If you think I'm going to fling his books at him and call him a liar—'

'No,' said Jin. 'Much better than that.'

'What, then?'

'You're going to seduce him.'

Chapter 14

Carmen Suite No 1 (Les Toreadores) – Bizet

'What was that?' asked Jin sharply. 'Nothing.' Andie glanced towards the bedroom from where the sound of a thud had startled both of them. Tom had obviously bumped into something. Or maybe collapsed with shock, if he'd heard what Jin had just said. 'The window's open,' she added. 'Probably the wind blew something. It's not important.'

'No,' said Jin. 'But this *is*, Andie.'

'Back up again,' her sister said. 'You and Kevin have come up with a plan which involves me seducing our mother's boyfriend and you think it's a good idea.'

'You see!' cried Jin. 'You're even calling him her boyfriend now. But it's not right. It's not!'

'What else can I call him?' asked Andie. 'They're a couple, aren't they?' She looked helplessly at Jin. 'Look, those books don't prove anything. He could just as easily be contributing under another name.'

'Oh, like that's really a possibility when he banged on and on about how he wrote them,' said Jin scathingly. 'Come on, Andie. Stop making excuses for him.'

'I'm not,' protested Andie. 'Really I'm not. It's just—'

'Everyone's laughing at her,' said Jin. 'Doireann said that she's the hottest topic of conversation in the social club ever. Not, of course, that she's even bothered to go to the club since the arrival of Jack bloody Ferguson. She hasn't been to her book club either, or to the bowling nights or anything. She's cut out all her old friends, she's

183

wandering round the city hand in hand with him like a lovestruck teenager, kissing him in the street and spending the rest of the time in bed with him . . . and you don't want to do anything about it.'

'She's not a child,' said Andie.

'She's behaving like one,' snapped Jin.

Andie's glance flickered to the clock on the table. Jin had already been in the flat for ten minutes and Tom had to leave soon. She'd have to get rid of her sister quickly.

'So what's this plan?' she asked.

Jin's face brightened. 'It's really clever,' she said. 'Basically, you seduce Jack.'

'I got that bit of it earlier,' said Andie. 'It's just exactly how and when and why you think this might be a good thing.'

'This weekend,' said Jin. 'We've been asked to a dinner in aid of a hospital trust. One of Kevin's friends, Andrew Comiskey, is on the board. He's hosting it in his house in Killiney. Gosh, you should see the house, Andie, it's absolutely fantastic. Quite old, with huge rooms, really gorgeous. You'll love it. Anyway, there are twenty tables of six to ten people and Kevin promised to take a table. He was going to get a gang from his office to go along but his idea is that we go instead. So there'd be me and him, Mum and Jack and you.'

'That's only five people,' Andie pointed out.

'Oh well, he'll be bringing people from the office too,' said Jin dismissively. 'We're going to take a table for ten. But I haven't mentioned the main man yet. His name's Trevor McAllister and he's a friend of Kevin's.'

'So what has he got to do with it all?'

'He's a widower,' said Jin. 'His wife was killed a few years ago. He hasn't been out and about much but lately he's been taking an interest again. He's fifty-five.'

'And you think . . .'

'He's in the same age bracket as Mum,' said Jin forcefully. 'He's an interior designer, not loaded, but worth a few bob, and Kevin thinks Mum would really get on with him.'

'So you're going to invite Mum and Jack to this do and then try and throw this Trevor character at her—'

'While you throw yourself at Jack!' concluded Jin happily.

'Jin, this is crazy.'

'No it's not,' said Jin. 'It's perfectly sensible. We're at the kind of bash that Mum loves – all that dressing up and mixing with the rich and famous, you know she's a sucker for it – and we introduce her to someone who actually moves in those circles all the time, someone far more suitable than Jack Ferguson. So she suddenly realises what a fool she's being over Jack. And that impression is reinforced when she sees you and Jack together.'

'Are you both out of your minds?' demanded Andie. 'Ma might have no interest in this Trevor bloke whatsoever; she won't believe you about the books – Jin, there must have been copies on the cruise, she knows that his name isn't on them so there's obviously some kind of explanation that we haven't thought of – and above everything, what d'you think the chances are that Jack would have the slightest bit of time for me anyway?'

'You get on with him,' said Jin.

'No I don't,' protested Andie.

'You do,' insisted Jin. 'He followed you to the kitchen on Sunday, didn't he? Wanted to have a private chat? What was all that about?'

'We were in the kitchen together for about a minute,' said Andie. 'There was no private chat. No nothing. He doesn't get on with me. I don't get on with him. He's our mother's bloody boyfriend, for God's sake, and I'm not going to throw myself at him in the vain hope that it'll wreck their relationship!'

'We have to wreck this relationship,' said Jin vehemently. 'He's worming his way into her heart and our home, Andie. We've got to stop it.'

'I don't like it any more than you,' Andie retorted. 'I really don't. Even though I'll confess that I don't dislike him as much as both Kevin and you seem to. Seeing her make a fool of herself – of course that bothers me, Jin. But I just *cannot* see that me getting involved will do anything other than make things worse.'

'It'll be a great evening, with good food and lots of wine,' said Jin. 'There'll be dancing too. All you have to do is cosy up to him a bit and I bet he'll be all over you like a rash. It'll suddenly click

185

with Mum how impossible her own situation is with him. Mind you, you'd better wear that dress you wore to the birthday bash. It's the only thing I've ever seen you in that made you look really sexy. And you'll have to look sexy for it to work.'

'Oh for heaven's sake!' Andie looked at her despairingly.

'Look, we're actually doing Mum a favour,' said Jin. 'We're going to introduce her to someone suitable. Someone decent. With a bit of luck she'll be captivated by Trevor McAllister. Kevin says he's quite attractive, and let's face it, she's bound to realise how much more appropriate it is to be with someone nearer her own age.'

'She could've got someone nearer her own age on the cruise in the first place,' Andie pointed out.

'Not at all,' said Jin firmly. 'All those cruises are swarming with totally ancient people. Mum was probably one of the youngest. That's why she ended up with Jack – maybe he was the only one on board who could actually move without a walking stick.'

'I really don't think—'

'We're not asking much,' cried Jin. 'The most important thing will be introducing her to Trevor anyway. Kevin says he's very distinguished and that Mum won't be able to resist him. You're just there to provide distraction.'

'I think it's mental,' said Andie. 'What if Ma can't stand this Trevor bloke? She's hardly going to appreciate seeing me throwing myself at Jack then, is she?'

'We're not expecting him to ravish you on the table top,' Jin pointed out. 'All we want is for Mum to see him and you together and for it to click in her mind that having a relationship with him is totally unrealistic.' She shook her head. 'It *is* unrealistic, Andie, surely you can see that.'

'Trying to set her up with someone else is equally unrealistic.'

'Just do it,' cried Jin. 'It's not asking too much, is it? And if it doesn't work then at least you'll have done something.'

'Oh, all right.' Andie's shoulders drooped in defeat. She thought that Kevin and Jin were being incredibly silly about the whole thing but there was nothing to be gained by arguing about it. Besides, she really did have to get her sister out of the flat in the next few minutes, and at least if she agreed to their ridiculous plan Jin would go. Tom was probably doing his nut in the bedroom waiting to get to work.

'Great,' said Jin. 'And don't forget to wear that blue thing.'

'I do have other clothes, you know,' said Andie.

'Yes, but you're supposed to be seducing him not boring him to death,' Jin told her.

'I know what my role is.'

'I'm only trying to look after her,' said Jin into the tense silence which had developed. 'You mightn't approve, but my motives are right.'

'It's not approval or disapproval,' Andie said. 'I don't think interfering does any good. Things have a habit of not turning out like you expected. But I'll go to the dinner and . . . and . . . we'll see how things go.'

'OK,' said Jin. 'It's next Friday night.'

'Friday!' Andie looked at her in horror. 'But—'

'Don't tell me you have something on?' Jin looked sceptical. 'You're always saying that you lead a boring life.'

'It's not that,' said Andie helplessly.

'Well, I'm sorry if it mucks up your plans, but even if you have a hot date you'd better cancel it. This is far more important.'

'But—'

'It's our mother's happiness,' said Jin. 'Don't you think that's important?'

'Of course I do, it's just—'

'Well then.' Jin stood up. 'We'll pick you up at seven sharp.'

Andie gestured helplessly. 'OK.'

'And make an effort,' added Jin as she let herself out of the flat.

As soon as the door closed behind her, Tom came out of the bedroom.

'Did I hear all that right?' he asked. 'She wants you to flirt with your mother's boyfriend? And they have someone else lined up for her instead?'

Andie nodded miserably. 'It's so stupid.'

'Not really,' said Tom. 'I can see where they're coming from. It makes sense.'

'No it bloody doesn't.' Andie looked at him incredulously. 'Ma might hate this Trevor bloke and I'm sure Jack Ferguson has no interest in me whatsoever so I'll look a complete fool.' She groaned. 'How is it I always let her talk me into doing things I don't want to? And,' she looked at him in despair, 'it's on Friday night.'

'That's all right,' said Tom.

'But you'll be leaving Elizabeth on Friday night,' cried Andie. 'I have to be here for you.'

'Don't worry,' said Tom. 'I'll sit outside in the car and wait. I've waited this long, a few extra hours won't make any difference.'

'But it could be really late before I get back.' Andie looked at him miserably. 'Tom, this was meant to be an important night in our lives and I really don't want to spend it fooling around with my mother's boyfriend!'

Tom burst out laughing and Andie couldn't help but giggle too, even though a tear threatened to slide down her cheek.

'It's ridiculous,' she sniffed. 'Only Jin would come up with a plan like this. Anyway, I'm certainly not going to seduce him.'

'You'd better not!' Tom smiled at her. 'I'll be the one waiting for your seduction technique.'

'I'll be thinking about that when I'm sitting beside the American gigolo.'

Tom chuckled. 'You'll have a laugh.'

'Why do you and Jin both think that?' she asked. 'How could it possibly be anything but a disaster?' She grimaced. 'Even if I was available to seduce him I don't know what makes Jin think that I could!'

'No bother to you at all,' said Tom. 'Sure, you seduced me without even trying.' He looked at his watch. 'I have to go, honey. I'm late as it is.'

'I know.'

'I'll get a key cut for you,' she said suddenly. 'You can let yourself in on Friday.'

'I won't see you before then to collect it,' said Tom.

'I could leave it somewhere,' she suggested.

'That's not a very secure idea,' Tom told her. 'Look, honey, don't fret about it. I don't mind waiting.'

'You sure?'

He nodded and she opened the door of the flat and let him out. As he hurried down the stairs she heard him exchange a greeting with someone on the way up. She didn't manage to close the door of the flat before Dominic Lyster appeared on her landing.

'Oh, hi.' She smiled at him faintly. 'Any news on your stolen briefcase?'

'Are you mad?' he asked. 'I'll never see it again. But I did get a snazzy new mobile phone. Only problem is that I've lost my entire phone book with the old one.'

'So you would,' she said. 'What a pain.'

He grinned suddenly, his eyes lighting up. 'Oh, not as bad as all that. A number of people had to be culled from the list anyway. And it's meant a great few days of not having to call people I don't want to talk to.'

Her smile was less forced this time. 'Not bad, I guess.'

'Doing anything tonight?' he asked suddenly.

She looked at him in surprise.

'It's just that I saw your boyfriend leaving. Thought you might fancy some company.'

'No thanks.' She shook her head. 'I've stuff to do.'

'Worth a try,' said Dominic.

'I don't think you need to try very much,' she told him. 'You never seem to be without someone.'

'They're only a comfort,' said Dominic lightly. 'I'm waiting for the next Ms Right to come along.'

'Well, I'm not about to be added to your comfort list,' said Andie sternly. 'And as you pointed out, there is a man in my life already.'

'Mr Right?' asked Dominic.

'Very, very Mr Right,' replied Andie as she went back into her flat and closed the door behind her. She flopped on to the sofa and gazed unseeingly in front of her.

She couldn't believe that she was allowing herself to get caught up in this insane plan. The more she thought about it, the crazier it seemed. It was hard to credit that Kevin, a clinical businessman who surely must have more sense, had agreed to it. If Cora really was besotted with Jack, it wouldn't make any difference how many suitable fifty-something men Kevin and Jin paraded in front of her.

189

If Jack really cared about Cora, Andie supposed she could flaunt herself all she wanted at him and he wouldn't even notice. And if he didn't care about her mother . . . Andie nibbled at her fingernail. If he didn't care and if he in any way expressed an interest in her . . . then she had no idea what she'd do but she certainly wasn't going to let it go any further. How on earth could Jin possibly think this was a good idea? She wanted to scream in frustration but that might only bring Dominic Lyster downstairs to find out what was wrong.

The worst of the whole thing, of course, was that it was on Friday night. Andie was a bit miffed that Tom hadn't been more annoyed about the fact that she was going out on the night he was supposed to be moving in with her. But then Tom was a very pragmatic sort of man and very few things bothered him. All the same, she'd planned on spending the day getting ready for him, soaking in the bath, plucking, exfoliating, perfuming, pampering – doing all the things that would make him realise what a prize he'd got in her. And she'd anticipated ordering an Indian meal, which they'd eat as usual on the squashy sofa, only this time Tom wouldn't be getting up to rush home afterwards because he'd be home already, so that when they went to bed it would be a completely different experience for them, knowing that they'd be together until they woke up again in the morning. Even after they woke up in the morning! Her heart beat quicker at the thought.

She picked up one of the books which Jin had left behind and then slammed it back on the table. Why hadn't she just told her sister that the whole thing was too silly for words and refused to have anything to do with it? Why was she so bloody weak?

Andie phoned Cora on the Wednesday before the dinner and her mother told her that she was looking forward to it because she always liked going to Kevin and Jin's events and she got invited to so few of them. Probably, Cora chuckled, because most of them had a fund-raising element and both Kevin and Jin knew that she didn't have any funds!

'It's nice of them to keep asking me and Jack to things too,' added Cora. 'It means a lot.'

'Ma—'

'I know you and Jin are a little bit put out by Jack and me, and I realise that Kevin probably has his concerns too, but I'm a grown woman and I know what I'm doing,' Cora interrupted her. 'And I'm looking forward to a nice occasion with all of us there again.'

Andie stayed silent. She couldn't possibly believe her mother had thought that the tension-filled lunch had been a 'nice occasion'.

'I believe it's a totally posh do,' continued Cora. 'Jin tells me she's persuaded you to get dressed up again.'

'For heaven's sake,' muttered Andie. 'I get dressed up often enough. Just because she doesn't see me in anything other than jeans doesn't mean that I don't have a decent wardrobe.'

'I don't see you in anything other than jeans either,' said Cora. 'So it's nice for me to see you looking good too. Though they were nice ones you were wearing to lunch. Flattered your bum.'

Andie grasped the phone a little tighter and clamped down on the desire to tell her mother exactly why Jin wanted her to get dressed up on Friday.

'Is Jack looking forward to it?' she asked eventually.

'Of course.' Cora laughed. 'He's looking at it as more research.'

'For what?' asked Andie. 'Twenty Things To Do or the Great American Novel?'

'God knows,' replied Cora cheerfully, 'but I suppose he'll get something out of it.'

He certainly will, thought Andie grimly as she replaced the receiver. He'll get out of it that we're an interfering dysfunctional family and that I'm the sacrificial lamb. She closed her eyes and allowed herself to think of Tom again and the fact that this time next week the two of them would be living together. It made everything else so much easier to bear.

But when Friday night came along, their plans were thrown into total disarray. Jin phoned Andie at six o'clock to tell her that Cora wasn't coming after all.

'Why not?' asked Andie, who was standing in front of the mirror wondering why she'd bothered to go to the hairdresser and get her hair put up when she disapproved of the whole idea in the first place.

'She's got a terrible cold,' Jin answered. 'I was talking to her earlier.

191

There seems to be a bit of a dose going around because Lara, my cleaning lady, is off with one too and Kevin is a bit sniffly though he's OK for tonight. Mum was hoping hers would ease off but it hasn't. She says she's sneezed her way through a box of tissues already.'

'Well if she's not coming I can't imagine Jack will.' Andie was suddenly hopeful that she too could back out of the evening and stay at home to wait for Tom. 'So there doesn't seem to be any point, does there?'

'That's where you're wrong,' said Jin. 'Jack said he didn't want to go but Mum has insisted. She told him that it was important for Americans to realise that social life in Ireland wasn't all about diddley-eye music and people hopping around doing *Riverdance* at every available opportunity. She told him that he should see us as we really are.'

'You think that a bash like this is seeing us as we really are?' asked Andie sceptically.

'Oh, you know what I mean,' said Jin impatiently. 'Anyway, Jack's coming and so are you.'

'But what about this other bloke? Trevor McAllister?'

'He's still coming too, of course,' said Jin. 'You can give him the once-over, see what you think. Only you can't fall for him, Andie!'

'For goodness' sake . . .'

'Well, your thing might be older men,' said Jin. 'But this man is earmarked for Mum. No harm that he comes along, and there'll be a few girls from Kevin's office anyway so we don't have to worry about the male–female ratio at the table. But the good thing is you can strut your stuff with Jack without worrying that Mum might be watching you. Maybe it's not such a bad thing that she can't come.'

'I've no intention of strutting any stuff with him. Look, even if she was there I wasn't going to throw myself at Jack, I told you that already. Now that she isn't, there's no real need for me to be there at all.'

'Don't be so selfish,' said Jin. 'Just for once can you think about someone else and not yourself?'

'I *am* thinking about someone else,' retorted Andie. 'I'm thinking about Ma.'

'So am I,' said Jin. 'And I'm thinking that we have a responsibility to look after her. Dad would want that, wouldn't he?'

'I suppose so,' said Andie wearily. 'But this is a crap plan.'

'Look, if he comes on to you then we'll know for sure what kind of shit he is and you can tell Ma.'

'Oh God!'

There was a silence at the other end of the phone and then Jin sighed deeply.

'Just do what you can,' she told Andie. 'Find out more about him. Maybe it's better you doing it all than Kevin trying to weasel information out of him. He hasn't found out anything else about him at all despite checking the internet. Perhaps you won't have to actually throw yourself at him. Maybe he'll just go for you anyway!'

'I think you and Kevin are in cloud-cuckoo-land,' said Andie despairingly. 'And I'm not sure that I shouldn't be carted off for agreeing to this stupid caper.'

'Oh, chill out,' said Jin. 'It's all in a good cause. Anyway, it'd be a lot more appropriate for Jack to fall for you than for Mum.'

'No it damn well wouldn't.' Andie poked at the knot of curls on the top of her head. 'I'm not interested in him, I'm sure he's not interested in me, and I'm certainly not interested in the type of relationship that me and Ma would have if she really thought I'd set out with the intention of snatching her boyfriend from under her nose. And I don't think much of the fact that you're convinced he's a complete shit and totally unsuitable for Ma but it's all right for me to have some kind of relationship with him!'

'Oh, lighten up,' said Jin.

'Easy for you to say,' muttered Andie. 'I had other plans for this evening, you know.'

'Oh yes, the hot date,' Jin remembered. 'Was it really important?'

'I guess not,' said Andie. She bit her lip. It was more than important, she wanted to scream. It was the most important night of her life!

'At least you know that you've stood him up in a good cause,' Jin told her. 'Though when this is all over I want to meet him.'

'Who?'

'Your mysterious boyfriend,' said Jin.

'I thought you wanted Jack to turn into my mysterious boyfriend,' said Andie drily.

'Only for a few minutes,' Jin told her. 'That'll be more than enough.'

The car arrived at exactly seven o'clock. Jin buzzed the intercom and got back into the car to wait while Andie locked up her flat. A clatter of footsteps on the stairs made Andie look up. Two pretty children, identically dressed in purple jeans and pink T-shirts, were coming down followed by Dominic.

'Hi,' he said as they stopped on her landing. 'You look great, Andie. Going anywhere nice?'

'Not really,' she said.

'If you get done up like that for not really I'd love to see you when you're going somewhere you want to go!'

She smiled at him. 'What about you?'

'Me and the girls are off to the movies,' he told her. 'It's our bucket of popcorn, portion of nachos and fizzy drink night.'

Andie wrinkled her nose.

'And if we don't hurry we'll be late, Dad,' said the elder girl impatiently. 'Let's go.'

Dominic gave Andie a resigned smile. 'Enjoy your evening,' he said.

'I'd rather be doing the popcorn and nacho thing,' she muttered as she followed them out of the block. As she clambered into the depths of the Mercedes Jin eyed her accusingly.

'I thought you were going to wear the blue dress.'

'*You* told me to wear the blue dress,' said Andie. 'I didn't want to.'

'That's not half as seductive,' said Jin as she looked at the maroon silk. 'It's much more prissy.'

'I don't need to be seductive,' said Andie sharply.

'Well you'd better do something to help end this ludicrous state of affairs,' said Kevin. 'If you can't seduce him you can at least find out useful information about him.'

194

'There's no way I can guarantee that!' cried Andie.

She shifted uneasily in her seat as the car swung to a halt in front of Cora's house. If Kevin thought that the seduction routine was a good idea, God only knew what his next step would be. Whatever it was, it would only make things even worse. If there was a worse, of course.

Kevin got out and walked up the path, followed by the two sisters. He rang the bell and Jack, wearing a black tuxedo, opened the door.

'Wow,' murmured Jin.

'Gosh,' whispered Andie.

Jack's Tom Cruise smile was as vibrant as ever and his blue eyes smouldered in his almost-scrubbed-clean face. His dark hair was spiked with gel. He looked, thought both the Corcoran girls, a million dollars. And Andie couldn't help but feel that for once Jin was right about something – there was no way a man who looked like this could really be interested in their mother. Regardless of the fact that Cora was looking about ten years younger herself these days, it just didn't work that way. Older men picked up glamorous girlfriends. Older women didn't have the same clout with attractive men – unless, perhaps, they were of the Joan Collins ilk, and even then, Andie thought, you had to wonder at the motivation.

She wondered even more as they went into the living room and saw Cora huddled in front of the fire, her nose shining red, a half-empty box of tissues on the coffee table beside her and her ancient navy-blue cardigan wrapped around her shoulders. She looked wretched.

'Are you OK?' Andie asked.

'Oh, fine, fine,' sniffed Cora airily. 'It's only a head cold.' She sneezed and grabbed a tissue. 'You should stay away from me,' she warned, 'unless you want it too.'

'Are you sure you don't want me to stay with you?' asked Jack.

'Absolutely,' she told him. 'I hate being fussed over.'

'That's true,' said Andie.

'Go and have a good time,' said Cora. 'I'll feel better being here on my own and thinking that all of you are enjoying yourselves.'

'Will you really?' asked Jin.

'Honestly,' said Cora. 'I want to wallow in my sneezing. I can't do that if you're all around me feeling sorry for me. I hate people around when I'm not feeling well.'

'If you're sure,' said Jack doubtfully.

'I am. Really.'

'OK then.' Kevin looked at his watch. 'Hope you're feeling better soon, Cora.'

'I'll be grand by tomorrow,' she assured him. 'Besides, I've got plenty of hot whiskey to treat myself with. Jack went down to the off-licence for me earlier.'

'Least he could do,' muttered Jin.

'Come on.' Andie pushed her sister in the small of the back. 'Let's get going.'

'See you later, Cora.' Jack dropped a kiss on the top of her head.

'See you later,' she said and took another tissue from the box.

Chapter 15

Polovtsian Dances – Borodin

A ndrew Comiskey's Killiney home was every bit as spectacular as Jin had said. Set in an enormous undulating garden which sloped towards the sea, it was a hodge-podge of styles. Originally a medium-sized Victorian villa with mullioned windows, it had been sympathetically added to over the years so that it was now much larger than before. It had a Tardis-like quality about it – while seemingly compact outside, once behind the heavy oak doors there were myriads of rooms all elegantly furnished and, that evening, all crowded with very glamorous people.

'Gosh,' murmured Andie as she slipped out of her wool coat, 'I thought your place was big, Jin, but this is something else.'

'It has real character, doesn't it?' said Jin enviously. 'And, of course, the views over the bay are fantastic.'

'It's pretty damn tremendous all right,' remarked Jack Ferguson. 'What's so intriguing about Europeans is that you have all these great houses in the middle of ordinariness.'

Andie laughed. 'I wouldn't say that too loud if I was you. Killiney is considered a very desirable address in Dublin. I'm not sure the people up the road want to be thought of as ordinary!'

'I guess not.' Jack looked around him. 'But we are only a five-minute drive away from less extravagant places, aren't we?'

'It's like Manhattan,' said Kevin drily. 'Walk two blocks in the wrong direction and you've moved from doormen to drugheads.'

'I'm not sure the Comiskeys would like to think that you could find someone dealing crack cocaine outside the gate,' remarked Jin.

'They're probably lashing out the ordinary cocaine in the kitchen,' said Andie.

'Andie!' Kevin looked angrily at her. 'Not at a function like this.'

'Sorry.' She looked contrite but her eyes danced with laughter.

'It's always in the staidest of places,' Jack murmured and squeezed her arm. 'It wouldn't surprise me in the least.'

She felt herself jump at the touch of his fingers. Bloody hell, she told herself, no wonder Jin thinks I'm hopeless with men if I almost leap out of my skin just because someone touches me.

'Are you OK?' Jack looked at her curiously.

'Fine, fine,' she said.

He smiled. 'You sounded just like your mother when you said that.'

Andie frowned. 'Did I?'

'Yes,' said Jack. 'Anytime I ask her if she wants anything or needs anything or if she wouldn't like me to do something round the house for her she always says no, it's fine, fine – just like you.'

'Oh.' Andie hadn't realised that she'd inherited any of her mother's mannerisms. She wondered if it was a good or a bad thing.

'Come on.' Jack put his hand on her back and steered her through a knot of people. 'Let's get ourselves something to drink.'

'Bingo,' muttered Jin as she watched the two of them move through the crowd.

'Told you it'd work,' said Kevin. 'The man's a complete opportunist.'

'He won't break Andie's heart too, will he?' Jin looked suddenly concerned.

'Your sister doesn't have a heart to be broken,' said Kevin. 'She's far too sensible to fall for someone like Jack Ferguson.'

'I hope so,' said Jin. 'Because, looking at him right now in that absolutely fantastic tux, I could fall for him myself!'

Kevin stared at her and she laughed. 'I'm joking, darling.'

'I hope so,' said Kevin.

There was much more wealth on display here than there'd been at the birthday party, thought Andie as she sipped a glass of white wine and observed the other guests. She guessed that many of the glamorous women spent their time flitting from charity event to charity event, showing off designer clothes and the latest in jewellery and always trying to outdo each other. It was a world that Andie found totally unreal, even though her sister actually lived in it. But though she found it easy to imagine that the other women in the room lived their exotic lifestyles she couldn't quite place Jin in the same bracket. She was her sister, for heaven's sake. She hadn't been brought up to take it all for granted. Maybe, she thought suddenly, feeling guilty, maybe none of them had. Maybe the expensively dressed women and their equally expensively dressed men had all worked hard to get where they were and she was just an inverted snob to feel a little bit put off by it all.

'You all right?' Jack, who'd disappeared in search of a men's room, rejoined her.

'Mmm.' She nodded. 'I was just feeling a bit superior because I'm the only one here who's broke.'

He roared with laughter. A number of people looked in their direction and Andie blushed.

'Does it really bother you?' he asked.

'What?'

'That your little sister is loaded and you're not?'

Andie grimaced. 'Sometimes it does,' she admitted finally. 'Sometimes – like when it's pissing rain and I'm at the bus stop and a car drives through a puddle and sends up a spray that soaks everyone there and when I get home I realise I haven't anything decent to change into because I forgot to turn on the dryer that morning – then I think that I should be the one with the Merc and the housekeeper and the jacuzzis. But when I see her fretting about the fact that one of her friends has a newer car or a bigger lump of jewellery I just feel sorry for her.'

'I've been rich and I've been poor and rich is better,' said Jack.

'That's a quote, isn't it?'

Jack nodded. 'I forget who, but he's right.'

'Oh, I don't know.' Andie shook her head. 'It doesn't really buy you happiness, you know.'

199

'Of course not,' agreed Jack. 'But if you're happy already it helps a lot.'

She smiled at him. 'Are you happy?'

'Right now?' said Jack. 'Right now, of course I am. I'm having a great time in Ireland and I haven't been at a bash like this since – well, since the captain's night on the cruise.' He made a face at her. 'A few of the repeat passengers get invited to cocktails with the captain. Very, very ostentatious. You could be totally disdainful there if you wanted.'

'Really?'

He nodded. 'There are wicked displays of jewellery that night.'

'What was it like, working on the ship?'

'Not bad,' said Jack. 'I wouldn't like to be actual crew. They usually share cabins and it's all pretty basic. I was a guest so I had my own. Nothing like your mom's and Doireann's but it wasn't bad all the same.'

Andie supposed that this was her cue. She still felt as though this was an insane idea but she'd said that she'd give it a shot. So she looked up into Jack's navy-blue eyes and smiled at him as seductively as she could. 'I'm sure you and Ma were good friends,' she said huskily. 'Still are. But I bet you're looking for a little fun with someone more your own age.'

Oh my God, she thought, as the words left her mouth. That's the most ridiculous thing I've ever said in my life. It sounds like dialogue in a porno film.

Jack stared at her in astonishment. 'What sort of fun?' he asked.

'Well, you know,' she said desperately. 'Fun.'

'Really?' Jack raised an eyebrow and then slid his arm around her waist. 'With you?'

She gulped. It was working. He was interested in her. Jin had been right after all!

'I – I – yes . . . with me. Fun. You know.' She felt beads of perspiration break out on her forehead. I must be out of my mind, she thought.

'What exactly were you thinking of?' He held her closer and she could smell his musky aftershave.

'Well, I suppose . . .'

'Because you're a lovely girl.'

She swallowed hard. 'I . . .'

'So, let me get this straight,' he said. 'You're asking me to go to bed with you?'

'No!' she squeaked. 'No. I didn't mean . . . not that sort of . . .'

'What then?' He took his arm from around her waist.

'I – I – oh fuck, fuck, fuck!'

She spun away from him and hurried out of the room and down the nearest corridor, where she spotted the open door of a downstairs bathroom. She fled inside, locked the door behind her and leaned her head against the wall. Of all the insane things she'd ever agreed to do, this was the absolute worst. *And* she'd made a complete mess of it! Although it didn't really matter, did it? Because it seemed to her that Jack Ferguson was perfectly prepared to go to bed with her. He really was, as both Jin and Kevin had insisted, an opportunistic bastard.

She opened her tiny handbag and realised that her hands were shaking. She took out her mobile phone. No message from Tom yet. Not that she'd expected one at this stage, but oh how she wished she was back at the flat and waiting for him instead of trapped in a nightmare of her own making. She wondered if she could sneak out of the Comiskeys' house without anyone noticing. She absolutely could not go back to the party and look Jack Ferguson in the eye. She really couldn't. She was mortified enough already as it was.

It took another five minutes and the sound of someone banging on the door before she felt able to leave the bathroom.

'Hello again,' said Jack as she turned the corner. 'You probably didn't hear Andrew make the announcement that it was time to go in to dinner.' He grasped her by the elbow and steered her in the opposite direction, along the corridor. Andie felt her heart sink into her boots as she fell into step beside him.

Dinner was being served in what could only be described as a ballroom. Once again Andie found herself overwhelmed by the sheer size and glitz of everything. She couldn't quite believe that the Comiskeys had room to cater for a hundred people at a sit-down meal in their home. She tried to visualise a hundred people in her flat and stopped after picturing them falling out of the windows.

'Hello again, you two,' said Jin archly as they sat down. Andie shot her a pleading look but Jin merely beamed at her and readjusted the diamante straps of her Betty Jackson dress. 'This is Trevor,' added Jin as an attractive man walked up to her. Andie smiled briefly at him as Jin introduced her. She had to admit that Trevor was much more the kind of man she could imagine having a relationship with her mother. He was medium height, with hazel eyes, and dark hair which was thinning on top. But he was still good-looking, though clearly not in the Jack Ferguson bracket. Andie glanced involuntarily at Jack, who was still standing beside her, his hand resting casually on the back of her chair. There was no easy escape. She felt her face burn with embarrassment even though Jack wasn't actually taking any notice of her but was looking round the room with interest. Probably sizing up additional people to have fun with, thought Andie angrily.

Then the other guests at their table arrived and everyone sat down. Andie established that Barbara was the one with the absolutely enormous breasts, Terri was the girl who looked shy and out of place while Clodagh was the epitome of style and elegance and, it turned out, Kevin's PA. Clodagh didn't have an escort with her but Barbara and Terri were accompanied by their husband and boyfriend respectively, both of whom worked for Kevin.

She wondered suddenly why Tom hadn't been invited. Barbara's husband, Eddie, ran one of Kevin's restaurant chains. Surely Kevin could just as easily have asked the man who ran his biggest bar? It would have been incredibly difficult, she knew, to sit across the table from Tom and pretend that he was a mere acquaintance but it would have been wonderful to have him here. Although, she thought gloomily, goodness knows what he would have made of my seduction techniques. Yet he'd actually thought the plot had a degree of merit! It was easy to imagine that a course of action made some kind of sense when you weren't involved. She wondered whether, if he'd actually met Jack, Tom would have been quite as laid-back about it all.

The next time I come to something like this, she told herself

202

– if there is a next time – it will be different, because Tom will have left Elizabeth by then and he'll be with me and we'll be a real couple. Her eyes darted towards Kevin and Jin, who were talking to Trevor McAllister, totally unaware that by tomorrow she would have someone permanently in her life and that she wouldn't be available for ridiculous seduction-of-hunky-American evenings. She glanced at her watch surreptitiously. Tom would be talking to Elizabeth now, telling her that it was over between them, explaining that he had to get on with his life. And Elizabeth – she wondered how Elizabeth would react. Badly, or perhaps simply accepting the fact that it was finished. Maybe she'd accepted it a long time ago. Perhaps, thought Andie, she and Tom had been worried about Elizabeth when there was no real need to worry at all. She rubbed the back of her neck.

'Are you all right?' mumured Jack, startling her.

'Fine, fine,' she said automatically, and then grimaced as he smiled knowingly at her. She'd never noticed her mother's use of the expression before. She'd have to stop it herself. No matter how things might turn out in the future, she certainly didn't think it was a good idea to be talking like a clone of her mother right now.

'I think they're getting along really well,' Jin whispered to Kevin, and nodded across the table at Andie and Jack. 'Though I wish Andie had worn the blue dress. It was fabulous on her – I didn't tell her exactly how great because I didn't want her to get a totally inflated opinion of how she could look.'

'She'd be very attractive if she tried,' agreed Kevin. 'Though not a patch on you, of course.'

'Just as well you said that.' Jin grinned. 'Anyway, she should make the effort more often. Maybe that way she'd get someone.'

'You don't think there must be someone?' asked Kevin.

Jin shrugged. 'She does date people apparently,' she told him. 'She said she was meant to be going out tonight. But Andie was never one for the big romantic relationship.' She leaned her head briefly against him. 'Not like me. Falling head over heels for you the moment we met.'

'You fell off your heels the moment we met,' he corrected her.

'I do love you,' she said.

'You'd scandalise the whole place if they heard you,' Kevin told her. 'Imagine admitting in public that you actually love your husband.'

'It's better than showing up in public with your mistress.' Jin nodded towards another table, where Ivor McDermott was accompanied by Adrienne, his Swedish air hostess. She looked stunningly beautiful in a long white dress which emphasised her slender figure and youthful good looks.

'I'm surprised at Ivor,' admitted Kevin. 'Especially since Bettina is here too.'

'Bettina is!' Jin looked round in surprise. 'I didn't see her earlier.'

'She's here all right,' said Kevin. 'Andrew told me that Samantha absolutely insisted on inviting her.'

'Is she with someone?' asked Jin curiously.

'A bloke called Mark Donoghue. Works in advertising. There they are,' he added, nodding towards another table. 'She's pulled out all the stops too.'

'Wow.' Jin's eyes opened wider. Bettina looked utterly wonderful in her understated little black dress, a single diamond hanging round her neck and matching drop earrings in her ears. She'd had her hair restyled into a flattering, younger look and she'd abandoned her usual pale-pink lipstick for a deep red which emphasised her full lips. But, thought Jin sadly, Bettina was still a woman on the wrong side of forty, no matter how fantastic she looked. Underneath the black dress she had stretch marks and cellulite. It didn't matter how many expensive creams you rubbed into yourself every day, time was the factor that influenced your body the most. Adrienne was a tantalising twenty-something. Bettina was a fabulous forty. How could she compete?

'I'll kill you,' Jin muttered to Kevin.

'Huh?'

'If you ever dump me for a Swedish air hostess I'll kill you.'

'Why would I dump you for a Swedish air hostess?' asked Kevin. 'You know I never liked blondes.'

*　　*　　*

Jack was talking to Barbara while Andie played with her green-leaf salad. She was afraid to look in his direction in case he tried to talk to her because she really had no idea what to say to him. She'd made him express some kind of interest in her and then she'd run off like a scalded cat. But it wasn't my fault, she muttered under her breath, seducing Jack had been a stupid plan from the start. They hadn't made any provision for what might actually happen after she turned on the charm! She pushed her food around her plate some more and wished that the evening was over.

'Could you pass the water?'

Andie jumped as Jack turned to her. She lifted the big jug of water and handed it to him wordlessly. He poured some into his glass and looked at her enquiringly. 'Want some?'

She nodded. Jack replaced the jug on the table and grinned at her. Andie swallowed.

'So, this is fun,' he said.

'Oh, please!' She gritted her teeth. 'I don't want to have fun with you.'

'But Andie, sweetheart, you said—'

'I know what I said! Forget it!'

'I'm devastated.' He grinned unexpectedly, his eyes dancing with amusement. 'What can I have done in such a short space of time to make you change your mind?'

'Look, it was a mistake,' she said. 'I shouldn't have said anything.'

'No,' he said, his voice suddenly much cooler. 'You shouldn't have.'

'But then you shouldn't have wanted to either,' she told him.

'I never said I wanted to,' said Jack. 'I mean, you're a gorgeous girl, Andie, and you look stunning tonight. But I'm afraid my affections are rather taken up somewhere else at the moment.'

'It sure didn't seem like that,' she said angrily.

'Oh, give me a break.' He laughed. 'You came on to me like the proverbial ton of bricks. I just played along.'

'Yeah, right.'

'Andie! You asked me to have fun with you. It was like – like something out of a B movie. A C movie even.'

'I know,' she admitted. 'I thought as much myself.'

'So what's a guy to do?'

She looked at him witheringly.

'After all, it isn't often that women throw themselves at me. And before dinner too!' He chuckled.

'I'd have thought it was an occupational hazard,' she said sourly.

'Sadly not,' said Jack. 'So you don't really want to have fun with me after all?'

'No,' said Andie.

'Why did you ask?'

'I think you know why.'

'Not really. Why don't you enlighten me?'

As Andie tried to think of what to say, the waiting staff began clearing away the starters and serving the main course. Barbara tapped Jack on the shoulder and asked him a question and, relieved at seeing him distracted from her, Andie surreptitiously checked her mobile again. Still no message from Tom. She nibbled anxiously at her bottom lip. It was turning into a really long night.

Everyone was suddenly engaged in animated conversation except her. Jack was now turning the full force of his megawatt smile on Barbara and seemed to have forgotten Andie existed. Terri and Clodagh were discussing the lifestyle of someone she'd never heard of. She suddenly felt gauche and out of place. She occupied herself by observing the other guests at the function, like the overweight man with the extremely red face who looked as if he might explode out of his tux at any moment and who, apparently, was on the board of trustees of the hospital that they were helping that evening. Andie wondered whether the man himself wouldn't be ending up in a cardiac ward pretty soon. Why was it, she asked herself, that so many medical people lived totally unhealthy lives? And how come such an unattractive bloke was accompanied by such a pretty woman? Or girl, thought Andie, as she looked at his companion, who couldn't have been more than twenty-five. There it was again, she mused, the older man and younger woman. Only an older man and a younger woman didn't look quite so out of place as Cora and Jack would have done. She sighed deeply.

'Bored?' Jack turned to her again.

'I – um . . .'

He looked at her quizzically. 'Why did you come here tonight? I get the feeling that this is really not your thing.'

'Jin asked me.'

'And do you do everything she asks?'

Pretty much, Andie thought with surprise. Despite the fact that she always considered herself to be a totally different person to her sister and despite the fact that they normally didn't have much contact with each other at all, she suddenly realised that whenever Jin wanted her to do something, she usually did it. Why? she wondered. And above all, why the hell had she agreed to this?

'Difficult question?' Jack's voice had lost the hostility of earlier and was suddenly warmer.

'Not really,' said Andie slowly. 'I do things if they're important.'

'And coming here tonight was important?' said Jack.

'I thought so at the time.'

'Why?'

'Oh, you damn well know why,' she said.

'Well, I'm guessing that it was to . . . to . . .' His blue eyes twinkled and once again Andie felt the force of his charm. 'To tempt me? Lure me away from Cora maybe?'

'Sort of,' she said honestly. 'Perhaps to find out more about you.' She didn't really want Jack going home and telling Cora that Andie had admitted to trying to seduce him. She wanted to have some semblance of a decent relationship with her mother after tonight.

'What more do you want to know?' asked Jack.

'Are you really here to do research?'

'Yes,' he replied. 'I told you. I'm a travel writer. I need to travel to new places. I've written a lot of books.'

'I've read them.'

'Huh?' He looked at her in surprise.

'Kevin ordered them from Amazon,' she told him. 'Twenty Things To Do in a whole heap of places.'

'I see,' said Jack.

'Your name doesn't appear on them, though.'

'It depends on which ones he ordered,' he said. 'I . . .' He hesitated, and Andie looked at him curiously. 'I knew the people who published them,' he said after a moment. 'And I suggested some style changes. The early ones are a bit drab. Still good, though,' he added hastily. 'But I was only involved in the later ones.'

'So you're saying that the ones Kevin ordered aren't by you?'

'Like I said, it depends,' said Jack. 'You can order them in sets too – East Coast, West Coast, you know the sort of thing. So if he got the Northern set, for example, I wouldn't have written them.'

She didn't know what to say. He sounded totally convincing.

'But you wrote other ones?'

'Of course,' he said. 'But a guide is different to other kinds of books. The person or people who wrote it don't have their names splashed all over the cover.'

'I dunno.' She frowned. 'I've read lots of travel books and the name of the author was on the front!'

He grinned. 'Guides are a bit different. They're not the same as describing your action-filled journey through the Rockies. They're more about imparting information.'

'We'd find your name, though, if we bought different guides.'

'Sure you would,' said Jack easily. 'Though not on all the ones I wrote. Sometimes I used another name.'

'Oh.'

'Thing is, most of the time you have a couple of people working on the guides,' he said. 'At least in the case of the Twenty Things that's how it works. Because you want to get a perspective from someone who lives in the city as well as someone who's visiting. And people don't necessarily like to see the same names over and over again. They think you haven't bothered.'

'I see,' said Andie.

'I'll get you one with my name on if it makes you feel better,' said Jack.

She shook her head. 'Of course not.'

'I do other things too,' he said suddenly.

'Like what?'

'Lectures, radio broadcasts, that sort of thing. I'm not a completely hopeless case.'

'I never said you were a hopeless case.'

'I kinda get the feeling that you and your sister and your scarily

208

chilling brother-in-law think I spend my life drifting round the place making free and easy with older women and doing very little else.'

She blushed and was about to deny it emphatically when Barbara suddenly interrupted them yet again by asking Jack a question about American men's attitudes towards women who'd had plastic surgery. Jin didn't need me to do any seducing, thought Andie, as she watched them chatter. Barbara is doing enough.

Was there even a grain of truth in what Jack had told her about the travel guides? she wondered, as she nibbled at a sliver of carrot. After all, he'd given them the impression that he'd written them all, but it wasn't the case. And now he was implying that having something to do with them was the same thing as writing them when it wasn't at all. He was difficult to fathom – sometimes appearing open and friendly and sometimes secretive. The bottom line, though, was whether or not Cora would ultimately be hurt by him. And Andie had the uneasy feeling that eventually she would. Which was why, despite the ridiculousness of the entire situation that evening, she couldn't help siding with Jin and Kevin and their concerns after all.

She looked at her watch and wondered whether Tom was waiting for her at the flat by now. She really wanted to go home. Jack was right. Even without the burden of trying to be seductive, she wouldn't have enjoyed tonight.

The desserts were being served before Jack turned back to her again. 'I'm sorry,' he said. 'I keep getting buttonholed by that woman and I can't get away from her.'

'That's OK,' said Andie. 'You're not my date or anything. We're just here together.' She winced after she spoke. Another absurd comment, she thought. Her intelligence seemed to have totally deserted her this evening.

'Poor Cora,' said Jack. 'She was so looking forward to tonight and she was really gutted when her cold got so bad. Until late this afternoon she was trying to convince herself that she should come but I told her that she'd be miserable.'

'And why did you come?' asked Andie.

'Because she insisted,' said Jack. His blue eyes sparkled. 'I think she might have wanted me to get to know both of you a little better.'

'And have you got to know us better?' asked Andie.

'Well, I've sure had my eyes opened by you.' He laughed, and this time Andie couldn't help smiling faintly.

'Look, we're worried about her,' she told Jack. 'She's very vulnerable. It's not that long since my dad died and, well, until now she hasn't gone out much. We don't want her to get into something that hurts her.'

'Everything hurts at some point,' said Jack. 'Bet you've been hurt yourself.'

Andie found her eyes suddenly flood with tears which she only stopped from spilling down her cheeks by squeezing her lids tightly closed. She'd been overwhelmed by a sudden sense of longing for Tom so deep it had been physical. And a sense of foreboding about the result of his showdown with Elizabeth tonight that had terrified her.

'Andie?'

'I'm OK,' she said as she recovered her composure.

'I'm sorry,' said Jack. 'Obviously there's someone, or something . . .'

'It doesn't matter,' said Andie sharply. 'Of course I've been hurt in the past. But I have a really good relationship now . . .' Her voice trailed off.

Jack looked at her with interest. 'Do you?' he asked. 'Hit me and tell me it's none of my business if you like, but all the gossip I ever hear about you is that you're a totally committed career woman who doesn't have time for a man. Which is why I was kind of knocked for six when you made your comment about having fun.'

'Career woman!' Andie laughed shortly. 'I'm a music teacher. It's not exactly a Wall Street type of thing.'

'It doesn't have to be,' said Jack. 'A career is a career. Music is as good as any.'

Andie shrugged. 'I guess. I don't think of my job as a career. I think of it as something I do, that's all.'

'Have you ever thought of doing anything else?'

'No,' she admitted. 'It's all I ever wanted.'

'Then it's definitely a career,' said Jack.

'Maybe,' conceded Andie. 'I actually can't imagine my life without music.'

'And a Wall Street honcho probably can't imagine life without a laptop.' Jack grinned at her. 'Personally, I prefer the music.'

'So do I.' She wished he didn't make her smile.

'Tell me about the boyfriend,' said Jack. 'I honestly didn't think there was one.'

'I don't want to talk about him really,' said Andie, who was suddenly aware that the conversation had somehow moved from Jack and Cora to herself. She wondered if this was Jack's secret, managing to switch topics before you even knew it so that he never had to answer awkward questions about himself.

'Is he a secret?' Jack frowned. 'Obviously he's a secret if nobody knows about him. Is he married?'

Andie flushed but said nothing.

'Will he leave his wife?' asked Jack. 'Or is it just a mad fling?'

She stared at him. How had Jack guessed that she was going out with a married man? 'It's actually none of your business,' she said sharply.

'I guess not,' said Jack. 'But I'm interested. It must have been going on for a while because Cora said that you haven't gone out with anyone for years, which, to be honest, I find very hard to believe.'

'Why?'

'Come on, Andie. You're an attractive woman even if you have an extraordinary way of behaving with men you barely know. I can't imagine you not going out with someone.'

'I really don't think you're in a position to discuss my love life.'

'Why not?' Jack grinned at her. 'You keep trying to discuss mine.'

Andie wished she could stop herself from liking him.

'Both Ma and Jin think I'm a hopeless case,' she said. 'Ma thinks I'm celibate. At one point Jin was sure I was a lesbian.'

'So why haven't you told them about the married man?' asked Jack.

'I haven't admitted that there is one yet.' Andie looked away from him.

'There is,' said Jack.

'Oh, all right,' she said tartly. 'There is. Hopefully we'll be

211

together soon.' She didn't want to tell Jack that tonight was the night it would happen. She hadn't spoken about Tom to anyone before now, not even her closest friends knew about him. She'd always felt that keeping it totally secret was the best policy.

'Sure he's not just stringing you along?' asked Jack.

'Not all men are bastards,' said Andie.

'True,' said Jack. 'But some of us are.'

'Are you?' she asked.

'No,' he replied.

'Good,' she said. 'We can stop talking about me and get back to the subject in hand. Which is my mother, actually.'

'Andie, I'm not talking to you about Cora and me because quite frankly it's none of your business.'

'OK, I know I acted like a fool earlier when really all I should have done was give it to you straight.' Andie took a deep breath. 'Kevin and Jin think you're after her for her money.'

'I wasn't aware she had any.'

'She hasn't.' Andie shifted uneasily in her chair. 'But they think that you think she might have. Or that somehow you can wheedle money out of them through her—' She broke off. 'This sounds terrible . . . as though you're a criminal . . . we don't think that.'

'Sounds to me like you do,' said Jack icily.

'No,' said Andie. 'But you haven't exactly told us the truth about everything. About the books, for example. It wasn't as though you'd written them like we thought at first. And maybe everything else is complete bullshit too.'

'I haven't lied to you about anything,' said Jack.

Andie bit her lip. 'We're worried. Even you must see how odd it is. You're so much younger than her . . .'

'You're all very narrow-minded.' Jack suddenly folded his white linen napkin and threw it on the table. 'Why shouldn't I care about her? Why shouldn't she care about me? Why do you have to stereotype everyone?' He looked at her and Andie could see disgust in his eyes. 'You pretend that you care about Cora, but if you did you'd have been round more when she needed you. Both of you. Until the day you dropped by to see me you hadn't been in her house for weeks.' He pushed his chair back from the table and stood up. 'I'm going for some air.'

Andie watched him as he strode through the room. She clenched her jaw at the unfairness of his comments. She might not have been to the house every day but she phoned Cora regularly. So did Jin. Surely their mother didn't feel abandoned by them? Surely it wasn't their fault that Cora had taken up with Jack? She bit her lip as Jin came and sat in his empty seat, leaving Kevin and Trevor McAllister to talk to each other.

'Well?' she demanded expectantly.

'Well he hates me,' said Andie.

'Why?'

'Because I told him we thought he was a money-digging bastard.'

'Andie!'

'What else could I have said?'

'We were looking for a bit of tact from you,' Jin told her. 'You were supposed to seduce him, not antagonise him.'

'That was always too ridiculous for words,' retorted Andie. 'He guessed what I was up to anyway and now he knows what we think. I suppose he's always known that. He's well aware that Ma hasn't any money and I'm sure he's well aware that he won't get any from you or Kevin either. So maybe he'll just fuck back off to America.'

Jin stared at her.

'I've really had enough,' said Andie tightly. 'I want to go home.'

'Don't be silly,' said Jin. 'Stay and enjoy yourself.'

'Enjoy myself!' Andie looked at her sister in amazement. 'This is the party from hell, our mother's boyfriend thinks I'm a selfish bitch with the seduction technique of an alley cat, and I don't know any-one here. So I can't see that enjoying myself is high on the agenda.'

'Why don't you ring the hot date bloke and ask him to drop by?' suggested Jin.

'What?'

'Your secret admirer. The one you were supposed to be with tonight.'

Andie felt her mouth go dry.

'Not suitable for a glam night out?' asked Jin.

Andie said nothing and Jin shrugged.

'Look, you can't go yet,' she said. 'It'd reflect badly on Kevin. You don't have to talk to the Hollywood Love God any more. I think we've made our point.'

Andie still found it impossible to speak.

'We won't stay late anyway,' Jin promised. 'Kevin's going to Oslo in the morning. They're still having problems getting the chain started there. He's spending more time in Norway than at home these days.'

'Maybe it's all those Scandinavian women.' Andie finally found herself able to speak.

Jin stared at her. 'You don't think so, do you?'

'Of course not,' said Andie, jolted out of imagining Tom arriving at the party by the sudden note of alarm in Jin's voice. 'It was a joke.'

'Yes, but . . .' Jin bit her lip. 'Ivor McDermott left his wife for a Swedish air hostess.'

'Who's Ivor McDermott?'

'You've never heard of him?' Jin looked shocked. 'He's the chairman of one of the biggest drinks companies in the country.'

Andie shrugged. 'Sorry. Still never heard of him.'

'That's him over there.' Jin nodded towards the table Andie had been observing earlier.

'The fat bloke?' asked Andie in amazement. 'I thought he was a doctor.'

'He's on the board of trustees,' said Jin. 'But he's a company chairman.'

'So the blonde bombshell is his Swedish air hostess?'

'Adrienne,' confirmed Jin. 'And that's his wife over there.' She waved her hand in the direction of Bettina's table. 'The woman in the black dress,' she told Andie.

'And both of them are here?' Andie looked questioningly at her sister.

'Bettina's always been active on behalf of the hospital,' Jin told her. 'And since Ivor's on the board . . .'

'But imagine!' said Andie in horror. 'Having to turn up at the event and see your ex with a Swedish air hostess draped all over him. Poor woman.'

214

'I think Bettina's great,' said Jin. 'I don't see her very often but I like her.'

'So why did the husband leg it with the blonde?'

'Why do any of them?' asked Jin.

'Total idiots,' said Andie. 'Don't they realise that the younger women are only interested in the money?'

'I don't think they let themselves consider that.' Jin pursed her lips. 'I think they like to believe it's because of their power and stamina.'

'What a load of old cobblers.' Andie snorted. 'I can't believe that a shower of middle-aged blokes, supposedly so intelligent, can really think that their arm-candy women are interested in them because of their looks.'

Jin giggled and Andie smiled. 'It's true,' Andie continued. 'People hook up with other people for a whole heap of reasons and nobody can ever make me believe that a gorgeous thing like Adrienne sees anything in that old fat fart other than a thick wallet.'

'Andie!' But Jin was laughing now.

'I hope Bettina has a good lawyer,' Andie said, suddenly serious again.

'I'm sure she has the best,' Jin assured her just as Andrew Comiskey announced that dancing was about to commence and would they mind leaving the tables until the staff had moved them to provide extra room.

Andie wandered off along one of the corridors again. She wondered where Jack had got to. Maybe, she thought anxiously, he was so annoyed at her for expressing what she and Jin thought about his relationship with Cora that he'd simply left the party and gone home. And if that was the case, he'd probably tell Cora exactly why he was back so early and she'd be hurt and annoyed with both Jin and Andie, which was the very last thing either of them wanted.

Andie sighed in despair. Why, oh why, was life so bloody complicated? Why didn't the right people meet and fall in love at the right time? Why was everything so difficult? And why the hell was she here when she should really be at home anyway? She checked the time. Nearly midnight. She took her mobile phone out of her

215

bag and dialled her message minder. There was no indication that any messages had been left but she wanted to check all the same. Because Tom should have called, or sent her a text message at least by now. She didn't know whether to be worried by the lack of communication from him. She hoped that things had gone all right with Elizabeth and that the other woman hadn't lost her head completely and tried slashing her wrists or something. Worse, thought Andie, maybe she'd taken a knife to Tom and stabbed him in a fury.

She squeezed her eyes tightly shut. She knew that she was being stupid and irrational having thoughts like that but she couldn't help it. It was so nerve-racking being here when she wanted to be at home with Tom as a couple at last.

Suddenly she realised that she'd taken a wrong turn, because instead of arriving back at the ballroom as she'd expected, she'd walked into another reception room. It was smaller than many others in the house and she guessed it must have been part of the original building. The walls were painted pale yellow, the carpet was a light mushroom and the furniture was squashed and well worn. But it was the piano that caught Andie's eye. A highly polished baby grand in the far corner of the room. She walked over to it and lifted the lid.

It was impossible for Andie to pass a piano and not play it. Although she insisted to everyone that she was merely a music teacher and that her own playing skills were mediocre, she loved to play when she was on her own. She sat down and ran her fingers up and down the keys in a variety of scales and arpeggios before sliding into Borodin's Polovtsian Dances.

'I wondered if you'd find the piano,' said Jack as she finished. 'I thought you might.'

She spun round in surprise, her heart thumping in her chest. 'I didn't see you here.'

'I was just outside. I *did* see you.'

'I thought maybe you'd gone home.'

'I was tempted,' said Jack coolly.

'I'm sorry about earlier.' She looked at him contritely. 'It was all so stupid. But if you only knew how concerned we are . . .'

'People say that all the time, but it's simply an excuse for being rude,' said Jack.

216

'I didn't mean to be rude,' said Andie. 'But I'm not sorry I made our position clear about my mother. We don't want her to make a fool of herself.'

'Why are none of you concerned about me making a fool of myself?' asked Jack.

'You don't look the sort of person who might,' said Andie. 'And you certainly didn't make a fool of yourself with me.'

'I've been an idiot about women in the past,' Jack told her wryly. 'There's no reason I won't in the future either.'

Andie shook her head. 'I don't see you being the one looked at as being the fool if – and when – it all goes wrong with Ma.'

'You know nothing,' said Jack.

'Perhaps.' Andie grimaced. 'As Jin will doubtless tell you, I'm not exactly considered to be an expert on people's love lives.'

'Because of the married man?' asked Jack.

'Nobody knows about him,' said Andie. 'And I don't want you to tell them.'

'I won't,' said Jack dismissively. '*I* don't interfere in other people's lives.'

'Please, please give me a break.' Andie closed her eyes. 'I've apologised to you. You don't need to snipe at me.'

'OK.' His voice softened and she opened her eyes again. 'Let's call a truce on both our relationships.'

She laughed tonelessly.

'I won't hurt your mother,' said Jack. 'I promise.'

'Fair enough.' Andie flexed her fingers.

'You said you weren't a good pianist,' Jack told her, 'but you play beautifully. I recognised the piece. It was lovely.'

'I'm not concert standard,' Andie told him. 'And that's what counts.'

'No,' disagreed Jack. 'What counts is whether or not someone enjoys listening to it. I did. Though I love "Strangers in Paradise" anyway.'

'Actually it's from the opera *Prince Igor*,' she told him. 'Adapted for the musical and not really a good piano piece at all.'

'*Kismet*, isn't it?' asked Jack. 'A favourite on the ship actually.

There were a couple of pianists on board. You're better than any of them. Play something else.'

She shook her head. 'I truly don't like playing for people,' she told him. 'I get flustered and I end up making mistakes.'

'Play something modern then,' suggested Jack. 'A song.' He looked at her quizzically. 'You do know how to play songs, don't you, not just versions of classical pieces adapted for musicals?'

She laughed. 'Not the latest stuff,' she told him. 'Not gangsta rap or garage – or techno, obviously.'

'I can see how that might be a problem all right,' said Jack. 'Anything else? Because if you play I'll sing.'

'Do you sing?'

'Not as well as you play.'

'That doesn't say much.' But she smiled as her fingers moved over the keys again.

Jack smiled too. He knew the song. He asked her whether or not she'd chosen 'Are You Going to San Francisco?' specially for him.

'No,' she told him as they finished. 'I bought a book of sixties hippie songs when I first started to learn the piano. It's one of my favourites. And you sing it really well.'

'Want to try another?' he asked.

'Know this?'

He nodded. '"Say a Little Prayer". Another one of my favourites. Though not entirely appropriate for a bloke to sing. Never mind, I'm comfortable with my sexuality.'

She laughed and continued playing. As they finished there was a quiet round of applause.

'An audience!' Jack turned around and smiled at the dozen people who were now standing in the doorway of the room. 'Come in. Join us. Any requests?'

'Jack, stop it,' said Andie. 'I can't . . .'

'I can,' said Jack as someone called out 'Strangers in the Night'.

'Oh, all right.' Suddenly Andie didn't care that she was playing the piano in public and that people were listening. They followed up with 'It's in His Kiss', 'Anything Goes' and then 'Raindrops Keep Fallin' on My Head', to which their audience, now swelled to about twenty, joined in.

218

'I'm finished now,' said Andie after the applause had died down. 'Really. I can't do any more.'

'I'd love to do one more with you.' Jack looked at her hopefully. 'My favourite song.'

'What?' she asked.

'"Summertime",' he told her. '*Porgy and Bess.* Know it?'

She nodded. It was one of her favourite songs too.

Jack had a great voice. Not properly trained, but strong nevertheless. And he could hold a note, something she was totally unable to do. She suddenly realised that everyone was singing along again and she laughed. Jack smiled at her. She closed her eyes and lost herself in the song, letting the emotion of both the words and the music sweep over her.

When they finished, Jack kissed her on the top of her head.

'More!' cried a couple of people.

'Not this time,' said Jack. 'I'm sure that the band is set up in the ballroom by now.'

When they realised they couldn't change his mind their audience filtered away, and suddenly Jack and Andie were left alone together.

'I really enjoyed that,' Jack told her.

'So did I,' she admitted. 'It's not normally my thing, but it was fun.' She made a face. 'Real fun. You know what I mean.'

'You're good,' he said.

'You're better.'

'Stop putting yourself down,' said Jack. 'You added all sorts of little fiddly bits to that music. I heard you! And it was great. They loved it.'

'They loved the sing-along,' Andie corrected him. 'But it doesn't matter. I had a good time. And I didn't expect to.'

She stood up and closed the lid of the piano.

'Are you going back to the ballroom?' he asked.

'I suppose so.'

'In which case, I'd love it if you'd dance with me.'

She smiled. 'Sure.'

'Great,' he said and slid his arm around her waist just as Jin and Bettina McDermott walked into the room.

Chapter 16

Hungarian Dance No 1 – Brahms

'I heard there was music.' Jin's eyes flickered from Andie to Jack and back again, her expression bewildered. 'And singing.'

'You're too late,' Andie told her. 'We were filling in a bit of time before the dancing started.'

'Samantha said that you were really good.' Jin looked at her sister in surprise. 'I thought you never played for people.'

Andie shrugged. 'Not normally. But with Jack on vocals it made a bit of a difference.'

'Multi-talented,' said Jin drily. 'Ship's lecturer, explorer, novelist, befriender of women on cruises . . .'

'That's me.' Jack kept his arm around Andie's waist.

'Are you a Fred Astaire on the ballroom floor too?' asked Jin.

He turned to Andie and winked at her. 'I'm the worst dancer in the world.'

Jin looked questioningly at her sister. Andie shrugged impercep-tibly. Jin furrowed her brow. 'Well,' she said eventually as she looked at Jack. 'Glad you're having a good time with at least one Corcoran woman tonight.'

There was an uncomfortable silence. Andie shot Jin a look of infuriated exasperation and then walked towards the door. 'Leave it,' she muttered to her sister as she brushed past her. 'Just leave it.' She strode quickly along the corridor.

'Hey, slow down!' Jack caught up with her. 'You're going the wrong way.'

'How do you know?' she demanded. 'You've never been in this house before so how do you know?'

'Sense of direction?' His blue eyes twinkled. 'I do write travel guides after all. Maybe if I get you back to the ballroom you'll believe me.'

She said nothing.

'And then you'll be able to tell your sister that I'm not a total sham.'

'She doesn't—'

'Oh, come on! She hates me even more than you do.'

'Nobody hates you,' lied Andie.

'This way.' He led her down another corridor and suddenly they were back in the ballroom, where the tables had been rearranged.

'I'm sorry she was so rude,' said Andie as they found their seats again.

'You've all been rude to me,' he replied casually. 'And you've explained why.'

'I know.' She filled her glass with water from the jug that was on the table. 'It doesn't make it right, though.'

'Don't worry about it,' said Jack. 'Make it up to me, let's dance.'

'Are you really the worst dancer in the world?' she asked as he led her on to the floor.

'Absolutely,' he assured her, and stepped on her toes.

Jin and Bettina sat in the piano room recently vacated by Andie and Jack. Bettina took a small silver box from her bag and opened it. She shook two small white pills into her hand and swallowed them with a gulp of champagne from the bottle she'd carried in with her.

'Valium,' she told Jin ruefully. 'I need it at the moment.'

'You're doing really well,' Jin said.

'I have to,' said Bettina. 'I'm not going to let people think that I care about Ivor and the tartlet.'

'She's fairly stunning,' admitted Jin. 'But you're much more attractive.'

Bettina smiled faintly. 'I used to be fairly stunning too,' she said. 'I hate the fact that I'm not any more. I hate the fact that gravity

221

has pulled my boobs and my bum down. I hate the cellulite on my thighs. I hate having to get my hair coloured because of the grey and not because I want a change. I don't want to be someone that people think of as well preserved. I want to look wonderful all the time.'

'I understand,' said Jin.

'Not yet, you don't,' Bettina told her. 'You, my dear, are still stunning yourself. There's no way Kevin will stray yet. Absolutely no way.'

'But you think he will one day?' Jin blinked.

'Don't they all,' muttered Bettina bitterly. She filled her glass again.

'Do they?'

'Oh, fuck it!' Bettina sniffed. 'I don't know. Maybe it's just Ivor. There have been women before and I tried not to get too worked up about it. Flings, that's what he always called them. He'd go to meetings and then a club afterwards and there'd always be someone who'd wrap herself around him and tell him he was wonderful.'

Jin bit her lip. 'That doesn't mean he had to have sex with them.'

'With Ivor it did.' Bettina took a tissue out of her bag and blew her nose. 'You know how it is, Jin. To me he was just my husband. I knew him before he made his money. I'd tell him to put out the rubbish or that his feet were smelly. I'd be normal with him. But those women, these younger models – they all make him think that he's God's gift. That he's special.'

Jin said nothing. She didn't know which category she fell into. The wife who would one day be betrayed or the younger model who flattered an older man's ego. She was both right now.

'Have you ever heard of Kevin being with anyone?' she asked eventually.

Bettina looked at her thoughtfully then shook her head. 'Not since he married you,' she said. 'Not that I'm aware of. There were one or two when he was with Monica, of course, though not serious as far as I know.'

'Why do they do it?' asked Jin fiercely. 'Why can't they just be happy with what they have?'

222

'Because they all like to have their egos massaged,' Bettina told her. 'As well as their other bits.'

Jin smiled sourly. 'I guess so.'

'Who was that gorgeous man with your sister?' asked Bettina after a moment in which she filled both of their glasses again.

'Oh, just a friend.' Jin kept her voice as light as she possibly could.

'A very attractive friend,' said Bettina. 'Though she's attractive too in a kind of down-to-earth way. But still, she'll struggle to hang on to him.'

And there you had it, thought Jin as she sipped her champagne. if Bettina thought that Andie would struggle to keep Jack, what on earth would she say if she heard that it was actually Jin's mother who was supposed to be the woman in his life? She'd laugh at the ridiculousness of it all. Jin shuddered internally at the sudden thought that Bettina and her friends might find out about Jack and Cora. Kevin was right, they'd be a laughing stock. And he couldn't afford to be a laughing stock when his business depended on him being the complete opposite.

'You're right,' Andie told Jack as they sat down after two dances. 'You *are* the worst dancer in the world. My toes are pulped.'

'Sorry,' said Jack, although he didn't sound in the slightest bit remorseful. 'I love it but I can't do it.'

'Bit of a disadvantage when you're the ship's lounge lizard,' remarked Andie.

'I was never the ship's lounge lizard,' he protested. 'There were, in fact, professional dancers on board and they looked after lonely passengers.'

'Really?'

He nodded. 'The cruise company wants everyone to have a good time. It's not a bad thing to do if you're on your own.'

'Maybe.' Andie shivered suddenly. 'I don't like the idea of someone being paid to dance with me.'

'Oh, I don't know.' Jack's tone was gritty. 'At least it's honest.'

'But a bit sad.'

'Why?' he asked. 'If you want someone to be with you, why not pay them?'

'But . . .'

'It's better than pretending,' said Jack. 'Like those girls and those men. They're only hanging out with each other because the girls know the men have money and the men want to pretend to themselves that they can still attract young women.'

'Jin and I talked about it earlier,' confessed Andie.

'So strip out all the pretence and just pay the person,' said Jack baldly.

Andie stared at him for a moment. 'Is Cora paying you?' she asked.

'For Christ's sake!' He sounded really angry now, and there was a hunted look about him that hadn't been there before.

'Oh God, I'm sorry, I'm sorry.' Andie pressed her fingers to her temples. 'I didn't mean . . .'

'You did,' said Jack.

She shook her head. 'I'm not apologising any more. I'm going home. I don't know if Kevin and Jin want to stay but I've had enough.'

'So have I,' said Jack sourly.

'You can't come with me,' Andie told him.

'What in heaven's name would make you think I'd want to?'

'Nothing,' said Andie. 'You wouldn't. I'll go.'

'Boyfriend waiting for you tonight?' he asked suddenly.

She swallowed. 'Yes.'

'Don't throw yourself away on him,' said Jack. 'It could be such a waste.'

'I'm certainly not throwing myself away on anyone,' she told him.

'Sure. Of course. You know what you're doing.'

'If only,' she muttered as she walked off in search of Jin to say goodbye.

Jin and Bettina were still in the piano room, the empty bottle of champagne on the floor beside them. They were playing 'Chopsticks' on the baby grand, giggling every time they missed the notes or hit the wrong ones.

'Andie!' Jin beamed as she saw her. 'Play this for us. Go on.'

'I want to go home now,' said Andie. 'I don't mind if you're staying a bit longer. But I want to leave.'

'Why?'

'Because I'm tired.'

'You're at a party,' said Jin. 'You work through the tiredness.'

'I want to go,' repeated Andie firmly.

'Well I'm not ready to leave yet.' Jin's words were slightly slurred. 'Me and Bettina – we're having a good time.'

'Good for you,' said Andie drily.

'You're such a party-pooper,' complained her sister.

'I can get a taxi,' said Andie. 'You stay if you want.'

'I don't know . . .' Jin squeezed her eyes shut and opened them again. 'Where's Kevin?'

'I haven't seen him in a while,' said Andie. 'I presume he's in the ballroom.'

'Probably with friends,' said Jin. 'Talking business. That's Kevin's idea of fun.'

'Used to be Ivor's,' muttered Bettina. 'But I don't care any more.'

'I'll see if I can find Kevin,' said Andie.

'OK.' Jin turned back to the piano and began tapping the keys again. 'Don't go without saying goodbye.'

Andie couldn't find her brother-in-law in the ballroom. She saw Kevin's assistant, Clodagh, happily sidestepping Jack Ferguson's size nine feet, laughing at him as he tried to move in rhythm with the music. Maybe Jack will fall for Clodagh, thought Andie sourly. Do everyone a favour. Although she wasn't sure how Kevin would feel about it. She didn't want to talk to Kevin. She didn't want to talk to anyone. She was tired, her head was beginning to ache and she wondered why on earth Tom hadn't left a message on her mobile to say that he was waiting for her. She'd been expecting something from him; she couldn't quite believe that he'd simply broken up with Elizabeth and driven to the flat without at least leaving a message.

Andie didn't want to think there was a possibility that Tom might have lost his nerve at the last minute. That, faced with Elizabeth sitting in front of him, his courage had failed him and he'd found it impossible to tell her he didn't love her any more, that Andie was the only woman in his life now. He couldn't have lost his nerve. He'd been so determined this time. She checked the phone again but there were no messages either on her voice-mail or in her message box.

Suddenly she saw Kevin, also on the dance floor, gyrating energetically with the blonde girl in the white dress. The fat man's air hostess. She was about to go up to her brother-in-law and tell him she wanted to leave but she changed her mind. She didn't need to talk to Kevin. She simply left the ballroom and went to get her coat. There was nobody at all in the main entrance hall. She let herself out of the house, pulling the heavy hall door securely closed behind her. The garden was well lit by lamps each side of the long driveway, but once outside, the road was narrow and dark. Andie hadn't a clue where she was. She turned to her left and hoped that she was heading in the right direction and that she'd shortly arrive at a major junction where she'd have a chance of picking up a cab.

She walked quickly though unsteadily, her heels too high for the uneven pavement. Her head was buzzing and all she could think was that the glitz and glamour weren't enough to offset the awfulness of her conversations with Jack Ferguson. She wished she could make up her mind about him – though he was definitely warmer and more likeable than Jin or Kevin would ever believe (playing the piano while he sang had been such unexpected fun), there was still something about him which bothered her. Maybe it was that he was a bit too warm and likeable when he wanted to be. Once or twice it had seemed to her as though she could have done what Jin suggested and thrown herself at him and she wasn't at all sure that he would have rejected her. And yet when he'd spoken about Cora it had been with real feeling. She shook her head. She didn't care any more. She was butting out and staying out. Let Cora do what she liked, get hurt if she liked. It was none of her business. Her mother was a grown-up, for heaven's sake, she could look after herself. They were being stupid by interfering.

She almost missed the taxi because she was walking with her head down, watching the pavement. But she looked up at the last minute when she heard the sound of the car engine and waved at it when she realised that the For Hire light was on. The car reversed back towards her.

'Drumcondra?' she said.

'Sure.' The driver nodded. 'You're a long way from home,' he added as she got into the back seat.

'Not by choice,' she told him and closed her eyes.

Tom wasn't waiting outside the apartment building. Andie felt her heart thud into her stomach as she paid the taxi driver (adding a substantial tip because he'd driven in complete and blissful silence) and then let herself into the block. She blinked in the harsh white light of the communal hallway as, once again, she checked her mobile for messages. She'd known there wouldn't be any. She would have heard it ring.

She let herself into her flat and switched on the old-fashioned standard lamp in the corner. Then she looked out of the window again. But Tom's car still wasn't there. She clenched and unclenched her jaw, wondering what had happened, why on earth he wasn't here and why he hadn't called.

What the hell had gone wrong? she wondered. Because he should be here by now. It was nearly one. If he'd spoken to Elizabeth like he'd said – like he'd promised – he'd have been waiting outside the apartment block for her. She opened the window and peered out into the darkness, knowing that it was impossible for her to have missed seeing him if he'd been there. So he wasn't there. And she didn't know why.

What could Elizabeth have said or done to stop him leaving? Threatened to kill herself? Threatened to kill him? Andie had berated herself for being over-the-top when she'd thought of it earlier, but now she shivered as she pictured the other woman with a knife in her hand slashing at Tom, yelling at him that he'd never be able to leave her. She closed her eyes and tried to switch off her imagination. These were the kind of things that happened on TV dramas, she reminded herself. This was real life. People didn't go berserk with knives in real life. And then she remembered news reports which proved that sometimes people did go crazy if they were confronted with a terrible situation, and perhaps she wasn't

227

being at all histrionic in visualising Elizabeth brandishing a knife at Tom.

Maybe he *had* left her, she thought suddenly. Maybe he'd arrived at the flat and realised that Andie was still out, and perhaps he'd called to the bar or something so that he wasn't sitting outside like a fool. That was a more likely turn of events. Andie felt better as she thought of it and she turned back into the room and filled the kettle. All the same, she thought as she switched it on, he should have called her. Not calling was what was making it difficult. Not knowing what had happened. What he'd said to Elizabeth and what Elizabeth had said to him. But surely the other woman must know that their marriage was a sham? Surely she was equally unhappy? And wouldn't she see the sense of them separating and starting all over again?

The kettle boiled. Andie poured water over the teabag she'd dropped into the big yellow mug and then wrapped her hands around it as she stood by the window again. What time would he arrive? Bar Tender stayed open until two. And it was at least an hour, usually more, after that before they finished up. But would he stay until closing time? Stay to tidy up? When he knew that she was waiting for him? She hated this feeling of uncertainty. In fact she couldn't bear it any more. They had an unwritten rule that he always called her, she never called him. But what was the point of it now? Hands shaking, she dialled Tom's mobile. But it simply diverted to his message minder. Not surprising if he was in the bar, she knew, because the volume of music and chatter made it impossible to hear. She said simply, 'Call me' and disconnected.

Perhaps he wasn't at the bar at all, he was still at home with Elizabeth and had switched the phone off because they were still talking. After all, when you had major discussions about your relationship they could take ten seconds or ten hours. In Tom and Elizabeth's case they might have had a lot to talk about. Although, right now, Andie couldn't really see what.

Alone in her flat, she now wished that she hadn't left the party. At least while she was there, being nagged at by Jin and irritated by everyone else and feeling bad about Jack Ferguson, she wasn't spending her whole time thinking about Tom and worrying about

228

their future together. Because no matter what excuses she could think up, she was worried. He should have been here waiting for her. The fact that he wasn't, no matter what the reason, was making her shake with fear. If only he'd call.

She sipped her tea and wondered suddenly how things were going at the party without her. Whether Jin and Kevin had decided to leave well alone or whether they'd decided to approach Jack themselves. Andie bit her lip. She had to admit that he wasn't bad company and she wasn't surprised that Cora liked him. She pursed her lips as she recalled his comments about not throwing herself away on the married man. Not that Jack would know anything about it, of course. It was funny, she thought, how everyone had totally biased views about other people's relationships. She and Jin were wary of Jack; Jack had his doubts about her and Tom even though he'd never met him; Jin was, she knew, occasionally troubled by thoughts of Kevin's first marriage. Then there were all those relationships about which Jack had been so scathing – the younger girls and older men at the party. Andie was in agreement with him there. The girls knew what they were doing. It was the men who were complete fools. But then, she said aloud as she looked out into the darkness, aren't they always?

'What d'you mean, she's gone?' demanded Jin.

She glared at Jack, who simply shrugged at her. 'She talked about going. I guess she went.'

'Why the hell would she do something like that?' asked Kevin. 'Why did you let her? We have a car, for heaven's sake, we were going to bring her home.'

'Her choice.'

Jin sighed in frustration. 'Why? It's not like she gets to events like this so often that she should want to leave early.'

'Maybe she simply wasn't enjoying it,' suggested Jack. 'She's a little shy, isn't she?'

'Not shy,' said Kevin. 'She just doesn't make an effort.'

'Actually, I think she's lovely.' Jack grinned wickedly at him. 'And I think she'd make a wonderful stepdaughter.'

'Stepdaughter!' Jin stared at him in shock. 'Stepdaughter?'

'As would you if I married Cora,' he added.

'You wouldn't.'

'Why not?'

'She's our mother!' Jin sounded scandalised. 'You couldn't possibly.'

'She's worth a hundred of the other women at this party,' said Jack. 'I could. Quite easily.'

Jin turned away from him and Kevin put his arm around her.

'Let's go,' he said.

'Do you want me to come too?' asked Jack.

'Not really,' said Kevin. 'But I suppose you'd better.'

'It's OK, Dixon,' said Jack. 'I'll stay here a bit longer. Make my own way back.'

Andie couldn't sleep. She lay on her back in the big double bed and stared at the ceiling. She'd broken the unwritten rule and phoned Tom's mobile but he hadn't returned her message. She felt powerless and hopeless and she suddenly couldn't help envying Cora and Jack. Even if their relationship went horribly wrong at least they'd spent full nights together. From the moment she'd started seeing Tom she'd wanted to wake up in the morning to see him beside her. She hated the way he had to leave her in the middle of the night.

Tomorrow, she told herself. Tomorrow he'd be here and everything would be OK. Whatever had prevented him from coming tonight would be irrelevant tomorrow. And maybe, she thought suddenly, maybe he'd decided to spend the night in a hotel or a B&B because he hadn't known how late it would be when she finally got home. Perhaps too he hadn't wanted to wait outside after all, knowing that Kevin and Jin would be dropping her home. It made sense when she thought about it for a little. Of course the only part that didn't make sense was the fact that he hadn't called or texted her. But maybe the battery in his phone was dead.

The rapid beep of her mobile's message alert made her sit upright in the bed, her heart thumping loudly. She almost dropped the phone in her haste to answer it but frowned as she realised that the message was coming from Cora's handset.

Did u get home OK? it asked. It was signed *Jack*.

230

Her eyes filled with tears. Where the hell was Tom? she demanded. Where? Why was Jack Ferguson sending her text messages but not the man she really cared about?

Yes, she sent back after a minute or two. *CU.*

The phone beeped again. *Ur mom says goodnight.*

Goodnight, she returned.

She waited for a moment in case it beeped again but it was silent. She replaced it on the bedside locker and tried to go to sleep.

Chapter 17

*Piano Sonata No 14 in C Sharp Minor (Moonlight): Adagio –
Beethoven*

Jin paced around the bedroom as she undressed, leaving her
clothes in scattered piles on the floor. Kevin followed her and
picked them up.

'For Christ's sake would you stop!' he cried eventually.

'Stop what?'

'Walking around like that. You're making me dizzy.'

'I feel dizzy already,' said Jin. 'He talked about marrying my
mother. Marrying her! I don't believe it.'

'I won't let it happen,' Kevin assured her. 'Somehow we'll bring
your mum to her senses.'

'Maybe.' But Jin's voice was full of doubt as she slid beneath the
covers and closed her eyes. Kevin continued undressing, then got
in beside her and turned out the lights. He pulled her closer to him
and circled her with his arm.

'Bettina looked well, though,' said Jin suddenly. 'I can see how
Trevor was taken with her.'

'She didn't look as well as Adrienne.'

'Kevin!' She turned around so that she was directly facing him.
'That's a horrible thing to say.'

'But true.'

'It doesn't matter. Ivor is a bastard.'

'For having someone else?'

'For behaving like every other middle-aged businessman in this
town.'

'Don't be so silly,' said Kevin. 'Not everyone is shagging someone as gorgeous as Adrienne.'

'Are you saying you'd all like to?'

'No.' Kevin sounded irritated.

'Why do so many of you do it?' she demanded.

Kevin didn't answer. She poked him in the ribs.

'Maybe because we get nothing but grief from our wives,' he said eventually.

Jin was shocked into silence. Did he think she gave him grief? Was he looking for someone else? She swallowed hard.

'But I'm not fooling around,' he said after a minute or two. 'Why would I when I have you?'

She allowed herself to relax into his hold and then snuggled closer to him. 'I love you,' she said.

'Why wouldn't you?' asked Kevin.

It wasn't exactly the response she'd wanted. She wished sometimes that Kevin would tell her that he loved her before she told him first. But he never did. She bit her lip. Maybe it was because he didn't really love her after all. Maybe, despite his protestations, he had someone else. Someone like Adrienne.

She slid beneath the covers and took him in her mouth. He gave a startled grunt and then exhaled loudly. It was hot and airless beneath the sheets but she wanted to give him pleasure. She wanted him to know that she loved him in many different ways. She wanted him to tell her that he loved her too.

He twisted her soft hair around his fingers and thrust against her. She heard him mutter her name and then cry that she was wonderful, that she was always wonderful. She waited to hear him say 'I love you,' but he didn't.

And afterwards, when he got back into bed after his visit to the bathroom, he simply said, 'That was great' before immediately falling asleep.

It was nearly five in the morning before Andie eventually drifted into sleep, but her dreams were uncomfortable and disjointed, so that when she woke up just after nine, she felt as though she hadn't slept at all. She got out of bed and pulled her dressing gown over her candy-striped pyjamas. She'd worn them last night instead of the slip of white oyster silk she'd intended if Tom had been there. She'd hung the slip on a padded hanger before pulling the pyjamas out of her bottom drawer. They were the least sexy garments she possessed but they were warm and comfortable. All the same, she thought, as she walked groggily into the kitchen, if he called round now he'd probably leave again straight away, shocked at how desperately unattractive she looked. He'd never seen her first thing in the morning before. She looked dispiritedly at her panda eyes and dull skin before getting under the shower. The tepid water (she'd forgotten to switch on the timer) didn't do much to revive her, but she got dressed in her most stylish trousers and her cranberry-coloured jumper, which made her feel a little less ragged. Then she rubbed some foundation into her skin, thinking that she really should have done the make-up thing before putting on her clothes, but anxious that she should look as though she'd had a decent night's sleep if and when he arrived. Of course he wasn't actually used to seeing her wearing much make-up – she normally only bothered with a dash of tinted moisturiser and a slap of natural pink lippy – so she didn't need to bother with it. Only somehow she felt as though she should.

Ring, she said fiercely to the phone, and then nearly jumped out of her skin as it did just that.

'Hello?' Her voice was anxious.

'It's me.'

She felt relief and anger wash over her. 'What happened? Where were you last night? Where are you now?'

'We need to talk.'

'Why? What's wrong, Tom?'

'I have to talk to you,' he repeated.

'Are you coming round? Have you packed?'

'I'll meet you in town,' he said.

'Why?' she asked warily.

'I can't come to your flat. Not right now. Meet me in the Jervis Centre.'

'Huh?' Andie was surprised. A shopping centre wasn't where she expected to have an intimate talk about their future. And it was public. Much more public than anywhere they'd ever met before. Although maybe that was the point. Maybe he wanted to make a statement about their new life together.

'We can have a coffee there,' he said.

'Has it all gone wrong?' she asked nervously. 'What did Elizabeth say? Is she all right?'

'We'll talk when we meet,' said Tom.

'Tom!'

'About an hour?'

'Tell me that everything's all right.' She couldn't keep the concern from her voice. 'I need to know, Tom.'

'Just meet me,' he said. 'We'll sort it out when you meet me.'

'An hour,' said Andie.

'See you then.'

She replaced the receiver and stared blankly at the wall opposite. He couldn't have backed out, could he? Lost his nerve? Surely not. Leaving Elizabeth, being with Andie instead – it meant everything to him. He'd said so often enough. He'd told her time and time again how much he loved her, how important she was to him, how great a part of his life she was. He couldn't have said all those things and not meant them. Besides, he wanted to leave Elizabeth. She knew that. He hadn't been lying about it, stringing her along.

Andie chewed at her already ragged thumbnail as a tear trickled down her cheek. She'd waited so long for this day. She didn't want to hear that it hadn't turned out the way she'd hoped. She didn't want to know that he'd lost his nerve. She wanted him to be with her. Tonight. Like he'd promised.

She took her coat from the hook on the back of the door and put it on.

'Hi,' said Dominic Lyster, who was coming up the stairs, a litre of milk and the Saturday newspapers under his arm. 'Did you have a good time last night, Andie? You look like you went on a complete bender.'

'Thanks,' she said shortly.

'Sorry. Didn't quite mean it like that. Are you all right, though? You're awfully pale.'

'I'm fine,' she said.

'Sure?'

'Oh for heaven's sake!' she snapped. 'Of course I'm sure. Not that it's any of your damn business anyway.'

'OK, OK.' Dominic stared at her. 'Take it easy.'

'Yeah, right,' she muttered as she clattered down the stairs. 'I will.'

She arrived at the Jervis Centre with twenty minutes to spare. She wandered aimlessly around Debenhams and Marks & Spencer, picking up clothes and looking at them without really seeing them before putting them back on the rails again. The stores were beginning to fill up with Saturday shoppers all eager to spend some hard-earned cash. She thought of the silk slip which had been breathtakingly expensive and hoped that she'd be wearing it tonight. But she was gripped with anxiety about her meeting with Tom, knowing in her heart that something must have gone wrong, because otherwise she'd have been wearing it last night instead of her sensible candy-striped pyjamas.

He was already waiting outside the café when she walked out of Debenhams and into the main concourse. She saw him instantly in the crowds, his dark hair tousled and unkempt, his hands thrust deep into the pockets of the casual jacket he was wearing.

'Hi.' She smiled uncertainly at him, wondering if he would kiss her. But he simply returned her smile and led her into the café.

'Why are we here?' she asked. 'We never meet in places like this.'

'I thought . . . it might be easier . . . with people around.'

She looked at him in astonishment as he placed two Danish pastries on a plate.

'I'm not really hungry,' she said.

'It's only a Danish.' His words were jerky.

She said nothing. She allowed him to pay for the coffees and the pastries and followed him to a table near the entrance.

'What happened?' she asked as soon as he sat down opposite her. 'What did she say?'

He took a sip of coffee, grimacing because it was too hot. He replaced the cup carefully on the saucer.

'For God's sake, Tom!' she cried, her patience finally snapping. 'What the hell is going on?'

'I – it's difficult,' he said.

'You didn't tell her.' Andie stared at him in sudden realisation. 'You said nothing.'

'It wasn't quite like that.'

'You told me you loved me,' she said. 'You told me that I was the only person in the world for you. You said that you were going to leave her, Tom. You promised.'

'It wasn't that easy,' he said uncomfortably.

'Nobody said it was going to be easy.' Her eyes glinted with tears. 'We always knew that.'

He rubbed his forehead.

'Didn't you say anything to her at all?' demanded Andie.

'I couldn't,' Tom told her. 'Not after what she said to me.'

'And what was that?' asked Andie scornfully.

'That she's pregnant again,' said Tom.

Andie thought she was going to faint. The bustle and clatter of the café had receded into the background, along with the piped music and the noise of the shoppers moving about the centre. Her vision seemed to have been reduced to the area directly in front of her – Tom's agonised face and a large sign that said 'No Smoking'.

'Andie,' he said urgently. 'Are you all right?'

She picked up her coffee cup, but her hand was shaking so much that she had to put it down again. Tom watched her anxiously, afraid that she was about to slide off her chair and on to the floor. The colour had completely drained from her face and her eyes were two grey-green smudges against the pallor of her skin.

'Andie, I'm sorry.'

She looked down at the paper napkin on her lap and began folding and unfolding it without saying a word.

'Andie, sweetheart, you know I love you.'

She tore the napkin in half and then tore the strips in half again.

'Say something,' begged Tom.

'Does she know you're with me now?' asked Andie.

He shook his head.

'Where does she think you are?'

He shrugged. 'I told her I'd things to do. She didn't mind me coming out. Besides, she's still in bed. She has to take it easy, you know.'

'Because of her pregnancy,' said Andie weakly.

'I couldn't believe it when she told me,' said Tom. 'I really couldn't.'

'She told you last night.'

He nodded.

'When you were supposed to be telling her that you were leaving her.'

'I can't leave her now,' said Tom. 'You know I can't. If I walked out on her while she was pregnant she'd probably lose the baby again. And I simply can't take that risk.'

'No. I know that.' Andie pulled at a strand of her hair and twisted it tightly around her little finger.

'I can hardly believe it,' said Tom. 'I'm in a state of complete shock. I never thought there was the slightest chance—'

'I don't know why you're so shocked,' she interrupted him sharply. 'I suppose that if you've been sleeping with her at the same time as you've been sleeping with me then it was always a possibility.'

'Andie!'

'How often?' she demanded. 'How often do you make love to her after being with me?'

'Never,' said Tom.

'You mean the baby isn't yours?'

'No,' he said. 'Of course I don't mean that. It's – I don't sleep with her when I've been with you. You know I don't. I couldn't.'

'But other times, then you can.'

'We *are* married to each other,' said Tom. 'It'd be a bit odd if I didn't.'

Andie knew that. She'd always known he was sleeping with Elizabeth too. She just hadn't wanted to believe it.

'You're not supposed to love her,' Andie said. 'And if you don't love someone you don't sleep with them.'

'Oh, be realistic,' said Tom. 'There are times when . . . well, I sleep with her. I just do. It doesn't mean I love you any less.'

238

'Doesn't it?'

'Of course it doesn't.'

Andie reached for her coffee cup again. She knew that her hands were still shaking. It clattered off the saucer as she lifted it and took a sip. It tasted terrible. She pushed it away.

'Look, just because she's pregnant doesn't mean things have to change,' said Tom.

Andie knew that her laugh had a touch of hysteria to it. 'Don't you understand that I wanted things to change?' she asked him. 'That I was tired of being your – your mistress?'

'You weren't my mistress,' said Tom. 'You aren't my mistress.'

'That's exactly what I am,' said Andie. 'You're married, you're sleeping with me, I'm your mistress.'

'You're melodramatic, that's what you are. Come on, Andie, we've never gone in for drama. We're not like that.'

'Tom, a couple of days ago you told me you were leaving your wife to live with me. Now you're telling me that you can't because she's pregnant. I'm entitled to feel a bit melodramatic.'

'I understand that it's upsetting,' he said. 'I can see how it's a problem. But—'

'It's a baby!' she cried. 'That's more than a problem, Tom!' She wiped at the tears that had begun to fall. 'How can you tell me that things aren't going to change – especially if she . . . if you have a baby of your own . . . if . . .' She broke off, unable to speak any more.

'OK, I know things change from that perspective,' said Tom. 'I'm not stupid. But we don't have to change, Andie. We can continue. We love each other. I love you.' He reached out and took her hand. 'I do love you. More than anything. You know that, don't you? God, Andie, what we have together is unlike anything I've ever known. We're right together. You know we are.'

'So you want to keep seeing me?' said Andie shakily. 'You want us to carry on the way we are?'

'Why not?' he asked. 'It's worked well for us until now, hasn't it? And you often said that you were happy with the arrangement, that it gave you space for yourself. Remember the first time I suggested that it would be great to be together all the time? You weren't so sure. You said that we shouldn't rush things.'

Andie stared at his fingers, twisted round her own. She wanted to scream and shout at him for being such a stupid sap as to believe that she'd ever been happy as his occasional lover. Of course she'd told him that she liked things the way they were. To say anything else would have driven him away! Of course she'd stressed the importance of her independence – she didn't want him thinking that she fell apart when he wasn't with her. And there were times when she liked being on her own. But it wasn't what she wanted for ever, for God's sake! It wasn't what anyone wanted in the end. She couldn't believe that he didn't understand that.

'I love you, sweetheart.' His words broke into her thoughts. 'I always will. I've told you that often enough. Surely you believe me.'

'I believe you,' she said slowly. 'It's just that I'm not sure it's enough any more.'

'Why? Why, when it was before?'

'I don't know.' She stood up abruptly. 'I don't know. Things changed and I had different expectations and now you've dropped this bombshell and . . .' She gritted her teeth. 'You need to be with her now. She's the one who matters most. Not me.' Her voice rose sharply.

'Andie,' he said softly. 'You're creating a scene.'

She wanted to create a scene. She wanted to throw the cup of coffee at him, to scream and shout at him and to rage out loud about the unfairness of everything. But she wasn't that kind of person. She never had been. So she said nothing as she turned round and walked out of the café, leaving Tom staring after her.

Chapter 18

Melancholie – Grieg

S he walked up Henry Street, pushing her way through the ever-
increasing throng of people who were strolling along the pedestrian thoroughfare. She didn't bother apologising as she banged
against the Saturday-morning shoppers laden with bags but simply
strode onwards, her head down, eyes glistening with tears.

Pregnant. Of all the things that Elizabeth could have done, all
the ways to keep Tom, getting pregnant was the big winner. Andie
knew that there was no way he could leave his wife when she was
pregnant, not with her history. Not even without her history. She
bit down on her lip so hard that it began to bleed. Why now? she
cried to herself. In all the time that she and Tom had been seeing
each other there hadn't been the slightest hint that Elizabeth could
or would ever get pregnant again. Andie had pushed the thought
that Tom must, at least occasionally, be sleeping with his wife to
the back of her mind, comforted by the fact that her relationship
with him was so strong that it didn't matter if he sometimes made
love to the other woman out of a sense of duty. But she'd never
expected Elizabeth to get pregnant. It wasn't an event that she'd
ever prepared herself for.

She wiped away the tears which trickled down her face. Harsh
though it was to consider, Elizabeth might lose this baby too. And
then what? Would Tom then decide to leave her? Or would he think
that he couldn't walk out when she'd had another tragic miscarriage?
Yet he'd clearly said that he wanted things to stay the way they were.
Was that what he'd really wanted all along? Andie swallowed hard.

She didn't think so. He was always the one who'd brought up being together. She'd never pressurised him. But if Elizabeth lost the baby she knew that Tom couldn't just walk out. If she didn't lose the baby, he might not want to walk out. And in the mean time he wanted things to go on as before.

A cry caught in Andie's throat. She could have allowed things to go on as before if she hadn't let herself believe that they were going to change. But now, with the hope of Tom being permanently in her life suddenly dashed, she couldn't see how she could go back to the way things were. She just couldn't. It was one thing thinking of him going home to a loveless marriage with a depressed woman. It was quite another to think of him spending his time with a pregnant Elizabeth. And yet another to think of him and Elizabeth with a child. How could she continue to have an affair with Tom if he had a child? It wasn't fair. On any of them.

Andie turned into O'Connell Street. The red and yellow single-decker bus had just pulled up to the bus stop. She got on and sat at the back, conscious that the other passengers were looking at her curiously, aware that her face was now tear-stained and blotchy. She wondered what advice they'd give her if she suddenly stood up and asked them. Would they see her as someone who was entitled to be unhappy for the loss of her dreams and her hopes? Or would they see her as a potential home-wrecker who might have helped to make a bad situation between two people even worse? It all depended on your perspective she thought miserably as she leaned her head against the grimy window. And right now she didn't know what her perspective was any more.

Cora was feeling a million times better. Her runny nose had dried up and the redness of her eyes had abated. She'd known that she'd feel much better today because her colds were always the same, violent and sneezy at first, but then clearing up rapidly. So she'd got out of bed early, leaving Jack deep in sleep, and gone downstairs to make herself some tea and toast.

She sat in the kitchen, her soft-pink robe pulled tightly around her waist, and contemplated her spiky orange decor as she nibbled at her marmalade-laden toast. Jack had laughed at her when she picked orange and had suggested a range of neutral colours instead, but she'd told him that it was orange or nothing. She'd been a bit surprised at first by how vibrant it looked on the walls, but she was starting to get used to it so that by now she couldn't imagine the room as it had been before. Biscuit-coloured and dreary, even though the off-white colour had been very fashionable when she and Des had picked it five years earlier.

She licked the crumbs from her fingers as she remembered watching Des painting the walls, doing everything in his methodical fashion, making sure all the furniture had been moved and the floor covered in paper before he started. Sticking masking tape around the skirting boards so that he wouldn't accidentally get paint on them. Washing the brushes thoroughly each evening. Having a plan and sticking to it. Painting with Jack had been different. They'd simply opened the tin and started lashing on the paint, which had meant some bright orange spots in places that bright orange wasn't meant to be. And then, when they'd finished the work, Jack had looked at the brushes and told Cora there wasn't a hope in hell they'd ever be used again and had thrown them in the bin. Something which Cora had found wasteful, but which Jack had laughed about.

They were so different, Jack and Des. She supposed it wasn't surprising because, of course, Jack was a completely different generation and had been brought up on a different continent, not to mention in an environment which was far, far removed from anything Cora had ever experienced. Yet when she'd struck up a conversation with him on the cruise ship, initially simply to tell him how much she'd enjoyed his lecture on Mayan civilisation, she'd been astonished at how easy he was to talk to and how much she enjoyed being in his company. He was relaxed and easy-going and he'd charmed her by insisting that she join him for a drink in the Crow's Nest Bar at the top of the ship. They'd sat beside the window and looked out at the black night sky pierced with silver starlight, and talked for ages. It had been a long time since Cora had talked to someone who didn't know everything about her. And a long time since she'd had a flirty kind of conversation with an attractive man. But she hadn't expected things to go any further than the couple of drinks they'd shared. Even when Doireann, who'd spent ages looking for her because otherwise they'd miss the midnight buffet, had found them in the bar together and told Cora that they'd looked remarkably close, she never expected anything more.

Cora cleared the breakfast dishes into the sink. She knew that Doireann had been shocked at her continued friendship with Jack. At first her sister-in-law had been amused by the fact that she'd caught them having a drink together and had laughed the next day when Jack had sought them out for a game of table tennis on one of the many decks, but she hadn't entirely approved of his joining them for drinks after dinner or insisting that they come to the ballroom-dancing extravaganza later that night. Cora smiled to herself as she remembered Jack's atrocious attempts at dancing with her.

'Guess I shouldn't have cut those classes,' he remarked after he'd trodden on her toes for the umpteenth time, and she'd laughed and said that he couldn't be good at everything, at which he'd looked at her quite seriously and said that he wanted to be good for her. She'd laughed it off, but she'd been shocked at the sudden fizzing of desire within her. She'd dismissed it as the somewhat pathetic urges of a woman who should have better things to think about. In any event, she'd thought later that night, even though she'd have to be a complete loss of a woman not to find Jack attractive, he was clearly just being nice to her.

But one night, as they'd sat on deck together chatting about Jack's experiences in Mexico, he'd suddenly turned to her and confessed that he found her very desirable, and that it was a bit of a surprise to him because he had to say that she wasn't his usual sort of woman. He'd grinned at her and told her that he normally went for leggy blondes – cheerleaders, he confessed, with athletic bodies and bronzed limbs. But she was so much more interesting. And, he admitted, she listened to him without judging him. In his experience, he told her, people were dreadfully judgemental, but she wasn't, and it was very, very refreshing. Cora had been extremely flattered but had reminded herself that people said all sorts of things they didn't really mean when they were on holiday. She'd doubted he'd have found her desirable the first day she'd come on board because then she'd been in her old persona of

244

a grey-haired fifty-eighty-year-old woman who'd recently lost her husband, even if she'd begun to feel OK about using make-up and lipstick again. It had actually been Doireann who'd arranged for them to go to the beauty salon on board the following morning, where the stylist had suggested the new cut and colour for her hair and where Cora had suddenly realised that she was tired of herself as a woman who was still in mourning. She realised too that in the months since Des's death she'd thought and acted as an older woman, even though she'd never felt old before. After she'd had her hair done she'd recaptured some of the spirit she'd always had and had suddenly felt happier and more willing to get involved in things again, which was why she hadn't minded asking a question at the Mexican lecture in the first place. It had been a real boost to her ego to realise that a man who was generally agreed by everyone on board to be the handsomest thing on two legs would want to talk to her. Especially since their conversations had been unexpectedly flirty, very challenging and extremely interesting. Jack was an intriguing person who'd packed a lot into his life. But she liked the fact that he saw her as someone worth talking to. Not, as so many of her friends at home seemed to think, someone to be pitied because she was alone.

Cora poured more tea into her cup. She was still astounded at the fact that she'd allowed any sort of relationship to develop between them. She knew that a lot of people would wonder about it and she guessed that they'd draw all sorts of conclusions about them. But on the ship, she hadn't cared. Because she hadn't really expected to see him once the cruise was over.

Jack had told her that his stint on the ship was finished after this trip, and as he'd talked about going to Europe, she hadn't been able to stop herself inviting him to stay. To be honest with herself, she hadn't really expected him to accept her invitation but she'd been excited when he did. And having him here, in the house with her, was wonderful. It had been so quiet in the last nine months and now Jack had brought new life and new enthusiasm into it. Cora was enjoying his company and enjoying the physical relationship she was having with him too. Even though she couldn't quite believe that it was happening.

She was sure that all of her friends were shaking their heads and saying that no good would come of it. She knew that her daughters were horrified. She was aware that Doireann, who hadn't said a word but had dropped broad hints from time to time, was uneasy about it. She promised herself that she'd get out of the relationship before it went wrong. She wasn't naïve enough to think that she could live like this for ever. But she wanted Jack to be a good part of her life, so that, no matter what, she'd always have memories of a man who made her laugh and smile and feel positively carefree if not downright silly again, when she'd believed she'd lost those kind of feelings for ever.

Jin had been up from early morning because Kevin's flight to Oslo departed at nine o'clock. She hadn't really wanted to get up but she'd woken when Kevin's alarm had gone off and had been totally unable to get back to sleep. So she'd gone down to the kitchen while Kevin showered and had hot coffee and toast waiting for him when he'd finished.

'Thanks.' He smiled at her absently. She knew that he was in work mode again, thinking about the business meeting ahead.

'You're back tomorrow?' she said.

'Hmm.' He looked up from the sheaf of papers he'd been glancing through. 'Tomorrow afternoon.' She could see him drag himself back to the present with difficulty. 'What are you planning to do?'

'I don't know,' she said. 'Go shopping maybe.' She realised that he wasn't really listening to her, that his mind was still on his work. 'Or open a rival bar,' she added blithely. 'Maybe set up my own modelling agency. Run off with the milkman.'

'Well, you do whatever you like, darling. I'll see you tomorrow.' Kevin kissed her briefly on the lips. 'I'd better go.'

'OK.' She followed him into the hallway, where he picked up his small overnight case and carried it to the car. 'Have fun.'

He grinned at her. 'Oh, I will. It's always fun doing these things. Once you get the desired result.'

'And will you?'

'I'd better,' he said. 'Otherwise I'll think I'm losing my touch.'

She smiled and closed the door behind him before going back to

246

the kitchen and pouring herself another cup of coffee. She flicked through a copy of *Glamour* magazine as she sipped the hot drink. But neither the fashions nor the celebrity gossip held her attention. Her concentration was ragged because of the late hour at which they'd arrived home from the party. And although Kevin had fallen asleep almost immediately after their oral sex, she hadn't been able to drop off herself. She'd kept wondering what Jack was doing at the party without them, worried that leaving him behind had been an incredibly stupid thing to do. People would ask questions, wonder why he hadn't left with them, wonder exactly who he was and what the relationship between them all actually was. And then the stupid gossiping would start. Jin clenched her jaw. She liked stupid gossip, but not when it was about her family.

She cleared the breakfast things into the dishwasher and switched it on. Its gentle hum made the house seem less quiet and deserted. It was odd, she mused, how it never seemed as solidly quiet when she knew that Kevin was coming home that evening, but whenever he was away, even for a night, the atmosphere changed completely. She went upstairs and into the bedroom. She didn't really like being in the house on her own. It was too big for one person. She walked out of her room and into each of the seven bedrooms. What was the point? she wondered. Why did they have seven bedrooms? When the estate agent had shown them around he'd talked about family and friends and plenty of space for guests, but the actual fact was that they never had people to stay and they didn't have a family.

Jin winced. She didn't want to go down this road again. She'd very deliberately avoided any thoughts of family other than her mother and Andie in the last week or so. Following her sudden swamping with baby images after her visit to Livia, she'd managed to avoid any references to them more recently. Anyway, she told herself as she walked out of the brightest and sunniest bedroom (the one the estate agent – though how would he know, thought Jin scornfully, and him a twenty-odd-year-old bloke – had insisted would make a lovely nursery), there wasn't any point in having baby thoughts because there would never be any babies with Kevin.

She wondered again what had made him decide on the vasectomy. Why he was so determined never to have another child, even though, at the time, he was apparently happily married to Monica. She'd never asked him because as far as she'd been concerned it was his decision to make, but now she wanted to know why he'd made it. Because it was such a final decision. She wondered if he'd expected to stay the rest of his life with Monica, and how the other woman had felt. And now she wondered whether, despite his protestations, he wouldn't like the idea of a second family. Especially with someone he loved.

Jin went back to their own bedroom and sat on the unmade bed. You'd think that someone would *want* a child to kind of cement the relationship, she mused. In fact lots of older men said that they got more satisfaction out of their second families, that they were around more for their children, that they had more time for them. But of course Kevin wasn't at that stage in his life yet and he didn't have more time for them. He barely had enough time for her, really, what with the business meetings at all hours of the day and having to fly to bloody Oslo at the weekend.

She resented the business meetings. The realisation came to her as a shock because she usually just accepted them as an inevitable part of being married to Kevin. But quite suddenly she knew that she was fed up with him being out of the house so much and fed up with the hold that his damn company had on him and fed up about the fact that he seemed to think that bringing her to multiple business dinners was enough of a social life for her. It wasn't even the social aspect of it, she told herself as her resentment grew, it was that they never went anywhere that wasn't populated by his business friends or acquaintances. They never went anywhere as a couple just to have fun.

She stared at her reflection in the mirror opposite as a chill feeling of unease began to envelop her. They never went anywhere as a couple, he was only interested in her as someone to attend functions with him, and he didn't want to have a family with her. Her perfect white teeth nibbled at her lower lip. Was that the way things were between them? Was she really just some kind of fashion accessory to him? She'd never thought about it like this before, but now that the notion had come into her head she couldn't get rid of it.

Yet he'd been good about the Cora and Jack affair. Jin felt herself

248

relax a little as she remembered how concerned Kevin had been. Concerned enough to go and see them. Concerned enough to have them over for lunch. Concerned enough to go to the trouble of inviting them all to Andrew Comiskey's. And to arrange for a substitute escort for Cora to be there. He wouldn't do all that if he didn't love her. And of course there was their physical relationship. Kevin could still barely keep his hands off her and was always anxious that she too was enjoying it. He'd even bought her a vibrator once, smiling with pleasure as she tried it out and then taking over, telling her that the real thing would be much more satisfying. (Which, she admitted, it most certainly was.)

She sighed deeply. Everything was fine with her and Kevin. It always had been and it always would be. She was fretting because she was worried about Cora and wondering what had happened to Andie last night and generally out of sorts because things hadn't exactly gone to plan. And all these worries were manifesting themselves in a sudden and irrational belief that everything would be all right if only she had a baby.

Her eyes opened wide. If only she had a baby. She had to get rid of these crazy thoughts popping into her head! She didn't want a baby. She'd never wanted a baby. If she'd wanted a baby she never would have married Kevin in the first place. She got up from the bed and went into the shower.

She was going to go shopping. There was nothing in her life that couldn't be fixed by signing a few credit card slips. And she planned on signing lots of them today.

Chapter 19

Piano Concerto No 2 in C Minor: Adagio – Rachmaninoff

This time Tom left a message on her answering machine. Andie saw the little red light blink at her as she opened the door of the flat and let herself in. But she didn't hit the play button straight away. She took off her coat and hung it up and then filled the kettle to make a cup of tea. She didn't really want any tea but she wanted to give herself a moment before listening to Tom's message. She knew it was from him because his mobile number had appeared in the caller ID display. He'd made the call only minutes after she'd walked out of the Jervis Centre. If he'd really wanted to speak to her, she thought, he would have called her mobile first.

When the kettle boiled she made the tea and took a sip before walking over to the phone. But she still hesitated before listening to the message. Right now, until she heard his voice, she could pretend that he was calling to tell her that it had all been a mistake. A joke that had gone wrong. Or that Elizabeth had lied. She could pretend that he was really calling to say that he was coming over because he'd left Elizabeth anyway, he wasn't able to stay with her regardless of anything. She wanted to believe that but she knew she couldn't. The trouble was that Tom was intrinsically a decent bloke, even if he had been having an affair with her for the past four years, which many people would think wasn't really the action of a decent bloke at all. But he wasn't going to leave Elizabeth for her now. Maybe he never would.

Andie sniffed and wiped away another tear. Her eyes were sore and so were her cheeks from the constant rubbing she'd done since she'd heard Tom's news. She took a deep breath and pressed the button.

'Andie, Andie, I'm so, so sorry. I didn't know how else to tell you. I couldn't believe it myself. After all this time . . . and the day that I'd chosen to tell her. I asked why she didn't tell me before, when she first suspected, and she said that it was because she couldn't quite believe it herself. So she didn't want to tell me until it was confirmed. The thing is, it's still very early days. We both know that it could go wrong again. What could I do, darling? I couldn't walk out on her. I just couldn't. Oh, Andie – I love you more than anything. Than anyone. I really do. You have to believe me. I know you're feeling hurt and probably betrayed by me. But I never expected this to happen. I really didn't. I don't know what to do now. I only know that I love you. I always will. Sweetheart, I'll ring you again later. I know you're not home yet. But I had to tell you how I feel. I don't want you to think that I'm an uncaring bastard because I'm not. Really. I love you.'

She was crying again but this time she didn't bother to wipe away the tears. She let them fall in heavy drops on to the telephone below. And then she hurled her mug of tea across the room.

Cora walked into the bakery on Phillipsburg Avenue and smiled at Mary Black, who was taking a tray of freshly baked scones from the oven.

'Morning, Mary,' she said cheerfully. 'Gorgeous day, isn't it?'

'How are you, Cora?' Mary returned the smile. 'Haven't seen you in a while. You were on a cruise, I hear.'

'Yes.' Cora nodded. 'Jin and Kevin organised it. Very good of them really. The Bahamas and Mexico.'

'It's well for some.' Mary sniffed.

'Oh, come on, Mary – you know it's far from cruising round the Bahamas I was reared!' Cora chuckled. 'But it was great fun.'

'And is it true?' asked Mary.

'What?'

'That you brought back a man with you?'

'Of course it's true,' Cora told her. 'A gorgeous hunky bloke who's staying with me for a while.'

251

'Well, not that I wouldn't want a gorgeous hunky bloke myself or anything, Cora, but is that a good idea? Having him staying with you?'

Cora shrugged. 'I've really no idea. But I'm having fun with him and I feel as though I deserve a bit of fun, Mary.'

'I suppose you do,' acknowledged Mary. 'I just thought that maybe it'd be a different sort of fun.'

'Well, who knows, another year, another sort of fun.' Cora grinned wickedly at her. 'Could I have a half-dozen croissants, please. And some sausage rolls if you've got them. A few fruit scones. And one of the batch breads would be nice too.'

She waited, enjoying the aroma of warm bread which filled the shop, while the baker filled brown paper bags with her requests. The door opened again. Polly Fitzsimons and Hester Madden walked in and stopped in surprise when they saw Cora.

'Hello, stranger,' said Polly after a second or two. 'We haven't seen you in a while.'

'I know.' Cora sounded suitably contrite. 'I just haven't had time to come to the book club meetings.'

'Because of her fancy man,' said Mary. 'The young fella.'

Cora laughed. 'Well, partly,' she said. 'I was busy before I went on the cruise, and since then I've been doing a bit of home decorating. Mind you, Jack is helping me.'

'Heaven help us,' said Polly. 'You're having an affair with a bloke half your age and he's handy round the house. What more could anyone ask for?' Her tone was a mixture of admiration, envy and censure.

'An affair sounds more dramatic than it really is,' said Cora mildly.

'I've seen him,' said Hester. 'How could you *not* be having a sizzling affair with him?'

'Sizzling?' remarked Cora.

'Jesus, if I thought for a second he'd look at me . . .' Hester winked at Cora, who laughed again.

'I thought people were a bit uncomfortable about the idea of me and Jack,' she said.

'Uncomfortable maybe,' said Polly. 'But we're also mad jealous.'

252

'Really?' asked Cora.

'Ah, Cora, of course we are,' said Hester. 'Look at you – you've lost about ten years in a couple of weeks. You look great.'

'So you don't all think I'm a mad old fool?' asked Cora.

'Maybe,' said Polly. 'But if you're a mad old fool who's having a great time, then who are we to begrudge you?'

'I wish my daughters would see it like that,' said Cora as she put her purchases into her shopping bag.

'Don't they?' asked Mary.

Cora sighed. 'Jin doesn't like him because to her he's nothing but a backpacking freeloader. Andie doesn't disapprove of him quite so much but she's still not happy about it. I guess they don't begrudge me, but what they really want is to see me settled with a clone of Des.'

The other three woman looked at her sympathetically. 'He was a great man, Des,' said Polly.

'I know he was,' Cora said. 'I'll never love anyone in the same way as I loved him. How could I? He was my life. But I don't want another Des in it. I'm not sure how much I want another man in it.'

'But you've got another man in it,' protested Mary.

'It doesn't seem like that,' confessed Cora. 'Jack's like a perfect present I've been loaned. I don't know whether he'll stay for long and I don't know if I want him to. But if the girls had anything to do with it he'd be out the door in a flash.'

'They'll never see it any way than the way they want,' said Hester. 'Look, Cora, is it true that he's a writer?'

'Yes.'

'Then why the hell didn't you bring him along to the last book club meeting? Aren't we always looking for something a bit more exciting?'

Cora looked surprised. 'I never thought of it.'

'You should have,' said Polly.

'But he only writes travel books,' said Cora.

'Sure it's writing, isn't it?' asked Hester. 'Why don't we set up a night?'

'I'll have to check with him first,' said Cora. 'Actually he is

253

working on a novel, only he's no idea whether or not it'll be published.'

'There you go,' said Polly. 'Travel writer and potential novelist. Bet you anything we'll have a full house that night. Especially if he's as sizzling as Hester seems to think.'

'Well, OK, then.' Cora smiled at them. 'I'll ask him. And I'll give you a call, Polly.'

'Do absolutely.'

'Right.'

Cora was still smiling as she walked back to the house. She had to admit that she'd avoided her friends since she'd come home from the cruise, partly because she was totally immersed in life with Jack and partly because she was unsure about their reaction to him. But whether it was simple curiosity on their part or whether they were perfectly prepared to accept the possibility that she was seeing someone younger, it was nice to know that they wanted to meet him. And, she chuckled to herself, nice to know that they were even a little bit envious. It was nice to be envied instead of pitied.

Jin was in the bookshop in Malahide. She'd already visited a number of boutiques and was laden down with exclusive carrier bags. She'd gone into the bookshop to see if she could find anything light and frivolous to read that evening. She intended to spend some time luxuriating in her jacuzzi and she wanted something frothy to keep her amused. She'd picked up a few and read the blurbs – they were all about girls looking for Mr Right but encountering Mr Wrong first. She wondered, as she skimmed through a brightly jacketed volume, whether or not Mr Right would stay Mr Right after the story had ended. After all, she thought, you could put 'the end' at the bottom of a page but how did you know that it really was the end? How did you know that just because the two love birds were finally together they'd actually stay that way?

What is the matter with me? she asked herself in sudden annoyance. Why am I being so gloomy? She kept the book in her hand as she moved through the shop and then stopped in front of the health section. Maybe I'm just a bit down, she thought, as she gazed at the titles telling her how to improve her outlook on life. Although

I don't know why I should be down. Everything in my life is exactly right. She picked up some hard-cover manuals about being happy and healthy but replaced them on the shelves. And then she picked up the mother and baby book that had caught her eye earlier but which she'd studiously ignored until now.

Why were they always so cute? she wondered, as she looked at the pictures of the babies. Why were their eyes so huge in their perfect little faces? Why were their expressions so beguiling? Why did they all appear so cuddly? She stared at the picture of the woman breast-feeding a child, her long blonde hair falling across her face, her expression one of complete serenity. And that's not right, thought Jin harshly, because everyone says that breast-feeding can be difficult and Saskia Barrett told me that it bloody well hurt.

'Hello, Jin!'

She whirled around at the sound of Áine O'Brien's voice.

'Oh, hi, Áine.'

'*Being With Baby*?' Áine looked at her enquiringly. 'Is there something you've got to tell me, Jin?'

'What? Oh, no.' Jin closed the book hastily. 'No, I was just looking at it.'

'Thinking about another little Dixon?' asked Áine wickedly. 'Must be about time. After all, you've been married four years and you're not getting any younger.'

'That's nonsense,' said Jin.

'Still, it's always a good ploy,' Áine told her. 'Keeps them on the straight and narrow.'

'Not from what I've been told,' returned Jin waspishly. 'It didn't help Kathy Jones, did it? Or Deirdre Summers. Or Sonia O'Neill.'

'Or even good old Monica,' agreed Áine. 'Who, I believe, turned down the invitation to Andrew Comiskey's bash last night on the basis that you'd be there.'

'Did she?' Jin frowned. 'Kevin never said anything about her being invited. Though I don't suppose he'd know.'

'Probably not,' said Áine. 'But isn't it nice to know that the ex knows her place?'

'I bet her nose is seriously out of joint.' Jin smiled faintly. 'After all, she's *the* charity woman this year.'

'And she's the mother of the children,' added Áine. 'Unless you're really going to change all that.'

Jin shook her head again. 'A friend of mine is pregnant,' she told Áine as she turned the book over and over in her hands. 'I wanted to be supportive.'

'You can be supportive without reading the books,' Áine said.

'I like to know that my support is grounded in fact,' said Jin. She smiled jerkily at the other woman and marched towards the till with the frothy novel and the mother and baby book still in her hands. She paid for them both and walked quickly towards the marina where she'd parked her car. Bloody hell, she thought, as she activated the remote, of all the people to bump into when reading a book about babies, Áine O'Brien is the one I'd've put bottom of the list. She'll start gossiping about it, I know she will. And next thing I know all sorts of people will be asking me if it's true and – God above! – someone will probably ask Kevin about it too. She groaned. It was stupid to have picked up the book in a Malahide shop anyway. She was well known in the town and even if Áine hadn't seen her someone else undoubtedly would. And she still didn't know what it was that kept making her think about babies anyway. She stood by the Mercedes and gazed across the estuary. She'd never wanted kids because of what they did to your body, and that hadn't changed one little bit. She was going through some ridiculous broody stage, clearly triggered by Livia's undoubted joy at her own pregnancy. She and Livia had always been friendly rivals in the modelling world. Maybe she was a little put out because Livia had had a change of view about the pregnancy thing. Maybe she simply felt as though she was being left behind. But being left behind was precisely what she wanted as far as this particular issue was concerned. And being left behind was what would happen. Because it was impossible for Kevin and her to have a baby together. So the sooner she put all these stupid thoughts out of her head for ever, the better.

Jack was re-grouting the bathroom tiles when Cora got back. She walked up the stairs and caught her breath at the sight of him in a sleeveless T-shirt and jeans. He could have passed for a male model in the Diet Coke or Levi's ads, she thought. And for some

256

extraordinary reason he was in her house, staying with her, telling her that he cared about her. She wondered how long the fantasy would last.

'Hi there,' she said. 'Fancy a cuppa?'

'I love the way you say that.' He turned and smiled at her. 'A cuppa sounds great.'

'You should know that all men doing work around the house insist on copious cups of tea,' Cora told him. 'Anything to delay the inevitable process of getting back to work.'

'I've only just started this,' he confessed. 'I slept for ages. You should have woken me earlier.'

'I thought about it,' Cora told him. 'But you looked so cute lying there with your hair mussed up and everything that I hadn't the heart.'

'Gee, thanks.' Jack laughed. He put his arm round her shoulders. 'You're too good to me.'

'I know,' said Cora. 'You finish up what you're doing while I put the kettle on.'

She'd just made the tea when Jack came downstairs.

'Oh, lovely,' he said. 'Scones and croissants. You know the way to a guy's heart.'

'Years of experience,' she said wryly.

'I've got years of experience of dealing with women,' Jack told her. 'But I still mess it up.'

'Do you?' She pushed the teapot over to him so that he could fill his own cup.

'You know I do.'

'Maybe we never get any sense,' she remarked.

'Maybe not. But who cares?'

'I met some of my friends today,' said Cora.

Jack glanced at her and then held her gaze. 'And?'

Was this the time to have a serious conversation with him? wondered Cora. Was now the moment to start asking the difficult questions about how much longer they had together? Was it time to confront their past and present lives and start talking about the future?

'They want to meet you.' It wasn't the time, she decided. She wasn't ready to give it all up yet. She simply wanted to have a good time with him, and that was still happening.

'Why?' asked Jack.

'Because you're a writer.' She explained about the book club and how she hadn't been since she'd come back from the cruise. 'We've never had a real-life writer talk to us before,' she told him. 'It'd be interesting.'

'Especially since they'll all be looking at you and wondering what it is about me that keeps such a good-looking woman with me.'

Cora laughed. 'You say the nicest things sometimes. Clearly you're a massive topic of conversation. Our book club would be like entering a lions' den. A dozen menopausal women and you. Could you possibly cope?'

'I can do my best.'

'Really?'

'Why not?' He smiled at her. 'I'm a bit pathetic like that, I actually enjoy talking about my books and the places I've been. I'd love to come.'

'Great,' said Cora. 'I'll phone Polly and she'll set it up.'

'So now I get to meet your friends,' he said mischievously. 'I wonder if I'll be as much of a smash hit with them as with your daughters.'

'Was it a bit of a nightmare last night?' she asked him. 'Did they try to "talk" to you?'

He nodded. 'Andie did it,' he told her. 'She said how worried they were. Apparently Kevin bought a selection of the travel guides and because my name wasn't on them they decided I was a total fraud.'

Cora made a face at him. 'Did you explain it all?'

'Not everything,' said Jack. 'But it wasn't the time or the place for meaning-of-life conversations, as you can imagine. I felt a bit sorry for Andie, who was doing her best to be nice to me while telling me I was a complete shit.'

'Jack!'

'Actually, Cora, she's sweet. She played the piano and we sang songs.'

Cora looked at him in astonishment. 'Andie did? In public?'

'Yes,' said Jack. 'I had to persuade her, of course, but she's really very good.'

'I know,' said Cora. 'But she never performs in public, Jack. Never.'

'Why?' asked Jack.

Cora explained that Andie had been burned in a tricky relationship with a fellow musician a few years earlier. She'd been crazy about him, she told Jack. And then they'd both auditioned for a place on an orchestral tour. Michael hadn't told Andie that he was going to the audition even though he knew that she'd been called too. He'd got it. She didn't. They'd split up. And she'd stopped performing in public.

'Well, she did last night,' said Jack.

'You can charm us like birds from the trees, can't you?' Cora was unexpectedly waspish.

He stared at her and she wondered if she was going to have a serious conversation with him after all.

'Andie played because I insisted on singing,' Jack told her.

'And Jin?' asked Cora. 'Where was Jin when this was happening?'

'She was moving and shaking with the rest of the loaded people,' said Jack. 'She's good at that.'

'That's true,' said Cora. 'She always wanted the lifestyle.'

'Really?'

Cora nodded.

'Is she happy?' asked Jack. 'I mean, they seemed to be last night, but you never can tell, can you?'

'He gives her everything she wants, which makes her happy.' Cora frowned. 'Jin was never very good at spartan living. Des was made redundant for a time when the girls were young . . .' She paused. 'We weren't poor or anything, but it was a sticky patch. Jin hated being told she couldn't have things that the other kids did. Besides, her tastes were always expensive. Andie never minded chain-store clothes but Jin used to save up her pocket money for the designer labels.'

Jack nodded. 'Well she's with the right man in that case.'

'He does love her,' said Cora, 'and she likes it to be shown by

259

constant gifts! Mind you, he gives himself everything he wants too, as you saw when we went to the house for lunch.'

Jack laughed. 'Billiards room and all! I thought he might offer to play so's he could whip my ass that day. But maybe he thinks I lead such a dissipated life that billiards would be too easy for me.'

Cora laughed. 'He's OK beneath it all,' she said.

'He also wanted to know my intentions towards you.'

'How old fashioned.'

'Cora, I'm living in your home. I've taken them all by surprise. They're worried,' continued Jack. 'They don't know why I'm with you and they're afraid I'm going to hurt you. There may well be other issues but they're the main ones.'

'Well, look . . .' She gazed at him with her vibrant green eyes. 'This is not the usual run-of-the-mill relationship, is it? For loads of reasons. It's not surprising that they're concerned about it and it's not surprising that they don't trust either of us.'

'I can understand why you might not entirely trust me, Cora, but I swear to you that I'll never do anything to hurt you.'

'I'm not expecting you to,' said Cora dismissively.

'You going to hurt me instead?'

She grinned. 'I doubt that somehow. I think you're a lot stronger than you pretend, Jack.'

'I got into the habit of trying to be vulnerable,' he told her. 'It seemed like the thing to do.'

This time she laughed, her eyes dancing with amusement.

'But your girls think that you're the vulnerable one,' he said. 'And they're right to think that way, Cora. I admire them for it even though I think they're completely crazy.'

Cora looked down at the cluster of engagement, wedding and eternity rings on her left hand. Then she looked up at him again. 'Of course I'm vulnerable,' she said. 'I was a wreck after Des died. You've changed all that, Jack, and regardless of why we're together or what's happened between us or whether or not you leave sooner rather than later, I'll always be happy about it.'

'I'm not planning to leave that soon,' said Jack.

'So you'll keep an old woman happy for a bit longer,' she teased.

260

'I keep telling you that you don't seem like an older woman to me.'

'You know, it's not that I feel old particularly,' mused Cora. 'I mean, I know I'm older in age but inside – it's true what they say about that. I don't feel all that different to when I was in my twenties and thirties. Of course then I probably wouldn't have thought much of a gorgeous bloke being snapped up by a woman twenty-five years older than him. I'd have thought she should've left him for me.'

'I wish you wouldn't keep telling me I'm gorgeous,' said Jack.

'Well, you are,' she said prosaically. 'No point in not admitting it. That's what has them all in a tizzy too. It'd probably be a different story if you were incredibly ugly. Then they'd think I was about right for you.'

'Oh, Cora.' He smiled at her. 'You're so – refreshing.'

'For a while,' she said. 'But maybe not for ever.'

'Do you always look on the down side?' he asked.

'No,' she said. 'Though sometimes you have to.' But she smiled at him as she popped her jam-smothered scone into her mouth.

261

Chapter 20

Etude in E Major (So Deep the Night) – Chopin

A ndie felt as though she was in a trance. After she'd flung the mug of tea across the room and seen it explode into pieces of bright yellow crockery she'd watched unwaveringly as the huge brown stain dribbled slowly down her pale green wall. She'd looked at the rivulets of tea sliding towards the skirting board, rolling over the edge of the wood and then finally dripping on to the silver-grey carpet, but she hadn't moved to do anything about it. It was as though the things that were happening in the real world weren't really connected to what was going on in her mind. She could observe events but they weren't able to touch her; she didn't care about the broken mug or the tea-stained wall and floor. None of these things were important any more.

She walked unsteadily to the sofa and sat down, pulling her legs up close to her body and wrapping her arms around them so that she could rest her chin on her knees. She hugged herself tightly as she slowly rocked backwards and forwards, wondering if she could ever quite deal with the pain she felt.

It wouldn't have mattered so much, she thought achingly, if Tom hadn't tried to move things to a new level. If he hadn't taken her to lunch in Ely Place and spoken of his utter misery with Elizabeth. If he hadn't made the decision to leave Elizabeth and told Andie of that decision. She'd been – if not happy about how things were before, at least accepting of it. She'd often told herself that she'd embarked on her relationship with Tom with her eyes wide open and that she'd always known that it would never come to anything.

And she'd grown used to that idea, built her life around it so that nothing about it could hurt her. But now, with all of her deepest, most innermost hopes suddenly raised and dashed again, now she felt as though she was in a black hole of despair from which she could never emerge.

She'd spent so much time in the last few days imagining what it would be like living with Tom, thinking that it would be such a short time until they'd finally be together, that she couldn't quite accept now that it wasn't going to happen any time soon. And the worst part of it all was that there was a tiny piece of her which acknowledged that if Elizabeth had felt the same kind of pain about the loss of her unborn children as she was feeling now, then it wasn't surprising that she'd spent the last few years in the deepest depression, because at this point Andie herself didn't know how she would ever be able to step outside the door again.

Tom was her soul-mate. What they'd had wasn't some brief and torrid affair. They'd connected on a much deeper level. She instinctively knew how he'd feel about anything before they discussed it. They often bought each other the same book as a gift, both thinking that the other would enjoy it. They even finished each other's sentences, for God's sake, and not stupid, silly sentences; complex, philosophical ones. They fitted together. She knew they did. She'd never felt so much a part of another person before. And now it was all over. Because she couldn't go back to the way they were. She just couldn't.

In the past she'd wondered whether Tom had had the same connection with Elizabeth as he had with her. He'd said that he'd loved Elizabeth dearly, had been attracted by her fragile beauty and gentle nature. He'd wanted to protect and nurture her, only, of course, he hadn't been able to because when it came to the miscarriages there was simply nothing he could do. He'd felt useless then, he'd told her. Useless and unnecessary and – more than that – somehow at fault because he was the one getting her pregnant and so he was to blame for the depths of pain she felt. And that, Tom had said to Andie one day as they sat on this self-same sofa together, was what had driven him and Elizabeth apart. He couldn't bear the fact that he'd been responsible for her grief. And she couldn't bear the fact that she hadn't been able to carry his children. Andie had replied that it was nobody's fault. He shouldn't blame himself. He shouldn't blame Elizabeth. Then he'd leaned against her and told her that since meeting her he'd been able to lose some of the burden of guilt and grief, and that he would always love her for that.

She shivered. Did he still love her? Now that Elizabeth was pregnant again, pregnant for the first time since she and Tom had begun their affair, did he still love her or had his affections shifted back to his wife? Did he want to protect and nurture Elizabeth all over again? Andie couldn't remember exactly what he'd said over coffee earlier that day. She knew that he'd talked about things between them staying the same, but how the hell could they with Elizabeth getting more and more pregnant with every passing second? How could he walk out, come to Andie's apartment, make love to her and go back to a pregnant Elizabeth? Maybe some men could do it, but surely not Tom.

The phone rang but she ignored it. She'd switched off the answering machine so the strident tone shrilled around the room for almost a minute before it eventually stopped. Then Andie got up and yanked the connection from the wall before going into the bedroom, pulling back the covers and climbing, fully clothed, into bed.

She drifted in and out of consciousness all day. Then, at eleven that night, she woke up with a jump, suddenly more alert than she'd been in the previous twelve hours. Her misery hadn't abated, her head ached and her whole body trembled. She was hot now because she'd left the heating on and the bedroom was like a sauna. She got out of the bed and stripped off her clothes, pulling on her candy-striped pyjamas again instead. Then she shuffled into the living room. She closed the curtains and switched on the standard lamp. She looked at the answering machine and frowned before remembering that she'd disconnected the phone. She stood immobile in the middle of the room, arms wrapped round her body, as though she didn't really know why she was there. Then she sat down at the piano and began to play.

She played her favourite composers, Chopin and Rachmaninoff

and Beethoven, concentrating on their gloomiest pieces, her mood reflected in the sombre music. And then she moved on to Holst and the more fiery Planet Suite, because she was suddenly angry. At herself. At Tom. At Elizabeth. When the last notes of Mars had died away, she allowed her fingers to glide aimlessly up and down the keys before finally settling into Bach's Toccata and Fugue in D Minor, the heavy march that she'd played at her father's funeral. She was in the last bars of the piece when the knock came on the door and she stopped, mid-phrase, in surprise.

Tom, she thought wildly and joyfully. He's come for me after all. And she allowed the lid of the piano to fall down with a thud before rushing to unlock the door and let him in.

Only of course it wasn't Tom, because she'd have had to buzz Tom into the block. It was Dominic Lyster, dressed in a sleeveless black top and a pair of leggings, his hair ruffled and his eyes gritty.

'Dominic.' She stared at him.

'Andie.'

'What's the matter?'

He looked at her, taking in her blotchy face and red-rimmed eyes. 'Are you OK?' he asked.

She didn't answer.

'Andie, it's two o'clock in the morning. I know I said that I didn't mind your music, that I actually quite liked it. But some kind of death march being played in the early hours is simply more than I can take.'

'I'm sorry,' she said tonelessly. 'I didn't realise.'

'Andie.' He reached out and put his hands on her shoulders. She recoiled. 'Andie,' he repeated gently. 'What's happened?' His eyes hardened. 'Has someone . . . did that bloke . . . have you been hurt?'

Through the mist that seemed to surround her Andie got the meaning of Dominic's words. She realised that he thought that Tom had hurt her physically. That, perhaps, he'd actually assaulted her. As if, she thought painfully, as if Tom would ever do something like that.

'I'm fine.' Her voice seemed to belong to someone else. Her tongue was huge in her mouth, unable to properly make the sounds.

But the words seemed to be OK. 'I'm all right. I'm sorry about the music.'

'Andie, I'm sorry too. You don't look OK to me.'

She shook her head. 'I am.'

'Is there anything I can do?'

Somewhere deep, deep inside her, she saw a thin thread of humour in the situation. She was standing in her pyjamas at two in the morning and her male neighbour was asking if he could help. On the cinema screen, she thought, this would be the cue for a romance. She could suddenly discover that Dominic was the man she'd really wanted, that Tom was nothing after all. And she could go up to Dominic's flat and they could make love and they'd live together happily ever after . . .

'Dominic?' The woman's voice was sleepy. Andie heard footsteps on the stairway and then saw her, an attractive girl in an oversized blue T-shirt. She almost laughed. Even now, she thought, even now she couldn't get it right, because Dominic had someone else too and there was no one for her, not in real life and not in some stupid fantasy life that she thought she could make work. She was a stupid, silly woman who really hadn't a clue. Just like Jin always said. It was simply that she'd never thought her sister could ever be right about it before.

'I'm sorry about the music,' she said again. 'I'll go to bed now.' She stepped back inside the apartment and closed the door firmly behind her. And then she went back to bed.

It was on Wednesday morning that the buzzer sounded, firm and insistent, dragging her back to the outside world. Dominic had knocked on the door on Sunday – she hadn't answered and he'd called out, asking her if everything was all right. So she'd shouted that everything was fine, there was no need for him to be concerned and would he just leave her alone. Then she'd curled up on the sofa again and watched Sky News for hours and hours so that she practically knew all the reports by heart. She kept telling herself that violence and hunger and deprivation in other parts of the world were much more important than how she felt, but it wasn't enough to make her feel any better. If anything, it made her feel worse.

266

When she heard the buzzer she was nibbling at a slice of dry toast. She hadn't eaten anything since Saturday – though she'd felt hungry she simply hadn't the willpower to eat. Besides there was hardly anything in the house because she hadn't bothered to go shopping. She'd planned to do it with Tom in a flurry of domesticity the previous weekend. But that morning she'd suddenly felt as though she could actually swallow food and she'd put on the toast even though she really wasn't enjoying it very much. She'd got dressed too, although all she'd done was to pull on an old T-shirt and a pair of jogging pants. She'd splashed water on her face and sprayed perfume on her neck but she hadn't done it with any degree of enthusiasm. And she hadn't bothered to brush her hair.

The buzzer sounded again. Her heart was thudding in her chest. Was it Tom this time? she wondered. The encounter with Dominic seemed like something that had happened in a dream, but she remembered the jolt of expectation she'd felt, the spurt of hope that the person knocking on the door was Tom. She didn't want to feel that again only to have it extinguished. Yet she couldn't help hoping. She hadn't wanted to talk to him on the phone, which was why she'd disconnected it and why she'd left her mobile switched off too. She hadn't quite known what she wanted.

She didn't use the speaker but simply hit the unlock button for the hall door. Then she squirted toothpaste on to a brush and ran it over her teeth until the knock came on the door of her flat, firm and impatient.

'Andie.'

She recognised the voice straight away. Hard not to: the distinctive American accent, the questioning inflexion at the end of the sentence.

'Andie, open the door.'

She walked slowly over to it and opened it. Jack Ferguson looked at her, his expression a mixture of anger and concern. 'What the hell is going on?' he asked.

She shrugged and he pushed past her into the apartment. He looked around, taking in the pieces of broken mug on the floor, the open bedroom door with its unmade bed, and Andie, pale-faced, still with red-rimmed eyes and wearing an old T-shirt.

267

'What's the matter?' he asked.

'Why are you here?'

'Why do you think?' He looked at her. 'You didn't go into work yesterday or Monday, Andie. The Academy phoned Cora. They were surprised you hadn't called. They tried your phone but couldn't get through. And they could only get your mail-box on your mobile. They thought something might be wrong. And Cora was worried. So I said I'd call round.'

'Nothing's wrong,' she said impatiently. 'I'm taking some time off.'

'Usually you tell your employers when you're taking time off,' said Jack.

'As if you'd know,' she returned. 'Given that you don't seem to work at all.'

'Come on, Andie,' said Jack. 'It's fortunate that I can be flexible enough in my work so that if the daughter of a woman I care deeply about doesn't answer her phone and doesn't turn up for work herself, at least I can check it out. Your mother is worried sick. She was afraid something had happened to you.'

'Why do people expect the worst if you do something a little bit unexpected?' demanded Andie. 'I don't know why Ma is getting her knickers in a twist. Surely you're enough of a distraction.'

'Andie!' Jack's tone was very angry. 'That's a horrible thing to say.'

'No it's not,' said Andie. 'You can say all you like, you can butter me up at Jin's flashy dinners, but bottom line is you have all sorts of ridiculous notions about Ma and none of them is right, 'cos you're not right for her and she's being a silly middle-aged woman.'

Jack ignored Andie and walked over to her telephone, which he replugged into the wall. Then he phoned Cora and told her that Andie had obviously caught a version of her cold, only much worse. She was on the mend now, he said, and sorry she hadn't been in touch. She was annoyed at the Academy for ringing Cora's number and worrying her. Jack said all this in a such cool and calm way that Andie almost believed it herself. Having reassured Cora a little more, he hung up and turned to face her again.

'Is this something to do with the married man?' he asked.

'It's none of your business,' she told him.

'It *is* my business,' he said. 'If you're unhappy and you're somehow going to upset Cora – then it is my business.'

'No,' she snapped. 'It's not. If I've messed up my life it's entirely my own concern and absolutely nothing to do with you. And I don't care what you think your relationship with my mother is, it doesn't give you the right to quiz me about my personal life!'

'I only want to help,' he said.

'Really.' She was glad she'd found her voice again. The last few days, only having called a few words through the closed door to Dominic, she'd begun to think that perhaps she'd forgotten how to speak at all. 'Well I don't want you to help me.'

'Maybe you need me to help you.'

'St Jack.' Her tone was scathing. 'I'll come and stay in your mother's house and sort out your lives while making a fool out of you all.'

'Oh don't be so bloody silly,' said Jack. He ran his fingers through his jet-black hair and looked at her in exasperation. 'Tell me what's happened. I promise not to try and help.'

'You don't need to know,' said Andie.

'Fine,' said Jack. 'Tell me anyway.'

She didn't want to talk to him but she wanted to talk. She rubbed her face with her hands.

'Come on,' said Jack. 'I'll make some coffee. Or tea if you prefer.'

'Coffee.' She slumped on to the sofa. 'Coffee is fine.'

He filled the kettle and spooned instant coffee into cups. While he waited for the water to heat, he picked up the pieces of the broken yellow mug and threw them into the wastebin under the sink. There was nothing he could do about the tea-stained wall or carpet.

'Here.' He handed her a cup. 'Tell me about it.'

'He was supposed to leave his wife,' said Andie. 'On Friday night.'

'When we were at the dinner?' Jack raised an eyebrow. 'Interesting timing.'

'I hadn't intended being at the dinner. Jin – Jin persuaded me.'

She shivered again at the flash of understanding in his eyes. 'He was to meet me back here.'

'I see,' said Jack. 'And what happened?'

Andie told him, in short, jerking sentences, about Elizabeth's pregnancy and Tom's decision to stay with her. And of his desire to have things the way they'd always been but her inability to accept that.

'Poor Andie.' Jack's navy-blue eyes softened and his voice was suddenly sympathetic.

'Not poor Andie,' she said fiercely. 'Nobody will think like that, Jack. You know they won't. It's always been poor Elizabeth. You know quite well that anybody who found out about Tom and me would be thinking of me as some hard-hearted bitch who was trying to rob a depressed woman of her husband.' She sniffed. 'And they'd be right. I shouldn't have got involved with him. I was the person in the wrong. I know that. But I couldn't help it.'

'It takes two,' said Jack mildly.

'Oh, don't give me that,' she cried. 'Just don't. Tom was vulnerable too. And deeply unhappy. I shouldn't have encouraged him.'

'Easy to say that now.'

'I should have left him to work things out whatever way he could with Elizabeth. Nearly four years!' She looked at Jack sadly. 'Nearly four years of my life and I would have kept going like that. I really would. Because I loved him and I felt sorry for her. Then he raised the stakes and now I don't know where we stand any more. And you know what – part of what really pisses me off about it is that he was having sex with her.'

Jack's look was still sympathetic.

'I mean, I knew he must be occasionally. But I could sort of pretend that he wasn't, which was pretty pathetic really. But now she's pregnant and I can't pretend, can I?'

'I guess not.'

'We were so right together.' She pushed her bedraggled hair behind her ears. 'We really were. We fitted. We had fun. I loved him. I still love him.' She started to cry again.

'And has he called you?' asked Jack.

'You're here because I disconnected everything so no one could call me,' she pointed out. 'He did phone on Saturday after I'd left him. But I didn't want to talk to him on the phone.'

'And what do you want now?' asked Jack.

She closed her eyes. 'I don't know.'

'Because if he wants to keep seeing you – even though that's not what you really want any more – will you decide that it's better than nothing?'

'I don't know,' she said again.

'I'm sorry,' he said. 'Really I am.'

She opened her eyes. 'You see, I don't have any right to be unhappy,' she told him. 'I'm the home-wrecker. She's the wife.'

'Of course you have the right to be unhappy,' said Jack. 'You thought you were in something that had a future.'

'I should never have thought like that.'

'Yeah, well, if we all thought the right things all the time the world would be a much duller place,' said Jack feelingly.

'I could cope with dull right now.' Andie sniffed.

'Come on.' Jack put his arm round her shoulders. 'You'll be all right.'

'Don't give me that time being a great healer bullshit,' she said.

'I won't.'

'Because it isn't.'

'No?' His blue eyes locked on hers, and he gave her the Tom Cruise smile. So that almost before she knew what she was doing, Andie leaned forward and kissed him.

He didn't pull away immediately. That was her first thought. He didn't pull away and maybe that meant that he found her attractive. Why shouldn't he find her attractive? Why shouldn't any man? And Jack had been good to her on Friday night. He'd sung songs while she played the piano, and danced with her (well, sort of), and he hadn't thrown a complete fit when she'd told him that neither she nor Jin thought he was a suitable companion for their mother.

Cora! Andie sprang back from Jack as though she'd suddenly received an electric shock. Jack was Cora's boyfriend. Her mother's boyfriend. Her mother's lover. Oh God, she thought wildly as

271

she stared at him, I've kissed my mother's lover. She turned away from him and fled into the bathroom, locking the door behind her.

By the time she came out again, Jack had gone.

Chapter 21

Bagatelle in A Minor (Für Elise) – Beethoven

Jin had hardly spoken to Kevin since he'd come back from Oslo on Sunday night. He'd spent the last few days in myriad meetings with his closest colleagues until finally, on Wednesday evening, he'd arrived home with a bottle of champagne and called out to her that it was celebration time.

She hadn't expected him home so early and she'd been in the jacuzzi listening to Mariah Carey, the water fizzing and bubbling around her. So when she walked into the kitchen as he popped the bottle of champagne she was wearing her white towelling robe and her copper hair fell in damp tendrils around her face, which was pink from the heat of the water.

Kevin grinned at her and kissed her hard on the mouth, his hand sliding beneath the fold of her robe, cupping her breast. 'Definitely celebration,' he said huskily.

'You think?'

'Without a doubt.' He pushed the robe from her shoulders so that she was naked in front of him. She stood straight, shoulders back so that her body looked long and lean, her breasts as pert as possible. Jin felt that there had been a noticeable sagging of her second-best assets (her legs, she felt, were definitely premium quality) over the past year or so, but Kevin had never said anything. And he wasn't saying anything now either. Instead, he dabbed champagne across her body and began to kiss it from her, his lips moving from breast to belly and down the insides of her legs. She moaned softly. He was so good at this, good at giving pleasure and good at taking it.

273

It was true, she thought, that the most successful people had skills and stamina in all areas of their lives.

She leaned back so that he could enter her and held him tight as he moved within her. And then, as he climaxed, her mind was suddenly filled with the type of images she'd seen so often on TV documentaries, tiny sperm swimming like crazy to be the first one to reach her eggs. Only, of course, in Kevin's case there weren't any tiny sperm. There weren't any sperm at all. And it wasn't because of anything wrong with him, it was because he'd chosen not to allow them to flood her body. He'd denied them access to her eggs. He didn't want to give her children.

She shuddered. She couldn't believe the direction her thoughts had taken. She was scared that she'd never be able to make love to Kevin again without thinking of him as a flawed sperm provider. She didn't know how to blank out the images and make things the way they were before. She wanted things to be the way they were before, when she was so certain of herself and of Kevin and of how much they loved each other. She still loved Kevin. She would always love him. Mad swimming sperm or no mad swimming sperm.

'The worst part of being away is not having you there,' he said later as they sat side by side in the chill-out room.

'You say the nicest things.' Her smile was forced.

'It's true,' he told her. 'At night I go to my hotel room and I miss knowing you're around.'

Suddenly she wondered if he ever had other women in his hotel rooms to ease the loneliness. Golden-haired girls like Ivor McDermott's Adrienne. Girls to give him the kind of pleasure he wanted. And maybe even needed. Jin tensed. If Kevin regarded having sex as simply a wonderful experience, why would he want to have it only with her? Why not with other women who moved in a different way or reacted in a different way? Why should it be an exclusive thing between them? If they were making love with the prospect of a child being a possible result, then that meant something else, didn't it? But making love, having sex, doing what they were doing for no other reason than physical pleasure – well, did it really mean anything after all? And if that was the case, did it really matter to Kevin whether it was her he was doing it with or someone else?

'Huh?' She looked up at him, not having heard his last words.

'You were in a daze,' he said.

'Sorry.' She shrugged her shoulders slightly. 'Lethargy set in.'

He laughed. 'As long as you're not lethargic beforehand! Anyway, I was just saying that Cian and I are playing in that father and son golf outing soon, so I'm going out to practise with him next week.'

'OK,' said Jin.

'He needs to think about his drive more,' explained Kevin. 'He just stands on the tee and thwacks it, hoping that brawn will overcome everything else. But you need to think a bit too.'

'Is he your favourite?' she asked suddenly.

'Huh?' Kevin looked at her in surprise.

'Of your children. Do you have a favourite?'

'No,' said Kevin.

'Do you really love them both exactly the same?'

'Why are you asking this?'

Jin shrugged. She rarely spoke to Kevin about his children because it was a part of his life that he kept separate from her. Besides, though they were usually polite on the rare occasions she met them, she knew that they didn't like her very much. She supposed that Monica had filled them with tales of her being Daddy's stupid trophy wife. Even though she'd never thought of herself that way, except, briefly, at the beginning of their marriage, when he used to introduce her so proudly to everyone while she struck a model's pose beside him, decked in designer clothes and lots of jewellery. Back then she'd sometimes thought that she was nothing more than an ornament, but Kevin had assured her that she wasn't. That she was gorgeous, attractive, desirable and great, great fun. She'd wanted him to mention that she was intelligent too, but he never did. But, she told herself, he knew that she was intelligent. He just didn't like her demonstrating it in front of him.

'They're two very different people.' Kevin answered her question. 'I love them equally but differently. That's the way it is with parents and kids, I suppose.'

'Perhaps we could have them over to dinner sometime?' suggested Jin.

'Here?' Kevin looked at her in astonishment. 'With us? Why?'

275

'Why not?'

'You'd be bored,' he told her. 'So would I. They're only kids, Jin, despite the fact that Clarissa dresses like a twenty-year-old and Cian swaggers round the place in that irritating macho way.'

'Cian's hardly a kid,' Jin pointed out. 'He's a young adult.'

'Well, I'm certainly not having them over to dinner,' said Kevin. 'It'd be a nightmare. You'd hate it.'

'Maybe I'd have fun.'

Kevin shook his head. 'Trust me. Only parents love their children.'

Jin stared at him in frustration. Why did he think that it would be such a bad idea for her to get to know Cian and Clarissa a bit better now? It might have been different when they were younger but surely they were old enough to accept her as part of his life? She wasn't asking to usurp Monica in any way, just to be acknowledged by them. Surely that wasn't so unreasonable?

'But—'

'Trust me,' Kevin interrupted her. 'We have a perfect set-up the way it is. Introducing those two into it would be a disaster.' He looked at his watch. 'I have to phone Bar Tender.'

'Why?'

'I need to talk to Tom about something.'

'How is Tom?' Jin knew that there was no point in pursuing the conversation about Cian and Clarissa. Kevin's mind was made up and he wouldn't change it unless he wanted to. Clearly, he didn't.

'Tom's fine,' said Kevin, who disliked talking about his children with Jin. They belonged to another part of his life. The responsible, drearier part. Not that he didn't care about them and want good things for them. Only he wanted to enjoy his life with his gorgeous wife more.

'And his wife?' asked Jin. 'The doll-like woman.' Who, she remembered suddenly, kept losing babies. She squeezed her eyes shut, desperately trying to block out the images of fat, bouncing babies with snub noses and chubby cheeks.

'Elizabeth's not too bad,' Kevin told her. 'They've been through a really tough time and, of course, Tom dealt with it so much better than her because he had another outlet, I suppose.'

'Other outlet?' Jin looked at him quizzically. 'What sort of other outlet? A woman?'

'Work, you dope,' said Kevin. 'Tom is devoted to Elizabeth. They went through a sticky patch after she lost the last baby and I was worried that they might not get through it, but they seem to have coped.'

'How did you feel?' asked Jin.

'Huh?'

'When Monica told you she was pregnant. How did you feel?'

'Amazed,' Kevin replied shortly. 'She was supposed to be on the pill.'

'Oh.'

'I didn't think it was a particularly good time, everything was breaking for me in the business sense, I was totally committed to what we were doing and I thought it would be unfair on the child.'

'But when Cian was born you must have changed your mind?'

He made a face. 'Well, of course when they put the baby in your arms and he's all red and wrinkled it's such a powerful thing . . . but people forget that kids are individuals. They want them for their own purposes.'

'Like what?' Jin looked at him curiously.

'Lots of men think of them as part of the dynasty,' he said. 'You know, proving you can do it and someone to pass things on to. I've never really felt like that. It wasn't important to me. I do what I do for my own satisfaction, not to pass it on to someone else.'

'But you will, won't you?' asked Jin. 'You'll leave everything to Cian and Clarissa.'

'Why are we having this morbid conversation?' asked Kevin. 'I hate talking about this sort of stuff and I thought you did too.'

Jin shrugged dismissively. 'I just wondered. No reason.'

'I don't wonder about things any more,' said Kevin. 'Except where the next deal is coming from.' He picked up the champagne bottle. It was almost empty. He poured the last drops into his glass and raised it to her. 'And I do wonder how it was I was so lucky to find someone like you.'

She smiled and drained the remainder of her champagne too.

277

Jack Ferguson sat in front of his laptop, staring at the screensaver, which was running looping whirls of acrobatic colours. He hadn't typed in anything from the pages of scribbled notes beside him, even though he'd been looking forward to the section he'd called 'Pub Crawling in Dublin'. In his efforts to bring the authentic Irish drinking experience to his readers he'd visited almost fifty different bars and had culled the list down to ten. Which was probably a lot to visit when pub crawling was just one of the Twenty Things To Do. He wondered how many people would manage to drink in more than two bars – he'd been a bit bleary after four himself. He was astonished that so many Irish people seemed to think that lowering pint after pint of beer was a matter of national pride – particularly if you went and did it all again in another bar down the road the exact same night.

Nor was he sure that he liked the typical authentic Irish bar of bare floorboards and dusty bottles on wooden shelves. According to Cora there were plenty of bars like this dotted round the country but not so many in the capital city any more, though he'd managed to find a few. And he'd concluded that maybe the dusty bar was something that fitted better into a rural setting but he personally preferred a modern, air-conditioned environment where he could sit down and read his paper and even order a coffee if he wanted without feeling out of place. Though, he mused, maybe that was his Californian experiences coming through. At the opposite end of the scale completely was the bar he'd last visited – the very high-tech glass and chrome Bar Tender, which had wall-to-wall TVs showing a variety of different stations as well as occasionally zooming in on the people in the bar itself. He'd wondered whether he'd meet Kevin Dixon there, but there was no sign of Cora's son-in-law either behind the bar or wandering around. Jack supposed that Kevin didn't really spend much time in the bars and restaurants he owned, and he didn't really think that a night in Bar Tender would be Kevin's idea of fun either. The average age of the drinkers seemed to him to barely hover around the legal drinking limit, but he had to admit that the place was jam-packed with very desirable women, even though it made him feel extremely old when he wondered if they weren't freezing in the barely-there clothes they seemed to favour.

He laughed shortly. Feeling old. That was an irony. Jack Ferguson, the man who was currently living with a woman twenty-five years his senior. He should never feel old. Right now, of course, he wasn't exactly sure what he was really feeling. He stared at the swirling colours on the screen again and thought about Andie Corcoran. Cora's daughter. A woman the same age as him and a woman who'd pulled him towards her and kissed him passionately on the lips a few hours earlier. If he closed his eyes he could still remember the feel of her mouth on his and the subtle scent of the floral perfume she'd been wearing. She'd looked awful, he thought, with her hair all over the place and her red eyes. But she'd tasted lovely. And her hot, hot body had trembled beside him as she kissed him so that it was all he could do not to slide his hands under her flimsy T-shirt and pull her closer to him.

Only she'd broken away from him and looked at him in shock and horror before hurtling into the bathroom. He'd waited in the flat for a couple of minutes, hoping that she'd come out so that he could talk to her. But she hadn't and he hadn't trusted himself to say the right thing. So he'd simply walked out and back to Cora's house in Marino. He'd reassured Cora that Andie was fine but just a little under the weather and then he'd come up to the guest room, telling her that he really had to work. Only, of course, work had been almost impossible.

'You OK up there?' Cora's voice floated up the stairs. He blinked and hit a key at random. The screensaver dissolved and the desktop appeared again.

'Nearly finished,' he called.

'Would you like coffee?' she asked.

'No. I'll be down shortly. I'll make us something to eat.'

'Whatever,' said Cora.

He double-clicked on the travel book icon and opened the piece he'd been working on. He stared at the screen in front of him, aware that he had no idea what he'd written earlier and no chance of making sense of it because he couldn't think of anything other than Cora and Andie.

279

He should have dealt with the situation better. He should be dealing with it now. He knew that he had choices to make and the time had surely come to make them and not faff around in front of his computer. He didn't know what he should do, what direction to take. What was the right thing to do. His therapist had always told him that he was essentially good despite his habit of doing the wrong thing, but then he'd spent a fortune on that damned therapist talking through his so-called issues, so what else was the man going to say? That he was irredeemably evil? That he was a disgrace to humanity? Anyway, talking through it all hadn't really made any difference in the end. He was still the same person he'd always been. And he wasn't sure that he liked himself any better now than he had before either. He wasn't sure he liked himself at all.

Chapter 22

Piano Concerto No 21 in C Major (Elvira Madigan) – Mozart

Andie's newest pupil was a solemn, dark-haired girl of ten who was barely tall enough to reach the pedals of the piano. But Andie knew that the brown-eyed Ella O'Hanlon was hugely talented and she'd looked forward to the lesson, glad that the day was a busy one because it meant that she could immerse herself in the music and not have to think about anything else. Since she hadn't been to work earlier in the week she'd missed Ella's last couple of lessons, and as she listened to the child's fingers dancing up and down the keyboard, sliding in and out of the various scales and arpeggios that she was practising, Andie felt very guilty. The little girl deserved a teacher who was there when she was supposed to be. She'd been thoughtless and selfish to lock herself away in her misery. If nothing else, Jack Ferguson's visit had made her realise that. She clamped down very firmly on the thought of Jack Ferguson and concentrated instead on her pupil. It cheered her up to know that in an age where most ten-year-olds wanted to be the next Britney or Kylie or Posh, there were some who still enjoyed a different kind of music. And as the thought popped into her head she made a face at herself and realised that was why Jin thought she'd end up as a dry old spinster. Because she was somehow outside the loop of what the modern world was all about. Yet what did Jin know? Andie asked silently. Nothing at all. Nothing about her and nothing about her life and nothing about the music that she really liked. Because (and despite the fact that she actually thought the beat to 'Hit Me Baby One More Time' was great) there was nothing quite as beautiful as a piece of classical music, perfectly interpreted. And she didn't care if that made her a bit of a misfit. She hoped, though, that as Ella grew up, she wouldn't feel a misfit either. She didn't think so. Andie was pretty sure that Ella had the opportunity of a good career ahead of her. If there'd been such a thing as *Piano Idol*, she guessed Ella would've won it hands down.

'*Andante*,' she reminded the little girl as she rattled too quickly through the Mozart piece she was playing. And Ella adjusted the pace exactly right, which made Andie nod in approval. Sometimes in her lessons she would be super-critical, picking over the student's work mercilessly, and occasionally reducing both of them to frustrated silence. But today she was content to let Ella play and simply to listen, to enjoy the composition and to let it soothe her.

'You've put in a lot of practice,' she told the little girl at the end of the lesson. 'And I'm very pleased with you.'

The button eyes gleamed in satisfaction. 'Thank you.'

'What else do you like to do?' she asked Ella.

The child frowned.

'When you're not playing the piano?'

'Red Faction,' said Ella.

'Huh?'

'On my PlayStation,' Ella explained. 'It's a game.'

'Oh.' Andie grimaced. 'I'm not very good at computer games.'

'You should be,' said Ella. 'It's all about speed and accuracy.'

Andie grinned. 'You also have to figure out what's going on. I can never discover what I'm actually supposed to do.'

'Blow up everything,' said Ella solemnly. 'It works most of the time.'

'Lovely.' But Andie laughed.

'Do you have a PlayStation?' asked Ella.

'No,' said Andie.

'A computer?'

'Nope.' Andie realised that her student was making her feel like a complete techno-phobe. She hoped the girl wouldn't ask if she owned a DVD. She did – Jin and Kevin had given her one for Christmas the previous year – but she still hadn't managed to figure it out. She'd never got past the stage of being able to either see the

282

picture or hear the soundtrack, but not simultaneously. Tom had offered to look at it for her but she'd always shaken her head and told him not to bother, she'd deal with it herself one day. She'd never wanted to waste her time with Tom by spending it plugging and unplugging the DVD.

'How do you get e-mail if you don't have a computer?' asked Ella.

'Well, I don't have an e-mail address,' said Andie. 'Although,' she added hastily, seeing the look of complete horror on Ella's face, 'we do have a computer with e-mail here at the Academy. So if you ever want to send me an e-mail you can.'

Ella looked at her pityingly. 'It's hardly the same thing. And of course you can't surf the net or anything.'

'You're right,' said Andie apologetically.

'The web is great for music,' said Ella. 'You can find out all sorts of stuff. You can download it and everything . . .' She looked hesitantly at Andie. 'I don't suppose you have an MP3 player.'

'Um, no.'

'It's going to be my job to teach you!' declared Ella.

Andie laughed. 'I think you'll have a lot harder job than I'm having with you,' she confessed. 'But I'll tell you what, I'll go to an internet café before our next lesson.'

Ella grinned at her. 'That's Monday afternoon.'

'I'll go before then,' promised Andie.

'OK.'

Andie looked at her watch. 'Come on,' she said. 'Let's go downstairs and see if your mother is waiting.'

Mrs O'Hanlon was already in the reception area. Ella skipped across the black and white tiled floor and hugged her.

'She's great,' said Andie in response to the woman's questioning look. 'And not only that, she's going to teach me how to use a computer some day. And possibly something called Red Faction.'

Sharon O'Hanlon smiled. 'She's been trying to teach me how to play that game for months. But I usually end up dead in the first level.'

'Oh, but you're hopeless!' exclaimed Ella. 'I bet Andie would be much better.'

'And I wouldn't put money on it,' said Andie. 'I'll see you Monday, Ella.'

'Don't forget to go to the internet café,' warned her pupil.

'I won't.'

She waved as mother and daughter walked out of the building and then walked over to the reception desk. Theresa Mannion looked up from the list of classes she was scanning through.

'Can I check if there are any e-mails for me?' asked Andie.

Theresa looked surprised. 'You never check.'

'I know,' said Andie. 'Not that there are many people who know my address here. Including me, to be honest. But I thought it would be a good idea to look.'

Theresa logged on to the computer and smiled at Andie. 'You've two,' she said.

'Really?'

Theresa nodded. 'Both from Kajsa.'

'Hell.' Andie wrinkled her nose. Her friend, Kajsa, a violinist, was currently on tour and had warned her to check for e-mails. 'When did she send them?'

'A month ago and two weeks ago,' said Theresa.

'Shit,' said Andie. 'I suppose she'll be thinking I don't care enough to reply. Can you print them off for me?'

'Sure,' Theresa said. 'D'you want to reply to them now?'

Andie shook her head. 'I've another lesson in fifteen minutes,' she told Theresa. 'I'd better read through what Kajsa's saying first.' She looked enquiringly at the young receptionist. 'Is there an internet café anywhere near here?'

'I'm not sure.' Theresa closed her eyes as she thought. 'But I bet there's more than one if you look. Try South William Street. Or Dawson Street.' She leaned towards the printer then handed the e-mails to Andie. 'You've got to get with the computer age a bit more, girl.'

'Oh, I know.' Andie sighed. 'I've got to get with everything a bit more.'

She read through Kajsa's e-mails before her next lesson, smiling at her friend's descriptions of skulduggery in the orchestra. Apparently the leader, a bloke named Cameron Morgan, was getting on everyone's nerves, and one of the flautists was having a messy affair with the conductor. Another hotbed of sex and vice, she thought. Maybe it's as well I never joined an orchestra. After all, I don't need to be travelling with other musicians to get into a personal life crisis, do I? I've managed it perfectly well on my own. She touched her lips with the tips of her fingers. She was astonished that Jack Ferguson's name wasn't somehow tattooed across them, a signal of her complete and utter disregard for any kind of appropriate behaviour. Early on in her relationship with Tom Hall she'd felt the same way about him. As though her face should somehow show the mark of her wrongdoing.

What is the matter with me? she wondered as she stood in her room and waited for Mia Moriarty to show up. Why the hell can't I have relationships like a normal person? She pulled at her hair, rewrapping the purple scrunchy around her loose pony tail. After all, she told herself, she'd conducted an affair for almost four years with a bloke whose wife was mentally unstable and then, as that crumbled into disaster, she'd thrown herself at the bloke who was sleeping with her mother. These were not the actions of a rational woman. They just weren't. And her face flamed again with the embarrassment of the kiss between herself and Jack. She'd stayed in the bathroom even after she'd heard the door of the flat close behind him, too shocked by her own behaviour to move. She'd half expected a phone call from him or from Cora later that evening but the phone had remained silent. And now, a couple of days later, she still hadn't heard from either of them. She didn't know what to do. It would be impossible to call around to Cora if Jack hadn't said anything, but equally impossible if he had. Andie felt sure that he'd kept silent, because she couldn't image her mother not contacting her otherwise. But perhaps Cora was too disgusted or too broken-hearted to call. Maybe, thought Andie, her heart leaping suddenly, maybe Jack had told her and they'd had a massive row and she'd thrown him out, only she wasn't ready to tell them about it yet.

Andie rubbed her eyes. She was dizzy with the permutations of it all and exhausted by her own inability to keep her mind on anything for more than about ten seconds. Anything except music, she thought with relief as Mia walked in and began one of Beethoven's piano sonatas. At least she always had that.

As she listened to Jack talk to the women in her book club about his travel experiences, Cora wondered whether it had been a good idea to let him loose among her friends. She could see Patricia Mahoney eyeing him up speculatively and could almost hear the cogs in the other woman's brain turning. Patricia was the glamorous one in the group. She was the flirtatious one too, the one who always preached the 'use it or lose it' gospel. Patricia had gone straight on to HRT the moment she'd experienced her first hot flush and dismissed any potential health worries by telling them that she wasn't going to have wrinkles when she didn't have to. Then, when a few wrinkles did appear, she'd immediately treated herself to what she described as a 'minor procedure' around the eyes. Cora had to admit that Patricia's minor procedure had worked very well, because the other woman didn't have the stretched and surprised look that gave away so many face-lifts. No, thought Cora, Patricia looked at least twenty years younger than the fifty-five she admitted to, and today she could probably shave another couple off that too. As she watched, Patricia elegantly recrossed her legs and ran her fingers through her shoulder-length golden hair. Unlike Cora, she'd never allowed it to go grey.

Would Jack find her attractive? wondered Cora. Would he be taken in by the shining tresses and the carefully made-up face and the casual combination of designer jeans and Lainey Keogh knitted top that Patricia wore to its best advantage? Would he fall for her seductive smile and undoubtedly sexy laugh?

Cora was startled to realise that she felt jealous. When they'd first arrived she'd basked in a superior glow as she saw the stunned expressions on the other women's faces. They couldn't believe that this handsome hunk was living with her. She noticed them suddenly standing a bit straighter and opening their eyes a little wider and she realised that they were reacting to Jack's looks and to his charm. (And, she mused, as she listened to his easy banter with the book club, he was very, very charming!)

Would he be attracted by someone like Patricia? She nibbled at her lower lip. She'd expect him to be tempted by a roomful of twenty-somethings, but if he found Patricia more desirable than her . . . yet why wouldn't he? Wasn't Patricia a million times better looking? Surely as he looked around them all he'd notice Patricia, while Cora herself would just merge into the crowd?

Stop it, she told herself sternly. Stop allowing yourself to feel this way. This was never what your relationship with Jack was all about!

He finished his talk and the women broke into groups. Cora watched as Patricia corralled him in a corner of the room. Of course, she remembered, Patricia had gone on holiday to Mexico a couple of years previously. She was probably giving him the benefit of her wide experience of Aztec culture. And then, quite possibly, inviting him to dinner. She sighed. She hadn't had these kind of thoughts since she was fifteen and had watched Veronica Keegan try to nab Paddy Brady from in front of her nose!

'Poor Jack.' Hester stood beside Cora. 'He'll need all of his experience to get out of that!'

Cora smiled at her friend. 'I was rather thinking something similar myself.'

'He's quite amazing, Cora.'

'I'd forgotten,' said Cora. 'It's astonishing how quickly someone becomes familiar. But seeing him with her . . .'

'She's impossible,' said Hester. 'I do feel sorry for her, of course, it couldn't have been much fun when her marriage broke up and I'm sure that bringing up the kids on her own wasn't easy, even if they were in their teens at the time. But she does so throw herself at men!'

'Why shouldn't she?' Cora asked wryly. 'She's clearly on a mission to find someone else.'

'Well she shouldn't try to muscle in on other people's territory,' said Hester staunchly.

Cora giggled. 'He's not mine, Hester.'

'Could've fooled me.'

'It's not long term.'

'Why not?'

Cora glanced at Jack. He was looking seriously at Patricia, nodding in agreement at whatever point she was making.

287

'Oh, Hester,' she said. 'He's young and free and single. And I'm too old for him.'

'Don't say that.' Hester shoved her in the ribs. 'Bringing him here, seeing you with him – it's given loads of us such a lift! If you can do it, Cora, why can't we?'

'In your case, because you're married,' Cora responded in amusement.

'Oh, I know,' said Hester. 'But it makes you think that perhaps men don't only have eyes for long tanned limbs and pierced belly buttons.'

They laughed together and Cora felt some of her gloom lift. Especially as Jack suddenly nodded at Patricia and left her in the corner while he made his way over to where the two women were standing. He kissed Cora lightly on the cheek.

'I don't want to rush you,' he said, 'but we're going out for dinner tonight.'

'Lucky you,' said Hester. 'I'm cooking for the whole family.'

'Jack's a great cook,' said Cora.

'You must lend him to me.' Hester winked at her. 'I'm sure I'd find a good use for him.' She smiled at Jack. 'It was nice to see you. Thanks for coming along today.'

'I enjoyed it,' said Jack.

'Hester, I'll make it to the next meeting,' Cora promised. 'I'm sorry I missed the last ones.'

'I don't blame you one bit,' said Hester. 'Curling up with a good book is all very well, but sometimes there are nicer things to curl up with.'

Jack laughed loudly and Cora smiled.

'I do like your friends,' he said as they walked back to the house. 'Though that Patricia woman was a bit of a tough nut.'

'You think?'

'Scary,' said Jack. 'She reminded me of the blonde one in *Sex and the City*. I thought she was eyeing me up for a quick romp.'

'I'm sure she was,' said Cora. 'Patricia's our love'em and leave'em member. Guess how old she is?'

'I've no idea,' said Jack. 'I couldn't see past the face-lift.'

'Jack!' Cora looked at him in surprise. 'Nobody ever knows about the face-lift.'

'I lived in California,' he reminded her. 'I know everything there is to know about cosmetic surgery.' He hugged her. 'And I prefer the natural look myself.'

'You're too sweet,' she said drily.

'I know.' He lapsed into silence and Cora glanced sideways at him. Despite the banter she knew there was something wrong. There had been for the past couple of days. That was why she had been so worried when she saw him with Patricia. She sighed. I'm too old for this, she thought suddenly. Too old to get tied up in knots about my feelings.

'What's the matter?' she asked abruptly.

He turned to her. 'What d'you mean?'

'You've been moping about the place for the last few days. Something's wrong. I thought maybe you were just nervous about the talk today, but it's more than that, isn't it? Have you had enough? Are you ready to go home?'

'It's not that,' said Jack.

'What, then?'

'I want to talk to you about it,' he admitted. 'But not just yet.'

'Why?'

'I need to sort out my own head first,' he told her. 'I haven't quite managed to.'

'Is that therapist-speak again?'

'Probably.'

'I'll get over it, you know.'

'What?'

'If you're ready to move on,' she said. 'Jack, I've had a great few weeks. I really have. You've made me feel like a completely different woman. But I knew it wouldn't last for ever. If today's the day, just tell me. I can live with that but I can't live with you being moody and depressed because you want to leave but don't know how to tell me.'

'I don't want to leave,' said Jack.

'But there's still something wrong?'

'Yes.'

'And it's to do with me? Or us.'

'No,' said Jack. 'It's more to do with me, actually.'

'Have they said something else?' Cora was suddenly angry. 'My two interfering daughters? Have they said something to upset you or annoy you or provoke you?'

Jack was silent.

'Because I'll bloody well kill them,' snapped Cora. 'I'm tired of my whole family thinking they know better than me about my own life. What do they know anyway? Andie's a hopeless case and Jin only loves Kevin for his money!'

'Cora!' Jack looked at her in surprise.

'Maybe that's a bit harsh.' Cora paused at the garden gate. 'I know she loves him, but she'd never have given him a second thought if he hadn't been well off. Andie spends her whole life wrapped up in dead musicians and either having no relationships at all or clearly having them with totally unsuitable people otherwise I'd know about them. Yet these are the girls who have the nerve to offer me advice! Huh!'

Jack smiled at her. He couldn't help it.

'If I've cheered you up I suppose that's something,' said Cora as she felt around the bottom of her bag for her key.

'You cheer me up all the time,' said Jack. 'That's the thing.'

'Come on then.' Cora suddenly felt happier. 'We can talk serious later. Let's go inside and do some very unserious sorts of things.'

Jin sat at the kitchen table and spread the glossy pages out in front of her. They were particulars of houses which had been sent out to her by an estate agency, and all of them were supposed to meet her demands of being an older house, preferably with sea views. Some were in Malahide, some in Howth and some in Sutton. She'd decided to stick to an area of the city she knew, even though the idea of something worth renovating along the canal was still enticing. But it wasn't really where she wanted to live. She liked it here and most of her friends, except Livia, lived within a five-mile radius. It would be crazy to move too far. Besides, town houses didn't have the same appeal as ones with gardens that swept down to the sea. The right house in the right location would help her to feel more settled, she thought. She'd never really felt comfortable in Briarlawns. It wasn't her. It really wasn't. She looked again at the photograph of a detached white house at the bottom of Howth Hill and thought that it was much more her kind of property. Sure, things might not be as modern as they had now, but that could be changed. And she'd enjoy changing it. Besides, it only had five bedrooms instead of seven. For the past few weeks, every time she'd walked past the empty bedrooms, Jin had felt a spurt of anger at the wasted space. OK, they didn't really need five bedrooms either but maybe one of them would have to become Kevin's billiards room because, looking at the house plans, she wasn't sure that they could put the table anywhere downstairs. Would it be too heavy to go upstairs? she wondered. She seemed to remember it had been a job to get it into the house at all.

She put the six brochures in order of preference. The house at the bottom of the hill; the house halfway up the hill (which would definitely end up more expensive because of the views, but which wasn't half as nice to look at); the detached dormer bungalow on the coast road ('bungalow' didn't do justice to its size, though, Jin knew); the old terraced house in Malahide – nice but maybe a bit too much in the centre of the town for her; and the two newer houses a little way outside the town which she really didn't think she was interested in but which might be worth looking at just to give her some ideas about Briarlawns.

She got up and poured herself a glass of filtered water. She hadn't said anything to Kevin about moving house. He wouldn't be crazy about the idea, she knew; he liked it here, liked the modern conveniences and the security system and everything else they had. He didn't really see his house as a home, just as somewhere to live. He had a better feel for the ambience of a bar than the ambience of a house. This house didn't feel like anything, thought Jin. It never really had.

She heard the sound of the vacuum cleaner come closer and realised that Lara had finished cleaning upstairs. Jin left the brochures on the table and walked past Lara, who was working in the hallway. She smiled absently at the Romanian woman, climbed the stairs slowly and went into the third guest bedroom. She opened the bedside locker and took out the book.

It was ridiculous to feel guilty about looking at a book, she thought. Stupid to feel a surge of nerves, as though if someone caught her reading it there would be trouble. It was her house, her book. She could read what she liked. Only she had yet to decide what possible purpose there was in devouring pages of a book about pregnancy and childbirth every day. Because that was what she was doing. Ever since she'd bought the damn book (and that was totally accidental and only because of Áine O'Brien's presence in the shop) she'd read a chapter every day. Actually she'd read the entire thing the afternoon she'd brought it home and then had shoved it in the guest-room locker where there was no chance of Kevin finding it. Then, the next morning, she'd had the urge to read it again and she'd tiptoed upstairs and sat down on the bed and read the chapter entitled 'Preparing for Pregnancy' over and over again. The next day she'd read 'Your Body Changes' and every day after that she'd read a chapter, not letting herself go any further, simply committing what she'd already read to memory.

Last night, as Kevin had reached for her and she'd turned towards him, she hadn't been able to rid her mind of images of his snipped tubes. She pictured the sperm wanting to break free, to do what they were supposed to do. She imagined what it was like for them when they found the way blocked. She wondered if it were possible that they would, over time, realise the problem and work to resolve it. If that was the reason that vasectomies sometimes didn't work – because the will of the sperm was so great that it forced the tubes to re-join. She knew, as she was thinking all these things, that she was being incredibly silly, but she couldn't help herself. And it wasn't until Kevin had rolled off her and muttered that she didn't seem to be with it and was anything the matter that she'd realised that the whole experience of lovemaking had completely passed her by and that he could really have been snoring away beside her for all the difference she felt.

She'd have to be more pro-active tonight, she thought, if she didn't want Kevin to start asking questions about why she wasn't responding to him like she normally did. The trouble was, she was finding it difficult to care. If sex between them had no real purpose, then what was the point in all the moaning and groaning? She knew that there had seemed to be a point to it before but she really wasn't sure what it was any more. Yes, there was the whole thing about love and pleasure and all that, but surely, at some stage, there was more to it than that? She turned the page and looked at the picture of the foetus sucking its thumb. It was a picture that seemed to be used the world over. And she wondered if she had sucked her thumb like that too.

'I want a baby.' She said the words out loud. 'I want a baby. I need a baby. I have to do something about it.'

She sat staring at the picture in front of her until she realised that Lara had switched off the vacuum cleaner and gone home. Then she reluctantly closed the book and put it back in the locker while she wondered what she should heat up for Kevin's dinner and whether she should start changing her diet. If she was ever going to get pregnant she'd need to be in tip-top shape. And somehow, someday, she knew it would happen. However she managed it. So there was no harm in getting ready in plenty of time.

Chapter 23

Carmina Burana: O Fortuna – Orff

There was an internet café in Exchequer Street. Andie pushed open the glass door and sat down at one of the terminals. She'd never used the café before but Theresa had told her what to do and so, after a couple of false starts, she managed to open the e-mail program and started writing a reply to Kajsa. She apologised for not having written until now and then asked for an update on the romantic and sexual conquests of the orchestra, as well as some info on how the tour itself was going. She thought for a while before giving her friend a brief history of Cora and Jack. She wrote about the party at Andrew Comiskey's and Jin's insistence on how she, Andie, could break up the relationship between her mother and her younger lover. She described how terrible she'd felt talking to Jack and how difficult the whole thing was. She didn't say anything about kissing him. To do that she would have had to explain why he'd come to the flat in the first place and she would have had to tell Kajsa about the break-up of her relationship with Tom. Despite being her closest friend, Kajsa didn't know anything about Tom either.

Andie reread the e-mail before she sent it, happy that it gave Kajsa an idea of what was going on in her life without telling her too much. Although, she thought as she pressed the 'send' button, Kajsa would never have criticised her about Tom. Kajsa would've been understanding and supportive because she was that kind of person. But Andie hadn't wanted her friend's support. She hadn't felt she needed it. Much as she sometimes had ached to talk about him, she didn't need to. And she always felt better for knowing that nobody else knew about them.

But now someone else did. Jack Ferguson. Her mother's lover. The man she'd thrown herself at for no good reason other than she'd wanted to kiss someone. That was what getting upset and talking things through did for you, Andie raged silently. You ended up blurting out things to the most unsuitable person and then, for whatever insane reason, you did the stupidest, craziest thing ever, like kissing them.

It wasn't as though she was particularly attracted to him, she told herself firmly. Yes, he was gorgeous. Yes, he was desirable. Yes, he made Colin Firth in *Pride and Prejudice* look like a sorry excuse for a sex symbol. But she didn't fancy him. She really didn't. She'd just wanted to kiss someone and he was available. He shouldn't have been, of course. He should have pushed her away before her lips had ever touched his. And the fact that he hadn't meant that he was the shallow bastard that Jin had always suspected. And yet . . . she touched her lips with the tip of her fingers as she'd done so many times since she'd kissed him . . . and yet she'd liked kissing him. She stared blankly at the screen in front of her as she re-lived it again. She'd known, even as she moved towards him, that she was going to like it, because she'd known that it was something she'd wanted for ages. Since the night of that terrible party, in fact, when he'd been so sweet and nice to her and sung songs while she played the piano in front of people she didn't even know. She hadn't been able to do that ever since she'd lost out on her place with the touring orchestra, but with Jack it had been different. She'd been confident and he'd given her that confidence, and for that alone she wanted to kiss him. And because he was so damn gorgeous and kissable anyway. Even though he was her mother's lover. Even though she was in love with someone else.

She closed her eyes and groaned softly. She was a horrible, horrible person. She was in love with a married man whose wife was precariously pregnant and she'd kissed her mother's boyfriend too. What sort of person did those things? Clearly, she told herself, she had the morals of an alley cat. Otherwise she'd have walked away from Tom and walked away from Jack and she wouldn't be sitting here with her head a torrent of conflicting thoughts and emotions. She bit her thumbnail furiously. Because of her piano-playing her nails were always short, but in the last few days they'd become even shorter because she couldn't stop biting them in fits of nervous tension. Every time she thought of Tom or of Jack she'd chew a nail or worry at her cuticles so that her fingers were a mess. Just like the rest of me, she reflected unhappily. I don't know what I'm doing with my life. And I hate myself.

A pop-up ad appeared on the screen in front of her and jolted her back to the present. She frowned suddenly, realising that she was sitting in front of a tool that might help her to find out more about Jack. Kevin hadn't turned up much, but then maybe Kevin hadn't tried very hard. Or maybe he'd gone about it the wrong way. She opened the Google page, which Theresa had shown her, and typed Jack's name into the search box.

There were loads of Jack Ferguson references. Andie was astonished to see how many there were. There were Jack Ferguson professors in a variety of different universities; a Jack Ferguson motor mechanic; two Jack Ferguson vets; Jack Ferguson, trombone player (she'd never heard of him); J. Randall (Jack) Ferguson the owner of some kind of US conglomerate; and still more. Andie knew that there wasn't any point in trawling through at least ten pages of Jack Fergusons. But she decided to try the next page and found a reference to the Charmed Cruises Caribbean schedule which promised nightly entertainment and lectures from the well-known traveller Jack Ferguson. If he was that well known, thought Andie sourly as she clicked on the link, he'd have a website himself.

She'd hoped that there'd be more information on Jack, but there was very little. There was also a link to the Twenty Things travel guides, but the only reference to Jack there was under contributors, along with at least another dozen names. He'd said, hadn't he, that he'd written under other names as well. Maybe she could find out something that way. And maybe his choice of pen-name was female. She tapped at the keys and typed in the name of Amy Smith. Like the Jack Ferguson search, there were plenty of Amy Smiths. But none who matched up as a contributor to travel guides. Andie made a face and typed again.

The Todd Hunters were more arty, she realised. There were three musicians, two sculptors and a Todd Hunter who specialised in body art. And then she saw the link that made her giggle – Executive Escorts: Willis Graham, Chet Broderick, Todd Hunter, Pierce Bogdanovich . . . and many others. Andie felt she was being cheap and tacky by wanting to look at a page about Executive Escorts, but she couldn't help herself. And besides, she justified it mentally, maybe Todd Hunter might give her a Jack Ferguson link.

The page, when it appeared on her browser, was coloured gunmetal and red. Executive Escorts provided a service to women who needed an escort for a function of any description. According to the home page, escorts could be hired who would accompany a woman to a business dinner, or meet her at the office to dissuade unwanted attention from colleagues; escorts would go to the theatre with women, or the movies or the opera. Just about anywhere, Andie chuckled. And it was lucrative for the escorts too. A range of set fees plus all expenses and meals. She remembered Jack Ferguson's comment to her on the night of the party, that paying for a companion was somehow more upfront than being with someone and pretending to care about them. She wondered whether he was right.

She clicked on the link to the Todd Hunter character. And then stared in shock at the black and white photo on the screen. Because there was absolutely no doubt in her mind that the man leaning against a pillar, wearing an open shirt and loose jeans and staring moodily at the camera, was Jack.

Jin had decided to bring the subject up casually. She wasn't going to make a big deal of anything and lead Kevin into thinking that she was totally obsessed when really she wasn't, but she'd decided that it was something they needed to talk about. He was due home early that evening, she knew, because he'd told her to make dinner. He never bothered with food if he was going to be late.

She drove to the deli and ordered a beef bourguignon, which she knew he liked, and she found the bottle of pinot noir Andie had brought to lunch a few weeks earlier. She shuddered as she remembered the lunch; such a difficult day, she thought. And we're really no further on despite everything. Cora is still letting Jack sleep in her house and none of the things we've tried has split them up. Jin sighed as she slid the bourguignon into the oven to heat. Maybe all their efforts had only made Jack even more determined. Perhaps he thought that since they disliked him so much there was an even greater reason to stay – although she had no idea what it might be.

Jin sat at the kitchen table and rested her chin on her hands. She'd phoned her mother earlier in the day but she hadn't been in, and then, when Cora had called back later because Jin had left a message, she'd sounded positively drunk. Jin had asked where they'd been and Cora had giggled about being at some lunch with Jack and that it had all been great fun, and no, sorry, she couldn't come shopping with Jin one day next week, she and Jack were actually going away for a couple of days.

'Where?' Jin had demanded, and Cora replied that they were heading off to Dromoland Castle.

'What!' The castle was one of the most exclusive places to stay in the country and Jin couldn't believe that Cora was paying for Jack to go there. It wasn't the sort of place her mother could afford to go and Jack clearly didn't have any cash himself.

'They're doing some really good offers,' Cora informed her when Jin had asked if it wasn't a bit extravagant. 'You're not the only one who wants to get pampered when you go away, you know. And you're not the only one who can afford it.'

Jin had stared at the receiver in shock. Cora was never usually so abrupt with her. That man's damn influence is getting worse with every passing day, she thought grimly as she hung up.

She heard Kevin's key in the front door and walked out into the hallway to greet him.

'You're looking lovely this evening,' he said, noticing how her slinky jade dress with its plunging neckline slid over the curves of her body. 'Are we going out?'

She shook her head. 'I felt like doing something nice for dinner,' she told him. 'So I thought I'd dress the part.'

'I love it when you do things like this.' He slipped his arm

298

around her and pulled her close to him. 'What are you wearing underneath?'

'You'll have to find that out.' She smiled at him.

'Before or after dinner?'

'Both?' she suggested.

His fingers pushed at the hemline of her dress, moving slowly up to the top of her thigh. They slid slowly towards the front of her body and stopped when they reached a small triangle of material. 'Green thong,' he guessed. 'Silk. Pear at the top.'

She laughed. 'Guess you'd better check to see if you're right.'

'I'm right.' He laughed too. 'I'm always right.'

They made love on the sweeping staircase, Kevin's eyes tightly closed, Jin's open, watching him. Then she closed her eyes too because she wanted to get caught up in the pleasure of what they were doing and she knew that she wouldn't if she was watching him and thinking of him being a non-provider of sperm. She didn't want to think of that part of it, not now. At this moment all she wanted was for him to love her.

'I don't know if many men are welcomed home by their wives like this,' he said afterwards. 'I doubt it, though, because if they were there wouldn't be any marital problems in this country whatsoever.'

'I'm glad you liked it.' She smiled at him, a coy, childish expression on her face, and he laughed before kissing her on the lips and telling her that she was one in a million.

'One in two million,' she corrected him. 'Because food is next on the agenda.'

He went into the dining room and she followed him in a few moments later with two plates of steaming bourguignon and the bottle of wine.

'Excellent.' Kevin rubbed his hands together. 'One of my favourite meals and . . .' he picked up the wine bottle and looked at it, 'one of my favourite wines. I didn't think I had any of this left in the cellar.'

'You didn't,' said Jin. 'Andie brought it.'

'Andie? Was she here earlier?'

Jin shook her head. 'When she came for lunch that day. She brought it then.'

299

'Very extravagant for Andie,' commented Kevin.

'Oh, no bother to our family to get extravagant all of a sudden,' muttered Jin. 'Cora and Jack are off to Dromoland Castle for a couple of days.'

'Jin!' Kevin stared at her. 'That'll cost her a fortune.'

'Doesn't seem to be worrying her in the slightest,' said Jin sourly.

'I hope they don't run into anyone we know there.'

'Please don't let's talk about them,' begged Jin. 'Not when we're about to eat. It gives me indigestion just thinking about it.'

'Me too,' said Kevin darkly. He poured wine into their glasses.

'I talked to Livia today,' Jin remarked.

'Oh yes, how is she?'

'Pregnant,' said Jin.

Kevin made a face. 'Poor girl. She had such a good figure.'

'She's happy,' said Jin. 'She told me when I met her for lunch a while ago, I just forgot to mention it to you.'

Kevin's eyes narrowed as he looked at her. 'Forgot?'

'It was the day I met Cora and Jack on the Dart,' she said. 'It pushed everything else out of my head.'

He nodded. 'Not surprising.'

'But anyway, I was talking to Livia today and she told me that they're getting someone in to decorate the nursery for them.'

'When's it due?' asked Kevin idly.

'Not for another few months,' Jin said. 'But she wants to be prepared.'

'Nesting,' Kevin said.

'Maybe.'

'A bit early for it,' he remarked. 'It's usually closer to the birth that women start getting ridiculous about cleaning the house and things like that.'

'Really?'

'Apparently.'

'Did Monica?'

'I can't remember.'

'Come on, Kevin, you must remember.'

'Why?' he asked. 'I wasn't there. She was the pregnant one. I've no idea.'

'But you've heard of nesting!'

'I heard far too much when she was pregnant,' said Kevin sourly.

Jin tried to smile at him. 'It couldn't have been that bad.'

'Are you trying to lead this conversation somewhere?' he asked. 'Because you know it's not something I want to talk about. And since there's no chance of me ever having more children I don't feel I need to talk about it either.'

'I know. I understand,' said Jin quickly. 'I'm just curious.'

'Why?'

'Well . . .' She twirled the stem of the wine glass between her fingers. 'It must be interesting, that's all.'

'Not interesting,' said Kevin. 'Inevitably disgusting, but not interesting.'

'Oh Kevin, you can't say that you were disgusted when your children were born.'

'I can't say I was overwhelmed either.'

'Why are you so anti-child?' demanded Jin.

'I'm not,' said Kevin. 'I just don't believe there's a necessity to think that everything about them is great. It isn't. And childbirth might be a glorious experience but it's also disgusting. Which your friend will find out for herself.'

'Do you ever regret the vasectomy?' Jin tried to sound casual but she wasn't totally sure she'd succeeded.

'What?' Kevin stared at her, recognising that the tone of the conversation had suddenly changed. Jin's eyes were bright, her face flushed.

'Well, don't you ever think that maybe you shouldn't have? That it was a bit radical?'

'No,' said Kevin. 'I don't.'

'It's just that, say you suddenly decided that you wanted another child . . .'

'Jin, they counsel you about that before you have the operation.'

'But do they give you enough time?' she asked. 'I mean, then you might have wanted it, but now . . .'

301

'What d'you mean, "but now"?'

'Just that you might sometimes wish you hadn't had it done.'

'I never wish I hadn't had it done.'

'Why?'

'Because I've never wanted more children,' he said. 'I am, however, getting the feeling that this is something that is beginning to bother you.'

'It's just . . . well . . . I wondered . . . just . . . why no more? Why would you not want kids with me?'

'I don't want them with anyone,' said Kevin. 'I'll remind you that I was living with Monica when I had the vasectomy so it had nothing to do with having kids by you specifically. I have two. That's enough as far as I'm concerned.'

'If you hadn't had them with Monica, though,' Jin persisted, 'then would you want them with me?'

'Maybe.' Kevin shrugged. 'Thing is, it's academic, isn't it? Because there aren't going to be any kids, Jin.'

'I know that,' she said. 'At least, I know that it would be difficult.'

'I've had a fucking vasectomy,' he snapped. 'That's somewhat more than difficult.' He looked angrily at her. 'Listen, because I'm not going here again. I had a vasectomy because I didn't want any more children. I hadn't met you then. Having met you, I still don't want any more children. I married you but that doesn't mean I want to go through the whole pregnancy thing with anyone. Is that enough?'

She looked at him uncomfortably. 'Sure. Sure. I just wanted to know. Sometimes you hear of people getting pregnant after their husbands have had vasectomies and I just wondered how you'd react if that happened.'

'That usually happens early on after the operation,' said Kevin. 'When there are still sperm left in the tubes. People are so stupid most of the time. It's clearly explained but they don't listen. There are no rogue sperm lurking around my body. You don't have to worry about accidental pregnancies.'

'I guess we'd have found out before now if there were any rogue sperm,' she said. 'We have sex often enough.'

'And what does that mean?'

'Nothing,' she said. 'Just that, well, we have it so often that if there was any chance of me getting pregnant I would've done, wouldn't I?'

'Probably,' said Kevin.

'And it just seems a bit – well – a bit wasteful.'

'Wasteful?' He stared at her.

'To have all that sex and no sperm.'

'Jin, are you out of your fucking mind?' he asked her. 'All that sex and no sperm? What the hell are you talking about?'

'Nothing,' she said hastily. 'Only, that loads of people try for babies and they don't have them and they probably don't do it as often as us . . . and . . .' Her voice trailed off. She knew she was talking utter rubbish and she knew Kevin thought so too.

'I have the feeling that this conversation, such as it is, is teetering dangerously on the brink of total insanity,' said Kevin. 'If there's a point you want to make, Jin, make it now.'

She felt herself blush. It was a long time since he'd talked to her in that tone of voice, the tone that implied she was a brainless twerp but that he was putting up with it because she was easy on the eye.

'I don't have a point to make,' she said. 'I – I just, I suppose I've been wondering what it would be like to have a baby. Because of Livia probably.' She looked up at him. 'You've had babies. You know. I don't.'

'Monica had them,' he said. 'I was a bystander.'

'Not in their upbringing,' she said. 'You're always there for them.'

'I wasn't when they were smaller,' he said. 'And I suppose a sense of guilt has made me good with them since the divorce.'

'But you don't love them?' She frowned.

'Of course I love them,' he said impatiently. 'They're my children. I just wouldn't have chosen to have them. At least, as I've said to you before, not when I did. I might have waited until a better time.'

'What would've been a better time?' asked Jin. 'Now?'

'As you know, we're very busy right now,' he said.

'So it wouldn't have been now.'

'I don't bloody know,' he said irritably. 'For heaven's sake, Jin,

303

I thought we knew where we were at with this issue. If talking to a pregnant friend messes up your head this much, you shouldn't talk to her any more.'

'Are you telling me who I should and shouldn't be friends with?'

'Christ, but you're being annoying tonight,' he said. 'I might have guessed when you met me wearing that dress. Looking great, giving me what you knew I wanted – and then this! Not very subtle, was it?'

Jin felt tears prick the backs of her eyes.

'I wore the dress because you like it,' she said. 'I cooked dinner because I knew you were coming home early. I wanted to talk to you but I didn't . . . it wasn't because of that that I made love to you. I made love to you because I wanted to.'

'But now you're thinking that making love to me is a bit of a waste of time because you can't get pregnant,' he said.

'I never said that.'

'It's what you're thinking.' Kevin shook his head. 'You're so transparent, Jin. You always were. And I'll tell you what the matter is, will I? You and Livia always did things around the same time. Modelling contracts, shows, that sort of thing. You got married within a year of each other. And now she's pregnant you feel that she's doing something you're not. That's all. It's not because you have the slightest interest in kids yourself. You'd be useless at it.'

'Why?' she demanded. 'Why would I be useless?'

'Let's face it,' he said. 'Bringing up children is a difficult job.'

'I can do difficult jobs.' Her eyes were bright as she looked at him.

'Prancing around in different clothes isn't difficult,' said Kevin. 'Knowing whether or not your child has meningitis is difficult.'

'A rash,' she said. 'And a temperature. And you can press a glass against them to check the rash.'

He stared at her. 'You've lost the plot completely, you know that.'

'I'm not a stupid person,' she said. 'I'm not. And I could raise kids just as well as bloody Monica.'

'Oh, well, that's not saying much,' said Kevin scornfully. 'She hardly ever sees Cian these days, and Clarissa has her driven demented.'

'They're teenage kids,' said Jin. 'That's what happens with teenagers. They drive everyone crazy.'

'But I can deal with them better than her.'

'Because you're not there all the time,' she said.

'I don't believe I'm discussing my children with you,' he said. 'We agreed that they were absolutely none of your business.'

'And they're not,' she said. 'I never get involved. You know that. Even when I think it might be a good idea. Because they're your kids, not mine, and – like always – I do what you want. All I'm saying is that maybe having a child of my own is something I'd be good at.'

'And I'm telling you that it's not possible for you to have a child of your own,' said Kevin. 'At least, not with me. And of course, if you have one with someone else . . .' He got up from the table. 'I'm going to watch TV. You can join me when you regain your senses.'

He walked out of the dining room, his rigid body indicating the depth of his anger. Jin sat at the table and watched the remains of her beef bourguignon congeal in front of her. She'd handled it so badly. Now there was no chance of him understanding how she felt. No chance of him considering a reversal of the operation. No chance of her ever having a baby of her own.

Chapter 24

Romeo and Juliet: Montagues and Capulets – Prokofiev

A ndie sat in the flat and looked at the printed sheets of paper in front of her. *Todd Hunter*, she read. *Six one, 182 lbs, blue eyes, dark hair. Available for all functions, any destination. Special interests include ancient civilizations, music and skiing.* There were two more pictures of Todd. Of Jack, she corrected herself. One of him wearing a tux and looking as fantastic as he'd done on the night of Andrew Comiskey's party, and another of him in a business suit, tie half undone, far too attractive to be a real businessman. He was much younger in all of the pictures but there was no question of it being anyone but him.

Andie's heart was thumping in her chest, hammering away at twice its normal speed as it had done ever since she'd seen the pictures. She couldn't believe that, of all the things that Jack could have been, it turned out that he was really some kind of sleazy escort bloke. So, she wondered in horrified amazement, had Cora paid him? Was she still paying him? If so, how much? And equally if so, how the hell could she afford it? Andie looked at Todd Hunter's rates again. The man wasn't cheap. Andie knew that Cora had some money from Des's insurance policy but it certainly wasn't enough to have full and exclusive use of Todd Hunter for more than a month. Andie almost gagged – how many other women had used Todd Hunter, and how far had he gone with them? Surely, she thought frantically, surely he wouldn't be a carrier of some awful sexually transmitted disease? God Almighty, didn't Cora have more sense? And surely she didn't think that spending Des's insurance policy money on an escort was what he had intended?

Andie felt her face go red as she recalled the night of Andrew Comiskey's party when she'd asked Jack (without really meaning it, but trying to be smart) whether Cora had paid him money. They'd been talking about the cruise company paying men to dance with lonely ladies and Jack had said that at least it was more honest than pretending, like the men at the party and their trophy wives. He'd been angry, she remembered, but she'd assumed he was angry at what she'd said. Now she realised that it was probably because she'd stumbled close to the truth.

The buzzer sounded, startling her so much that she dropped the pages, which wafted on to the floor. She answered the intercom.

'It's me,' said Tom urgently. 'Let me in, Andie.'

She didn't want to see Tom now. And yet she did. Of course she did. She closed her eyes.

'Please, Andie, let me in,' he repeated.

If she weakened now she'd regret it for ever.

'Please.'

She buzzed the entrance door and then opened the door to the flat.

The flowers appeared before he did, the biggest bouquet she'd ever seen, all roses, in reds and yellows. It was spectacularly beautiful. She swallowed hard.

'Oh, Andie.' He stepped into the flat, put the roses on the small table and turned to her. 'Christ, I've missed you.'

She moved back from his embrace and looked at him. A flash of hurt crossed his face and he dropped his arms back to his sides.

'Why are you here?' she asked.

'I couldn't leave you,' he said. 'Not the way it was. Not hating me.'

'I don't hate you.'

'You should,' he told her. 'Oh, Andie, you should. It was wrong of me to tell you about Elizabeth the way I did. It was wrong of me to let you walk away.'

'You didn't let me walk away,' she said. 'I walked away myself. It was nothing to do with you.'

'It was my fault,' he said. 'I broke this news to you in a damn café, sweetheart. I was all of those things that I try to tell myself blokes aren't – thoughtless and selfish.'

'You had to tell me somewhere.' She shrugged. 'It doesn't matter.'

'I should've handled it better.'

'Makes no difference to the situation,' she said shortly.

'Andie, if I ask you to wait for me . . .' He looked at her pleadingly. 'You know I can't leave her now. But I can't live without you either.'

She grimaced. 'Sounds good in a song. But in real life you can.'

'Maybe I can *live* without you,' he told her. 'But life wouldn't be the same.'

She felt a tear topple from her eye and slide down her cheek.

'Oh, honey, don't cry.' He moved towards her.

She wanted to back away again but she couldn't. She allowed him to hold her.

'I love you,' she whispered. 'But I don't know if that's enough any more.'

'It has to be,' he told her fiercely.

'But what are we going to do?' She looked up at him. 'You can't leave her. I can't go on like this.'

'Just give me some more time,' he begged. 'Think of how long our lives are, Andie. What's another few months?'

It was so good to be back in his arms again. She moulded into the familiar warmth of his embrace and rested her head on his shoulder. Another few months. He was right, really. It wasn't such a long time. It was just that so much would happen during it. She wasn't sure she could cope. She breathed in his cedarwood smell. Warm and familiar. It was comforting to have him hold her again. It felt so right after the nights she'd spent without him, missing him. She wanted things to work out. She really did. She sighed deeply and wrapped her arms around him. He held her even tighter and suddenly she allowed herself to believe that it was OK again and everything would be all right. He tipped her head up towards him and brought his lips down on hers, fierce and demanding. Her response was equally fierce. Then he carried her to the bedroom, where he dropped her on to the unmade bed and made love to her quickly and intensely, both of them coming together in a turbulent wave of mutual passion.

'I missed you,' he said gently as he eventually rolled over and then sat on the edge of the bed.

'I missed you too.'

'You mean everything to me.'

Andie didn't speak. She couldn't.

'We *will* be together, Andie,' he said. 'I promise you.'

She bit her lip.

He looked at his watch. 'I have all night,' he told her. 'Elizabeth is in hospital today.'

She turned to him quickly, a questioning look on her face.

'Nothing wrong,' he said. 'Just tests. They're keeping her over-night.'

She was still finding it difficult to speak.

'So I can stay,' he told her. 'You and me together, Andie. All night.' He kissed her gently on the cheek. 'What would you like to do?'

'I don't know,' she whispered.

'What I thought would be nice would be if we went for something to eat,' he said. 'Somewhere around here? Nobody knows me. And then we could come back and have a bottle of wine and I'll get your damned DVD to work. And then we could go to bed together. What d'you think?'

She felt suddenly overwhelmed. A few hours ago she'd believed that he was out of her life for ever. And now he was here with her again. Not only that, but he wanted to take her out to a public place. And stay the night afterwards.

'I don't know,' she whispered again.

'I want us to do ordinary things,' he said. 'Like an ordinary couple. I want you to know that it can be normal between us.'

'You think?' She bit her lip.

'Oh, Andie, I know it's hard on you. I truly do. But one day it'll be different.'

She swallowed the tears that threatened to fall again. This was the date she'd always dreamed of with him. The date on which he

309

could stay the night. Quite suddenly she didn't care any more. She was entitled to be with him if she wanted. He loved her. And she loved him. She smiled and rubbed at her eyes.

'Give me two minutes in the bathroom,' she said.

She slid off the bed and walked into the living room, where she hastily picked up the printed pages showing Jack Ferguson as Todd Hunter and shoved them beneath that day's newspaper. Then she went into the bathroom and splashed her face with water. She cleaned her teeth, put drops in her eyes and then, with a little more care than usual, dabbed tinted moisturiser over her cheeks and forehead. She thought about taking ages over her mascara and ending up with the kind of lashes that Jin always had, but she couldn't be bothered in the end and just slicked on a daub of Maybelline.

Tom was still sitting on the bed when she came back into the bedroom. She sprayed herself with Gio and then pulled on a moss-green jumper and her bargain-basement Stella jeans.

'How do women do that?' asked Tom.

'What?'

'Turn into going-out-type creatures so quickly.'

She laughed. 'Trade secret.'

'You look great,' he told her. 'Which makes me wonder about going out at all.'

'D'you want to stay in?' she asked. In her dreams of their first night spent together they were always in the flat. But the idea of been taken out by him was utterly appealing.

'I'd love to stay in and do what we just did all over again,' he told her. 'But I know that I'm starving and might not be up to scratch until I get food inside me.'

She smiled. 'Come on then.'

'Where will we go?' he asked. 'I've passed by the occasional restaurant near here but I was kind of hoping that you'd have the low-down on where's good.'

'There's a lovely Chinese place about ten minutes' walk away,' she said.

'Excellent.'

She opened the door and they walked down the stairs hand in

hand. As they reached the bottom the entrance door swung open and Dominic Lyster came in.

'Hi, Andie,' he said. 'How're you doing?'

'Great, Dominic, thanks.'

'Feeling better?'

She shot him a warning look.

'Were you sick?' asked Tom.

'A bit of a cold, wasn't it?' Dominic smiled at her.

Andie had to admit that Dominic was quick on the uptake. She didn't want Tom to know how upset she'd been, and he'd certainly find out if Dominic kept on that particular line of conversation.

'Yes, Dominic,' she said gratefully. 'But I'm over it now. Everyone had it.'

'I probably gave it to you,' said Tom apologetically. 'Remember when I came over and—'

'Yes,' she interrupted him. 'Yes, you probably did.'

'Out anywhere nice?' asked Dominic.

'Chinese,' said Andie succinctly.

'Have a great evening.'

'Thanks. You too.'

They all smiled at each other again and then Andie and Tom walked out of the building.

'I didn't know you had a cold,' said Tom.

'Because at the time I wasn't speaking to you,' Andie told him.

'But you are now?'

'I must be.' She tucked her arm in his. 'I'm going out to dinner with you, amn't I?'

They walked along Griffith Avenue in silence. Andie allowed herself to revel in the fact that they were here together, even if only for one night. And then she wondered whether Elizabeth would spend much time in hospital and if so whether Tom would be able to come over for even more nights. Oh God, she thought, I do love him so much. It can't be wrong when I love him, can it?

The restaurant was nearly full, but they got a table tucked away in a corner. Tom ordered drinks while they looked at the menu. I'm out on a date with him, thought Andie happily as the words

311

on the card danced in front of her eyes. We're like a real couple. And it's wonderful!

They didn't talk about serious things. Andie told him about Kajsa's e-mails and the torrid affairs of the orchestra. Tom told her about the hen party in Bar Tender where the bride-to-be had jumped up on to a table and proceeded to take off all her clothes before anyone could stop her. They laughed and joked together and Andie felt all the tensions of the last few days dissolve around her.

'So how did things go at that party with your mother's boyfriend?' Tom asked as the waiter took away their plates and brought cups of green tea.

Andie flinched. Remembering the party made her remember how she'd felt as she waited in vain for Tom to call and how she'd felt the next day when he told her about Elizabeth's pregnancy.

He didn't notice her discomfort. 'Did you seduce the red-hot lover?' he asked lightly.

She shook her head and hoped that in the dim light of the restaurant he couldn't see that her cheeks were burning. 'Of course not. We talked about him and Ma but that was all.'

'And is she still seeing him?'

'Yes.' Andie nodded. And it turns out that he's some kind of escort stud, she added mentally, and God knows how many women he's been with and how much my mother is paying him for the privilege. Oh yes, and I kissed him. Passionately. But that's all. Nothing to worry about.

'Andie?'

'What?'

'You've gone into a daze.'

'Sorry,' she said.

'Are you all still really upset about him?' asked Tom.

'He's very unsuitable,' said Andie.

'Maybe he's OK,' Tom said. 'Maybe you just haven't given him a chance.'

'I can assure you he's very unsuitable,' she said tightly.

Tom's gaze was curious. 'I thought you felt it was all a bit of a laugh.'

'I never felt that,' she said. 'I did think we shouldn't interfere, which is completely different.'

'Well, you obviously didn't try to seduce him very hard, thankfully.' Tom grinned at her. 'Otherwise I'm sure it would have worked.'

She smiled faintly. 'I doubt that, somehow. I think his agenda is completely different.' *Like he wouldn't be available for seduction unless I had the money. Which is probably why he didn't try to take it any further, because he knew I wouldn't be able to pay him.* And then she was suddenly struck by a thought. *What if his sights were really set on Jin? What if Cora had told him so much about Jin and Kevin on board the ship that he'd decided he could come to Ireland and eventually become a kept man by her filthy-rich daughter? Could that have been in his mind all along?*

She unwrapped a dark chocolate mint from the tiny salver on the table. *Surely not,* she told herself. *There must be plenty more really rich people in the States for him to try. After all, he advertised on the bloody internet, didn't he! There was no reason for him to come to Ireland on the off-chance that Cora's well-off daughter was ripe for a bit of a fling. Besides,* thought Andie, *Jin didn't need to have flings with anyone. She had all she needed in Kevin, didn't she?*

'So what's going to happen with your mother?' asked Tom.

'I've no idea,' she replied. 'I haven't been talking to her much since, though I know Jin has.'

'Is it bothering you?'

'On and off.' Andie couldn't get the image of an open-shirted Jack leaning against a pillar and calling himself Todd Hunter out of her mind.

'She has to do what's best for her,' said Tom.

'Don't we all.'

They didn't speak for a moment, then Tom reached across the table and caught her hand in his. 'Andie, I'm really sorry about Elizabeth. I never dreamed she'd get pregnant again.'

'Neither did I,' said Andie shortly.

'You'll never really know how badly I felt that day,' said Tom. 'I wanted so much to grab you and run away with you and forget about everything, but – I couldn't do that, darling. I just couldn't.'

313

'I know.'

'Eventually things will work out,' said Tom. 'They have to.'

'I know,' she said again.

'Come on.' He signalled for the bill. 'Let's go back to the flat.'

'Have you built up your strength?' she asked.

He laughed. 'Well, yes, but I'm sorry, my love, because I'm going to reek of garlic!'

'I like the smell of garlic,' she said valiantly.

He signed the credit card slip and they got up from the table. They waited at the cash desk while the waiter got their coats. They were still waiting when Jack and Cora walked in.

Oh. My. God. Andie squeezed her eyes shut as she saw them, as though by doing so she could make them disappear. Not here. Not now. Not them.

'Andie!' Cora's face lit up as she spotted her daughter. 'I didn't expect to bump into you here.'

'We're just on our way out again. We were having a meal.' Obviously, she thought wildly, obviously we were having a meal, what the hell else would we be doing in a restaurant? Christ, I'm losing it altogether! She half turned to Tom, who was standing behind her. She couldn't not introduce him and she thought that if she did it quickly and casually Cora might not take much interest. 'This is Tom,' she said. 'Tom, this is my mother.'

Cora's green eyes observed him appraisingly. 'Hello,' she said.

'Hello,' replied Tom.

There was an awkward little silence.

'So, you guys have a good time?' asked Jack, his look flickering between Andie and Tom.

'Great, thanks,' said Andie. 'Lovely food.'

'I know,' said Cora. 'That's why we're here.'

'I didn't realise it was one of your haunts,' said Andie, wishing as she said it that she'd kept her mouth shut because it sounded like she'd have avoided the restaurant if she'd known Cora might be here. Well, of course, she would have!

'Indeed.' Cora smiled. 'So who's Tom?' She looked at Andie and then at Tom.

'A friend of Andie's,' explained Tom.

'Good friend?' asked Jack.

Andie wanted to slap him. He knew – she knew he knew. And he was mocking her, she was sure of that. But how dare he? How fucking dare he, she raged internally, when he was doing whatever he was doing with Cora and maybe targeting Jin and generally messing up everyone's lives and just being a complete and utter bastard.

'We've known each other a while,' said Tom. 'And you are?'

Andie hid a smile. Even though Tom didn't know about Jack's secret life he clearly had the measure of the man.

'Jack Ferguson,' replied Jack. 'An equally good friend of Cora's, although I don't think I've known her as long as you've known Andie.'

'You never mentioned Tom to me before,' said Cora. 'Why not?'

'No need,' said Andie succinctly.

'But why don't you call round with him sometime?' asked Cora. 'I'd love to see you.'

'Maybe she doesn't want to,' said Jack. 'Maybe Tom doesn't want to either.'

How dare you judge me, thought Andie furiously. You, of all people!

'I'd love to drop round some time, Mrs Corcoran,' said Tom politely.

'Are you going anywhere nice now?' asked Cora. 'It's such a shame we didn't come earlier. We could have joined you.'

Andie managed to keep her face totally impassive. She couldn't begin to imagine how awful her date with Tom would have been if Cora and Jack had turned up halfway through instead of at the end.

'It's a pity we didn't time it better,' agreed Tom easily. 'I'm just going to see Andie home, we're not doing anything else.'

'I'm sure it's enough,' said Jack.

'I'm really pleased to have met you,' said Cora. 'I never get to meet Andie's boyfriends.'

'He's not a boyfriend,' said Andie hastily. She realised that she'd sounded like a gauche teenager. 'He's a good friend, that's all.' She felt mean as she said the words. Tom was more than a good friend. Tom was the light in her life, the man who made her feel complete. It wasn't fair to have to refer to him as a good friend, as though he was just one of many.

Cora smiled knowingly. 'Well, whatever, it's nice to have met you. Tom.' She frowned slightly. 'Though I can't help feeling that we've met before. There wasn't anything—'

'You haven't met before,' said Andie. 'Really you haven't.' She didn't want Cora to possibly remember Tom at Jin and Kevin's wedding, unlikely though that might be. Because if she did remember then she'd be bound to say something to Jin, who might somehow put two and two together and realise who Tom actually was . . . and God only knew where that would lead! Andie felt herself shiver at the thought.

'We'd best be off,' said Tom. 'It was nice meeting you too.'

'You guys have a good night,' said Jack laconically.

'You too,' said Andie. Her eyes met his and she looked steadily at him. 'See you again, Todd,' she added under her breath.

It gave her immense satisfaction to see a look of undiluted horror cross his face.

'So that's the Hollywood Hunk,' said Tom as they walked back along Griffith Avenue towards Andie's flat. 'He's regrettably good-looking all right.'

'He's a shit,' said Andie.

'I can see why you and Jin think it's a pretty unlikely set-up.'

'Could we not talk about them?' asked Andie irritably.

'Sure.' Tom glanced at her. 'Sorry.'

'It's just that this is our night,' she said. 'I don't want to waste it thinking about other people.'

Tom chuckled. 'Neither do I.'

He put his arm around her and they walked in silence together. Andie willed herself not to think of her mother and Jack. Her mother and Todd. Her mother and a bloke who was paid for sex. Because there was no question about it, that was what the man was. A male prostitute. Sleeping with her mother. Andie's chicken satay turned over in her stomach.

316

But back inside the flat she resolutely put them out of her mind. She curled up on the sofa while Tom tinkered with the DVD. After nearly an hour fiddling around with it while she sat and watched him, he managed to get it working. He sat beside her and they watched *Titanic*, which was the only DVD she possessed. She fell asleep before it ended, her head resting on Tom's shoulder, suddenly totally at ease. It was nearly one in the morning when he shook her awake and asked if she didn't want to go to bed. She nodded sleepily at him and stumbled into the bedroom. But by the time he got in beside her she was thoroughly awake again. She reached for him and they made love, while she thought that this was what she had always wanted, an uninterrupted night with Tom. And then, as he moved rhythmically with her, she couldn't help wondering what would happen if Elizabeth's condition suddenly worsened and someone needed to contact him. She couldn't believe that she was thinking this when he was doing such wonderful things to her but she couldn't put the thought out of her head either.

'Tom?' she whispered.

'What?'

'What if she needs you?'

'Huh?'

'Elizabeth. What if there's a problem?'

Tom paused for a moment. 'Not now,' he said tightly.

'No, but Tom, listen, what if she needs you?'

'Andie!'

'Well, I just wondered.'

Tom suddenly flopped on to his side. 'Jesus, woman,' he said. 'You sure pick your moments.'

'I'm sorry, I'm sorry.' Andie was close to tears. 'I didn't mean . . . it was just – how will she contact you?'

'My mobile,' said Tom. 'I put our phone on call divert to it. Though she nearly always rings the mobile directly anyway. It's there. On the bedside locker.'

Andie followed his look. Sure enough the Nokia was within arm's reach. He hadn't forgotten about Elizabeth even though he was with her. She felt a twinge of bitterness and of guilt.

'I'm sorry,' she whispered again.

317

'Doesn't matter.' He hugged her briefly. 'I'm knackered now anyway. Let's get a bit of rest.' He yawned widely and then rolled on to his back. It was only a matter of seconds before his breathing became slow and steady and Andie knew that he was asleep.

She lay beside him in the darkness, wide awake. She was angry with herself for thinking of Elizabeth, for ruining the moment between them. Tonight was meant to have been perfect, but how could it be when she started asking him questions about his wife? How could it be, either, when images of her mother and the male escort kept popping into her mind too? It was hard to know which was worse, she thought miserably. She moved closer to Tom but he turned on to his side, his back towards her. Was this the way he was with Elizabeth? she wondered. Did they sleep back to back or did Elizabeth do what Andie was doing now and slide her arm around him? Did he even notice?

What time would he leave in the morning? Would they have time for a leisurely breakfast together? Would he make love to her again? She wasn't sure whether she would want to make love to him first thing in the morning with her unfreshened breath and dishevelled hair.

He snored gently. She moved closer to him. It didn't matter, she told herself fiercely. It didn't matter about Elizabeth or about Cora and Jack or about what might happen in the morning. All that mattered was here and now. And the fact that he was with her. At last.

Chapter 25

Piano Concerto No 1 in B Flat Minor – Tchaikovsky

The morning was better than the night before. She woke at nine and, still half asleep, turned over in bed. Tom was out for the count. Andie felt her heart well up with her love for him and with the pleasure of his being in the bed beside her. He'd stayed. He really had. For the whole night. And even though she'd messed up their lovemaking last night it was good to know that he cared enough about her to be here in her bed this morning. She snuggled closer to him and he opened one eye.

'Morning,' he said.

'Hello.'

'Good night's sleep?' he asked.

She nodded.

'Me too.' He reached for her and kissed her. And this time she didn't think for one second of Elizabeth.

Afterwards they had breakfast together, and then Tom went for a shower while Andie sat at the round table beside the window. The wind outside was whipping the trees from side to side, sending brown leaves whirling to the ground so that they spun in frenzied circles around the car park. She hated it when the leaves began to fall and the swathe of green from the trees was replaced by bare branches poking at the grey sky. She shivered, suddenly cold despite the fact that the heat was on full. She got up and pulled an old grey jumper over her silk slip. She was glad she'd finally had the opportunity to wear it; she'd begun to think that it was doomed to spend its time hanging on the padded hanger at the back of the wardrobe. She wondered when she'd have the chance to wear it again. If Elizabeth was going to spend a lot of time in hospital, maybe Tom would be able to spend more and more time with her. She stood by the window and allowed herself the luxury of imagining him staying with her for a few days. A week maybe. Of getting into a routine with him so that she'd have to say things like 'Can you pick up a litre of milk on your way home' or 'What have you done with the bathroom cleaner?' They were silly things, she knew, but they were togetherness things too. And she wanted them to be together.

She heard his phone ring in the bedroom. He'd left it on the locker. Her mouth went dry. It stopped just as she walked into the room and the message on the screen was '1 missed call'. She hit the list option. The call was from Lizzie. Lizzie! He never referred to her as anything but Elizabeth. Andie had always considered it to be a very formal name, suited to the kind of relationship that Tom and his wife appeared to have. But Lizzie was much more intimate. Lizzie implied sitting beside each other watching movies and snacking on microwave popcorn, or cuddling happily together in bed, or simply being friends with each other. Lizzie was caring and relaxed. Elizabeth wasn't.

Tom walked out of the bathroom wrapped in her big blue bath towel.

'Elizabeth called,' said Andie.

He looked at her, a worried frown on his face. 'Did you talk to her?'

'Don't be so silly.' She shrugged. 'Her name came up on your mobile, that's all.'

'Oh.' He sighed. 'I guess that's it then, Andie. She's ready to come home. She said she'd call after the consultant had seen her this morning.'

'You have to collect her?'

'Of course.'

Andie didn't want to feel the band of jealousy that had twisted itself around her heart, but it was there all the same. How could she not be jealous of Lizzie, the woman who was going to have Tom's baby, the woman who only had to click her fingers to make him come running? The woman he didn't love any more, she reminded

320

herself. The woman he was going to leave. The woman who had tricked him by getting pregnant again. She clenched her jaw in the sure knowledge that she was being unfair. Elizabeth had suffered deeply, for God's sake! She was entitled to a level of support from Tom now. She needed support. And so Andie knew that she wasn't going to say anything that would make her appear petty and narrow-minded and, above all, that would reveal the depth of her jealousy. She would be the way she always was. Understanding. Accepting. Support for Tom while he supported Lizzie.

'I'd better call her back,' he said apologetically.

Andie nodded. She stayed in the living room while he went back into the bedroom and called his wife. She hadn't heard him speak to her since the day of Jin and Kevin's wedding. He'd sounded vaguely solicitous of her then. He sounded ultra-gentle now. Andie pulled at a piece of loose skin around her middle finger and winced as it went deep. Tears pricked the back of her eyes.

'She's ready to leave now,' said Tom as he emerged from the bedroom again. 'I have to pick her up, sweetheart.'

'I know,' said Andie.

He put his arms around her and pulled her towards him. His skin was still damp from the shower. 'Last night was wonderful,' he said.

'Yes,' she whispered.

'And there will be other opportunities,' he told her. 'Plenty of them.'

'I suppose so.'

'It's not just the sleeping with you.' He buried his face in her hair. 'It's simply being with you.'

Andie blinked to hold back the tears. She allowed herself to stay in the circle of his arms for a while and then pulled away. 'You'd better get dressed.'

'Sure.' He kissed her gently. 'I'll call you.'

'OK,' she said.

She played Rachmaninoff after he left, her eyes tightly closed as she let the music take hold of her. Her tears dripped down her cheeks and slid on to the keys. She was a bad, bad person, she told herself. She was bad for having an affair with Tom in the first place

321

and bad for letting him back into her life when there had been an opportunity to let him go, and really, really bad for hating the fact that he secretly called his wife Lizzie.

What's going to happen to us? she asked herself despairingly. And the tears fell harder at the thought that if he'd left her sooner, if she herself had given him an ultimatum earlier, maybe they wouldn't be in this situation now. As Jin had often told her, she'd let things drift, and now they'd drifted into something she couldn't cope with any more. She brushed her fingers across her cheeks and then segued into Tchaikovsky's Piano Concerto No 1, which allowed her the satisfaction of thumping the keys really hard and venting anger, frustration and the ever-present guilt all at the same time. Tchaikovsky probably hadn't intended it to be quite so loud and angry, she thought, as her fingers raced across the keyboard, but he knew about sorrow and depression all the same.

She allowed the last notes to fade gently into the air and then closed the lid of the piano. She felt better already. Though she'd have berated any of her pupils who'd done the same, thumping the keys was a fantastic release, and the music itself was so inspiring that it allowed everything inside her to be liberated. She wondered if she'd have managed to carry on her affair with Tom for so long if she hadn't had the escape of music to help her through it.

The knock at the door startled her. She got up and answered it.

'Hi, Andie,' said Dominic. 'Hope I'm not disturbing you.'

'No,' she said. 'Come in.'

'Thanks.' He looked at her apologetically. 'I was just wondering if by any remote chance you had a copy of Thursday's newspaper? The one with the property supplement? Apparently they've put an ad in for a house I'm selling and they've got all the information wrong. I nipped down to the newsagent's but they don't have any left and I want to see it myself before tearing a strip off someone.'

'Oh, right. I think I have.' She nodded towards the pile of papers on the coffee table. 'Take your pick.'

'Thanks,' he said. 'I heard you playing, by the way. It was wonderful.'

She smiled faintly. 'You think? It was too loud and too heavy really.'

322

'Sounded kind of passionate to me,' said Dominic idly as he flicked through the papers.

'Wrong sort of passion,' said Andie.

Dominic laughed. 'I don't know. I thought it was fiery. Oops, sorry,' he said suddenly as A4 pages slid from the paper. 'You have something in here.'

'Oh God!' Andie remembered the printouts she'd made of the Todd Hunter website pictures. She grabbed at them but didn't get them all. Dominic caught a page as it fell and looked at it. Then he looked at Andie. Her face flushed crimson. 'It's not what you think,' she said.

'I'm not actually thinking anything,' said Dominic. 'Other than this guy has some package.'

'Dominic!' Andie wouldn't have believed it was possible for her face to flame any further but she could feel herself growing hotter with embarrassment with every passing second.

'So – should I ask?' He looked at her enquiringly.

'Not really,' she said uncomfortably.

'Like, when he says "any destination", does he mean he'll travel from California or wherever it is all the way to Dublin?'

'Of course it doesn't,' said Andie. And then she pressed her fingers to her cheeks. 'Well, I don't know, do I? I mean, I haven't . . . I don't . . . it's not . . .'

'Hey, Andie, I don't mind.' Dominic's voice was full of suppressed laughter. 'I didn't realise that you, well . . .'

'OK, look, Dominic, you know quite well that I don't have any kind of relationship with this bloke. You've met my relationship man already.'

'Maybe there's one for the relationship and one for – more physical matters?' suggested Dominic.

'No!' she said forcefully. 'No. Tom and I are fine in that department, thank you. This guy – it was research I was doing, that's all.'

'Cool,' said Dominic admiringly. 'I get to research crumbling old houses with mildew and stuff and you get to research blokes who look like this. Is he a musician?'

'I doubt it.' Andie heaved a sigh. 'Oh, Dominic, if you must know, he's my mother's boyfriend.'

323

Andie had never seen anyone rendered so utterly speechless before. Dominic opened and closed his mouth but nothing came out. He stared at her.

'It's true.' Actually, thought Andie suddenly, it was quite a relief to tell someone else about Cora and her gigolo. Someone other than hysterical Jin and uninterested Tom. She frowned. Why did she think Tom was uninterested? He wasn't. They just didn't have much time to talk about it, that was all.

'So how did your mother hook up with this?' asked Dominic.

Andie told him, and when she'd finished, his laugh was deep and infectious.

'You Corcoran women sure are something,' he said. 'And fair play to your mother.'

'Yes, well . . .' Andie grimaced. 'We don't think that's quite the way to look at it, Dominic. Goodness knows what sort of spin he's put on things to her, and to be honest with you, both Jin and I are quite worried about it. More than worried after seeing this.' She bit her lip. 'I haven't told Jin yet but I know that when I do she'll throw a complete wobbler.'

'I guess it's a bit of a problem all right,' he agreed. 'But still, how many women of your mother's age do you know who've got either the resources to pay someone like that or the wit to get it for free?'

'I never quite thought of it like that,' said Andie, 'and you do have a point, Dominic. But we have to tell her.'

'Andie, if she's paying him you don't have to tell her anything,' said Dominic. 'She already knows.'

Andie clenched and unclenched her fists. 'She isn't paying him,' she whispered. 'She couldn't be. Not Ma.'

Jin was in the spare bedroom looking at the picture of a newly born baby. It was quite off-putting really, she thought, because it was still covered in blood and attached to its – no, *his* mother, she corrected herself, by the bruised-looking cord. 'Totally and utterly disgusting,' she said out loud. And she wondered how it was that she could ever have thought that having a baby would be a wonderful thing. It would be horrible. She'd get fat and bloated (Livia had rung the other day to say that her ankles were starting to swell)

324

and the whole thing would be a complete nightmare. So it wasn't something she wanted to do. It really wasn't. Women didn't get pregnant on a whim. And that was all this was on her part. A whim. A passing fancy. She didn't really want it at all.

She turned the page. In the next picture the baby had been cleaned up and was wrapped in a lemon blanket while his mother held him close to her. His head didn't look angry and squashed any more. His button nose was pert in his smooth-skinned face. Jin could almost smell the soap and the talc and the essence of baby from the pages of the book.

Why was Kevin so against it, though? Why? It was unfair of him to say to her that she knew how the land lay before she married him and unfair of him to expect her not to want a child of her own at some stage. He should never have even suggested marriage given the circumstances. Surely he must have realised that one day she'd change her mind.

She stared at the page again. She couldn't change her mind. It wasn't possible for her to have Kevin's child. He'd had a vasectomy. It was as simple as that. She pressed her hand against her stomach. *She* could have babies though. But if she waited much longer then maybe it would be harder to conceive. You heard about it all the time, those women who'd ignored the ticking of their clock and who'd had their glittering careers and wonderful lives and then discovered that it was too late to have anything more. She didn't want to be one of those women. She wanted to be a mother. She closed her eyes. That was the truth. She *had* changed her mind. It wasn't just a whim and it wasn't just a passing fancy. She really, really wanted to have a baby.

She snapped the book closed and replaced it at the back of the bedside locker. Then she walked across the room and looked out over her spacious back garden with its manicured lawn, sheltered patio area, kidney-shaped fish pond and hypnotic fountain. It wasn't a children's garden. If she had kids the lawn would be scuffed and the patio area a dumping ground for brightly coloured pedal cars or footballs or whatever else happened to be the flavour of the day. She wouldn't be able to grow elegant agapanthus flowers or delicate roses. Her house, her garden – they wouldn't be her own.

Were they now? she wondered suddenly. Were they really her house, her garden? Or were they Kevin's? She swallowed. What would happen if she and Kevin ever split up? Without children there'd be no question of him leaving her a seven-bedroomed house in Malahide, would there? Not that she'd want him to leave her anything. God almighty, she thought suddenly, I don't want him to leave me at all. I love Kevin. I've always loved Kevin. She glanced at her watch. He was playing golf with Cian this afternoon in the club's father and son competition. He wouldn't be back until late. She was alone in the house. As usual.

She gritted her teeth and went back into her bedroom. Their bedroom. She took her cashmere coat from the wardrobe and pulled it on. She wanted to go out and look at other houses. Ones in which she'd feel more content and settled than Briarlawns. Houses that were less stately, perhaps, and more homely.

The phone rang as she stood in the hallway checking her hair.

'It's me,' said Andie as she answered it. 'I'm on the bus.'

'What bus?' asked Jin.

'The one that goes past your house,' Andie told her. 'I'm about halfway there. I know I should've rung earlier but I was a bit distracted. I have to see you.'

'Here?' said Jin in surprise. 'Now?'

'Yes.'

'Is anything wrong?'

Andie glanced at the pages in the manila folder she'd brought with her.

'I don't know,' she said eventually as her mind raced over all the possibilities. 'Everything could be fine. Or it could all be a complete disaster.'

On the rare occasions she found herself standing at the closed double gates of Briarlawns, Andie couldn't help making faces at the video camera mounted on the pillar. She knew that it was incredibly juvenile of her but she simply couldn't stop herself, even today when her heart really wasn't in it. So as soon as she'd pressed the buzzer she scrunched up her nose and widened her eyes into a passable imitation of a living gargoyle.

326

'Careful you're not left like that.' Jin's disembodied voice was dry.

Andie made another face as the pedestrian gate swung open. She slipped through and walked up the driveway. She frowned to herself as she realised that she'd never simply dropped over to Jin's before. Any other time she'd been here it had been because of an invitation – the excruciating lunch with Cora and Jack, the triple birthday celebrations which had irked her so much, the uncomfortable Christmas dinner of the previous year. She never called in to see her sister for the hell of it.

Jin opened the hall door and greeted her.

'Hi,' said Andie. 'I forgot to ask if Kevin was around.'

'Does it matter?' Jin's voice was tight and Andie looked at her in surprise.

'Not really. Not at all actually. Probably better that he's not here under the circumstances.'

'For heaven's sake, Andie, what's it all about?' asked Jin impatiently.

'I'll get to it,' said Andie as she followed her sister into the chill-out room.

'You don't come here for no reason.' Jin echoed Andie's own thoughts. 'So it must be something pretty awful.'

'I guess,' said Andie.

'D'you want a drink?' asked Jin. 'We've a nice chardonnay in the cooler.'

'Is chardonnay particularly nice?' asked Andie. 'I really don't have a clue about wine. I know I should but I usually pick whatever the house red or white is and I never bother looking at the label.'

Jin pursed her lips. 'If you buy cheap wine you're spending more on tax and less on the wine itself,' she said.

'Anything will do me,' said Andie. 'But yes, a drink would be wonderful.'

She sat back in one of the leather armchairs while Jin got the wine. Comfortable chairs, she thought enviously. Gorgeous room. It would be nice to have the money. Really it would.

Jin returned with a bottle and two glasses. She poured the wine, raised her glass in a half-hearted toast and looked at Andie.

'Well?' she said.

Andie sipped the wine. 'Lovely,' she agreed. 'Good choice.'

'Andie!' Jin couldn't hide her impatience.

'I know, I know, I'm sorry.' Andie put her glass on the coffee table. 'It's just – well – look.' She handed the manila folder with the Todd Hunter pictures to her sister. Jin stared at them, her eyes growing wider as she read about Todd and looked at his photographs. Then she looked up at Andie again.

'Is this for real?' she breathed slowly.

'Looks real enough to me.'

'She'll throw him out after this.'

'If she doesn't know already,' said Andie.

Jin looked at her sister in horror. 'She couldn't possibly know,' she said furiously. 'Our mum? Deliberately letting this – this sex-for-sale merchant stay in her house?'

'She could be paying him to stay.'

'Andie!' Jin's voice was full of shock. 'You can't believe that. Not Mum. Paying for . . . paying . . . I just don't believe it.'

'Well, neither do I really,' agreed Andie. 'And what's really creepy, Jin, is that I actually joked to him about it at that party. You know, half seriously but not really meaning it. He was furious with me. Now I know why.' She rubbed her temples. 'Thing is, if she doesn't know and if she isn't paying him, then why else would he have come back with her?'

'There must be another reason,' snapped Jin. 'Because there's absolutely no way Mum could possibly know about this.'

'But does it explain the situation?' asked Andie. 'After all, both of us were totally amazed that Jack would spend any time with her at all. If she's paying him then it all makes perfect sense.'

'Andie, she can't possibly afford to pay him.' Jin's eyes scanned the Executive Escorts fees. 'And he's been here for ages. She'd be bankrupt!'

'I thought perhaps she was using the insurance money,' said Andie.

'No!' Jin's eyes reflected her total disbelief. 'Why would she do that? That money was to keep her comfortable.'

'Maybe she didn't want to be comfortable any more,' suggested Andie. 'Maybe she just wanted a bit of fun. And sex.'

'Andie!' cried Jin. 'It's Mum you're talking about. Not some crazy woman.'

'She's been pretty crazy this last while,' Andie pointed out. 'What about the facials and the manicures and the new clothes?'

'I know, I know.' Jin looked distracted. 'But she's still Mum! She surely hasn't lost her mind completely!'

'Maybe she wants sex and thought this was a good way,' said Andie. 'I know the whole idea horrifies both of us but we have to be realistic.'

'Well if she just wanted sex I'm sure there are plenty of men who'd be happy to sleep with her for free,' said Jin sharply.

Andie smiled faintly. 'Probably. But maybe she didn't want to sleep with them. Maybe she *did* want to sleep with Jack. Or Todd. Or whatever his real name is.'

'Oh God.' Jin looked at the A4 pages again. Todd Hunter's lean body seemed to taunt her. 'I just don't believe it.'

'Neither do I,' said Andie. 'But it's a fact. That's why I called out here to show you, Jin. I felt we needed to think through all the possibilities.'

'There are only two,' said Jin. 'One is that she's paying him, like you said; the other is that she doesn't know and he's stringing her along because . . .' She shrugged. 'I've no real idea why, but maybe he has his reasons. And there must be reasons, Andie, because blokes like this don't give it away for free, do they?'

'If she knows, she'll be humiliated if we say anything,' Andie told her sister. 'And if she doesn't she'll still be humiliated.'

'We have to find out without asking her,' said Jin.

'And how do we go about that?'

'Talk to him,' said Jin firmly.

Andie shuddered. 'I'm not doing it.'

'You have to,' said Jin.

'I can't.'

'Of course you can. You got on with him at the party, didn't you? Even though you argued with him you still ended up playing the piano with him.' Jin looked at Andie curiously. 'You know, I've never quite figured that out, Andie. You don't play for anyone. How come you did for him?'

329

'It was because he was singing,' said Andie dismissively. 'It made it less important somehow.'

'Well it seems to me that you two have a better relationship than him and me,' said Jin. 'And I certainly don't want Kevin talking to him – the whole thing would end in violence, I know it would. Kevin might seem placid to you but he has a foul temper when he's really goaded, and he's furious enough about the entire situation anyway. I keep having to stop him rushing down to Marino to clock Jack and tell Mum that she's a menopausal old fool who should know better. So you have to do it, Andie. There's no one else.'

The idea of meeting Jack Ferguson again made Andie's head spin. How could she call the man and speak to him after what had happened between them? How could she ask him if the relationship between himself and her mother was purely businesslike when she'd practically thrown herself at him? He couldn't possibly take her seriously. Although . . . A thought suddenly struck her.

'I don't think she knows,' she said out loud.

'Huh?'

'Ma. I don't think she knows about him.'

'What makes you so sure?' asked Jin.

Andie didn't say that it was because Jack had looked so horrified when she'd whispered the name Todd to him the previous night. And because he'd glanced at Cora, a worried expression on his face, immediately afterwards. Although, she thought now, maybe it was just that he didn't want Andie to realise what her mother was doing. She bit her lip. She didn't want to tell Jin about meeting them because then Jin would have to know that she'd been out with someone and she'd start asking questions and eventually worm Tom's name out of her. It was bad enough, Andie felt, having to worry about Cora's relationship without having to tell Jin about her own.

'Maybe I'm wrong,' she said. 'I just had this feeling . . . but my feelings are pretty hopeless most of the time, so let's ignore it.'

'Whatever you say.' Jin looked at her curiously.

'Oh, this is too absurd for words!' cried Andie. 'Our mother isn't some dotty old fool trying to relive her youth. She really isn't. So what the hell is going on with this bloke, and why?'

Jin shook her head. 'I've no idea. But Kevin will blow his stack at this. He truly will. It was bad enough when it just seemed as though Mum was behaving irrationally. But if she's actually handing over money . . .' She shook her head. 'It's impossible. Can you imagine what his colleagues would think? What our friends would think?' Jin closed her eyes and then opened them again. 'There'd be horrible little innuendos in those gossipy parts of the papers and everyone would know exactly what was going on. I wouldn't be able to walk down the street in Malahide ever again.'

'I'm more thinking that Ma wouldn't be able to hold her head up among her friends if they ever found out,' said Andie.

'Which is worse?' Jin asked. 'Her paying him or her being in total ignorance?'

'I don't know,' wailed Andie. 'Either prospect is awful.'

'Why the hell did she catch a cold the night of the party?' fumed Jin. 'We had such a great guy lined up for her in Trevor McAllister.'

'The older man?'

Jin nodded. 'He's really nice. I talked to him that night, we danced together too. I liked him a lot. He would've been perfect.'

Andie's laugh was hollow. 'Too late now. I can't see any bloke wanting to hook up with a woman who's spent the last few weeks with a male escort.'

'Even if one of them could get over the idea, they'd never get over the comparisons,' said Jin.

This time Andie's laugh was more genuine. 'I know it's not funny really,' she said. 'But can you imagine it – Ma having the greatest sex of her life now?'

'OK, Andie, that's not something I ever want to imagine,' said Jin firmly.

'True,' said Andie. She looked ruefully at her sister. 'You know, I was wrong to say we should stay out of it earlier. You're right about him, Jin. He's a bastard. And whether or not she's paying him is irrelevant. She's clearly not herself. He's exerted some kind of influence over her and it's a bad one.' Although, she thought suddenly, Cora had seemed so happy last night. Pleased to be out with someone who was looking after her. Not looking after her,

Andie reminded herself, looking after himself. Insinuating himself into Cora's affections. Or into Cora's clearly dwindling savings.

'She's taking him to Dromoland Castle next week,' remarked Jin.

'You're joking!' Andie looked horrified.

'I asked her to come shopping with me. Arnott's are doing discounts for card-holders and I thought she might want to take advantage of mine. But she said she was going away with him.'

'We have to stop it,' said Andie fiercely. 'We have to. But the idea of confronting him . . . Oh, Jin, I don't know if I can do it.'

Jin had never seen Andie so strung out before. 'Well, maybe I should talk to Kevin first,' she said doubtfully. 'I suppose it's clear now that money is this guy's thing. Whatever's going on between him and Mum, however they're playing it at the moment, anyone who works as a male escort is in it for the money. Perhaps Kevin can just write a cheque without hitting him.'

Andie nodded. 'I suppose this bloke will do anything for cash. Especially leave.'

The thought that had suddenly come into Jin's head was so impossible she dismissed it immediately. But she knew it was still there, lodged in her brain, even though she wasn't allowing it to come to the surface again. She'd explore it later, when she was on her own and had time to think about it.

'You think Kevin will offer him enough?' Andie broke into her reverie.

'I don't know how much is enough,' said Jin. 'But he'll do something. All I have to do is make sure he doesn't freak out too much.'

'Where is he now?' asked Andie.

'Golf,' said Jin.

'He plays a lot of golf, doesn't he?'

'They all do.' Jin snorted. 'It's like some kind of rite of passage for businessmen, you know. Once they get into a club they feel accepted.'

Andie raised an eyebrow at the scathing tone of her sister's comments. 'I thought you approved of him playing golf.'

'I don't approve or disapprove of anything he does,' said Jin. 'It's a fact of life. And today it's a match with Cian, so I can't object to a father–son bonding kind of thing.'

Andie nodded.

'Anyway, he won't be back till much later,' Jin added.

'Bit lonely for you,' commented her sister.

'Not really,' said Jin. 'I've lots to do.'

Like what? wondered Andie. When she was on her own she always had her music, whether it was for work or for pleasure. It didn't make any difference to her; she could lose herself in it just the same. But if you didn't have a particular interest, she thought, if there wasn't anything that was specifically important to you, what did you do when you were on your own? And then she felt bad for assuming that Jin didn't have any interests. How the hell would she know?

'Am I disturbing you?' asked Andie. 'Will I go now?'

'No,' said Jin. She reached for the bottle of wine and refilled their glasses. 'You might as well stay for a while. Look at some brochures with me. I was going to go house-hunting before you rang.'

'House-hunting?' Andie looked at her in surprise. 'Why? I thought you liked it here.'

'It's OK,' said Jin. 'But it has no character. And it's a bit big.'

'Of course it's big,' said Andie. 'It's a status symbol, isn't it? It's meant to be big.'

'Too many bedrooms,' said Jin.

'Not if you eventually have kids,' Andie said lightly.

Her words stabbed Jin in the heart. She took a large slug from her glass of chardonnay.

'Any sign of that?' asked Andie. 'I know you said ages ago that you weren't really thinking of it, but have you changed your mind at all?'

Jin shook her head wordlessly.

'Because it can come at you suddenly, can't it?' asked Andie. 'The old clock thing hits you and the next thing you know you're going gaga over romper suits.' She giggled and then bit her lip as she suddenly thought of Tom and Elizabeth – no, Tom and Lizzie – as proud parents. The pain was very real.

'It's not funny,' said Jin sharply.

'I know it's not funny,' said Andie shakily.

'Exactly.' Jin took another gulp of wine. So did Andie. The two of them sat side by side and stared at the gas-effect fire.

Andie wished she hadn't thought of Tom and Elizabeth. Rushing out to Jin had helped her forget that he was with her now, that he'd brought her home from hospital, full of concern about her and their unborn child. Dammit, she thought furiously, I don't want anything to happen to their baby. I want Elizabeth to have it. I want it to be healthy. I want things to work out for her.

And I still want Tom.

Jin was thinking of being pregnant. Of the hormonal changes that would flood her body. Of getting fat. Of having swollen ankles. Of being sick in the morning. And she thought of what it would be like to hold her very own child in her arms and know that she was totally responsible for it and that she could love it unconditionally. She knew that loving a child was different to loving anyone else. She wanted to give that love to her own baby. She just wasn't sure how she could possibly achieve it.

Rain started to beat against the French doors. Jin got up and pulled the heavy drapes, then switched on the lamps and lit some scented candles.

'Would you like something to eat?' she asked Andie.

Her sister shook her head. 'I'd better get home,' she said. 'I'm sure Kevin will be back soon.'

'Not for ages yet,' said Jin. 'Even in a downpour they'll still play. And it's lashing down out there right now. Stay for a bit longer.' She picked up the wine bottle. 'Let's finish this anyway.'

Andie shrugged. 'OK.'

'Why don't I ring for a pizza?' suggested Jin. 'I'm hungry. I bet you are too.'

Not really, thought Andie. Because in the back of my mind there are thoughts of Tom and Elizabeth and they take the edge off any feeling of hunger that hits me. But she nodded at Jin, who picked up the phone and dialled in an order for a large pizza with everything.

They sat in unaccustomed though surprisingly restful silence. Then Jin picked up the remote control and switched on the TV, settling on an episode of *The Simpsons*, which made both of them giggle.

The pizza arrived just as the cartoon was ending and they took it into the kitchen, Jin explaining apologetically that Kevin didn't like the smell of food in the chill-out room. Andie said that it wasn't a problem and that it was easier to eat at the table anyway. While they ate she looked at the brochures for the houses that Jin had intended to go and see that afternoon.

'Barrington Properties,' she said as she looked at the brochure for the house on Howth Hill. 'My upstairs neighbour works for them.'

'Does she?' asked Jin. 'Any fantastic properties at exceptional prices I don't know about?'

'She's a he.' Andie wiped tomato sauce from her chin. 'I could ask.'

'Good-looking?' asked Jin.

Andie shrugged and thought of Dominic's rangy body and easy smile. 'OK, I guess. Nothing special.'

'Married?'

'Divorced.'

'Well off?'

'He lives in the same block as me,' Andie pointed out. 'Hardly rolling in it.'

'Not worth your while then,' said Jin dismissively.

'Jin Corcoran!' Andie glared at her. 'That's a horrible thing to say. Dominic's actually very nice.'

'Oh?' Jin looked at Andie with interest. 'Jumping very quickly to his defence there, aren't we?'

'Don't be stupid,' said Andie. 'He has loads of girlfriends. I'm just saying that he doesn't have to be loaded to be nice.'

'Have you ever gone out with him?'

'Oh, for heaven's sake . . .'

'Well, have you?'

'No,' said Andie.

'Has he ever asked you?'

Andie tore at another slice of pizza. 'Actually, yes.'

'So why didn't you accept?'

'Because I had better things to do,' she snapped in reply.

Jin studied her sister's face, which was red and angry. Andie

335

picked off the pieces of pepperoni and arranged them on the side of her plate.

'What's the story?' asked Jin. 'Has the hot date become more serious? Why won't you tell me?'

'Because it's none of your bloody business!' Andie knew that she was overreacting but she couldn't help herself.

'I only asked,' said Jin mildly. 'There's no need to get into such a state over it.'

'You're always asking,' snarled Andie. 'Always pointing out that I have this dreary, depressing life while you're so happy in your cocoon of wealth and designer things. Well, it's not me, Jin, and it never will be.'

'I never said it was!' Jin was annoyed now.

'I couldn't bear to be like you,' Andie continued furiously. 'Knowing that I could have everything I wanted but never really being happy with any of it.'

'Who gave you the right to decide?' snapped Jin. 'Who made you the arbiter of what's a good kind of life to lead? And how do you know whether I'm happy or not?'

'How could anyone be happy rattling around this place on their own?' demanded Andie. 'For heaven's sake, Jin, you're even talking about buying a smaller house!'

'A house with more character,' said Jin. 'Not smaller because I want smaller.'

'You said this one had too many bedrooms!'

'I know I did. But that's not the point.'

'What's the point?' asked Andie. 'What's the point of you living the kind of life you lead?'

'The point is I like it,' Jin said shortly. 'I like my life. I like my stuff. I like everything I have.'

'And you like Kevin too?'

'I love Kevin.' Jin's bottom lip trembled. 'I love him. He gives me everything!'

Except children, she added to herself. Except what I really want. She pressed her fingers to her eyes. She wasn't going to give Andie the satisfaction of realising how upset she was. Andie, who hadn't a clue about anything!

'At least I have someone who's there for me,' Jin went on shakily. 'Someone who cares enough to get involved in the mess that our mother is making of her life. Someone who will pay for our problems to go away. Someone practical. I'd rather have Kevin than no one at all. And I'd certainly pick my life any time over yours because yes, Andie, yours is dreary and boring and all the things I said. You're a loser, you always will be.'

'I'll go.' Andie got up and pushed her chair away from the table. 'Coming here was a mistake.'

'Fine,' said Jin.

'I'll call you,' said Andie. 'Talk to your precious all-providing Kevin and see what he says or what sort of cheque he can write to sort it all out. But if Jack says it's not about money then – then I'll confront him myself and I will sort things out once and for all no matter how difficult it is. Because at least I can do things myself, I don't need to ask anyone's permission first!'

'They'll be in Dromoland for a couple of days,' Jin reminded her sharply. 'So we can't do anything straight away.'

'Oh yes,' said Andie. 'Getting through what's left of Ma's money.'

'You don't have to worry about her money,' said Jin. 'At the end of the day Kevin can sort that out too.'

'Of course he can,' said Andie bitterly. 'Write a cheque, solve everything.'

She stalked out of the kitchen, collecting her coat as she went. Jin followed her but Andie left the house without another word.

Chapter 26

Piano Concerto No 2 in C Minor: Moderato – Rachmaninoff

The rain was tipping down in bucketfuls and Andie was drenched before she made it to the curve in the driveway. Bloody bloody hell, she thought furiously, as her hair plastered itself to her head and face. Why did I ever come out here in the first place? I should've known that Jin and I would argue about something. We always damn well do. And she bit her lip because she knew she shouldn't have said the things she had said to her sister. Jin's life was hers to lead and it wasn't as though Andie's own was anything much to write home about. At least, she thought bitterly, at least Jin actually has a husband and a home of her own and all the things she apparently wants. What have I got? Someone else's husband, that's what. And then only when she doesn't need him.

She stumbled on the wet gravel and winced as pain shot through her ankle. That was all she needed, a twisted ankle to go with everything else. But it wasn't too badly hurt and she was able to limp down the rest of the driveway to the huge wrought-iron gates.

They were locked. There was a keypad beside the pedestrian gate but Andie didn't know the combination. She shook her head in disbelief at the fact that her own sister lived in a house where you had to have an entry code to get out! And she chewed her lip as she tried to think of what it might be. Jin's birthday, she thought, as she pressed the keys. But nothing happened. Dad's birthday? She had no success with any of the dates she used, and then she realised that the code was probably something to do with Kevin. But it wasn't his birth date either. She looked at the keypad in frustration. She'd

338

have to ask Jin. Then she saw that there wasn't an intercom on this keypad. She supposed there didn't need to be – clearly most people leaving the house knew the code. She groaned and rattled the gate just in case it opened. But it remained obstinately shut. There must be a way, she muttered to herself. She didn't want to have to go back to the house again. Yet she couldn't see an alternative. The wall was too high to climb and she was half afraid that if she tried, Kevin's famed security system would kick into action and before she knew where she was she'd find herself arrested. Which would definitely lower her stock with her brother-in-law.

'Oh shit,' she said out loud. 'Shit, shit, shit.'

She leaned indecisively against the wall while the rain soaked her even further and she fought back tears of frustration. She was wet enough already, she told herself sternly, without giving in to a desire to put her head in her hands and sob! Then she heard the low roar of a car engine and the swish of tyres on the wet surface. She realised that the car had stopped in front of Briarlawns. There was a muted clunk and the main gates began to swing slowly open.

She stepped away from the wall as the car drove through the gates and then came to an abrupt halt. The electric window slid down and Kevin leaned out.

'Andie? What the hell are you doing here?'

'Trying to get out,' she said as nonchalantly as she could. 'I didn't know the code.'

'But why were you here in the first place?' asked Kevin. 'Not that it's a problem, of course, only Jin wouldn't be too happy to think you were wandering round the garden getting drenched.'

'You think?' muttered Andie.

'Come back to the house,' said Kevin, 'and dry off.'

'No point,' Andie told him. 'I need to get home and I'll only get wet again anyway.'

'Don't be so silly,' said Kevin. 'Come back to the house, dry off and I'll drive you home.'

Andie hesitated. If she arrived back at the house now she'd probably annoy Jin even more.

'Hurry up,' said Kevin. 'I'm getting wet myself.'

She opened the door of the Mercedes and settled gingerly

into the cream leather seat. It was a gorgeous car, she thought enviously, what with the soft leather and the walnut trim and the air-conditioning. So much nicer than Tom's battered Ford, whose heater was permanently stuck on cold. She could see how anyone could get used to travelling in style.

Kevin pulled up outside the house and unlocked the front door.

'I'm back,' he called. 'I've got a visitor with me.'

Jim emerged into the hallway. Her face was pale, her green eyes dull.

'Have you been drinking?' demanded Kevin abruptly.

'With me,' said Andie. 'Earlier. We shared some wine.'

'You're back early,' said Jin. 'I wasn't expecting you yet.'

'Part of the course was waterlogged,' Kevin told her, 'so we finished early. The bar was crowded too and I wasn't in the mood to stay.'

'Oh.'

'Kevin met me at the gate,' Andie explained. 'I didn't know how to get out.'

'There's a keypad,' said Jin.

'I know,' said Andie. 'But I didn't know the code.'

Jin's eyes flickered into life again as she smiled faintly. 'It's the same one as the one to get in.'

'Only I didn't know that either,' said Andie. 'You always let me in, remember?'

'I told her to come back to the house and dry off,' Kevin said as he strode towards the kitchen, the girls following behind him. 'She wanted to get the bus.'

'That's Andie for you,' said Jin drily. 'Ecologically sound as well as a woman of the people.'

'Sod off,' Andie told Jin.

'Disapproves of wealth and luxury,' Jin continued. 'Disapproves of me.'

Kevin frowned as he looked at Jin and then glanced at Andie. 'You two have a row?' he asked.

'Not really,' said Andie. 'A difference of opinion.'

'So she slagged me off like she always does.'

'I didn't mean to,' said Andie. 'You were getting at me first.'

'How?' demanded Jin. 'How did I get at you?'

'Asking me about my love life,' snapped Andie, 'when it's none of your concern.'

'I don't think this is getting us anywhere,' said Kevin coolly. 'Andie, if you're going to dry off you'd better do it now. Jin, darling, you look a bit under the weather yourself. Would you like to change too?'

'No,' said Jin tiredly. 'And I'm not under the weather. You always say that if I've had a drink.'

'You drink a lot,' said Kevin.

'I don't,' snapped Jin. 'Andie and I shared a bottle of wine. I'm a bit tired, that's all.'

'You're always tired these days,' said Kevin.

Andie looked at them uneasily. She'd never seen them snipe at each other before. Usually their habit of fawning and smiling and holding hands was enough to drive her demented. But this was different. And unpleasant.

'I'll dry off,' she said hastily.

'Third room on the right upstairs,' Jin said. 'There are towels in there. I'll get you a change of clothes.'

'Nothing you have will fit me.'

'I have clothes to fit everyone,' said Jin dismissively. 'I'm sure I'll find something.'

Andie shrugged and hurried up the stairs. She let herself into the bedroom Jin had mentioned and shivered as she peeled off her wet clothes. Honestly, she thought, how daft can the two of us get? Me stomping off down the garden in a flipping rainstorm just because I got annoyed with her? And her getting the hump with me for . . . well, she admitted to herself, for not being very nice, I suppose. I should keep my big mouth shut about Jin's lifestyle and simply leave her to it. But she frowned as she remembered the needling between Jin and Kevin and she wondered if everything in paradise was quite as idyllic as she supposed.

Kevin and Jin were in the kitchen, where Jin was putting the remains of the pizza into a black refuse sack.

341

'You and Andie were eating pizza?' he asked in amazement.

'What's so strange about that?'

'Everything,' said Kevin. 'She's here in the first place. You were drinking wine and eating pizza. You and she don't do that!'

'Well we did today,' said Jin. 'Not that it was an experience I particularly want to repeat.'

'Why?'

'She's a stupid cow,' said Jin. 'She hasn't a clue about life. Not a notion. Frigid bitch.'

'Jin!'

'Well she is,' muttered Jin.

Kevin shrugged. 'Maybe. I can never quite figure her out myself. What was she doing here anyway?'

Jin rubbed her eyes. 'You're not going to believe this,' she said. 'It was about Jack.'

Kevin looked at her in astonishment and fury as she told him about Jack's alter ego.

'I don't believe it!' he cried as he looked through the printed pages that Jin had given him. 'What the hell does your damn mother think she's playing at?'

'Well, if she doesn't know—'

'Of course she bloody knows!' snapped Kevin. 'Men like that don't accompany women for free. She must have paid for him to come back here and she's paying him now. And you know what, Jin, when she's run out of money she'll come looking to us. Just as we bloody suspected all along!'

'Yes, well . . .' Jin bit her lip.

'To think that I cared about her!' raged Kevin. 'When she was simply taking us all for fools!'

'I don't think—'

'Jin, listen to me.' Kevin looked angrily at his wife. 'Your mother is paying a man to live with her and have sex with her. Do you really think I can allow that?'

'It's not for you to allow or disallow,' said Jin. 'I don't want this situation to continue either, but you can't talk about allowing it as though my mother would take a blind bit of notice of what you thought.'

'I – we – have a position in the community,' said Kevin. 'Your mother will turn us all into laughing stocks!'

'She might not realise—'

'Don't be more stupid than you really are,' retorted Kevin.

Jin stared at him. 'I'm not stupid.'

'I didn't mean – oh, you know what I meant!' Kevin shook his head.

'You said I was stupid.'

'I am not going to get into an argument with you when there are far more pressing matters for us to worry about,' said Kevin. 'What I will say is that you have to face facts and realise that though we all thought Cora was an innocent pawn, she's actually been pulling the strings. And I don't know why she's invited this man to stay with her, but he's not going to spend another night under her roof if I can help it. We'll be the laughing stock of the country if this gets out!'

'Kevin, we can't barge in on them,' protested Jin.

'Oh can't we?' His voice was grim.

'I told Andie you'd look after things, but Kevin, she's my mother, and I don't care how silly she's been, you can't treat her like an employee or something, you have to be nice to her.'

'Silly!' Kevin snorted. 'More than silly. She's having sex with a man and paying him. That's criminal, not silly.'

'She's been through a lot in the past year,' said Jin.

'Darling, other women lose their husbands. They don't rush around with a chequebook in their hands paying for blokes to hop into bed with them. They have some dignity.'

'You're making it sound sordid.'

'It *is* sordid.'

'No worse than Ivor McDermott and his blonde bimbo bombshell,' snapped Jin.

'Hi there.' Andie, a blue robe wrapped tightly around her, walked into the room. 'Sorry, Jin, but you said you'd get me something to wear and I really have to go home now.'

'Oh, right. Sure.'

'What do you think, Andie?' asked Kevin. 'Should we call in to see Cora and Jack on the way back to your flat?'

343

She stared at him.

'I take it you don't think so?' he said into her horrified silence.

'Well, it's not that, it's just . . . what would we say?' she asked. 'I mean, don't you think we have to be sensitive about it?'

'As sensitive as Cora's being by pretending this guy is just a friend?'

'Look, it must be embarrassing for her,' protested Andie.

'Embarrassing is hardly the word,' said Kevin. 'Expensive, maybe.'

'Kevin, can't we all just sleep on it?' suggested Jin. 'Not rush into doing something we might regret?'

'If you ask me, we've all pussyfooted around the issue far too much already,' said Kevin. His face was red with anger as he cracked his fingers. 'But I'm prepared to leave it temporarily while you think of sensitive ways to deal with your mother's total insanity. Only because if I went there now I'd probably hit him and then he'd sue me for assault. Which he probably wants.'

'Surely not,' said Jin.

'You're so naïve,' said Kevin tautly. He turned to look at Andie. 'How long will it take you to get dressed?'

'As long as it takes me to squeeze into something belonging to Jin,' replied Andie wryly.

'I'll see what I can do,' said Jin sourly. 'Come upstairs with me again.'

Andie trudged after her sister, wincing at the pain in her ankle. 'I'm sorry,' she said. 'I didn't mean to come back.'

'How did you intend getting out?' asked Jin.

'I was debating climbing the wall,' said Andie.

Jin looked at her and shook her head. 'Sometimes you're still ten years old,' she said.

'Don't get at me.' Andie was suddenly tired.

'OK.' Jin didn't want to argue any more either. 'Let's find you something to wear.'

'An old tracksuit?' Andie suggested as Jin pushed open her bedroom door.

'Do you spend your time *wanting* to look like a frump?' Jin slid open the doors of her wardrobe and took a pair of soft caramel-coloured trousers from the rails. 'These are very loose-fitting,' she

344

told Andie. 'Too big for me actually, I haven't worn them. But I have the perfect top to go with them.' She began sorting through a rail and then spun around to look at Andie. 'What the hell are those you're wearing?'

'A bra and knickers,' said Andie defensively. 'What d'you think they are?'

'They look like you've washed them a hundred times with a pair of blue socks,' said Jin. 'For heaven's sake!'

'I do have other underwear,' retorted Andie. 'This is my slouching-around-in stuff.'

'And when does the other stuff get an airing?' Jin opened a drawer and took out a pale cream bra embroidered with pink and blue flowers and matching embroidered briefs.

'Regularly,' said Andie.

'Really?' Jin handed her the bra and briefs.

'I'm not wearing your knickers!' Andie sounded scandalised.

'They're new,' said Jin. 'I haven't worn them before. They'll fit you. They're kind of broad.'

'Gee, thanks.'

'Oh, stop it,' said Jin. 'If you're going to wear my clothes you'd better wear something good underneath too. Here.' She proffered a chocolate-brown V-neck top. 'This goes well with the trousers.'

'Pity about my boots,' said Andie after she'd dressed in Jin's clothes and brushed out her copper hair. 'They will rather spoil the elegant look.'

'You look great,' said Jin critically. 'Which you could do all the time if you bothered to make the slightest bit of effort.'

'I told you,' said Andie as she admired her reflection (elegant, she thought; her sister really did know about clothes) in Jin's full-length mirror, 'I do dress up from time to time. Just not usually when you're around.'

'You looked lovely at the birthday celebrations,' said Jin.

'You said that before.'

'It's true.'

'There must be a man,' said Jin, 'for whom you wear decent underwear and sexy clothes.'

Andie swallowed the lump that materialised in her throat. But this time she didn't snap at her sister. 'I don't know if it will last.'

'Why?'

'There are reasons.'

'What sort of reasons?'

Andie shrugged.

'Maybe it will work out even if it's not going great at the moment. Maybe you're just not giving it a chance!'

'No,' said Andie slowly and thoughtfully. 'I think I've given it every chance. I'm just not so sure we're ever going to make it. I don't know if we can.'

Jin looked at her curiously. But then Andie bundled her damp clothes together and shoved them into the paper carrier bag on the bed. 'I'd better go,' she said.

'Don't waste that look on sitting in tonight.' Jin smiled crookedly at her. 'Slap on a bit of foundation and lippy and get out there.'

Andie smiled and hugged her sister. 'Maybe,' she said. 'I doubt it, but maybe.'

As she'd suspected, her clunky boots ruined the overall effect of the stylish clothes. But Kevin whistled appreciatively as she walked into the kitchen and then held up one of the For Sale brochures and asked Jin what the hell they were all about.

'Ideas,' she said easily.

'Hope you're not getting any ideas about moving,' he told her darkly.

'Only ideas,' she repeated.

Andie raised an eyebrow in her direction, but Jin ignored her.

'I'll call you tomorrow,' she said. 'We'll decide on what to do about Mum then. Me and Kevin will talk it over tonight.'

'OK.'

'Let's go,' said Kevin.

Andie got into the car beside him and settled into the luxurious seat again. He opened the gates by remote control and they were soon speeding down the Malahide Road towards the city.

'Is Jin actually thinking of buying a new house?' he asked Andie abruptly.

'Oh, I don't know,' she replied airily. 'I suppose everyone looks at houses for sale from time to time.'

Kevin grunted. 'I know her. She gets ideas into her head.'

'Don't we all.'

'She likes to act on them.'

'I'm sure she wouldn't do anything without consulting you first.'

Kevin's eyes flickered over to her but Andie was looking straight ahead.

'Briarlawns is a perfect home,' he said.

'It's lovely,' agreed Andie, 'but I think it's on the big side for two people. I asked Jin whether you were thinking of starting a family but she didn't seem to want to talk about it very much.'

'It's our own business,' said Kevin coldly.

'Sure it is,' said Andie. 'But you know, Kevin, it's getting on a bit for her.'

'She's only thirty-one,' he said scornfully.

'I know. I know. But sometimes it takes time before you strike lucky.'

'Did she put you up to this?' he asked.

'Up to what?'

'Baby talk.'

'Of course not,' said Andie. 'I was just making conversation.'

'Well don't,' said Kevin. 'Especially when you don't have the faintest idea what you're talking about.'

They drove the rest of the way in silence. Andie could feel Kevin's annoyance hanging in the air and she was glad to get out of the car and let herself in to her building. She sighed in relief as she closed the entrance door behind her.

Then she stopped in shock when she saw Jack Ferguson sitting on the stairs in front of her, watching her.

Chapter 27

Impromptu in G Flat Major – Schubert

As soon as Andie and Kevin had gone, Jin went back upstairs and took out the mother and baby book again. She knew that her behaviour was becoming obsessive but she couldn't seem to help herself. She was totally beguiled by the baby pictures now, even the ones that only a few hours earlier she'd thought were horrible and disgusting. This time they were beautiful to her, an affirmation of the power of love. Tears slid down her cheeks and on to the glossy pages of the book. There would be no baby to cement her love for Kevin. No child that they would create together. No one to carry on after they'd gone.

She was being silly, she told herself for the hundredth time. She'd always despised people who thought that having children to carry on your line was important. She'd told them that it was living your own life as best you could that mattered, not hoping you lived on through someone else. And she still believed that. Only she couldn't bear the idea of there not being someone else. Of not having a baby of her own.

The phone rang and startled her so much that she dropped the book. Its spine cracked and the by now well-thumbed pages came away from the covers. She gathered them up and put the book back in the locker before lifting the receiver.

'Is my husband there?'

Jin bristled at the clipped, arrogant tones of Monica Dixon-Smith. It drove her mad the way the woman still called Kevin her husband, but she refused to rise to the bait by arguing the point.

'Kevin is out at the moment,' she said. 'Do you want me to pass on a message?'

'Where is he?' asked Monica. 'I thought he was back from his golf.'

You really are such a cow, thought Jin. It's no wonder he left you.

'Actually he's dropping my sister home,' she said sweetly. 'She was here earlier but of course the weather turned bad so Kevin offered to give her a lift.' And fuck you too, she thought, I do hope you like knowing what a cosy little family we are. As if.

'Get him to call me when he gets back,' said Monica. 'I need to speak to him.'

'I'll tell him you rang,' said Jin.

'Make sure he calls me.' Monica's voice was firm. 'It's important.'

'I'll tell him you rang,' repeated Jin.

'By the way,' said Monica casually, 'what's this I hear about your mother?'

Jin stiffened. 'Pardon?'

'Your mother,' said Monica again. 'I believe there's a new man in her life.'

'My mother has lots of friends,' said Jin.

'But much younger friends?' Monica's voice was laden with innuendo.

'I really don't think what my mother does is any business of yours,' retorted Jin.

Monica laughed. 'There's no such thing as a private life,' she said smugly.

'I'll get Kevin to call you.' Jin's hand was shaking as she hung up the phone. The last thing she wanted was gossip about her mother. But it was already starting. When the true nature of Jack and Cora's relationship became common knowledge Kevin would go ballistic. And she wouldn't, couldn't blame him.

'What are you doing here?' Andie's voice was harsh as she stood in front of Jack.

'I'm here to talk to you,' said Jack. 'To clear the air.'

349

'There's no air to be cleared,' said Andie. 'I apologise for my behaviour in throwing myself at you the other day. I apologise for expecting you to reciprocate. Especially without a fee.'

'Andie!'

'And I apologise for muttering your other name last night,' she continued. 'I realise that it was uncomfortable for you.'

'I was surprised,' said Jack.

'I bet you were.'

'And that's why I'm here,' he told her. 'To have a few words.'

'It'll take more than a few words,' said Andie.

'I realise that.' Jack looked uncomfortable. 'I want to explain some things to you.'

'It's my mother you should be explaining to,' said Andie.

'Your mother doesn't need any explanations,' said Jack. 'She knows what she's doing.'

Andie felt her stomach turn over. He was standing in front of her and admitting that Cora was paying him for sex. She couldn't really believe it, even now. And, quite suddenly, she didn't want to talk to him on her own. She hadn't been looking forward to some big confrontation scene with Kevin and Jin attacking him, but she wasn't going to have this conversation with him by herself. She might find him attractive, but he was still a male escort, for heaven's sake! She really didn't think she wanted to spend her evening talking to a male escort. A male escort she'd kissed!

'Look, whatever you and Ma are doing is your own concern,' said Andie. 'I won't deny that my family aren't happy about it. I won't deny that Kevin isn't planning to have a deep discussion with you about it. And I won't deny that we really, really want you out of her life. But whatever the arrangement is between you, that's nothing to do with me and I'm not going to talk about it.'

'There isn't an arrangement,' said Jack forcefully. 'Not the kind you think anyway.'

'Jack . . . Todd – whatever your actual name is – I don't care what kind of arrangement it is. I really don't. All I care about is the fact that she's making a fool of herself and she'll get hurt. At first it was more that she'd get hurt than that she'd make a fool of herself, but maybe we were all wrong about that. Maybe she's a lot more clued up than we gave her credit for. It doesn't matter. But we're not keen on you hanging round much longer.' She looked him straight in the eye. 'We don't think she can afford to keep you hanging round for much longer either.'

'That's exactly where you're wrong!' Jack raised his voice and looked helplessly at her. 'That's what I'm trying to explain to you.'

'I don't want to hear some kind of pathetic explanation that it took you all of a day to come up with,' snapped Andie. 'You don't seem to understand. Whatever you and she have agreed, whatever's happened, it doesn't matter. It's the future that matters to us.'

'You are *so* wrong about me,' said Jack. 'And if you'd let me come up to your apartment I'll explain it. But not here.'

'You are *not* coming up to my flat,' said Andie firmly. 'And it's not because I don't think I can resist your charms or anything like that. As I said, I was upset the other night and I didn't know what I was doing. Well, I did actually but it was a big, big mistake. Now I don't know how much you're clocking up in talking to me and whether that's going on Ma's bill too, so just forget it!'

'You are the most pig-headed woman I've ever met.' His eyes flashed in anger. 'And possibly the most stupid too.'

'Oh, I don't know.' She shrugged. 'I got a free kiss, didn't I?'

'Andie—'

'Is everything all right?'

Andie hadn't heard the door open but suddenly she realised that Dominic Lyster was standing on the stairs looking down at them, his dark eyes full of concern.

'Everything's fine, Dominic,' she said. 'Jack was just going.'

'But—'

'You heard her,' said Dominic. 'You're just going, apparently.'

'Andie, you're being really stupid about this. You need to call round to the house. Talk to Cora and me together.'

The idea of sitting in front of them, discussing their financial and sexual arrangements, was revolting. She shuddered. Dominic walked down the stairs and put his arm on her shoulder.

'I was going to ask you in for a cup of tea,' he said to her. 'I was supposed to be picking up the girls tonight but Charlotte changed

351

the arrangements, so I'm on my own this evening and I'd love the company.'

'That's really nice of you.' She stood closer to Dominic. 'Well, Jack, I'm sure we'll talk again. But not now.'

Jack looked at her in frustration and then shook his head. 'You're all crazy, you know,' he said. 'You and that sister of yours and her freaky controlling husband. None of you has a clue.'

'Thanks for sharing that with me,' she said. 'Now, as you can see, I've things to do.'

'Right.' He turned and opened the entrance door. 'Have it your way. Go round thinking complete rubbish if that's what you want. Only Cora deserves better!' He walked out and slammed the door behind him. Andie winced.

'That cup of tea?' suggested Dominic.

'Would be really, really welcome,' she told him in relief.

When Kevin got back to the house Jin was in the chill-out room flicking through the TV channels with the remote control. She'd changed into a pair of black Calvin Klein sweatpants and a matching sweatshirt and had tucked her legs under her body so that she was cocooned into a corner of the leather sofa. Kevin slid his shoes from his feet and flopped into the armchair opposite.

'God, but your sister is irritating,' he said.

'I know.'

'So why was she here again?'

'I told you. She'd found out that stuff about Jack. Or Todd. She wanted to tell me.'

'So why'd she come out. Why didn't she just phone?'

'I don't know,' said Jin.

'A bit unusual.'

'Yes.'

'And you sat around, ate pizza, drank wine, looked at houses and talked about having children.'

'What?' Jin stared at him. 'No we didn't. We sat around, talked about Jack and Mum, ordered pizza and had two glasses of wine each. I showed her some brochures of houses for sale and she wanted to know why I'd think of moving and I said this house

352

was a bit big maybe and she asked if we were having kids and I said no.' The words came out in a tumbled rush. 'We didn't talk about anything. We just said things. It's different.'

'Because she asked me about it in the car,' said Kevin.

'About what?'

'About us having a family,' he said grimly. 'I told her it was none of her business but she clearly thinks it is.'

'You're getting it all wrong,' protested Jin. 'It was all very casual.'

'Really.'

'Yes, really,' said Jin. 'I didn't tell her there was no chance of us ever having a baby because you'd had the snip and I didn't tell her that you hated kids and I didn't tell her anything at all about our private life because that's exactly what it is and I don't go round sharing it with people, even my sister.'

She glared at Kevin for a moment, then looked away. He said nothing and she turned towards him again. 'Monica phoned.'

'Huh?'

'Monica. Your ex-wife. She phoned looking for you.'

'What did she want?'

'I don't know,' said Jin. 'She didn't tell me. But she passed a remark about Mum.'

'What sort of remark?'

'That she was seeing someone.'

'Oh bloody hell!' Kevin got up from the armchair and stalked out of the room. Jin rubbed her forehead and picked up the remote control again.

Andie's teeth were chattering as she sat at Dominic's square table and wrapped her fingers around the mug of hot tea he'd just handed her.

'Crisis?' he asked. It was the only thing he'd said other than to tell her to sit down.

'Oh, Dominic.' Andie pressed the mug against her forehead. 'I can't believe the things that are going on in our family at the moment.'

'All to do with your mum and the guy with the six-pack abs?'

353

She looked up at him and smiled faintly. 'I know. It's so insane. It was bad enough when he was just a freeloading bum from the States, but now that he's . . . he's . . .'

'He wanted to explain to you,' said Dominic.

'Like he actually could,' Andie retorted. 'Oh, maybe he could come up with something like "It's so different this time, I really love her" or "I charge your mother half-rates".' She groaned. 'It's so horrible. I can't believe she's doing it.'

'Neither can I, to be honest,' said Dominic. 'She's a nice lady, your mum. Any time I've bumped into her when she's called around she's always friendly and – well, normal.'

'That's just the point,' cried Andie. 'She's a fifty-eight-year-old suburban woman. They don't go around picking up men and paying them for sex.' She sighed. 'Or maybe they do. Maybe I'm as hopeless and out of date as everyone seems to think and I've absolutely no clue about what goes on up the garden path any more. Maybe they're all bloody well at it!'

He laughed. 'I don't think there are gangs of women shelling out cash for blokes,' he told her. 'At least, I haven't heard of it myself, unfortunately.'

'You have enough women of your own,' she said sharply.

'You said that to me before,' he told her. 'And not that many, Andie. In the year there's only been three. Don't hit me over the head, but one of them was a one-night stand and the other two both lasted a couple of months. Kathryn, the most recent, gave me the push a few days ago. She said I wasn't ready for commitment.' He laughed wryly. 'Actually I think I was far too ready, you know? Trying to get someone to fill Charlotte's place. But that was silly. So maybe I should do what you seem to think I was doing and bring a different woman here every night.'

'I'm not getting involved in anyone's relationships any more,' she said tiredly. 'You could have a harem up here for all I care.'

'Chance would be a fine thing.' He smiled lightly at her. 'Can I refill that for you?'

She nodded. 'Thanks.'

'So what's the word with your own man?' His back was to her as he filled her mug and he didn't see the shadow that crossed her

354

face. He turned and handed the mug back to her. 'Not good?' he suggested into her silence.

'I still love him,' she said tightly. 'But it's not as easy as just loving.'

'I'm sorry,' said Dominic.

'We'll work it out.' Andie sighed. 'Maybe. Someday. Somehow.'

'Don't you think you're wasting a lot of time?'

She shook her head. 'I don't want anyone but him.'

'Maybe you could give someone else a chance,' suggested Dominic. 'Maybe you're blocking out other potential boyfriends because of him.'

'You tend to do that when you're in love with someone,' remarked Andie.

He smiled at her. 'True.'

'Why did your marriage break up?' she asked suddenly.

'The usual,' he said. 'We did it for the wrong reasons. We thought we loved each other but it was just a mad lust kind of thing. As well as the fact that her best friend was getting married and she thought it'd be nice to do it too.'

'So you're blaming her?'

He shook his head. 'I was equally thick. I kept thinking it'd be a good day out, and we booked a great place in Thailand for our honeymoon . . .' He sighed. 'I think I knew as soon as we came home it was a mistake.'

'But you stayed together,' said Andie. 'You had kids.'

'I might have known it was a mistake but I certainly wasn't going to admit it,' said Dominic. 'Besides, the lust thing was still going strong. And then when we had Amelie – well, I was besotted with her, of course. So I didn't leave. Charlotte got pregnant again very quickly. So it wasn't until the girls were a bit older that I realised that she and I barely had a word to say to each other.'

'Were you horrible to her?' asked Andie. 'Did you have affairs?'

Dominic laughed. 'Nothing so dramatic. I came home one evening and she'd left a note to say she and the girls had gone to stay with a friend for a couple of days. That's all it was from her point of view, a weekend away. But she hadn't discussed it with me, hadn't asked me what my plans were . . . I realised we were living totally separate lives.'

'But it wasn't amicable, your split? You said that you and she can talk civilly now but it wasn't like that before?'

'Oh, well, when I said I thought it was all over, she went nuts. And we had massive rows about custody of the girls and the house and all of those kind of things. She got a much better solicitor than me, I'm afraid. But you get over it in the end, Andie. And now we're . . . well, not friends, I suppose, but we do our best for the girls and we're getting on with our lives.'

'Only you can have women in yours but it'd be a lot harder for her to have a man,' Andie pointed out.

'Possibly,' conceded Dominic.

'She's pregnant.'

Dominic looked at her in puzzlement before realisation dawned. 'Your boyfriend's wife?'

'Yes.'

'Oops.'

'She's been pregnant before but she kept losing them.'

Dominic said nothing.

'So he won't leave her.'

'That's hard luck,' said Dominic carefully.

'Depends on your point of view, doesn't it?' Andie pushed her hair out of her eyes. 'And I know I shouldn't resent her and her damn pregnancy and resent him for not being around when I want him, but I am so fucked up with guilt I don't know what to do next.'

'How about another mug of tea?' suggested Dominic.

Chapter 28

Serenade No 9 in D Major: Rondo – Mozart

'I have to go out,' said Kevin as he walked back into the chill-out room, the cordless phone still in his hand.

'Huh?' Jin looked up at him. 'Why?'

'I have to call over to Monica's.'

Jin felt herself stiffen. In all the time they'd been married he'd never called over to Monica's. As far as Jin was concerned, he barely even knew where Monica lived.

'What's the matter?' she asked.

Kevin looked unseeingly at her, his eyes focused on the middle distance, clearly miles away.

'Kevin,' she repeated more loudly. 'What's the matter? Why do you have to go to see Monica?'

'It's not Monica.' His voice crackled with anger. 'It's Cian.'

'Cian?' Jin looked at him in puzzlement. 'But you were playing golf with Cian earlier and everything was OK, wasn't it?'

'I know,' said Kevin. 'He was supposed to talk to me. But he didn't.'

'Talk about what?' asked Jin.

'About the fact that he's managed to get his damn girlfriend pregnant!' snapped Kevin. 'The stupid fucking idiot.'

The magazine she'd been reading slid from Jin's grasp and landed on the cream carpet. She stared at Kevin in disbelief.

'Fool, fool boy!' cried her husband. 'I can't believe he was so dense as to let some little tart trick him like that.'

Jin felt as though she'd been slapped in the face. Cian – Kevin's

357

son – had slept with a girl and got her pregnant. A girl who was a whole generation younger than Jin herself. The next Dixon baby wouldn't be hers and Kevin's. The next Dixon baby would be Kevin's grandchild. She closed her eyes and saw the image of Kevin's dark-haired son leaning over his new-born baby.

'Little tramp!' Kevin's voice shook with rage.

'Oh, come on!' Jin suddenly found her voice, although it seemed to her that the words were being spoken by someone else. 'Girls don't trick blokes by getting pregnant any more.'

'According to Monica they'd split up,' said Kevin. 'And got back together again at some friend's birthday party. I cannot believe he was so thick.'

'Maybe he loves her.' Jin flinched under Kevin's withering glare.

'I don't care whether he thinks he loves her or not,' he retorted. 'And I'll damn well kill him when I see him. I wondered why the hell he was rushing off after the golf. To get out of the danger zone. Monica had insisted he tell me today himself but he bottled it.'

Seeing the fury on Kevin's face Jin couldn't really blame Cian for wimping out.

'I need to see Monica and discuss what's to be done about this,' said Kevin. 'I'll be back later.'

'Sure,' said Jin. 'What do you think you'll come up with?'

'How the hell should I know?' demanded Kevin irritably. 'Well, I do know. The bottom line is that as far as we're concerned this is an unwanted baby. Cian told Monica that much anyway. He said it was a mistake. So if this girlfriend of his thinks that we're offering unlimited support she has another think coming.' His jaw twitched. 'I'll support her in getting rid of it but that's as far as I'll go.'

'Kevin!' Jin looked at him in horror. 'You can't mean that.'

'What can't I mean?'

'You'd pay for an abortion?' Jin's eyes were wide. 'Kevin, it's a baby.'

'Jin, my sweet, at this point it's nothing more than a few random cells,' said Kevin. 'And if this girl is sensible then we can deal with this in an equally sensible manner.'

'But she might want to keep it.' Jin was conscious that her head was throbbing with the enormity of the shock that Kevin's son had made his girlfriend pregnant. And she was gripped with an envy of this girl so intense that she almost cried out.

'If she elects to keep this child then she'll do it without my blessing,' said Kevin. 'And without any help from me either.'

'You can't carry on like this any more,' said Jin hotly. 'You can't just blame her and tell her that she has to get an abortion or suffer the consequences. Cian's the father. He has responsibilities.'

'Oh, get real!' Kevin glared at Jin. 'You think it was responsible of him to get her pregnant in the first place? Monica says that she's a little social climber from Donnycarney and that the only reason she went out with Cian was because he had a car of his own.'

'That's a terrible thing to say!' Jin's voice was shaking with anger too now. 'You don't know her. And what the hell is wrong with Donnycarney? It's not far from where my mother lives and where I was brought up, and don't you dare imply that our family is somehow beneath you!'

'Well, your mother *is* paying a bloke for sex,' retorted Kevin. 'I think that says it all.'

Jin stared at him, stunned. She clenched and unclenched her fist, holding back the impulse to physically assault him.

He looked at her for a moment then shrugged. 'Sorry,' he said. 'I'm angry.'

'So am I.'

'I'll be back later,' he said.

He picked up his car keys and walked out of the room.

'I can't drink any more tea.' Andie looked ruefully at Dominic. 'It's really nice of you to keep plying me with it but I've had enough.'

Dominic smiled at her. 'I'm enjoying your company,' he said.

'You always seem to be looking for company,' Andie told him. 'Are you lonely?'

'Sometimes,' he said frankly. 'You know those surveys which say that married men are the happiest people of all? Unmarried men rate low in the satisfaction stakes.'

'I've heard that all right,' said Andie. 'Seems strange when most of you simply want to keep on with your single lives after you get married.'

Dominic laughed. 'Not really. Just sometimes. But it's those times that land us in trouble.'

'I guess.' She stared into her empty mug and then looked up at him. 'Why do we all make such a mess of it?' she asked. 'Why is it when we have something good we let it slip away? Why do we want what we can't have?'

He regarded her sympathetically. 'You really love him, don't you, your married man?'

Andie picked at her fingernail. 'He's been part of my life for so long,' she whispered. 'And such a good part.'

'But perhaps you have to let him go,' said Dominic.

'Why?' Her grey-green eyes glittered. 'Why should I? If I want to keep on living my life the way I've been living it till now, that's my business, isn't it? It's just some stupid convention that makes us think that all men should be faithful to their wives all the time and that all wives should expect it.' She made a face. 'Yet loads of people have affairs, long-term ones too. And it works out perfectly fine for them.'

'You think they're happy?'

'I was happy,' she said fiercely. 'I *am* happy.'

'No you're not,' said Dominic.

'Yes I am,' she repeated forcefully.

'You weren't one bit happy that day in your flat,' Dominic told her. 'You were devastated.'

'Everyone goes through bad times,' said Andie.

'But you don't need to,' Dominic told her. 'And you'll end up going through even more of them in the future, won't you? When this woman has her baby? You really think you're going to be able to cope with that?'

Andie gritted her teeth. 'Yes.'

'Wouldn't it be so much better fun just going out with a bloke who has no strings attached?' asked Dominic.

'If a decent one existed,' said Andie.

'I like to think of myself as decent,' remarked Dominic.

Andie laughed. 'You're tied up with strings,' she said. 'A wife, two kids? No strings? Don't make me laugh.'

'But closure, so to speak, with the wife,' Dominic said. 'And a

360

good relationship with the kids. I've dealt with it, Andie. Your Tom hasn't.'

'I like you,' she said. 'I really do. But you're the bloke who lives upstairs.'

'I know,' he said. 'Look, why don't you come out for a few drinks with me tonight? Just as friends. But see what's going on in the city. See what it can be like when you're not afraid of being spotted with someone. See how much fun it can be, Andie.'

'It was never fun,' she said sharply.

'Oh, come on.' He made a face at her. 'You're all dressed up tonight. The least you can do is show it off a bit.'

She glanced down at Jin's trousers and jumper. It was amazing how people were so swayed by clothes, it really was. She sighed. She didn't want to sit in her flat and cry. But she knew that was what she'd do if she went downstairs now. 'Let me just change my shoes,' she said eventually. 'These boots don't go and I hurt my ankle earlier. I need something flatter.'

'OK,' he said. 'I'll be waiting for you.'

'I must be mad,' she said. 'I really must.'

Jin sat on the bed, the mother and baby book open again, the pages which had come away from the spine when she'd dropped it spread out on the duvet in front of her. It wasn't right, she thought, as the longing hammered away inside her, it wasn't right that Cian had got this girl pregnant when he hadn't even wanted to while his father had deliberately made sure that he'd never make anyone pregnant ever again. It wasn't right and it wasn't fair and she couldn't live with it any more. She picked up the picture of the baby boy nestling in his mother's arms and held it to her face, pressing it against her cheek so that she could almost believe that the child was beside her, touching her, part of her. She wondered what his name was and where he lived and, suddenly, how old he was now. And she wondered how he was growing up and whether he was a happy child and how his mother felt about allowing his picture to be in a book where it could be seen by anyone. 'When I have a baby,' Jin said out loud, 'I'll take millions of photos but they'll all be private ones, for me and for him.'

She got up from the bed and pulled open the top drawer of the chest in front of her. She took out a selection of tops and blouses and laid them on the bed. None of them would fit her when she became pregnant, but it wouldn't matter. Anyway, maternity clothes were much more stylish these days. She wasn't sure that she was the sort of person who could wear cropped T-shirts over a bump that hung out over cargo pants (she felt the look really only suited very young women), but she knew she could make herself appear well all the same. She put her hand to her stomach. It wasn't impossible, she told herself. There were ways it could be done. She just had to believe in it, that was all.

Dominic took Andie to a new bar on the quays. She looked around with interest as she managed to squeeze herself on to the last available stool near the plate-glass window. She hadn't even known this place existed. She was, she thought ruefully, totally out of touch. Dominic went to the bar and returned with her requested bottle of Miller and a pint of Guinness for himself. He stood beside her, gazing out at the brightly lit street, which was thronged with people.

'This was one of the things that instantly lost its appeal after I split up with Charlotte,' he said.

'What?'

'Being "out there",' he told her. 'Being available again. Going to bars. Meeting people.'

'I think you do pretty OK,' she remarked.

'It's not the same,' he said. He took a sip of his drink. 'When you've shared your life with someone it isn't easy to give it all up.'

Andie looked at him speculatively. 'Are you lecturing me?' she asked.

'Of course not.'

'Because I get the feeling we're having a multi-stranded conversation here.'

'No.' He shook his head. 'I suppose I'm just . . . musing.'

'I love Tom,' Andie told him. 'I've loved him for nearly four years. It's not some mad, passionate lust thing. We connect.'

Dominic nodded.

362

'We do,' insisted Andie. 'I love simply being with him. And he loves being with me too. We don't need to be out and about all the time. We're happy in each other's company.'

'Great,' said Dominic.

'You think I'm kidding myself.'

'No,' he said. 'I think you do love each other. I just don't know that there's much future in it. Not after what you told me.'

Andie bit her lip. 'He stayed the night,' she said softly. 'He stayed with me and he made me breakfast the next morning.'

Dominic said nothing.

'I don't think this was a good idea.' Andie looked up at him. 'I'm sorry. I'm not in the mood to be out tonight.'

'I'm not in the mood to be in,' said Dominic.

She frowned. 'Why?'

'I hate being in the flat on my own,' said Dominic. 'Not all the time, of course, but sometimes. And occasionally I drink too much. Which makes me start to think that I'm a sad old geezer who had it all and let it go. And whether it was my fault or hers doesn't really matter because in the end it all got fucked up.'

Andie looked at him sympathetically. Until now she'd never really thought about Dominic as anyone other than the bloke upstairs who had lots of girlfriends. But she realised that her reasoning for his lots of girlfriends and his were completely different. Besides, three in a year wasn't many for a fairly good-looking available bloke. He could easily have had more. It was strange, though, to think of him as a lonely person. He always seemed perfectly happy to her.

'I'm sorry.' She smiled at him and her eyes lit up. 'I've been really horrible and miserable and no fun at all to be out with. Let's just have a good time tonight and not think about ex-wives or bastard lovers or anything at all.'

Dominic laughed. 'OK.'

'But no falling into bed together later as friends with no strings attached,' warned Andie. 'I've never thought that was a good idea.'

'Nor have I,' said Dominic.

Jack and Cora sat in the orange-painted kitchen. Jack's laptop was open in front of him and he stabbed at the keys from time to time before lapsing into inactivity again. Cora was doing the newspaper crossword, although she was currently stumped by the clue for twenty-one across, which she knew was an anagram of 'rioted'. It was easy, she knew, but she simply couldn't concentrate tonight. She scratched the top of her head with her Biro and glanced at Jack.

He'd been frowning for most of the evening, Cora had noticed, and his brow was still furrowed as he looked at the screen in front of him. He'd gone out for a while earlier, telling her he needed to sort something out, and had come back in a temper. Although they'd originally intended to go out for something to eat he had cooked instead, the sizzling prawns in oil seeming to mirror the crackling tension around him. Cora hadn't said anything as he chopped and stir-fried and finally ladled the food on to her plate. Nor had she tried to talk to him afterwards when he'd gone upstairs and returned with the laptop, hunching into the armchair beside the fire.

Whenever Des had been in a temper, or had been upset for whatever reason, Cora had always cajoled him out of his black mood. She would work hard to entice him into a conversation by asking him questions or seeking his advice or simply chatting to him so that quite suddenly his humour would change and he'd be back to his normal sunny disposition. But it had been difficult and wearing. She didn't feel like starting it with Jack.

He looked up and caught her gaze.

'Not getting much done,' he said ruefully.

'No,' she agreed.

'I'm making a mess of it.'

'What are you working on?' she asked.

'The Great American Novel,' he told her. 'Only it's complete shit.'

Cora laughed. 'I'm sure it isn't.'

'Oh, it is,' said Jack definitely. 'It's one of the few things I can't blag my way into doing properly. I think I need talent for it but I don't think my talents really lie in that direction.'

'So what are you going to do?'

'Sometimes the skill is in knowing when to give up,' said Jack.

'Sometimes.' She nodded.

364

'Only I'm not sure that I want to give up.'

She shrugged. 'It's your choice.'

'You don't ever want to make me do anything.'

'Why should I?' asked Cora. 'You're an adult.'

'I know.' He laughed shortly. 'I haven't always behaved like one, though.'

'How should adults really behave?' asked Cora.

'Sensibly,' suggested Jack.

'Ah, rubbish.' Cora grinned at him. 'I've been sensible my whole life. Except maybe the last few weeks. And though the sensible part was great I haven't had as much fun in ages.'

'My coming here has caused you nothing but trouble,' said Jack.

She shook her head. 'Not at all. Sure, the girls are all in a heap, but that's their problem, not mine. And I suppose I was a bit off-hand with my friends because I didn't know how they'd react, but as you discovered, all that happened was that they loved you!'

Jack grinned lop-sidedly. 'I don't know about that.'

'They did. And why not? You're very lovable.'

'But I'm not a very good person,' said Jack.

'You told me,' Cora said.

'Not everything.'

She looked at him questioningly. 'There's still more about you?'

'I told you the important bits,' said Jack. 'At least, I told you the bits that I thought mattered. Only I think there are other issues that maybe matter more.'

'Do you have a dark, dark secret I know nothing about?' Cora sounded amused.

'It's not the sort of dark, dark secret you'd expect,' said Jack uncomfortably.

'You'd better tell me,' said Cora.

'I'm not sure I know how.' Jack closed the lid of the laptop and looked at her. 'But I'll do my best.'

Cora raised her eyebrows. 'Hang on a second,' she said as she printed the word 'editor' neatly in the space for twenty-one across before folding the paper and putting it on the table beside her. 'Now,' she said and regarded him thoughtfully with her emerald-green eyes. 'Tell me the worst.'

Chapter 29

Salut d'Amour – Elgar

It was late by the time Kevin arrived back from Monica's. His temper hadn't been improved in the time he'd spent listening to her wailing about the fact that Cian had ruined his life and that he'd never have been so stupid if Kevin had stayed around. He'd pointed out that Cian's life was hardly ruined and that everyone made mistakes. But when Cian had come into the room he'd yelled and shouted at him in a way he never had before, shocking himself with the intensity of his anger at his son. He'd been shocked too at how much older Cian had suddenly seemed, taking Kevin's fury and turning it back on him, telling him that there were worse things in life than getting a girl pregnant and that he would take responsibility for what had happened and that he didn't love Shona but that she was entitled to something from him. When Kevin had sneered at Cian, asking what something the boy could possibly mean, since as far as Kevin knew Cian didn't have much of his own, his son had calmly told him that he could get a job and offer some support to Shona and the baby.

Cian had dismissed Kevin's suggestion that he would pay for an abortion, telling him that it wasn't what Shona wanted and that it wasn't what he wanted either. And they'd argued fiercely about the whole concept of life and pregnancy and what was right until Kevin's head was spinning. Finally he'd yelled at Cian that there were two ways of looking at the future – one in which everything could be dealt with quickly, quietly and discreetly so that he could get on with his life, and the other which would be a mess of conflicting ideas and obligations and in which he would be forever bound to some girl with whom he had nothing in common – and that it was as clear as day which was the better option to take. Cian's retort, that Kevin had always taken the unemotional route, annoyed him more than he could say, especially as he saw Monica's own expression change from frustration and anger to a level of sympathy and understanding. Cian told Kevin that the decision whether to have the child or not wasn't up to him but to Shona, and he'd respect whatever choice she made.

In the end Kevin had left the house feeling that his relationship with his son had been fractured for ever and telling himself that children always were more trouble than they were worth, especially when they got a bit older and started making the sort of mistakes that you knew they could avoid. What was the point, he asked himself, in trying to share your experience of life with your children when they had no respect for it whatsoever?

He let himself into the house and pushed open the door to the chill-out room. There was no sign of Jin, who he assumed had already gone to bed. He went into the kitchen and made himself a cup of tea, which he drank sitting at the big pine table while he looked at the brochures of the houses for sale he'd spotted earlier. Why would she want to move? he asked himself as he glanced round the room. Briarlawns was as perfect a house as she could get. So what if it had a lot of bedrooms they didn't use? It was hardly a reason to move, was it? He frowned as he recalled his conversations with both Jin and Andie. The sisters had clearly discussed babies and children and Kevin was uneasy at the fact that this was becoming a recurring topic with Jin. Ever since she'd first told him about her friend Livia's pregnancy she'd dragged babies into the conversation whenever she could. And the evening she'd directly brought up the subject, the evening he'd made love to her on the stairway, he'd known that it was becoming a big issue with her. But he also knew that Jin blew hot and cold on ideas and that the entire baby thing was just a product of envy. She was always like that – when Saskia Barrett's husband had given her a new car as a present, Jin had complained that her Merc was out of date. When Lily O'Shea turned up at a party wearing a diamond necklace, Jin had wanted one too. He was convinced that this entire house-moving thing was simply because one or other of Jin's crowd of friends had moved and she was feeling left out; and as for the baby idea – as soon as Livia actually produced her child and ended up tired and exhausted he knew that Jin would go off it altogether. She wasn't the maternal type. He'd known that from the moment he first set eyes on her. That was why he'd fallen for her.

He drained his mug. Jin was a lovely woman to be with, absolutely fantastic in bed and usually an excellent wife, but there were times when she was extremely irritating. Her constant need to have the same as, if not more than, everyone else (while nice when he could gratify her every whim) could become very tiring. So could her desire to appear intelligent. He didn't need intelligence. He needed someone to look after him.

He put his mug in the dishwasher and walked up the stairs to their bedroom. Then he stood in surprise at the open door and looked at the empty bed. He walked through the bedroom and into the bathroom, but it, too, was empty. He frowned as he checked out the other six bedrooms, wondering if for some reason his argument with Jin earlier in the day had caused her to decide that she wanted to sleep alone. Yet even when they had their worst arguments they always slept together. He could think of nothing to make her want to be on her own. But there was no sign of her. He went back to the main bedroom and opened the walk-in wardrobe. It was impossible to tell whether any of her clothes were missing. She had so many that it would have been easy for her to take a caseful and for him not to know. But, he thought, why would she have done that? There was no reason for her to walk out. He scratched the top of his head.

Her bloody mother, he thought suddenly. Something must have happened with her bloody mother and her bloody toy-boy and Jin had gone racing down to Marino to sort it out. He gritted his teeth. He'd always known that man would be nothing but trouble. He picked up the phone and was about to hit the speed-dial for Cora's number when he hesitated. If there was some major dust-up going on then maybe he shouldn't just phone. Maybe he should go there. And yet if he did that and Jin wasn't at Cora's . . . He stood indecisively beside the phone. Why the hell hadn't she left him a note? Why did she have to act so impetuously? It was one of her biggest failings but one which he'd managed to almost eradicate over the past few years. He shook his head. He wouldn't ring. He'd wait for Jin to call him. Sooner or later she'd let him know what was going on.

Andie was drunk. Not horribly falling-down drunk, not hammered out of her skull drunk, but silly drunk so that everything Dominic Lyster said seemed incredibly witty and funny and made her giggle uncontrollably. He was laughing too as he helped her walk along the uneven pavement, mindful of her still-aching ankle as he steered her out of the way of oncoming pedestrians.

'One more,' she told him as they stood at the junction of O'Connell Street. 'One more drink and then we'll go home.'

'I think you've had enough,' said Dominic. 'I don't want to be responsible for your pounding head in the morning.'

'I am totally responsible for everything I do,' Andie told him solemnly as she pushed a lock of hair out of her eyes. 'I am in complete control – oops,' she added as she slipped off the edge of the pavement.

'You're not in complete control,' said Dominic. 'You're pissed.'

'A bit,' she admitted. 'A tiny, teensy, minuscule little bit. But I haven't been drunk in ages. And it's nice.'

Dominic grinned at her. 'You're not supposed to think that way,' he said sternly. 'You're meant to—'

'Oh, hell, Dominic, I don't care what I'm meant to do or meant to feel!' Andie interrupted him. 'You said come out and have a good time and that's what I'm doing. So I want one more drink.'

'OK, OK,' he said. 'Where?'

'There.' She pointed to the glass and chrome building that was Bar Tender. 'That's where I want to have a drink.'

'Whatever you like,' he said. 'Though I wouldn't have thought it'd be your thing.'

'It's exactly my thing,' she said as the pedestrian lights went green and she launched herself across the road.

Cora and Jack sat opposite each other. Neither of them spoke. Cora stared at a point on the wall past Jack's head while he fiddled with the stainless-steel chain of his watch-strap. Eventually the strap opened and Jack's watch clattered to the floor. He picked it up and replaced it on his wrist.

'Genuine?' asked Cora.

Jack looked at her uncomfortably. 'Yes.'

'Des bought one when we were in Turkey,' she said. 'It looked great. But it was called Bolex.' She smiled faintly. 'Caused great amusement among his mates.'

'I guess,' said Jack.

'The difficulty for me is that I thought I was helping you out.' Cora looked at him steadily. 'But now I see that you didn't really need my help at all.'

'I did,' said Jack, 'only not for the reasons you thought.'

'I think I feel foolish,' Cora told him. 'But I'm not sure I care.'

'I'm sorry I didn't tell you until now.'

Cora shrugged. 'What difference would it have made?'

'You wouldn't feel foolish. And you would have been able to keep things straight between yourself and Andie and Jin.'

'Oh, I kind of enjoyed that part of it,' said Cora. 'D'you know, they were so protective after Des died . . . at first I needed it and then I found it a bit overwhelming. Yet when they didn't call all the time I resented that too. So to be honest with you, Jack, I got a laugh out of seeing them so churned up about us. It was nice to have them looking at me as a completely different person. I was always just their mother before.'

'You were a good one, though,' said Jack. 'You still are.'

'I was an average mother,' Cora said. 'I don't think you ever believe you were good enough. I love them both but I can be super-critical of them sometimes. I don't mean to be – but I see them making mistakes and I want to interfere but I don't and then I think I should've said something . . . I don't praise them enough for the good things they do. When I was younger it was always about not letting your kids get big-headed about themselves and so I hold back from telling Andie that she's incredibly talented and acknowledging that Jin had a really good career . . . No, Jack, I don't know that I'm doing that good a job with them at all.'

370

'They care about you,' said Jack.

'Well, they're certainly consumed with worry about me!'

'I like that.' Jack smiled. 'I like the way Andie freaked out at me both at that awful party and tonight. She despises me now.'

'Oh, she'll come round,' said Cora briskly. 'If there's anything she needs to come round to, I suppose . . .' She looked at him quizzically. 'Where do we go from here?'

'I don't know,' said Jack. 'I guess I was using you, Cora. Being with you was – is – so simple. And I didn't want to complicate things. You're so relaxed about your life, it made me feel relaxed too.'

'And I was using you,' she said. 'To become relaxed. To get over Des.'

He smiled again. 'And have you?'

'Yes,' said Cora. 'I'll never stop loving him. But I'm over losing him. And that's because of you. So quit putting yourself down.'

'I don't always,' said Jack. 'I boast about the guides and my travels and that whole aspect of my life. I guess it's because it's the part I did right.'

'Jack, *you* were the reason the guides did so well,' said Cora. 'The ones you designed are a million miles better than the others. If you ask me, they have a lot to be grateful to you for. That's why you deserve the success you have now and that's why your family should be proud of you.'

'But no one can forgive the escort time,' said Jack. 'Because everyone thinks the same thing no matter why I did it in the first place.'

Cora gazed into the distance. 'Of course they can forgive it,' she said. 'I can't honestly say that I would have chosen that career for a son of mine either, but I can understand your motivation.'

'Yeah, but it just shows how stupid I was.'

'Not at all.' She grinned. 'I think it's a hoot really. Honestly I do. Though obviously you looked a lot better in those photos than you do now. Gorgeous and all though you are, I suppose it was hard work keeping the abs in photo-shoot condition.'

'Actually it was waxing the chest that was the worst,' he confessed.

She winced.

'As a matter of interest, what was your best night?' asked Cora.

'OK, but don't freak out or anything,' said Jack. 'I took the ex-wife of an oil-company zillionaire to the opera. In Milan. All paid for.'

'Did you sleep with her?' asked Cora.

'Cora—'

'I just wondered,' said Cora. 'After all, you told me why you did it and what it was all about but surely the temptation was there. On both sides.'

'Sleeping with the customers was never included in the price,' said Jack. 'Any arrangements are strictly personal. But, you know, we weren't that sort of agency. And I – it wasn't why I did it. I tried to explain that to you, Cora.'

'So did you sleep with her?' she asked again.

'No,' replied Jack. 'She was a lovely woman but she didn't want to sleep with me, she only wanted to show me off.'

'Did you sleep with any of them?'

'I—'

'I'm not judging you,' said Cora. 'Honestly I'm not. But I'd like to know.'

'I slept with a woman called Sheralyn,' said Jack eventually. 'She hired me for an office party. She was a really nice woman. And I slept with Tabitha.' He looked at Cora. 'I can't say that I didn't enjoy it but I suppose I thought that it was what they wanted too.'

'I slept with one man before Des,' she said. 'At the time I would've been branded a scarlet woman if anyone had found out! It's amazing how things change.'

'I guess.'

'If you'd gone out with them but not as an escort would you have slept with them?'

'Yes,' said Jack.

Cora sat back in the chair again and stretched her legs out in front of her. 'So what d'you think Andie is going to do?' she asked.

Jack looked surprised at the change in topic but his reply to Cora was thoughtful. 'Well, she clearly holds me in about as much esteem as a poisonous snake,' he said slowly. 'And she's really upset about her own relationship . . .' His voice trailed off as Cora frowned.

372

'With Tom?' she asked. 'What's the matter with him?'

He nodded uneasily. 'It's her private life, Cora. I can't talk about it.'

Cora's frown deepened. 'What's the matter with Tom?' she asked again.

'Nothing,' said Jack. 'Really, Cora, he's a nice bloke, but I'm not sure that Andie and he . . . Anyway, I think that's why—'

'She kissed you,' finished Cora.

'Makes me seem very escort-ish,' said Jack uneasily.

'Was she a good kisser?'

'Cora!'

'I'm hoping she was,' said Cora.

'I didn't kiss her back,' said Jack. 'Not in the way you mean.'

'Is there anything else you're keeping from me?' asked Cora.

'That's everything, I promise,' said Jack.

Cora nodded. 'OK. Well, I don't know how I feel about things right now,' she said. 'I'm going to bed. I need to sleep on it all.' She smiled at him. 'You need to sleep too. Because when Jin hears about the—'

'She'll hate me too,' he interrupted her. 'More than anyone, I reckon.'

'You might be right,' said Cora. 'Of all of us she'll resent not knowing your background. But she'll forgive you, you know she will!'

She got up from the chair and kissed Jack on the cheek. 'Don't wake me,' she said.

Andie hadn't been in Bar Tender since the opening night. Once again she stared in amazement at the TV screens hanging from the shining chrome pillars and winced at the pulsating noise of the music coming from the speakers. Alongside Dominic, she pushed her way through the throng of fashionable twenty-somethings who were dancing and drinking and chattering away over the deafening beat. How could Tom work somewhere like this? she wondered. His previous bar had been on much more traditional lines and he'd known many of the customers as regulars, had learned about them and always had something to say to them. There was nothing he could talk about to the throng of people here tonight and nobody he could possibly remember even though they were probably all regulars. Bar Tender was the in place to be in Dublin at the moment and Andie supposed that the mass of people who were here tonight always went to wherever the in place was.

'Wouldn't you rather go somewhere quieter?' yelled Dominic.

Andie shook her head and continued to make her way towards the huge circular bar, which was entirely made up of glass blocks with coloured lights illuminating them from behind.

'It's like something out of a sci-fi movie,' said Dominic as he followed her.

'It's interesting,' said Andie.

'I wouldn't have pegged you for a place like this,' Dominic told her. 'I'd have thought you were into elegant piano bars.'

'You don't know me at all,' said Andie.

'I realise that now.'

The crowd was three deep around the glass-blocked bar. Andie looked at the barmen in search of Tom. She knew that he was working tonight, though she supposed he wouldn't necessarily be behind the bar every minute. But no wonder he enjoyed coming to her flat after a night here, she thought as the music pounded in her head, this would tire anyone out. Then she saw him as he walked around the pillar from the far side of the bar, a cocktail shaker in his hand.

'Andie!' She realised that Dominic was pulling at her arm. 'What do you want to drink?'

Dominic had the attention of another barman. Andie glanced from him to Tom.

'A banana daiquiri,' she said.

'What?' Dominic looked at her in surprise.

'That's what I want.'

'Sure. OK.' Dominic turned back to the barman and ordered the drinks. He looked at Andie curiously. 'What's with the cocktails all of a sudden?' he asked.

'We weren't anywhere that did them until now.'

'Are you all right?' he asked.

'Of course.'

'Only you seem . . . oh!' His gaze followed hers and he watched as Tom poured the cocktail he'd been mixing into a tall glass. 'I didn't realise,' he said. 'I'm sorry.'

Andie turned to him. 'I've never seen him at work before,' she said.

'Right.' Dominic took his pint from the barman and sipped deeply.

'I didn't plan to come here,' she said. 'It just seemed like a good idea.'

'Sure,' said Dominic.

'I mean, I had a good time with you and everything, it's just . . .'

'I understand.'

'Do you?' She kept watching behind the bar. Tom hadn't seen her yet but she knew that eventually he would. He was mixing the cocktail now, her cocktail. She hadn't known for sure that he would when she ordered it – after all, they could probably all shake it with the best of them – but she'd hoped he might. And now he was pouring the daiquiri into a wide glass and placing a maraschino cherry on the top, but he still had no idea that the drink was for her.

It was weird, Andie thought, to watch him at work and to know that she had slept with him, had explored every part of his body, had seen him sleeping and had held him close. Nobody else in the bar knew that. To them he was just a barman. To her he was her meaning for living.

Tom looked up and saw her. His eyes widened and then he frowned.

'What's up?' he mouthed at her.

She shook her head. 'Nothing.'

'Why are you here?'

She shook her head again. Tom turned and spoke to one of the other barmen, then slipped out from behind the bar and pushed his way towards her.

'You never come here,' he said as he reached her.

'I know.' She shrugged. 'I was out tonight. I thought—'

'Out?' He stared at her.

She nodded. 'With Dominic.' She turned towards him but Dominic wasn't beside her any more. She shrugged. 'The bloke from the flat upstairs. He asked me for a drink.'

'And you came here with him?'

'We went to a different bar first.' Andie smiled.

'Are you drunk?' demanded Tom.

'A bit.'

'Andie, it's not a good idea to be here,' said Tom. 'Anyone could see you.'

'Well they could, but would they give a toss?' asked Andie. 'So what if anyone sees me? Nobody we know will see me. Nobody I know comes here.'

'Did you want to talk?' asked Tom. 'Only I'm working, Andie. I don't have time to talk to you. Not right now.'

'Do you love me?' she asked.

'Now that's a silly question.' Tom looked around him but nobody was taking any notice of them. 'You know I do.'

'But will you leave Elizabeth?'

'Some day.'

'When?'

'Andie, I don't know right now. And this isn't the time or the place, you know that.'

'I'm tired of the time and the place,' she said. 'I'm tired of everything.'

'You'll feel different in the morning,' said Tom. 'You've had too much to drink. You should get home.'

'Will you come back to the flat later?' she asked.

'I can't,' said Tom.

'Why?'

'Andie – I just can't.'

'Because you have to be with her. With Lizzie.'

Tom rubbed his face with his hand. 'Sweetheart, please.'

'She's the one really, isn't she?'

'You know how I feel about you,' said Tom. 'I've told you often enough.'

'But you can't do anything about it,' said Andie miserably. 'Because of Lizzie and the baby.'

'I'm doing what I can,' said Tom. 'You're the most important person in my life.'

'Yeah,' said Andie. 'I know.'

'Look, it's busy tonight, you can see that. I have to get behind the bar again.'

'Sure.'

'I'll call you tomorrow,' promised Tom. 'Just because I'm not with you every second of the day doesn't mean I don't love you. You must know that, darling. You must.'

'I know.' She closed her eyes. When she opened them Tom was already behind the bar again.

Jin sat on the bed. As usual the mother and baby book was open in front of her. It was too late to call him now, she thought, she should have done it earlier. She'd worked it all out, what she'd say to him, how she'd put the whole package together. She realised that it was different to what he normally did. She understood he might be a bit put out about it. But it all came down to money in the end, didn't it? And fortunately she had some money of her own. Enough, she hoped, to make it worth his while. Enough to make her dreams come true.

Chapter 30

Nocturne No 20 in C Sharp Minor – Chopin

K evin woke up at his usual time of six o'clock and rolled over in the bed, instantly awake as always. He sat upright in surprise as he realised that Jin wasn't there beside him and that she clearly hadn't come home at all the previous night. He'd lain awake until about two in the morning listening for the sound of her key in the lock but had finally fallen asleep, telling himself that she'd be home soon whatever the hell she'd got up to. He threw back the covers and got out of the bed. Maybe he was wrong and she was home. Maybe she'd seen him sleeping and decided not to disturb him by getting into bed beside him.

She wasn't in any of the guest bedrooms. He opened and closed each door noisily in the hope of waking her if she was there. He stood, indecisively, at the doorway of the last empty bedroom, a spot of worry gnawing at his stomach. Then the glossy page of a book, poking out from beneath the bed, caught his eye. He picked it up, looked at it and frowned deeply. The page was all about preparing for pregnancy. He exhaled sharply and frowned again. Silly, silly woman, he thought. What the hell are you up to? Then he screwed the loose page up into a ball, which he threw into the cane wastepaper basket beside the locker, and stomped down the stairs to fill the kettle with cold water.

Andie didn't wake until eleven, and when she did she immediately wished she hadn't. Her head was pounding, her eyes hurt and her mouth had the stale taste of too much drink. She lifted her head from the pillow and let it fall back straight away, wincing as the small army of men with Kango hammers started drilling again inside her skull. She remembered that it was precisely because she always had such horrible hangovers that she rarely got blitzed out of her mind. And she wished with all her heart that she hadn't ordered at least another two cocktails at Bar Tender last night and drunk them quickly while Tom worked the other side of the bar.

She couldn't actually remember getting home. She remembered looking around for Dominic and realising that he'd probably gone without her. She hadn't blamed him for that; she was feeling guilty about having dragged him into the pulsating bar in the first place. Beyond registering the fact that he was no longer anywhere to be seen, she hadn't been too upset at his disappearance. She vaguely recalled an unsteady walk to the entrance of the bar and then – nothing. She assumed she must have managed to get a cab home, but she shivered at the thought that she had absolutely no idea whether that was what had actually happened. But she was safely here in bed – still, she realised, wearing Jin's fancy underwear. She didn't remember getting undressed, even less hanging up Jin's trousers. She must have done, though, because they weren't on the floor as she'd expect if she'd simply stumbled into bed. She tried to sit up properly again and failed. Her whole body was a trembling mass. She groaned aloud and wondered why it was that she always seemed to do such stupid things.

Kevin normally played golf on Sunday mornings even if he'd already played the day before. The tee-off time was eight o'clock and he usually left Jin curled up beneath the covers. He didn't know what to do this morning. It was pretty pointless sitting round the house, but she wasn't answering her mobile phone and he had no idea where she was. He grunted in frustrated annoyance. He'd known she was getting into a state about the whole pregnancy thing and he supposed he should have been more alert to it, but honestly, what did she expect him to do? He couldn't understand women and their sudden changes of mind, especially when it came to family matters. It was one of the things that had unravelled his relationship with Monica. When he'd first married her she'd been

379

as enthusiastic about the business as him, working for a while as his unpaid secretary as he'd struggled to get his vision off the ground. And for a time she'd enjoyed the whole buzz of the new bars and new restaurants, meeting people, entertaining them . . . She'd been as much a part of it as he was. But then she'd lost interest, finding so-called better things to do, telling him that it was more important to spend time with the kids and get involved in all kinds of groups in the neighbourhood than worry about what she called his 'business empire'. She'd been dismissive of the money he'd made, telling him that the most important thing was being happy and having a healthy family. It had always surprised him that she didn't, in the end, spend more on clothes and make-up and having a good time.

Jin had been much more the kind of wife he'd expected in that regard. She positively glowed every time she signed a credit-card slip. And she'd been as anti-baby as him at the start, revelling in the fact that they could have limitless sex without any worries about conception. Now she'd apparently been brainwashed by that silly friend of hers, who'd clearly made her believe that all things infantile were worth it. He shook his head. No parent would ever admit that their children weren't worth it, but he sometimes wondered whether the supposed joy they brought wasn't entirely overrated. Clarissa, for example, had caused him nothing but grief as a child, mischievous, rebellious, just plain bold as far as he was concerned. And although he'd allowed her to wheedle money and clothes and goodness knows what else out of him when she was older, it didn't blind him to the fact that she was a pretty but vacuous teenager whose main aim in life was to be comfortable. Cian, on the other hand, had been a good kind of son to have, even though many of his interests weren't Kevin's own. But Kevin thought he got on pretty well with him, especially when they played golf together. Which was why he was angry that Cian hadn't told him about the trashy girlfriend, and why he was irritated by his son's desire to 'do the right thing' even though having an unplanned and unwanted child clearly wasn't the right thing at all.

Kevin rubbed his finger along the side of his nose. Had this business with Cian precipitated Jin's mad dash from the house? She'd been shocked at the news but surely it couldn't have upset her that much? Yet if she was already on edge about baby issues . . . He sighed deeply. He didn't know how she was thinking, didn't see that it mattered so much. Children were children and they grew into adults. It wasn't such a damn big deal, was it?

An hour later Andie finally made it out of bed and staggered into the kitchen, where she drank a pint of water and swallowed a couple of paracetamol tablets. Never again, she told herself sternly. Never, ever again. She slid her soothing Chopin nocturnes CD into the player and allowed the sounds to wash over her, easing the headache from behind her eyes and helping the tension to slip from her body.

If only she could remember, though. She curled up on the sofa and chewed at her bottom lip. She'd wanted to talk to Tom about their relationship but she knew she couldn't have said anything because she was certain she'd remember having any kind of proper conversation with him. She knew that he was, if not annoyed with her, then certainly disturbed at the fact that she'd shown up unexpectedly at Bar Tender. She wrinkled her nose. He'd been the one who occasionally wanted a whiff of excitement and danger from their relationship by bringing her to out-of-the-way public places where there was an outside chance of being seen. And then taking her to the bar in Ely Place, which wasn't out of the way at all. He'd done those things and he hadn't wanted her to get upset or annoyed with him, but she knew that it had been different last night. She wondered, suddenly chilled, if she'd blown it by showing up, if he felt he couldn't trust her any more.

The knock on the door startled her and caused the pounding in her head to start all over again. She got up from the sofa and opened it, a pained expression on her face.

'Hi,' said Dominic.

'Oh, hi.' She looked at him unenthusiastically. It was all very well for him to have got into a huff with her, she couldn't really blame him for that, but the fact was he'd abandoned her in the centre of the city when she was pissed out of her skull and that hadn't been a very neighbourly thing to do.

'I heard your CD and I realised you must be awake,' Dominic said. 'I called to see how you were.'

'Fine.'

'I was worried about you,' he said. 'You seemed to be so out of it.'

'Well I managed to get home, thanks, so everything's OK now.' She made to close the door but stopped at the expression on his face. 'What?' she added.

'Don't you remember?' he asked.

'Remember what?'

'I brought you home, Andie.'

She opened the door a little wider. 'Did you?'

'Yes. You were . . . disoriented. Upset even.'

'Why?' She held the door open some more. 'You'd better come in.'

'You were upset because that bloke, your married man, kept working and ignored you and you belted back a couple of those daiquiris and then insisted on a vodka martini, which, to be honest, tipped you over the edge.'

'I don't like vodka,' she said.

'Well, you drank it all the same.'

'I don't remember.' She looked at him irritably. 'I remember having another couple of drinks. I looked round for you. You were gone.'

'No I wasn't,' said Dominic. 'I thought at first that maybe your bloke would look after you. But he was working.'

'It wasn't his fault,' said Andie defensively. 'He couldn't leave the bar.'

'No,' said Dominic. 'But you were getting into a state. So I brought you home.'

'I'm sorry,' she said unhappily. 'I hope I didn't make a complete show of myself. And I really didn't mean to cause you any inconvenience.'

He smiled at her. 'You didn't on either account. And bringing you home wasn't a problem – we were going in the same direction.'

'True.' She rubbed her neck. 'Actually, I think I vaguely remember falling into the flat, but . . .'

'You tripped over that table.' Dominic indicated a small lamp table.

382

'Ah.'

'Then you fell down and couldn't get up again.'

'No.' She looked at him, aghast.

'Yes.' He grinned. 'So I tucked you into bed and said goodnight.'

'You what!' This time her look was horrified.

'Clearly it was the only place for you.'

'You put me to bed?' she asked. 'As in . . . Dominic, I was sort of undressed. Don't tell me you undressed me.'

'Only as far as your underwear,' he assured her. 'I didn't do anything.'

'I should hope not!' she cried, wincing as her headache bounced between her ears.

'What else could I do?' he asked. 'You were in a bad state, Andie. And part of that was my fault because I'd taken you out and told you to lighten up.' He looked at her curiously. 'Did you always intend to go to Bar Tender?'

'I don't know,' she replied. 'Not at first. I don't think so anyway. But after a while – then I wanted to go.'

'That man sure holds some deep attraction for you,' said Dominic.

'I told you before.' She shrugged. 'We belong together. I know you probably think it's crazy and impossible and maybe I think it is too – but we're right for each other, Dominic. We really are.'

'And what about his wife? And the baby?'

Andie frowned. 'I don't want to talk about them. Not now. I feel like shit and thinking about it will make me feel worse.'

'Because you know it's an impossible situation and always will be?'

'Oh shut up, Dominic!' Her eyes were bright as she turned to look at him. 'Don't preach at me. Don't moralise. You don't even know me that well.'

'I have seen you in your undies, though,' said Dominic lightly. 'And very pretty they were too.'

Another part of me that belongs to someone else, though, thought Andie bitterly. Looks like I can't have anything for myself.

Kevin thought about phoning the police but he knew that the first question they'd ask was whether he'd had a row with Jin and he

383

wasn't exactly sure how he'd be able to answer that one. Then he thought about ringing Robert Carlisle, his lawyer, to see whether they could make the guards believe that perhaps Jin had been kidnapped. After all, he thought, it could have happened. He was a prominent businessman and it wasn't entirely outside the bounds of possibility that someone would target Jin as a kidnap victim. Only, Kevin realised, if she'd been kidnapped he would've had a ransom demand by now. It didn't really make sense to get the guards involved when he knew what was going on. She'd clearly decided to stay away from him for a while to make him realise how much he wanted her and to somehow make him think harder about her desire for a child. Well, he thought, she could want all she liked but it just wasn't going to happen, and running away, even if only for a few days, wasn't going to change that. It wasn't as though he could simply turn the tap back on and suddenly start producing sperm for her. Things didn't happen that way. And she was out of her bloody mind if she thought he'd even consider having his vasectomy reversed. He shook his head in irritation. That was the problem with Jin, of course. She always thought she could have everything she wanted. She had to find out that there were some things she simply couldn't. Even if she was married to a man who could give her every material thing she could possibly desire.

He rang her mobile again but got her message minder. The last time he'd simply left a message saying 'Call me' but this time he spoke for longer.

'I know you're upset about something,' he said as calmly as he could. 'I realise that you're going through a bit of a crisis at the moment. It seems to be linked in with the whole baby issue. You know that it's impossible, Jin. So there's no point in staying away from home and trying to punish me in some way for not being able to give you just one thing out of the many things I've already given you. I want you to come home and come home now. Stop this nonsense. You know you matter to me.'

Jin wished she'd brought more stuff. It had been stupid to walk out of the house like that, with only a change of clothes hastily flung into her leather bag. But she'd thought that she could phone him

384

last night and sort everything out and that she might even be back this morning with the deed already done. Only there hadn't been any reply when she'd phoned Cora's and she'd wondered whether her mother and the playboy escort were already in bed together. She wasn't sure how Cora would react when and if Jack told her about her request, but she reckoned, if Cora was simply paying for him to be with her as they now suspected, there wasn't very much she could say. After all, a service was a service, wasn't it? She simply wanted Jack for a different purpose than her mother. She reckoned that he would have good healthy sperm. He was such a hunky kind of man she couldn't believe that his sperm wouldn't be kind of hunky too. And asking him to sleep with her and get her pregnant, well, that would kill two birds with one stone, wouldn't it, because however Cora reacted initially she'd be bound to get rid of Jack in the end. It simply wouldn't be possible for her to stay with the father of her daughter's baby.

Jin squeezed her eyes shut and rocked from side to side on the hotel bed. It sounded weird. Strange. People wouldn't really understand, would they? But it was a good plan. Use Jack for sperm. Andie had said she might consider using a bloke just to get pregnant. Jin had been shocked at the time but the thought had lodged in her brain. And then resurfaced when she'd discussed Jack with her sister. Why shouldn't he get her pregnant? It wasn't as though she was asking anything else from him. She didn't need him to be involved in anything to do with the child. It wasn't as though she needed a father figure. Kevin would be the father figure, wouldn't he?

She wrapped her arms around her knees. It wouldn't be easy to sell it to Kevin, of course. But maybe she could persuade him that it was one of those freak of nature things. Perhaps she could get him to think that the operation hadn't been as successful as he'd first thought. And once she had the baby he'd feel differently. She knew he would. He had children of his own. He must understand. OK, he was mad at Cian now but he still loved his son. She lay back on the bed. Kevin couldn't have meant what he said about Cian's girlfriend and the abortion. He couldn't. He'd come round to that too, wouldn't he?

She shivered suddenly. What if he didn't? What if she did get pregnant and he insisted on getting a test and discovered that he couldn't have fathered the child? What then? Would he throw her out? Say horrible things about her? Tell everyone that she'd slept with someone just to have a baby? He couldn't do that. His reputation would be ruined. She knew that she was considered to be a good catch. Kevin couldn't live with the idea that his wife had needed to get something – anything – from somebody else.

She opened the mother and baby book again and looked at the picture of the little boy nestled against his mother's breast. It would be worth it, she told herself, in the end it would definitely be worth it.

Chapter 31

Piano Sonata No 2 in B Flat Minor – Chopin

T he phone in Cora's house rang and rang but there was no answer. Jin bit her lip and wondered where her mother could be. She didn't want to call her on her mobile, somehow it would seem stranger to ask to speak to Jack on the mobile than it would have been at the house. Jin didn't know why this should be so but she knew it was.

And then she remembered. Cora and Jack were going to Dromoland Castle for their midweek break. Only it wasn't exactly midweek, it was Monday to Wednesday, which Cora had said worked out very inexpensively. Huh, thought Jin as she gazed out of the bedroom window of the hotel which overlooked the sludge-green river Liffey, inexpensive for whom? She wondered at what point Cora would simply run out of money, causing Jack to walk out. But, she thought to herself, it still really didn't make a whole heap of sense. After all, he'd actually talked about marrying Cora at that awful evening at Andrew Comiskey's. Why would he say something like that if he was only paid on a day-to-day basis? As part of his cover, so to speak? And he'd baited her about her becoming his step-daughter too, which had annoyed her beyond belief. What was the point in saying that? Surely if he was being paid to act a part he would have done it a little more graciously?

Well, it didn't really matter. She only had one part she wanted him to act. But she wasn't sure how or when she was going to be able to contact him. She looked at the screen of her expensive mobile phone and bit her bottom lip. There were three messages in her mail-box and she was pretty sure they were from Kevin, given the time that they'd been sent. She wondered at what point he'd discovered she'd left the house and at what point he'd realised she hadn't come home. And she wondered how upset he was at her departure. She sat back on the bed again. Her head was beginning to spin. She felt – as she had the previous night in her sudden mad dash from the house – disconnected from the world and very, very tired. She closed her eyes and allowed herself to drift into sleep again.

It was Wednesday morning when Kevin finally rang Andie. She was between lessons and reading a book about the mathematics of music (it was an undisputed fact that many people who were good at music were also good at numbers) when her phone chirped in her bag and caused her to jump in surprise.

'Andie, it's me. Kevin.'

'Kevin?' She certainly hadn't expected to receive a call from her brother-in-law. 'What's up?'

Kevin cleared his throat. 'I was wondering if you'd heard from Jin at all.'

'Jin? No. Why? Is anything the matter?'

He cleared his throat again. 'She isn't at home,' he said.

'Huh?' It took a second for Andie to register what Kevin was actually saying. 'Not at home? D'you mean she's left you?' Her voice rose to a squeak at the end of the sentence. Whatever might occur in her sister's life, Andie had never factored in Jin leaving Kevin as part of it.

'Not exactly,' he replied evenly. 'It's just that she was a bit upset, I think, and she's gone away.'

'Upset? About what?'

'It's not something I want to talk about over the phone,' said Kevin.

'Kevin!' Andie exploded at him. 'Don't be so bloody stupid. If she's upset and she's left you I'm entitled to know.'

'I forgot you overdramatised things,' said Kevin sourly.

'No I don't,' retorted Andie. 'You're the one who rang me looking to find out where she was. The least you can do is tell me why you think she's gone!'

'I don't know that she's gone exactly,' said Kevin. 'She hasn't taken any stuff. At least, if she has, it's not much.'

'Are you sure she's gone at all?' Andie suddenly felt herself begin to worry. Jin would never go anywhere without a ton of make-up and a caseful of clothes. 'Kevin, she couldn't have been attacked or anything could she?'

'No,' said Kevin. 'I know she's gone.'

'Well, did you guys have a row?'

'Look, I really don't want to go into all this right now,' said Kevin. 'I'm trying to sort things out. If you're telling me that you haven't seen or heard from Jin that's fine. I'll find her myself.'

'But Kevin . . .' Andie's voice trailed off.

'It's not a serious thing,' he told her firmly. 'It's something that I can work out with Jin myself. She just needs to see sense about it. Let me know if you hear from her, though.'

'Of course. But . . .' Andie realised she was talking into thin air. Kevin had hung up. She sat down in front of the piano and ran her fingers up and down the keys as she so often did when she was agitated. What the hell had happened between Jin and Kevin? When had Jin disappeared? Andie had been so shocked by Kevin's phone call that she hadn't asked him any of the important questions. And if Jin had left him, where on earth had she gone? Andie thumped the keys a little harder. Had Kevin called Cora yet? Had Jin and her husband argued about it? She worried her bottom lip as she remembered that Cora and Jack were away this week. But due back when? Today or tomorrow, she thought. She couldn't remember if Jin had actually told her.

She stopped playing scales and took her phone out of her bag again. She hit the call register menu and picked out Kevin's number. He answered it immediately.

'Dixon.'

'Kevin, it's me again.'

'Andie. Has she been in touch already?'

'No,' said Andie. 'But I need to know if you've talked to Ma.'

'Your mother is away until later today,' said Kevin.

'So you haven't called her?'

'No. I will.'

389

'Let me,' said Andie. 'If Jin has been in contact with her . . . well, she hasn't called you, has she, so maybe she's said something to Ma . . .'

'All right,' Kevin agreed after a pause. 'I don't know exactly when she's due back.'

'I'll call her now,' said Andie. 'Maybe Jin decided to join her.'

Kevin laughed shortly. 'Your mother and the paid escort? I hardly think so.'

'No, well, you're right, I suppose not,' said Andie. 'But you never know, do you?'

'Indeed,' said Kevin.

'What *did* you argue about?' asked Andie.

'It's none of your business,' snapped Kevin.

'Oh for heaven's sake!' she cried in exasperation. 'I'm trying to help you here.'

'You've done quite enough already,' returned Kevin. 'I'm not entirely convinced that this whole thing isn't your fault.'

'*My* fault?'

'Yes, your bloody fault,' snapped Kevin. 'You rushed out to our house last Saturday and you fed her some line about not being pregnant or about having kids and you upset her.'

'Is that what this is about?' demanded Andie. 'Because if so I don't know where you're getting your ideas from, Kevin Dixon, but I said nothing to her about getting pregnant.' She paused. 'I did say something about her clock ticking but it was harmless.'

'You might have thought it was harmless but of course that's you all over, isn't it, Andie? You only see things from your perspective. You don't know what's going on in other people's minds.'

'That's complete rubbish,' said Andie angrily. 'We chatted. That's all. I didn't talk about anything from my perspective. And you're a fine one to talk when your only perspective is your boring business.'

'That's ridiculous,' said Kevin. 'My business, my boring business as you put it, is what's kept your damn sister in the style to which she's allowed herself to become accustomed over the last four years, and if it wasn't for me she'd be still hawking her body round tacky catalogues.'

'Kevin!' Andie's grip tightened on her phone. 'How can you say that? You know that Jin was successful before she married you. She'd still be successful if she hadn't given it all up.'

'She's thirty-one years old,' said Kevin. 'She's getting long in the tooth for that sort of work.'

'Have you ever said this to her?' demanded Andie. 'Because if you have I can quite see why she's walked out on you, you pompous fucking prick.'

She winced as she realised she was talking to thin air again. Not surprisingly, Kevin had hung up.

Andie sighed deeply. She got up from the piano and walked across the room to the big window which overlooked the street below. People hurried by, wrapped up against the cold easterly breeze that chilled the air despite the cloudless blue sky. Where the hell are you, Jin? she wondered as she scrolled through her phone book to find her sister's mobile number. And what in heaven's name is the matter?

It was interesting how many times her phone rang, thought Jin, as she sat in the hotel bath and listened to it buzzing just out of reach. She was secretly pleased that Kevin had rung so often, even though his messages, which she'd eventually decided to access, had become sharper and sharper. She knew that he was annoyed with her but she didn't care. It was about time he realised that he wasn't the only person in the world with dreams and ambitions. It was about time he thought a little bit about her and her feelings. For the last few months their lives had revolved completely and utterly around the Oslo deal and she was sick of it. She'd been delighted when things finally came to a successful conclusion and had hoped that it would give him a bit more time to be with her again. A part of her had even welcomed the débâcle of Cora and Jack because it meant that Kevin had to focus on family rather than business matters. But it had all been overshadowed now by Cian and his girlfriend and the news of her pregnancy.

Jin gazed at her own body beneath the oil-scented water. It was still trim and firm thanks to her daily workouts and strict diet. She knew that she was a very attractive woman. She could see how Kevin might be put off by the idea of her flat stomach suddenly becoming rounder and rounder as her baby grew. But surely he could understand that the time had come when she wanted that to happen? Or maybe, she thought, he could understand it but he didn't want to do anything about it. She added more hot water as a tear trickled down her cheek. She was being unfair to Kevin. He'd had a damn vasectomy, hadn't he? What did she really expect him to do about it?

She expected him to sympathise with her, she realised. She expected him to regret the vasectomy. She expected him to, at the very least, say that he'd go to the doctor and talk about a reversal. But he'd done none of those things. He'd talked to her as though she was a child. He'd patronised her. And then he'd stormed off to discuss the probability of Cian's girlfriend having an abortion. Which was enough, in Jin's view, to make her see that there was no way Kevin would ever change his opinion on his vasectomy and no way he would ever understand the need she had for a child of her own.

She felt the longing surge up within her again, so strong that it was a physical sensation and made her draw her knees to her stomach involuntarily. She wondered if this was what had happened to Livia, if this was why a girl who had once shrieked with horror when a toddler had grasped her trouser leg with a chocolate-covered fist was now happily talking about easy-care clothes and sloppy T-shirts. She'd heard about women suddenly wanting children and feeling that it was an almost unstoppable force, and she'd never believed it. But now she felt that if she didn't have a baby of her own she would shrivel up and die with the longing within her. She wished she understood it. She wished she understood herself. But all she knew was that having her own child was the most important thing in the world to her. And nothing could stop her. Nothing.

Andie left a message on Jin's phone telling her that Kevin was a bit worried and that although she was perfectly entitled to disappear for a bit of R&R could she just ring home because she, Andie, was anxious too. Owing to the fact, she added, that Jin had apparently legged it without taking half her wardrobe. Andie felt as though this was a comment Jin would expect her to make. She didn't want to sound overanxious and nagging. She wanted her sister to call her and not feel pressurised about it.

After she'd left the message she dialled Cora's number. But her mother's phone was switched to her message minder too. Honestly, thought Andie irritably, what was the point of so many people having mobile phones if they didn't bother to have them switched on? She left a message for Cora to give her a shout when she got home and then switched her own phone off. She had a lesson in five minutes. At least she had a good reason to be out of touch for a while.

Chapter 32

Vocalise – Rachmaninoff

Andie didn't ring Cora until after she'd finished lessons for the day. She was pleased when the phone was answered after the third ring, but dismayed to hear Jack's voice on the line.

'Is my mother there?' she asked abruptly. The sudden fuss about Jin had pushed thoughts of Cora and Jack (and especially thoughts of Jack's disgusting profession) completely out of her head. She hadn't exactly forgotten about him, but he'd become irrelevant in her mind. He was hardly irrelevant now, though, asking her whether anything was the matter.

'Why should anything be the matter?' she asked irritably. 'I want to talk to my mother.'

'Cora's asleep,' said Jack. 'She got a headache on the way home from Dromoland. I didn't realise she suffered from migraine.'

'Oh, poor Ma!' Andie forgot about her dislike of Jack in her sympathy for Cora. Her mother didn't get the blinding headaches very often, but when she did she was totally wiped out. 'Did she eat chocolate, by any chance?'

'Actually, yes,' confirmed Jack.

'Silly woman.' Andie sniffed. 'She knows that it triggers it and she's usually really good at avoiding it. But every so often she gives in to the urge for a Flake.'

'It's my fault,' said Jack contritely. 'I bought it for her. She didn't say anything.'

'Typical Ma,' said Andie. 'She never does say anything.'

There was an awkward silence while Andie wondered whether she should confide in Jack and Jack wondered what on earth he could say to a woman who despised him for a whole variety of reasons and who now undoubtedly blamed him for Cora's migraine.

'Look, there's something I have to talk to you about,' he said abruptly. 'We haven't talked, Andie, and we need to.'

'No we don't,' she said and then stopped. 'Well, actually, yes we do. Because there are outstanding issues that need to be dealt with, and soon. But that's not why I'm ringing, Jack, and I'm not going to talk to you about them now either.'

'You can't keep pushing me out,' he said.

'Oh yes I can,' she said sharply. 'You're nothing but a – a . . .' She didn't quite know what to call him. 'Look, it doesn't matter at the moment. Maybe it's as well I'm talking to you. I want to know if Jin has been in touch with Ma.'

'Jin?'

'Yes, Jin. My sister. You know.'

'Of course I know,' said Jack testily. 'And she hasn't been in touch. She may have called earlier but she didn't leave a message. Cora turned off her phone when her headache started. Why? What's up with her?'

'Oh, nothing,' said Andie as lightly as she could. 'I just thought she might have contacted Ma, that's all.'

'About what?' asked Jack.

'It's none of your business,' replied Andie.

'Quit telling me what is and isn't my business.' Jack was annoyed. 'I want to explain things to you but you won't let me. So until you know the full facts you can take that self-satisfied, patronising tone out of your voice and get with the programme. You're hardly the best kind of person to be lecturing anyone else about their lifestyle.'

'And you're a complete faker,' said Andie. 'As soon as we get the chance, you're toast.'

'You don't have the faintest idea what you're talking about,' returned Jack.

'Oh yes I do,' she snapped. Then she sighed. 'Look, Jack, I know that you've made my mother happy. I do realise that. Although clearly at a financial cost to her. But I just don't think you're the

395

right route for her to take. I can't approve of what she's doing. You've got to understand that. I can't approve of you either and the kind of lifestyle you lead.'

'You kissed me, by the way,' said Jack shortly. '*You*. Kissed. Me. I didn't make any moves on you. So if anyone has a suspect lifestyle you'd want to check your own out first. And if anyone is doing anything to upset Cora it sure as hell isn't me.'

'Did you tell her?' Suddenly Andie was anxious. 'Surely you didn't tell her I kissed you?'

'I don't have *any* secrets from Cora,' said Jack. 'Which might be a bit of a surprise to you, Andie.'

'Oh my God!' Andie's hand flew to her cheek, which had begun to burn. 'You're joking. You couldn't have told her.'

'Why couldn't I?' asked Jack.

'Because – because . . .'

'Because it's showed you up?' he asked.

'I would have told her myself,' said Andie.

'I know. But I wouldn't have come out of it half as well, would I?'

'Jack . . .' She exhaled slowly. 'Jack, I didn't want to get involved in you and Cora. Not in anything. But Jin and I – we couldn't help ourselves.'

'Is there a message you want me to pass on to Cora?' he asked shortly.

'No,' said Andie. 'But if Jin calls please let me know.'

Jack replaced the receiver and frowned. He had no idea what that was all about. Why was Andie so anxious to know whether her sister had phoned? What mad, bad scheme had they cooked up now? A scheme that was probably backfiring on them in some way, only neither he nor they knew how.

He walked into the kitchen and sat down at the table. It was all his own fault, he supposed, for teasing them so much and making such a big thing out of his relationship with their mother. He hadn't intended to but they'd been so indignant and Cora had been so amused . . . He stared at the orange walls. It had all started out as a bit of a joke but somehow none of it was funny any more. He

396

hadn't intended to get entangled in their lives – hell, he thought, Cora hadn't intended him to get entangled in her life either. It was supposed to have been a bit of fun. Sure, he'd grown unexpectedly fond of her on the ship and he'd been surprised at himself when he'd kissed her, but he hadn't imagined things would go this far. Yet somehow they had. And somehow . . . he rested his head on his hands . . . somehow he was less convinced about finishing his research and heading back home to the States than he'd been at the start.

The phone rang again. He leaped out of the chair and hurried into the hallway. Cora didn't have a cordless phone and still kept hers in the hall. He didn't want the strident ringing to waken her.

'Yes?' he said softly.

'Jack? Is that you?'

'Yes,' he said.

'This is Jin Dixon,' said the voice. 'I need to see you and I need to see you now.'

Jack left a note for Cora to say that he'd gone to meet Jin and let himself out of the house. He didn't bother to ring Andie to tell her that her sister had called. After all, he reasoned, Andie had expected Jin to be looking for Cora and not for him. He walked slowly along the narrow residential roads bordered each side by the neat little houses until he reached the bus stop. Jin had asked him to meet her at the Morrison Hotel, which Jack knew was about as stylish a place as you could find in Dublin. He wasn't surprised that it would be Jin's choice of location, but he was intrigued as to what the meeting was all about.

He didn't have to wait long for a bus and the journey into the city took less than fifteen minutes. Jack liked being this close to the centre of things. When he'd lived in New York he'd rented a couple of rooms near Washington Square, which he'd loved. But his family home was out of town. Way out of town. He squeezed his eyes shut and tried to block out the sudden pictures of the house and the garden, his parents and the kind of life they'd wanted him to live. Not that he cared any more about what they thought, of course, but he knew that Marnie Ferguson would flip completely if she thought he was living with a woman only a few years younger than herself.

He got off the bus in O'Connell Street and then turned on to the quays and followed the boardwalk until he reached the hotel. Jin had said that she'd meet him in reception but he didn't see her in the darkened area until she stood up and walked towards him.

She looked wretched, he thought, despite her undoubted beauty. Her face was pale and without a trace of make-up. He hadn't seen her without make-up before. Her copper hair hung limply to her shoulders and her fabulous emerald-green eyes were dulled.

'Hello,' she said.

'Hi.' He looked at her curiously. 'What's with you, Jin? What's all this about?'

'I have a room,' she said, walking towards the lift. 'We can talk there.'

He followed her, looking around to see if he could spot her control-freak husband lurking behind a planter. It wouldn't have surprised him to discover that he was being set up in some way by the Dixons. He just wasn't exactly sure how yet. Cameras in the bedroom, he thought, as he followed Jin out of the lift. Perhaps she'd throw herself at him and then Kevin would jump out from the wardrobe with a video tape in hand. Jack laughed to himself. He was beginning to lose it completely, thanks to this crazy family.

Jin opened the door and stepped inside the room. Jack looked around to see if he could spot anyone secreted in a wardrobe or anywhere else, but it appeared quite normal. Jin sat in the chocolate-brown armchair beside the window.

'So, you're wondering why I've asked you here,' she said.

'I've given up wondering about you and your mad sister.' Jack kept his voice cheerful.

'We're not mad,' said Jin.

'Could've fooled me.'

'She told me all about you.'

'I guessed.'

'Do you make a lot of money?' asked Jin.

'As I tried to tell her—'

'Actually that doesn't really matter,' she interrupted him. 'I suppose what I wanted to do was to use your services.'

'Huh?' He stared at her.

'You're not cheap,' she said. 'Those prices – steep, aren't they? And that's without the sex.'

'Look, Jin, as I've tried to explain—'

'I don't want you to explain.'

'Why do neither of you want me to tell you what I actually did?' demanded Jack. 'What is it with you girls?'

'I'll tell you what it is with me,' said Jin. 'I want to get pregnant.'

Jack stared at her wordlessly.

'I want to get pregnant and my husband can't do it for me.'

'Kevin's impotent?' Jack's eyes opened wide.

'No,' said Jin sharply. 'He's actually very, very potent indeed. He's good in bed. Great, in fact. But he can't get me pregnant.'

'So . . . ?'

'So you can.'

Jack was speechless again.

'At least, I presume you can.' Suddenly Jin looked concerned. 'I didn't think of it before. You haven't had a vasectomy, have you?'

'And Kevin has?'

'He doesn't want kids,' said Jin forlornly. 'He has them already. And a grandchild on the way, though he doesn't want that. He thinks that his son's girlfriend should have an abortion. It's not up to him, though, is it?' She looked at Jack.

'No,' he said slowly. 'But listen, Jin—'

'I want a professional person to do a professional job,' she said. 'I'll pay you whatever you want. I don't need you to contribute to the child afterwards. My only condition is that after being with me you leave my mother alone.'

'If you seriously thought I could get you pregnant and then go home and play happy families with Cora you're even more deranged than I already think,' said Jack. After he'd spoken he wished he hadn't been so harsh. Her eyes filled with tears.

'It's a business proposition,' she said shakily. 'That's all. You must be used to it.'

'No,' he said. 'I'm not.'

'Maybe not this sort,' she agreed. 'But don't tell me that all those women you've escorted haven't asked you for a few additional services.'

Jack sighed deeply. 'Jin, I can't possibly do what you're asking.'

'Why?' she demanded. 'It's not so difficult. A few minutes, that's all.'

'You might not get pregnant,' said Jack drily.

'That's a risk I'm prepared to take,' she told him.

'Jin, I think you're really upset.' His voice was very gentle this time. 'I think that somehow things must have gotten a little too much for you. You're clearly not thinking straight. Even if I were to sleep with you and by some extraordinary chance you ended up pregnant, how on earth would you go back to Kevin and explain it?'

'I thought I'd worry about that later,' she said.

'You can't worry about it later,' he told her. 'Let's face it, Jin, your husband's had a vasectomy. It's not conducive to you suddenly discovering you're pregnant!'

'Sometimes it happens,' she said obstinately. 'I've read about it.'

'It's very rare,' said Jack, 'and even then usually quite shortly after the procedure. I'm guessing it's a while since Kevin had it done?'

'Ages,' confirmed Jin. 'After Clarissa was born.'

'He was pretty sure about things.'

'He always is.' Jin's tone was bitter.

'Maybe he's not the right person for you,' suggested Jack. 'Maybe you need to be with someone else.'

'He's perfect for me,' she said fiercely. 'He loves me. We have great sex. We have a lovely home. I have everything I want.'

Jack said nothing.

'Please, Jack!' Suddenly her arms were around him, her body pressed against his. 'It's important to me. I have to have a baby. I really do.'

'Jin—'

Her lips were close to his. He tried to move but she was quicker than him. Suddenly she was kissing him, her lips soft and warm, while her fingers frantically worked at the buttons of his shirt.

400

I don't believe it, he thought desperately. Not another Corcoran woman! Why does this keep happening to me?

Andie didn't know whether to ring Kevin again. She sat in front of the TV and watched the news, although none of it really got through to her. She was running through her conversation with him, picking over the pieces where he'd talked about Jin and pregnancy and wondering exactly what it was that had annoyed him so much and apparently upset Jin too. Because, Andie realised, there was something not quite right there. She just didn't know exactly what it was. She picked at her thumbnail as she worried about her sister and her brother-in-law. And she worried about Cora and Jack too.

The buzzer sounded and she leaped up from the sofa, certain that the caller was either Kevin or Jin or perhaps both of them. She was surprised to hear Tom's voice. She hadn't spoken to him since Monday, when he'd phoned her and she'd apologised for calling into Bar Tender. He'd been abrupt at first and then forgiving and he'd said that he'd drop by at the weekend, he was busy during the week. So why, she wondered, was he here now?

She buzzed open the entry door and then opened the door to the flat. His tread on the stairs was heavy and tired and his face, when he appeared on the landing, was equally tired.

'What's wrong?' she asked immediately.

He walked into the flat. 'Elizabeth lost the baby,' he said starkly.

Andie felt the room revolve around her and, to her complete shock, tears began to slide down her cheeks. 'Oh, Tom,' she said. 'I'm so, so sorry.' She held out her arms and he allowed her to hug him and draw him close.

'I thought it would be different this time,' he said, his voice muffled. 'I don't know why. It's never been different before.'

'What happened?' she asked.

He lifted his head and she saw that his cheeks were tear-stained too.

'She started getting cramps,' he said. 'I brought her into hospital straight away. But we both knew . . .' His voice trailed off.

'How is she?'

'Exhausted,' he said.

'How is she otherwise?'

'I don't know,' said Tom. 'I thought she'd be more broken up about it than she is. I'm afraid it's delayed shock.'

'I'm sorry,' whispered Andie again. 'I truly am.'

Tom sighed and broke away from her. He sat down on the sofa and rubbed his face with both hands. She watched him, uncertain of what to do. So she filled the kettle to make tea, even though she didn't feel like drinking it.

'I can't go through this again,' said Tom.

'No,' agreed Andie.

'Neither can Lizzie.'

She stopped, tea bags in her hand, and turned towards him.

'Lizzie,' she said. 'Elizabeth.'

Tom looked up at her. 'I call her Lizzie at home.'

'I know.'

'So why are you looking at me like that?'

'You never call her Lizzie in front of me.'

'Don't I?'

'No.'

'Well, Elizabeth,' he said impatiently. 'It doesn't matter what I call her, does it? She can't do this again and neither can I.' He bit the end of his finger. 'She'd talked about adopting, you know.'

Andie felt her stomach shift. 'Do you want to adopt?' she asked.

'It's not easy,' said Tom. 'Loads of tests and then you hardly ever get a baby, which is what most parents want.'

'How badly does she want a baby?'

Tom shrugged. 'You know what? At the start we didn't care. We assumed it would happen. And when it all kept going wrong it became a thing of desperation. It made both of us feel inadequate, I think.'

'You're not inadequate,' said Andie. The kettle clicked and she poured boiling water into the mugs. 'Either of you. You've gone through terrible experiences together.' She swirled the tea bags around in the mugs and then added milk to Tom's before handing it to him. He took a sip then put it on the coffee table.

402

'You need a break,' she added.

'I don't know what I need any more,' said Tom. 'Except you.'

Andie wrapped her hands around her mug, suddenly chilled, while conflicting thoughts whirled around in her head. 'You need to be with her,' she said bleakly.

'They sent me home,' said Tom. 'I was at the hospital all day.'

'Why did you come here?' asked Andie.

'Where else would I go?' he asked.

She stared into her tea, unable to speak as she tried to get her emotions under control.

'I thought you were mad at me.' The words came slowly.

'Why?'

'For coming into the bar. For being at your workplace. For getting drunk.'

'I was annoyed,' he admitted. 'I didn't think it was a very sensible thing to do.'

'You were right,' she said.

'Why the bloke from upstairs?' asked Tom.

'Dominic,' she told him. 'Spur-of-the-moment thing.'

'And are you and Dominic—'

'How could me and Dominic be anything,' she interrupted him, 'when for the last few years it's been me and you?'

'I just wondered,' said Tom. 'He seemed concerned about you.'

'He brought me home,' said Andie. 'We'd gone out to . . . to . . .' She shrugged. 'His idea really. For me to have a good time without you.'

'Why?' asked Tom.

'Because he didn't think that I was happy in my relationship.' Her smile was sardonic.

'And are you?'

She put the mug beside Tom's on the coffee table. 'You are the best thing that ever happened to me.' She stared at the table before looking up at him. 'You make me feel good about myself, make me confident. You give me loads of pleasure and, oh Tom, I love you so much . . .'

'Sounds like there's a but coming.'

She looked at him miserably.

403

'You're going to say that Elizabeth needs me now,' he said bitterly. 'Like I said she needed me when she found out she was pregnant.'

'Of course she does,' said Andie. 'This is a really hard time for her.'

'And it's not for me?'

Andie bit her lip. 'I didn't mean that,' she said. 'I know it's awful for you too. I can't even imagine how awful.'

'No,' he said. 'You can't.'

'And if it's awful for you . . . it must be twice as awful for her.'

'Why would you think that?' Tom sounded angry. 'Why should it be worse for a woman? Why can't I be just as heartbroken?'

Andie swallowed hard. 'I'm sorry,' she said. 'I truly, truly am.'

'The only thing that keeps me going is you,' said Tom fiercely. 'Knowing I can depend on you. Knowing that you love me.'

'I never loved anyone like I loved you,' she said after a charged silence. 'But—'

'Like I said,' Tom interrupted her. 'There was a but coming.'

'But Tom, we can't go on like this. We really can't. I knew you couldn't walk out on Elizabeth when she told you she was pregnant. I hated it, but I understood it. And you absolutely can't walk out on her now either.' She stared at him, horrified at what she knew she was saying.

'I don't want to walk out on her now,' said Tom. 'You know I don't. You know I can't.'

'Yes,' agreed Andie. 'The thing is, there'll always be something.'

'No there won't,' said Tom. 'Eventually we'll get over this somehow and then I'll leave.'

'But maybe by then something else will have happened,' said Andie. 'And you won't be able to leave then either.'

'Nothing else can happen,' said Tom fiercely. 'It's bad enough already.'

Andie felt sick. She wanted to love and comfort Tom but she didn't know how. She knew that she couldn't begin to understand how he must feel at this moment, neither could she possibly know how Elizabeth must be feeling. What she did know was that she didn't want to be between them right now when they really needed each other more than anyone else.

'You have to talk to her,' she said eventually. 'You have to find out how she really feels about what's happened. You can't just let her sit in a room and be depressed for the rest of her life.'

'She never wants to talk about it,' said Tom. 'I have tried. But there's no point in trying any more.'

'If there was no point then you'd have walked out before now,' Andie told him.

'Don't bloody well try to analyse me,' he snapped. 'Just don't.'

'I'm not,' she said unhappily. 'Really I'm not. But it seems to me that there are more issues between you and Elizabeth than I ever really understood. You're angry with her for losing the babies and she's angry with you about it too. So angry, maybe, that neither of you wants to discuss it. And you're right – you feel a failure over it, but so does she. Oh, Tom, you really need to talk to some professionals about this. Both of you. Together.'

'We already did that,' said Tom shortly. 'I told you. After the first. They said we'd be fine.'

'But you're not fine,' said Andie. 'Neither of you is fine.'

'I'm fine with you,' said Tom.

'The thing is,' said Andie shakily, 'oh, Tom, the thing is – I'm not fine with you any more.'

'I don't believe this.' Suddenly Tom stood up and faced her. 'I came here because I needed to be with you. And now it suddenly seems like you're finding ways to break up with me.'

'I don't want to,' whispered Andie. 'But I think we're breaking up all the same.'

He put his arms around her and pulled her close. His lips found hers. She kissed him. Then she looked into his grey eyes.

'You can't break up with me,' he said. 'You know you can't. Not now.'

It's my heart that's going to break, thought Andie, as she held his gaze.

'I know now is the wrong time,' she said miserably. 'I feel such a shit. But there's never going to be a right time. And I just can't go on like this any more.'

He said nothing.

'Loving you was great,' she told him. 'Special. Really special.'

'You still love me,' he said.

'I know.' She bit her lip. 'But sometimes it just isn't enough. It's supposed to be, isn't it? Love conquers all and that sort of thing. But maybe it doesn't, in the end. Maybe sometimes you have to know when to call it a day.'

'So after all this time you want me to go back to Elizabeth and try to work things out? Is that it?'

'I don't know if you and Elizabeth can work anything out,' said Andie. 'Maybe it's too late for that. But I know that you still have feelings for her. You always thought of how your actions would affect her. That's why we had an affair, Tom. That's why we aren't together now.'

'It wasn't – isn't – an affair!' he cried. 'It's much more than that.'

'I know,' whispered Andie. 'But it has to end now, Tom. You have responsibilities towards Elizabeth, and I – it's time for me to move on.'

'Look, we can still work something out,' he said desperately. 'I know I have to be with Elizabeth right now. But later . . .'

'I can't wait for later any more,' she told him as she fought the impulse to wrap her arms around him. 'I can't hope that I'll be happy because of something that goes wrong between you and her.'

'It's gone wrong over a long time,' said Tom.

'Maybe,' agreed Andie. 'But you always cared about her. No matter what your reasons.'

'Andie, I've just lost a baby,' said Tom. 'Please don't tell me that I'm losing the person who means most to me as well.'

She wanted to hold him and never let him go. She wanted to tell him that he was the person who meant most to her too. She wanted to cry that she loved him and that she would always love him. But she simply stood in front of him, fighting the tears and saying nothing.

'You think you can force Elizabeth and me to work something out,' said Tom. 'But you can't.'

'This isn't about you and Elizabeth,' said Andie wretchedly. 'It's about you and me. I need to get on with my life and I won't ever do that as long as I'm with you. You won't leave Elizabeth right now and if you did you wouldn't be the man I love anyway. You and she need to work it out. I don't mean that you need to stay together in the long term,' she added as he began to speak, 'just that you need to resolve the issue about the miscarriages. You both have to deal with it in a different way to how you've done up to now. And maybe then you'll leave her.'

'But you won't be there for me if I do.'

'No,' she said sadly. 'I won't.'

'Oh God!' He put his arms around her and she wanted to lean her head on his shoulder. But she didn't.

'You'd better go,' she said. 'Please.'

'You've made up your mind,' he said in wonderment. 'Had you decided this before I ever came here?'

She shook her head. 'No. No. I didn't even think it when we began to talk. I always felt you'd be in my life for ever, Tom. But things change and I can't . . . I can't . . .'

'It wasn't just about sex.' He looked at her urgently. 'I didn't use you, Andie.'

'I know.'

'Lizzie and I . . . it's because I made love to her, isn't it?' There was a sudden flash of understanding in his eyes.

'Of course not,' said Andie. 'I felt bad about it at the time but I always knew . . .'

'Then what?' he asked. 'I need to know why, Andie.'

'I don't know,' she whispered. 'I'm so sorry. I know it's the wrong time. But there never will be a right time.'

'So I leave here and I go back to Elizabeth and you fondly believe we can work it out,' said Tom bitterly. 'Even though we haven't worked it out before.'

'Oh, Tom, I don't know whether you can work it out or not. So much has happened that maybe it's utterly impossible. But don't you see that regardless of what happens between you and Elizabeth I think we've come to the end.' Andie's voice shook. 'Maybe it would've happened whether or not she'd got pregnant and whether or not she'd lost the baby. Maybe we were just a long, long fling.'

'Not a fling,' he said. 'Never just a fling.'

'I know that really,' she told him. 'I'm just trying to . . .' She shrugged. 'You know.' She walked over to the door and unlocked it. He looked miserably at her. 'I want what's best for you,' she said. 'I really do.'

'Does anyone ever get what's best for them?' He opened the door.

'I'm sorry,' she said again. 'About the baby. About us. About everything.'

'So am I.' He walked across the landing to the stairs and stopped for a moment.

She wanted to call him back. She wanted to beg him not to go. But she lifted her hand in a half-wave and then walked back into the flat and closed the door behind her.

Chapter 33

Scherzo No 1 in B Minor – Chopin

Jin was in shock. She couldn't believe he'd walked out on her like that – had spoken to her like that. She couldn't believe he'd suggested that she needed help. How dare he, of all people, say something like that? She didn't need help. She needed a baby. She opened the door to the minibar and took out a bottle of gin. She poured it into a glass and added a splash of bitter lemon. Then she swallowed it back in a quick gulp which left her spluttering and coughing because she'd never been very good at throwing back drinks in one go. She took another gin from the bar and filled the glass again. She managed to swallow most of the drink this time. Then she slid on to her knees in front of the bar, curled up in a ball and cried harder than she'd ever cried in her life before.

Andie was in shock too. She sat on the sofa looking at the blank TV screen, her arms wrapped around her legs, which she had drawn up to her chest. She was playing Chopin's intricate Scherzo No 1 in B Minor in her head, her fingers racing along her mental keyboard, playing the piece to absolute perfection before finishing with a flourish that made her lean forward so violently that she almost fell off the cushion.

She blinked back into the room and the present and the fact that she was alone. She couldn't quite believe what had happened, couldn't believe that she'd let Tom go. Not let him go, she told herself, made him go. Made him realise that Elizabeth needed him. She clenched her jaw. Maybe Elizabeth didn't need him. Maybe she needed something or someone else completely. Andie couldn't be sure about that. What she was sure of, though, was that right now Elizabeth and Elizabeth's needs were a whole heap greater than her own. And she wondered again, with mounting guilt, whether Tom and Elizabeth might not have worked things out before now if she hadn't been there in the background.

There was no point in thinking that way, she told herself. The Halls had their problems and they might be insurmountable. But if they were they had to be insurmountable because of Tom and Elizabeth themselves, not because of her.

She got up from the sofa and walked over to the piano. She stuck with intricate pieces – Bach's Art of the Fugue, which she always felt was a showpiece for technical skills, Beethoven's Für Elise, one of the first pieces she'd ever learned to play competently, and finally one of her favourites, Tchaikovsky's Piano Concerto in B Flat, which was lighter and more cheerful and suddenly lifted her mood so that although she still felt utterly bereft she didn't feel as though she wanted to lock herself away for ever.

She'd just completed the final chord when her phone rang. At least, she thought, as she got up to answer it, I'll be able to speak to whoever it is now. I wouldn't have been half an hour ago. And she was grateful for the music that she could always depend on to calm her.

'Hello.' All the same, she was surprised to find that her voice was steady.

'Hi, Andie, this is Jack Ferguson.'

She tensed. Jack bloody Ferguson. What could he possibly want? And then, with a sense of shock, she realised that it was only a couple of hours ago that she'd called him to find out if Jin had been in touch. She was horrified to realise that she'd totally forgotten about her sister's disappearance from Briarlawns and that she'd been in a world of her own since then. Maybe, she thought frantically, I do only see things from my own perspective, like Kevin said. I only think about me and the things that happen to me, and how, how, how could I have forgotten about Jin?

'Has Jin been in touch?' she asked.

'Yes,' said Jack.

'Oh, great.' Andie felt a sense of relief wash over her. 'I was worried and I know that Kevin is frantic.'

'Really?' asked Jack. 'Frantic?'

'Yes, well, I guess Kevin's definition of frantic and ours might be a little different,' conceded Andie. 'Where's Jin? Is everything OK?'

'I'm not entirely sure,' said Jack.

'What?' Andie felt her heart race. 'What's the matter?'

'I'm calling you from the Morrison Hotel,' said Jack. 'Your sister has a room here.'

'She's left Kevin?' Andie was bemused. 'She's staying there because she's left him?'

'Look, Andie, I know you hate me and you think I'm a complete shit and there's a whole heap of unresolved issues about me and your mom that we need to talk through, but can you put all that to one side and meet me here?'

'Why?' asked Andie.

'Believe me when I tell you I'm not trying to be overdramatic or anything like that, but I think it would be best if I talked to you face to face.'

Andie didn't want to meet Jack face to face. But she could hear a real sense of concern in his voice. She paused indecisively and then sighed.

'OK,' she said. 'But this better not be some wind-up.'

'Thanks,' said Jack. 'I'll be in the lobby.'

She managed to get a taxi on Griffith Avenue and was deposited outside the hotel ten minutes later. She hurried into the reception area and immediately saw Jack standing there anxiously. He looked different, thought Andie, less Hollywood Dream God and more ordinary bloke. His dark hair wasn't a study in carelessness but spiky from having run his fingers through it so many times. And his sweatshirt, spotted slightly with orange paint, was rumpled over his faded jeans.

'Hi,' she said. 'What's the matter?'

She listened in utter amazement as Jack told her about Jin's request for him to sleep with her so that she could become pregnant. She could almost feel her jaw drop as Jack said, uneasily, that her

411

sister had almost thrown herself on him when he'd refused and that he'd had to practically peel her off him. She was speechless when he said that he'd let himself out of the room as quickly as he could and gone down to the lobby to phone her because he had no idea what else to do.

'Jesus Christ,' she gasped as he finished speaking. 'Does Ma know all this?'

'No,' he said. 'She was sleeping when I left and I didn't want to call her and set off her headache again. That's why I called you.'

'We'd better talk to Jin right now,' said Andie.

'We can't.' Jack looked at her despairingly. 'She's not in her room. I went back upstairs because I was worried about her but she must have legged it while I was on the phone to you.'

'Are you sure she's gone?' asked Andie urgently. 'She's not in there unconscious or anything, is she?'

Jack shook his head. 'I managed to persuade them to go up and check,' he told her. 'She's gone.'

'Bloody hell.' Andie chewed at the corner of her lip. 'Any idea where?'

'No,' said Jack. 'Have you?'

Andie rubbed her temples. 'I can't imagine.' She smiled ruefully. 'Maybe she's come to her senses and gone home.' She took her phone out of her bag. 'I guess I should call Kevin.'

Her brother-in-law answered after the fifth ring.

'Dixon.'

'Hi, Kevin, it's me, Andie.'

'Any news?' he asked abruptly.

'Yes and no,' said Andie. 'She was in the Morrison but she'd gone by the time I got here.'

'Why didn't you call me first?' demanded Kevin. 'I'd have made sure she didn't go anywhere.'

'I'm sorry,' said Andie. 'When Jack phoned—'

'Jack?' interrupted Kevin. 'Jack Ferguson?'

'Well, yes,' admitted Andie. 'He was here.'

'What was he doing there?' asked Kevin. 'How did he know she was missing? How did he find her?'

Andie was glad that video-phones weren't readily available,

because she knew her expression was a study in uncertainty. 'Jin phoned home,' she said eventually. 'Jack was talking to her and he came here to see her.'

'Why?'

'I guess he thought it would be a good idea.' Andie looked awkwardly at Jack.

'Put him on,' ordered Kevin.

'There's no point,' said Andie firmly. 'The fact is that Jin was here but she's not any more. Perhaps she's on her way back to Malahide.'

'Perhaps,' agreed Kevin reluctantly. 'You stay there, Andie, until I call you again.'

'OK,' she said. She put the phone back in her bag and looked at Jack. 'He wants me to stay here while he waits to see if Jin turns up at home.'

'Did he say what he wanted me to do?' asked Jack.

She smiled uncomfortably at him and shook her head.

'Would you like a coffee?' he asked.

'I was thinking that maybe you should get back to Ma's,' she told him. 'In case she turns up there.'

'I guess that wherever she turns up the last person she wants to see is me,' said Jack.

'You must be getting used to that.'

'Story of my life,' said Jack.

'I'm sorry,' said Andie.

'What for?'

'Some of the things I've said to you. And the way we've behaved. We've no right to judge you.'

'You've every right,' said Jack. 'But you need to be judging me on all the facts not some of them.'

She nodded. 'We'll talk. Once all this is sorted out.'

'I'm looking forward to it,' he said. He hugged her briefly and then walked out of the hotel.

Andie sat in one of the deep leather chairs and gazed around her. From her vantage point she could see the bar and lounge areas, which were thronged with people despite the fact that it was a

413

midweek evening. Will this be me in the future? she wondered, as she watched a giggling group of girls stride past her and make straight for the bar. Will I be out there doing single-woman things again? She sighed. She'd never been very good at the single-woman thing anyway. She just wasn't very good with men full stop. None of her pre-Tom boyfriends had been anything very exciting, though she had a sneaking suspicion that the reasons had been more to do with her than with them. Michael, of course, had been the longest-lasting and a relationship of which Cora had approved. But that hadn't worked out, what with Michael getting a place in the orchestra while she'd had to resign herself to teaching. She wondered whether things would have been different if she'd been the one to tour with the orchestra. Would Michael have felt as bitter and useless as she had? Or would he have been supportive? She twirled her fingers through her hair. Actually he would just have applied somewhere else. Michael had always been convinced of his talent.

The thing was, Andie realised suddenly, she really liked teaching. She got a kick out of listening to her students improve and now she revelled in their success as once she would have revelled in her own. She didn't want to perform in public any more, although since playing the piano at Andrew Comiskey's party she didn't feel that thrashing out a few impromptu tunes was such a big deal. Maybe she could play a bit more for people she knew without feeling as though they were judging every fudged note or every quaver that should have been a crochet. Maybe they didn't care very much just as long as it sounded OK. Maybe wanting perfection was wanting too much most of the time.

She looked at her watch. A half-hour had passed since Jack had left. Clearly Jin wasn't at Cora's because he would have phoned to let her know that by now. It would take her longer to get to Malahide, though, and even if she'd left while Jack had been on the phone to Andie, she wouldn't necessarily be there yet. Andie shifted in the seat and wondered what the likelihood of Jin returning to the hotel was. Poor Jin, she thought, she must be in a complete state. Andie hadn't known about Kevin's vasectomy, of course, but she could see why, in the first flush of love and excitement, Jin would think it didn't matter. Especially because she hadn't been a

414

particularly maternal sort of person. Even when they'd been children and played with dolls, Jin had spent most of her time dressing them up, pinning ribbons to their clothes and marching them along in a fashion parade, while Andie had lined hers up against the wall and lectured them about hard work. Bloody hell, she thought, are our lives already mapped out for us no matter what?

Her mobile rang and she answered it straight away as she saw her sister's name on the screen.

'Jin!' she cried immediately. 'Where the hell are you?'

'I'm at your place,' said Jin. 'Outside your door. Where are you?'

'Not far.' Andie didn't want to tell Jin that she'd made an emergency dash to the Morrison. 'I'll be home in a couple of minutes. Wait for me.'

'OK,' said Jin wearily.

Andie hurried out of the hotel and was lucky enough to get a taxi, which had just dropped a couple of girls outside. More single women, thought Andie, it's going to be a bloody nightmare on my own! She gave the driver her address and barely managed to keep from saying 'Step on it' as though she were in a movie. She hit her mother's number.

'Hello,' said Jack.

'Me again,' said Andie. 'Apparently she's at my flat. I'm on my way there now.'

'Your flat?' Jack sounded puzzled. 'I didn't think you two were close enough for her to appear on your doorstep.'

'Well there you go,' said Andie tartly. 'You don't know everything about us.'

'Sorry,' said Jack.

'It's OK,' said Andie. 'I'll phone you later.'

'Cora's awake now,' said Jack. 'She's feeling fine again. So I told her.'

'What did you tell her?'

'That Jin and Kevin had had an argument and Jin had checked in to the hotel, but that she'd phoned looking for Cora and I came to see her instead. And that she left without telling me.'

'I presume Ma is looking for greater detail than that,' said Andie.

'She knows there's more to it. I'll tell her, but not till I hear from you again.'

'OK,' said Andie. 'I suppose I'd better phone Kevin.'

'I'll do it if you like,' offered Jack.

'Would you?' asked Andie gratefully. 'Only, Jack, don't let him come to the flat in a great steaming rage. If Jin is as upset and confused about everything as we think, Kevin turning up in one of his moods isn't going to help things.'

'I'll do my best,' said Jack. 'Don't you worry.'

'I'm nearly there now,' said Andie. 'I'll call you later. And thanks for everything.'

'You're welcome,' said Jack.

There was no sign of Jin outside the building. Andie looked around her frantically, afraid that her sister had headed off again and completely at a loss to know where she could possibly have gone this time. She unlocked the main door and hurried up the stairs. As she reached her landing she heard a door open and Dominic's head appeared over the hand rail.

'You got here,' he said.

'Yes, but I'm in a rush.'

'Your sister is up here.'

Andie stopped mid-stair, a wave of relief washing over her. 'Is she? With you?'

'She was waiting outside for you,' Dominic told her. 'I let her in. Couldn't leave her out there.'

Jin appeared from behind him and began walking down the stairs.

'Thanks for letting me in,' she told him. 'And for showing me the house brochures. I'll see you again.'

'Sure,' he said. 'Nice to have met you.'

'Thanks, Dominic,' called Andie, but he'd already gone back into his flat and closed the door.

Andie and Jin looked at each other uncertainly and then Andie walked up the last few stairs to her landing and unlocked her door. The two of them went inside. She couldn't remember the last time she'd seen her sister without make-up. Even without it, though, and despite the dark circles under her eyes, Jin's natural beauty was still evident. She's still stunning, thought Andie, in surprise. She could still get out there and strut her stuff if she wanted to.

'Would you like anything to drink?' asked Andie.

'Coffee,' said Jin. 'Black. Strong.'

'Sure you wouldn't prefer something else?' Andie looked at her quizzically. 'A gin and tonic maybe, or a glass of wine?'

Jin made a face. 'I stupidly drank far too much earlier,' she said. 'I couldn't possibly.'

Andie filled the kettle, took two mugs out of the cupboard and ladled a large spoonful of coffee into each. 'Want to tell me what this is all about?' she asked.

Jin sat down on the sofa and covered her face with her hands. 'I don't know if I can,' she said.

'Why?' asked Andie.

'It's all so – so embarrassing. And demeaning. And just plain awful.'

'How embarrassed can you be?' asked Andie. 'After all, I'm the one who watched Ma comb nits out of your hair in the bathroom.'

Jin's laugh was strangled.

'And I was there when Pierce Noonan pulled down your knickers in the playground.'

Jin uncovered her face and smiled uncertainly at her sister.

'Plus I intercepted that ridiculously soppy Valentine's card from Magnus Larsson,' Andie reminded her. 'As I recall, you found that very, very embarrassing.'

She made the coffee and handed a mug to Jin. 'So don't talk to me about embarrassment.'

'This is different.' Jin squeezed her hands around the mug and stared at the floor.

'I know,' said Andie gently. 'Jack called me. From the Morrison.'

'Jack!' Jin was so startled that she splashed coffee on to the carpet. 'Oh hell, Andie – sorry!'

'It doesn't matter,' said Andie. 'This carpet has seen more than its fair share of coffee stains. One more won't make any difference.'

'What did he say?' Jin put the cup on the side table and wiped ineffectually at the stain with a paper tissue.

'He said that you were very upset,' said Andie carefully. 'He said that you're unhappy that Kevin doesn't want children.'

Jin scrubbed at the coffee stain a little harder. Her face was flushed when she looked up. 'That all?'

'He said you wanted to get pregnant but that Kevin has had a vasectomy.' Andie put her arm around Jin's shoulder. 'I'm really, really sorry.'

'Did he say that I jumped on him?' asked Jin harshly. 'Did he say that I completely lost it? That I'd gone to the hotel and taken a room and that I wanted him to get me pregnant?'

'He kind of implied that,' admitted Andie. 'But he knew that you didn't quite realise what you were doing. Jin, honey, this is clearly a huge issue for you.'

'It wasn't,' said Jin bitterly. 'I never even thought about it before. But then Livia, my friend, got pregnant and suddenly . . .' Her eyes swam with tears. 'Suddenly I realised that this was something I wanted too. It became an obsession. I kept thinking that maybe Kevin would understand and would get the vasectomy reversed. I know that's crazy. And then . . .' She rubbed her eyes with the back of her hand. 'Then Monica phoned.'

'His ex-wife?'

Jin nodded. '*Cian* has managed to get his girlfriend pregnant,' she said bitterly. 'And both Monica and Kevin were furious about it. Kevin wanted the girl, Shona, to have an abortion.'

'Oh, Jin!' Andie hugged her even tighter. 'No wonder you flipped.'

'It just seemed so unfair.' Jin sobbed. 'She was pregnant and I so desperately wanted a baby. And I know it's a completely different set of circumstances but there was Kevin, wanting her to have an abortion and never wanting me to have kids at all. And I suddenly realised that all my fantasies about having babies with him were just that. Fantasies.'

'So why did you think that asking Jack to . . . you know . . . why did you think that was a good idea?'

'Oh, look, Andie, it was a fucking insane idea!' cried Jin. 'I know

418

that now. I knew it then only I couldn't help myself. It was as though my body was acting completely independently of my mind. I kept thinking that he's so virile he's probably loaded up with billions of healthy sperm just waiting for the chance . . . and then I thought that if I did this and told Mum she'd throw him out there and then. Besides, I reckoned that it'd all be in a day's work to him. I thought . . . oh shit, I know this is crazy . . . I thought I could say to Kevin that I'd done it for Mum . . . and that he'd understand. I don't know what possessed me, I really don't. It all seemed totally logical right up to the point where Jack arrived at the hotel.'

'But he said no.'

'I couldn't believe it,' said Jin. 'I said I'd pay him whatever he wanted. He looked at me as though I was completely off my head.'

'Which you were, actually,' said Andie.

'I know that now,' said Jin. She covered her face with her hands again. 'I've messed up big time, haven't I?'

Andie grimaced. 'Nothing we can't sort out,' she said optimistically.

'I'm not so sure about that,' said Jin.

The buzzer rang and startled both of them. Andie got up and pressed the intercom.

'It's me and Cora,' said Jack. 'Let us in, Andie.'

She hit the unlock button and looked at Jin. Her sister was crying again.

Chapter 34

Rhapsody on a Theme of Paganini – Rachmaninoff

'I thought you were going to wait till I called,' hissed Andie as Jack arrived at the door of the flat.

'I insisted,' said Cora. 'Jack wanted me to wait but that was ridiculous.' She pushed past Andie and into the flat, where Jin sat huddled on the sofa, her face tear-streaked. Cora immediately sat down beside her and put her arms around her while Jack and Andie stood awkwardly at the door. Andie couldn't help but notice that Cora looked remarkably elegant in a slim-fitting pair of trousers and soft-knit jumper which she'd never seen before.

'We'll give you a few minutes on your own,' she said.

Cora nodded and held Jin even closer. Andie sat at the top of the stairs and sighed deeply.

'Exciting day,' said Jack.

'I'm too old for this kind of trauma,' said Andie.

'She'll get over it,' said Jack. 'I think she just lost it completely.'

Andie nodded. 'She said that wanting a baby became an obsession and she'd do anything to make it happen.'

'Even jump the bones of a man she despises,' said Jack.

'You've been really good about this,' Andie told him.

'Oh, I'm just trying to ingratiate myself with you all.'

Andie glanced at him and he made a face at her in return. He really was kind of sweet, she thought, it was just a pity about his past. Or his present. She really had no idea where things were with him and Cora. But suddenly she really wished that it would work out for them. Only what did working out for them mean when he was

420

only in it for the money? Perhaps, though, it was easier than being in it for anything else. Unbidden, thoughts of Tom came back to her and gripped her, making her hurt physically. She still couldn't quite believe that Tom was no longer in her life. She couldn't entirely grasp the fact that he wouldn't be calling her later or dropping round to the flat at inconvenient times which were nevertheless so important to her. Damn it, she thought, I don't want to have broken up with him. I do love him.

'You OK?' asked Jack. 'Has it been a bit much for you?'

She shook her head, unable to speak.

'Something else the matter?' he asked.

'Not really.' She tried to be nonchalant but her voice shook. 'I split up with Tom today.'

'Andie!' Jack looked at her in surprise. 'I thought that you and he were going to live together?'

'So did I at one point,' she said. 'But circumstances changed.'

'He's decided to stay with his wife?'

'It was a joint decision,' she told him. 'The reasons were good ones. I'm not sorry about it. But I feel a bit . . . a bit . . .' She broke off and scrubbed at her eyes, unable to finish the sentence.

'It's been an eventful day for you,' said Jack. He put his arm round her shoulder and hugged her. It was a friendly hug and it made her smile.

'You know, me and Jin have spent the past few weeks worrying about you and Ma,' she said ruefully. 'But it's our own lives we should've been worrying about.'

'Oh, Andie – everyone worries about their family,' said Jack. 'Even me.'

'Do you have family to worry about?' she asked curiously. 'I mean, I suppose you do but I kind of thought that that – well, given what you do – you wouldn't be exactly close to them.'

'I've never been exactly close to them,' Jack said. 'It doesn't mean that we don't worry about each other.' He grinned at her suddenly. 'You know, it's cost me a fortune in therapy to be able to say that.'

'Huh?'

'I had issues,' he told her. 'Since I was a kid.'

'Why?'

'At this point let's just say that my goals and theirs were completely different.'

'I can see that given your career choice,' said Andie. 'It's just that – well, Jack, you're actually a rather nice person. So I don't know why—'

She broke off as the stairwell was suddenly flooded by the bright lights of a car's headlamps. 'Kevin,' she said immediately. 'I thought you told him not to come.'

'I did try,' said Jack ruefully. 'But I suppose I was the last person he'd listen to.'

'I'd better let him in.' Andie stood up. 'You go and warn Jin and Ma.'

She hurried down the stairs and opened the door to the building. Kevin strode past her. 'She's upset,' Andie said to his back. 'Don't lose it with her, Kevin.'

He turned to her. 'She's a fool,' he said. 'And she's trying to make me look like a fool too.'

'No she's not.'

'I have better things to do with my life than traipse around Dublin looking for my wife,' said Kevin sharply. 'She doesn't even realise how much trouble she's caused me.'

Andie bit her lip and hurried up the stairs after him.

Cora and Jin were still sitting on the sofa as she followed Kevin into the flat. Jack was standing by the window. Kevin looked at him in disgust, then at Jin, whose face was pale and tired.

'Come on,' he said. 'Let's go. Do you have a coat?'

'I'm not going anywhere yet,' said Jin.

'It's late,' said Kevin. 'I don't know exactly what's been going on in your head for the last few days but I certainly don't want to hear it all now. Maybe tomorrow in the privacy of our own home. But I'm not going to get into some kind of truth-fest about how unhappy you think you are or what a shit you think I am or whatever it is that's caused you to act in such a damn fool way.'

'Kevin.' Cora's voice was measured. 'Jin is extremely upset. There's absolutely no need to talk to her like that.'

'Jin is a cosseted, pampered woman who hasn't ever needed to

422

worry about anything in her life,' said Kevin. 'And whatever's upsetting her can easily be sorted out. But I'm not doing it here and I'm not doing it now.' He looked at his wife again. 'Come on,' he repeated. 'Let's go.'

'No,' she said.

'Jin, if I walk out of this room and you're not with me I'm not coming back for you,' said Kevin. 'I think I've been really patient and understanding, and despite your ridiculous disappearance and the trouble it's put me to I'm prepared to take you home and talk it through with you. So don't sit there like some tragic drama queen, get your coat.'

Jin stood up. 'I love you,' she said. 'At least I think I do. I always thought we were good together and right for each other, and the fact that there's been a problem has been my fault, not yours. I'm not blaming you for anything.' Her eyes held his as she spoke. 'But the thing is, Kevin, I was wrong when I married you thinking that children didn't matter to me, because I've realised over the last few weeks that they do.'

'Oh for heaven's sake!' exploded Kevin. 'I knew that it was all about this baby nonsense. I thought we'd resolved that.'

'Of course we haven't resolved it,' said Jin. 'How could we?'

'I told you.' His eyes flickered between the people in the room. 'It's not possible.'

'I know,' said Jin. 'And what I have to decide is whether I can live with you knowing how impossible it is, or whether it means so much to me that I can't accept it.'

'Jin.' Kevin's tone softened. 'Think about this for a moment. You're talking about giving up a gorgeous house and a wonderful lifestyle for what? The possibility that sometime in the future you might meet someone and have a baby with them. How likely is that?'

'Well, not that unlikely,' she said. 'I'm only thirty-one!'

'So who do you intend to meet?' he asked. 'Someone like Jack?'

'I could do worse,' said Jin wryly. 'He was good to me today.'

Kevin laughed harshly. 'Presumably because he thinks he can make something out of it.'

'Kevin Dixon!' Cora's face was flushed. 'That's a disgraceful thing to say.'

'Oh, come on, Cora,' said Kevin. 'We all know that you're paying him to be with you. Why else is he here?'

There was a horrified silence in the room. Andie twisted her fingers together. Jin looked anxiously at her mother. Jack moved from his position at the window. Then Cora laughed. 'Do you really think that?' she asked. 'Even now?'

'I don't know whether you're handing over cash or whether there's some other agreement between you,' said Kevin. 'But we know that he advertises himself for sale on the internet. I wanted to do something about it, Cora, but I was mindful of your recent bereavement and I gave in to the girls' wishes to take things easily. But I can tell you here and now that I have to insist that this – this – that Ferguson leaves here tonight and doesn't return.'

'No,' said Cora.

Andie wondered how often people said no to Kevin Dixon. He was certainly hearing it enough tonight.

'Come on, Cora,' he said. 'This is a totally unsuitable arrangement. It's time to end it.'

'I've never paid Jack for anything,' said Cora. 'Nor would I expect to. I'm surprised that you think it's something I'd even consider.'

'He *does* advertise on the internet.' Andie felt that she had to say something.

Jack grinned at her. 'But I don't kiss on the first date.'

'Really, Ferguson!' Kevin looked disgusted.

'Tell them.' Cora looked at Jack resignedly. 'We could be here all night otherwise.'

Jack pushed his hands deep into the pockets of his jeans and observed the rest of the family with equal resignation. 'You're right to think that I worked as an escort, but you're wrong to think that it was anything sordid.'

Kevin looked sceptically at him. Jack ignored him.

'And yes, I advertised on the internet site. It's run by a friend of mine.'

'Your friend in the sex industry,' said Kevin scathingly.

'Well, maybe,' said Jack. 'She doesn't think of it quite like that

424

and it's not the original intention behind why she set it up, but there's no doubt that some escorts do have sex with some of their clients.'

'And this is your job?'

'No,' said Jack. 'But it was for a while.'

Andie covered her eyes with her hands. She realised that somewhere, in the darkest recesses of her mind, she'd hoped there was a chance that Jack wasn't really a male escort and that when he'd said he could clear up everything he really would have another explanation. But he hadn't.

'Look, I know it has all sorts of connotations,' continued Jack. 'Obviously it does. But when I signed up with Brenna it was because she really was providing blokes for women as . . . well . . . old-fashioned escorts. She's a good and decent woman. She used to go to a lot of company functions but hated going without someone on her arm if she wasn't in a relationship. Someone, she said, who'd deflect unwanted attention. And she thought that perhaps there was a market for men to accompany women to events.' He shrugged. 'She was right. There is. Sometimes, of course, it becomes something else. But the original idea was simply to have a member of the opposite sex by your side.'

'And you signed up for this?' Kevin looked at him incredulously.

'Why not?' asked Jack. 'I told you. Brenna's a decent woman. She thought I'd be good at it. And I was. I needed the money too.'

'So you'll do anything for money?' asked Kevin contemptuously.

'No,' replied Jack. 'Mostly I did it because I knew that it was something my father would've hated to think I was doing.' He shrugged. 'I didn't do it to sleep with the clients. And actually, being an escort isn't bad at all. You go nice places, people treat you well and you get paid at the end of it all. Not everyone was looking for sex, you know.'

'Regardless of how you look at it, you were still paid to sleep with them,' said Kevin scathingly.

'No I wasn't,' said Jack. 'As I told Cora, I did sleep with two of the women I met. But that was a personal thing and they didn't pay me. I'm not totally proud of myself but I'm not ashamed either. Those women were good women. All of the women I met were.

425

Sure, some of them *were* looking for sex, but most of them just wanted someone to bring to an event with them. One girl took me to a school reunion. Her ex-boyfriend's eyes nearly fell out of his head. It was fun.'

'Are you still an escort?' asked Jin.

'Of course not,' said Jack.

'But your name is still on the site,' objected Andie.

'Sure, but if you try to book me you get a message that I'm not currently available,' Jack told her. 'Brenna, my pal, wanted to leave my picture on it. She said I looked smouldering and it was good for business. She helped me out, so why not.'

'You knew this?' Kevin looked at Cora.

'Well, not immediately,' she admitted. 'As far as I was concerned, Jack was the ship's lecturer. We did discuss our lives and our families and he told me a certain amount, but not about the escort thing. I guess he thought I wouldn't understand. Too old maybe.' Her eyes twinkled at them. 'You know, when you get older you understand more, not less. So when he did tell me about it, it didn't bother me as much as you'd expect. After all, as he said, it wasn't some seedy outfit, and I did, in fact, check out his story with Brenna Chaplin. Jack insisted I call her. She was a charming person. She said that she persuaded him to do it.'

'She's probably in cahoots with him!' Kevin snorted. 'With an alias of her own. Heidi Fleiss perhaps.'

'You said you did it because you needed the money and you thought your family would disapprove,' said Andie as though Kevin hadn't spoken. 'Though I'd imagine everyone's family would disapprove. So why did you want to piss them off so much?'

'I left home because my – my father wanted me to stay working in the family business. I didn't. There was a row. My father and I – well, we didn't see eye to eye about anything. I decided to leave. I didn't have any money saved, mostly I'd spent it on beer and coke. The coke you snort, not the sort you drink, though I gave that up after I left! The night I walked out I went into my father's study and took a wedge of cash from his safe. It didn't take long to get through it. I travelled around, went to Mexico, started to get my act together and then I met Brenna. I agreed to the escort thing

426

because it paid well and because it was fun and because I knew it would really bug my father when he heard about it. Because he'd believe that it was seedy and horrible.' He grinned. 'And I was right. When they found out they freaked. He called me and told me that I was a disgrace. He sounded a lot like you, Kevin.'

'Well, it's not exactly the occupation anyone would want for their child,' said Kevin.

'I made that money honestly and through my own efforts and I was proud of that,' said Jack starkly. 'Besides, approving of my career wasn't necessarily his call to make.'

'Perhaps not,' Kevin conceded. 'However, as his son you should at least have acknowledged that he had your best interests at heart.'

'Ah, well, that was part of the problem.' Jack shrugged. 'I wasn't too sure that I was his son in the first place.'

'Not sure?' Jin looked at him in confusion. 'Why not sure?'

'My father – still a lot like you, Kevin – was always obsessed with the family business. My mom had an affair with one of the office staff. When I was born there was some doubt as to who the father was.'

'Yes, but you could find out easily enough,' said Andie. 'Genetically speaking, anyway.'

'Thirty-odd years ago it wasn't as certain as it is now,' said Jack. 'Besides, he didn't want to do it and he wouldn't let my mother do it either. He decided to accept me straight away as his own child when he found out about Mom and her pregnancy. He didn't want to entertain the possibility I wasn't. Even if she hadn't had an affair there were problems in the marriage because she hadn't got pregnant before then. So I was both welcome and unwelcome. It made for an – an interesting upbringing.'

'And was your mother in love with the other guy?' asked Jin. 'Did she ever think of divorcing your dad to be with him?'

'No,' said Jack baldly. 'She liked the kind of life she had with my father. She was just lonely, I guess.'

'So what was your problem with him?' asked Andie.

Jack shrugged. 'He was happy that everyone could see a young Ferguson at last. Put rumours about his lack of firepower to rest. But the nagging doubts were always there. I was never good enough for him. Sometimes he referred to me as the spawn.'

'Oh, Jack!' Andie looked horrified.

'So my life was a whirl of sometimes being in his good books and sometimes being in his bad books and never being able to do enough to please him, although as a kid I really and truly tried. But whenever I did anything wrong he'd look at me and mutter about bad genes. It took a long time before my mom told me why.'

'You need to find out for sure,' said Jin. 'If not for him, for you.'

'The thing is,' said Jack, 'when I learned that there was a question over my paternity I became twice as hung up as him. I was in my teens by then. My mom sent me to a shrink but I didn't want to be analysed and I didn't want to spend time talking about my feelings – very few blokes do, I guess. Anyway, I was pretty sure that he wasn't related to me. I don't much look like him, you know. And to be honest, there was a part of me that didn't want to know for sure either. I know you might find that hard to believe but I was afraid of learning the truth. I reckoned that if I wasn't his son it meant that I wasn't entitled to live where I lived or do the things I was doing. Of course that left me completely fucked up in my own mind. I joined the company because I thought it would make him happy, but it didn't. In the end I used to sit in my office and roll joints all day. That was where the row came from. He said I didn't deserve to be paid and I said I knew, but what was he going to do about it, and he said he'd fire me . . . all stupid macho stuff. I said I'd leave and that's what I did. But I took the money and I hated myself for that afterwards. Made me think that I'd tried to break away but in the end I hadn't walked out on my own. Didn't stop me from blowing it all, though. I rang my mom. She told me to come home. I said I couldn't. She told me to grow up.' He sighed. 'She was right. I was thinking of myself all the time and how unfair life was . . . and then I met Brenna. She'd had a really tough background – her mom was a single mother, raised her on her own with not a lot of cash – but Brenna didn't spend her time moaning about her absent father or the unfairness of life. She made me feel so bloody self-indulgent! She set me up with the escort work, suddenly I made some money – I sent a cheque back to my father and spent the rest on the analysis that I hadn't wanted when I was younger. And even though I'd believed that those therapy guys are a complete waste of time, he actually did me a bit of good. He made me see that it isn't who we are genetically that counts. It's what we make of ourselves and our lives that really matters.'

'You still need to know,' said Andie.

'Oh, I do now,' Jack told her baldly. 'It may sound daft to you, but because my father hadn't wanted to get a test done I'd believed that I couldn't either. And, like I said, there was a bit of me that didn't want to find out. But then I realised that I had to know. I had the test done a few months ago.'

'And?' Both girls looked at him expectantly.

'I really am the son and heir.' Jack laughed shortly. 'I truly didn't believe I was. I spent most of my life convincing myself that I wasn't and resenting him for wanting to turn me into someone like him. Plus I always thought of him as a complete shit. I used to comfort myself by thinking that my real dad was some great guy who'd been shipped somewhere else simply because he'd loved my mom.'

'The guy she had an affair with was sent away?' Andie looked at him in amazement. 'How? Why? That surely doesn't happen in real life.'

'He left the company,' said Jack. 'With a big fat pay-off.'

'Your father could do that?' asked Jin.

'My grandfather, actually,' said Jack. 'My father took over later.'

There was an edgy silence.

'So how did you move from being an escort to a travel writer?' asked Andie eventually.

'Well, fun though it was, I didn't want to do escorting for ever. Kevin is right about that. It's not a long-term career choice. I'd travelled a lot by then so I got a job with a publishing company and started work on the guides. Eventually that company was bought out by another one.' He shrugged. 'I wasn't sure that I wanted to keep working with them then so I took some time out, which is when I went on the cruise. The concept of the European Twenty Things was to help me decide. It was a compromise that we worked out.'

'Why didn't you want to work for the new company?' asked Andie. 'And why did they agree to you doing the cruise thing instead?'

Jack looked at Cora.

'Because Jack's father now owns the publishing company,' said Cora simply. 'As well as the cruise line.'

Three pairs of eyes stared at Jack, who shrugged again.

'Who the hell *is* your father?' asked Kevin.

'J. Randall Ferguson,' said Jack. 'He's well known at home but you probably wouldn't have heard of him.'

'His name was on the internet,' Andie remembered. 'I saw it.'

'Yes, well, that's good old Pops,' said Jack.

'The company is called Randall Ferguson,' said Kevin slowly.

'Got it in one,' said Jack.

'I didn't associate it with you.'

'Obviously not.' He grinned. 'I wouldn't expect you to.'

'So – Jack . . .' Andie looked at him curiously. 'Are you reconciled with your dad now?'

He squirmed. 'Reconciled isn't really the right word. I still think he has problems. But after a long time working it out, I know his problems are his and mine are mine. Though I'm still not sure about being able to work with him. I thought that he'd deliberately targeted the company because I worked there. Reckoned it was him doing his control freakery thing again. And I told him about the DNA test. Turns out he'd had it done too, a few years ago. Only he decided not to tell me then, because of course he knew about the escort work and everything. He wanted to see how I'd turn out because there was the whole issue of my inheritance and all that sort of nonsense.'

'Inheritance?' Jin opened her eyes wide.

'Does this mean you're not an impoverished beach bum?' asked Andie.

'Afraid not,' he said easily. 'Actually, since Jack Senior decided to cough up some of his loot, I'm loaded.'

'Really?' Jin sounded unconvinced.

'Really.'

'Randall Ferguson is in the Fortune Top 500 companies,' said Kevin slowly. 'It's worth billions.'

'Are you worth billions, Jack?' Jin was staring at him in utter disbelief.

'Well, given that my father is still with us, not billions,' he replied. 'But – put it this way – I certainly don't need to do the escorting any more.'

'Oh shit,' groaned Andie.

'Andie Corcoran!' Cora glared at her. 'Language!'

'Sorry, Ma,' said Andie, 'but you and Jack have made fools out of all of us.'

'Actually, it's Ferguson who's made fools of us,' said Kevin sourly. 'Including you, Cora.'

'Jack never made a fool out of me,' said Cora. 'Of course I didn't know that he had money to burn, but I never thought he was on his uppers either. You were the only one who seemed to think that he was ready to fleece me, Kevin. Well, you and Jin both.' She turned to her daughter. 'You were so scathing when you met him, you clearly thought he was on the make, and then you were all flapping around getting into a panic – and, to be honest, it was funny.'

'We were worried!' cried Jin.

'I know,' said Cora. 'But I was a bit miffed that you seemed to think I couldn't look after myself.'

'So . . .' Andie was still curious. 'What's the relationship between you and Jack? I mean, we thought – and sorry, Jack, but we couldn't help it – we thought Jack was freeloading. Then we thought that you'd hired him—'

'Where the hell did you think that first I'd have the money and second have the nerve to hire a bloke?' demanded Cora. 'I mean, darling, what sort of a mother do you think I am?'

'I know, I know.' Andie looked at her in distraction. 'It was just . . . oh, bloody, bloody hell, we're such eejits, the lot of us!'

Jack laughed. 'Not really. Like I said to Cora, you care about each other. I suppose when I was growing up I felt that everyone cared more about the business than anything else. My father only wanted me to carry it on. The way I looked at it, he wasn't even bothered whether I was really his as long as I could keep it going. It seemed so creepy to me. Of course, I was nervous about telling Cora everything, but I didn't need to be. She's the most relaxed person I've ever met.'

'I've got to the stage in my life where I'm relaxed about most things,' said Cora. 'Besides, I wanted someone like Jack in my life. He makes me feel—'

'Oh, please don't say he makes you feel young again,' Kevin interrupted her. 'Really, Cora, I would still think you had more sense. You know what people must think when they see you with him. Although, perhaps, knowing his background they might be somewhat more generous in their opinions.'

'D'you know, Kevin,' said Cora easily, 'I couldn't care less.'

'And is this a real relationship?' Jin looked at both Cora and Jack.

'I don't know,' Cora answered. 'I care about Jack a lot and I know he cares about me. But there are difficulties. Not least the fact that I'm old enough to be his mother!'

'If you love each other it doesn't matter,' said Jin softly.

'You're saying that with the knowledge that Jack isn't the broke backpacker you first thought,' said Cora wryly.

Jin shook her head. 'I'm saying it with the knowledge that he's a decent person who did the right thing by me.'

'Thank you.' Jack was taken aback.

'He *is* a nice bloke,' said Andie. 'He was nice to me too, at the Comiskeys' party, when I was very, very *not* nice to him. And later when I was unhappy about something.' She looked at Cora. 'I behaved badly but Jack didn't.'

'You caught me off guard,' said Jack.

'All this is very interesting,' said Kevin, 'and I'm delighted, Cora, that you haven't been ripped off by anyone. But I'm quite horrified, Ferguson, that you led us all up the garden path and that you caused both Andie and Jin some considerable distress in the process. There was no reason not to come clean.'

'You would have treated me differently,' said Jack.

'Of course.' Kevin looked surprised.

'But that's one of my many problems,' Jack told him. 'I hate people treating me differently. I hate them fawning over me because they think I can throw them an extra tip at the end of the day. That's why I bummed around for so long. I don't like lots of trappings, it's not me.'

'There's nothing wrong with a nice house and a decent car

432

and people to look after you if you work hard,' said Kevin frostily.

'That's the point,' Jack said. 'I hadn't worked hard. People did this for me because of my father. And yet as far as I was concerned he might not have been my father at all. That's why I wanted to lead a different kind of life.' He grinned at Kevin. 'Thing was, the travel guides began to do so well that everyone was calling me a publishing genius! They wanted to make me a director of the company. That's when Dad made the bid for it. I couldn't bear it.'

Kevin turned towards his mother-in-law. 'As I said, I'm delighted, Cora, that regardless of what happens with Ferguson in the end, you haven't been put to a whole heap of unnecessary expense.' He looked at Jin. 'The discussion has rather wandered off the point, hasn't it? It's late, Jin. Let's go.'

'I can't,' she said.

'I beg your pardon?'

'I can't.'

'Why?'

'Because . . .' She squeezed her eyes closed and then opened them again. 'Because it's not enough, Kevin. Yes, I do have lots of good things with you. Yes, we've had some great times together. But I've changed. I didn't realise I'd change. I'm sorry. It's not you, it's me. I thought that all the things you could give me were enough. But they're not.'

'Oh, for heaven's sake!' He looked at her in exasperation. 'Your head has been turned by listening to all this stuff from Ferguson. I suppose you think the story of his mother having an affair is romantic instead of a bit sordid.'

'You know, Kevin, I'd kind of ease up on throwing around words like that about my mom,' said Jack.

'I didn't mean it personally,' said Kevin impatiently. 'Now come on, Jin. Stop thinking nonsense and come home.'

'No,' she said.

Kevin's jaw tightened. 'You think you'll find someone else who'll give you a baby? You're living in hope, Jin. Not expectation.'

'I know,' she said. 'But I have to take the chance.' She looked at him anxiously. 'Besides, it's not just about children, even though I thought it was. I just don't love you enough, Kevin.'

'What?'

'I don't love you enough.' Jin's voice was stronger. 'I thought I did but I don't. I love being with you. I love the life we lead. And I do love you. But not enough. I'm sorry.'

'You're not thinking straight,' said Kevin angrily. 'By tomorrow morning you'll have come to your senses. And you'll be banging on the door to get in. I'm not sure that I'll be forgiving, Jin.'

'My thinking is fine,' she told him.

'I gave you everything!' he cried. 'Everything! And you're telling me it's not enough.'

'I'm sorry,' she said. 'I really am.'

'OK.' Kevin looked at her in disgust. 'Whatever you want. Let me know the name of your solicitor.'

Jin watched him as he opened the door to the flat and winced as he banged it closed behind him.

'Are you sure that's what you want?' asked Cora gently.

Jin nodded. 'It was great while it lasted,' she said shakily. 'It really was. But there's more to life.'

'You might feel different in the morning,' said Jack. 'He's right about that.'

'I don't think so.' Jin's voice was a little stronger. 'I know that Kevin was great to me. I owe him a lot. But, like I said, I've changed.'

'He's also right about the fact that you might not find someone else,' said Cora.

'I know,' said Jin with a sudden flash of spirit. 'But let's face it, Mum, if you can find someone like Jack at fifty-eight, there's hope for me yet!'

Cora laughed. 'I didn't mean that there was no hope. Only that it'll take you time to get over this and . . . well, there are no guarantees, that's all.'

'I know,' said Jin.

'But I'm glad,' said Cora. 'I was happy when you married Kevin because I thought he would be the right person for you. And even when I occasionally thought that perhaps he wasn't, I comforted myself with the fact that you still seemed to be happy. All I want is for you to be happy. Both of you.'

'We're pretty all right with the idea of you being happy too,' said Andie, although her stomach had spasmed at the sudden realisation that she wasn't happy at all. That the man who had made her happy was out of her life for ever and that she had been the one to tell him to go.

'You all right?' Jack had noticed the fleeting expression cross her face.

'Yes, sure,' she said. 'A little tired, that's all.'

'Oh God, yes – it's late!' Cora looked at her watch and opened her eyes wide.

'And I have to get up in the morning,' said Andie. 'Some of us are still working gals, you know.'

'Well, I'll have to get a job myself now,' said Jin. 'I can't see Kevin being overly generous. Besides, I don't want his money anyway.'

Andie giggled. 'Jin Corcoran as a commuter. It's not an easy image.'

'Hey, modelling wasn't easy either,' Jin reminded her. 'Very competitive, very cut-throat. I can hack it with the best of them.'

'I know you can,' said Cora staunchly as she put her arm around her daughter.

'I'm in the middle of a girlie moment, aren't I?' said Jack plaintively.

'Sure are.' Cora laughed. 'But come on, let's go. Leave Andie in peace.'

'Do you want to stay here tonight?' Andie asked Jin.

Her sister rubbed her eyes. 'You don't have the space,' she said.

'You could kip down on the sofa,' said Andie. 'It's been done before.'

'I can book into the Morrison again,' said Jin. 'Kevin won't have had time to cancel my card yet.'

'Oh, don't be silly,' said Andie. 'Stay.'

'Are you sure?'

'Sure I'm sure.'

'You can come home with Jack and me if you prefer,' said Cora.

Jin looked at her hesitantly.

'We won't be noisy.'

'Mum!'

'And I do have a spare room.'

'It was the idea of you and Jack . . . well, you know.' She looked at Cora uncomfortably. 'I can't get to grips with it.'

'Neither can I,' admitted Andie.

'We're not at it morning, noon and night, you know,' said Cora.

'It's the fact that you're at it at all,' said Jin glumly.

Cora laughed.

'Well, it's hard,' Andie said defensively. 'You're our mother. He's still the Hollywood Dream God. Worse now, he's a stonkingly rich Hollywood Dream God.'

'Dream God?' asked Jack.

'Your looks,' explained Andie. 'We thought they were movie-star variety.'

Jack grinned. 'I always thought that's why Jack Senior wanted my picture in the corporate reports,' he said. 'I added glamour.'

'Come on,' said Cora. 'Let's go and give Andie a bit of peace. What do you want to do, Jin?'

'I'll stay with Andie,' said Jin. 'If she's sure she can spare the sofa.'

'Absolutely,' said Andie.

'OK.' Cora kissed both of them on the cheeks. 'Why don't you call round for dinner tomorrow evening? Jack can cook.'

'Oh, can I?' He grinned at her.

'Sure can. Make yourself useful.'

'We'd love to come,' said Andie.

'I'll do something special,' Jack promised. 'Right, Cora. Let's go.'

Andie closed the door after them and then leaned against it and sighed deeply.

'What a night,' she said.

'I'm sorry,' said Jin. 'I caused a lot of fuss.'

'Worth it,' said Andie succinctly. 'So much got sorted out.' She looked at Jin. 'Are you all right?'

Jin nodded. 'I feel a lot better,' she said. 'I don't know what it was before. And I do realise things might not turn out the way I want. But I couldn't pretend they would with Kevin either.'

'He isn't a bad person,' said Andie.

'You never liked him,' Jin told her.

'He's not my kind of guy,' agreed Andie. 'But he *was* yours.'

'For a time,' said Jin. 'Then I needed a different sort of person. I'm sorry it's happened like this. It really wasn't his fault.'

'Maybe that's the best a lot of us can hope for,' Andie said. 'To have the right person for a time.'

She swallowed the lump that had come into her throat as she thought of Tom again. He'd been the right person for her. He still was. But their time was up. She clenched her fists tightly and stared into space.

'Andie?'

She didn't hear Jin. She was thinking about Tom. Wondering why she'd made him leave, wondering if, perhaps, she'd made a terrible mistake.

'Andie!'

This time she heard her sister. 'Sorry,' she said. 'What?'

'Is everything OK? You were in a complete daze just then.'

'Oh, sure,' said Andie. 'Fine, fine.' She realised she was using Cora's expression again.

'You don't actually look fine,' said Jin. 'You're very pale.'

'Probably tired,' said Andie. 'It's late and it's been a bit of an ordeal.'

'I know, but . . .' Jin looked at her curiously. 'You seem . . . upset to me.'

'Just because you're happy about how you've worked things out doesn't mean—' Andie broke off. She bit her lip.

'What is it?' asked Jin anxiously.

A tear rolled down Andie's cheek, followed by another and another. And then suddenly she was sobbing uncontrollably while Jin looked at her in horrified concern.

'Andie!' She caught her sister by the shoulders. 'Talk to me.'

'Too much talking tonight,' sobbed Andie. 'We don't need any more.'

'I think we do,' said Jin.

'It's silly. Not important.'

'Why?'

'Honestly.' Andie hiccoughed. 'I split up with someone today too. But really, it doesn't matter.'

'Andie Corcoran! Of course it matters.' Jin pulled a tissue out of the box on the coffee table. 'Who did you split up with? The hot date? The mystery man?'

Andie's smile wobbled through her tears. 'I guess so.'

'Why?'

'Because his wife . . . Oh, Jin, you're not going to want to hear this now. Really you're not.'

'I am,' said Jin firmly. 'And what wife, Andie?'

Her sister blew her nose and took a deep breath. 'I was going out with someone and his wife was pregnant and she lost the baby,' she said.

Jin stared at her. Andie took another tissue from the box and blew her nose again.

'Why did she lose the baby?' asked Jin eventually.

'She's had problems in the past,' said Andie. 'It wasn't her first miscarriage.'

'It isn't your fault,' said Jin. 'It's not like she found out about you and lost it, is it?'

Andie shook her head. 'But I broke it off with him when I found out,' she said.

'Did he blame you?' asked Jin. 'Not that he should have, but did he?'

'Of course not,' said Andie. 'But they needed to be together.'

'Well, yes.' Jin looked at her sympathetically. 'Some women do have problems in carrying a baby to term,' she went on. 'One of Kevin's employees, Tom Hall, is married to a woman who's had a couple of miscarriages—' She stopped abruptly as she saw the expression on Andie's face.

'Not Tom?' She looked at her sister in utter disbelief. 'Don't tell me you were seeing Tom Hall? You couldn't have been seeing Tom Hall!'

Andie nodded wordlessly.

'But Kevin thinks the world of him!' cried Jin. 'And of . . . of . . .'

'Elizabeth,' supplied Andie. 'Lizzie.'

'I've met Tom,' said Jin. 'Lots of times. Elizabeth too.'

'I know,' said Andie. 'I was always terrified you'd put two and two together.'

'How long?'

'Nearly four years.'

'I don't believe you!'

'Since your wedding,' said Andie. 'Well, not exactly since your wedding. I first met him at that. But since the barbecue you invited me to in the hope I'd meet an eligible single guy.'

'And you never said anything, anything at all.'

Andie shrugged.

'All the time I've been asking you about boyfriends and you've been having an affair with Tom Hall!'

'I told you you didn't want to know,' said Andie.

'I don't mind knowing,' Jin said. 'I'm just kind of shocked.'

'Yeah, well, it's over now, so there's no need to worry,' said Andie.

'You've been seeing him for four years and you've just broken up with him and you think I shouldn't worry?' said Jin.

'What's there to worry about?' Andie blew her nose again.

'You, for starters. God knows, Andie, you've been in this relation-ship nearly as long as Kevin and me. And you must have known that it'd all go wrong in the end.'

'It was meant to be a fling. Look, Jin, I really don't want a lecture from you about the sanctity of marriage or anything.'

'You're hardly likely to get that from me,' said Jin. 'And I certainly wouldn't lecture you. I care about *you*, Andie. Not Tom.'

Andie looked up from the pattern on the carpet she'd been staring at.

'Four years is a long time. Especially to keep it a secret. Especially since whenever I met you I gave you grief . . . Oh, Andie. He's a shit.'

'No he's not.' Andie smiled wanly at her. 'He's doing his best in a difficult situation. Maybe one neither of us should have let develop. He's got problems. So has she.'

439

'So have we all,' said Jin. She exhaled sharply. 'Looks like the entire Corcoran family has had a day of upheaval today.'

'I know.'

'But things will get better,' said Jin. 'They always do, don't they? I felt so terrible earlier. And now – now I honestly feel as though a weight has been lifted from my shoulders. I mean, I know that there are problems ahead of me but I'm sure that I can cope with them. I realise I'll have to worry about Kevin and his team of lawyers and about the fact that children are a really important issue for me, but regardless of how it turns out I feel better about it. You'll cope too, Andie.'

'Sure I will,' said Andie. 'I know how to cope. But tonight . . . tonight I just want to cry.'

Jin reached out to her and the two of them hugged each other.

'A bit like the time we were both in deep trouble for covering the kitchen wall with crayon.' Andie's tone was muffled. 'And Dad was so, so angry with us. Remember? He shouted at me that I should have known better. And he shouted at you too. And we both burst into tears and ran up to our room . . .'

'And you told me he'd get over it,' said Jin. 'But we were terrified at the time.'

'Glad we can still tell each other we'll get over things.' Andie lifted her head from Jin's shoulder and rubbed at her eyes.

'I can't get over the fact that your hot date was Tom Hall,' said Jin. 'Gosh, and I asked you to phone him the night of the Comiskey party.' She giggled suddenly. 'Can you imagine what Kevin would have said?'

'It was imagining Kevin's reaction that made us so careful to keep things quiet,' Andie told her. 'And then one day we met Ma and Jack.'

'No!'

'In that Chinese restaurant at the end of Griffith Avenue,' said Andie. 'I was scared out of my wits that Ma would remember who he was and realise . . . I was terrified she'd mention to you that she'd met me with a bloke called Tom and that you'd realise too.'

'I wouldn't have,' said Jin. 'At least I don't think so anyway. And even if I had—'

'Jin, you'd have freaked out. Especially because Tom worked for Kevin. That was what made it so difficult.'

Jin nodded. 'Well, at least Mum doesn't have to know.'

'She probably does,' said Andie resignedly. 'Jack knows.'

'Jack does! Andie, how the hell did he know and I didn't?'

'He guessed. The night of the party when I threw myself at him and made such a hash of it.' She sighed deeply. 'He was nice to me all the same.'

'He *is* nice, isn't he?' Jin frowned. 'D'you believe that he only escorted women to functions and didn't have sex with them?'

'He said he slept with two of them,' said Andie.

'Which is not very comforting when you think of the future.'

'I'm not making any judgements,' said Andie. 'I suppose all of us do things we're not especially happy about . . . it doesn't mean we should harp on about them for ever.'

Jin nodded. 'But I'm still not convinced about Mum and him. Not long-term.'

'Oh well, neither of us has managed long-term either,' said Andie, 'so we can't really get into a knot over her, can we?'

Jin chuckled and then yawned widely. 'Sorry. I'm just so knackered now,' she said.

'Go to bed,' said Andie. 'I'll sleep on the sofa.'

'Absolutely not,' said Jin.

'Do,' Andie told her. 'I'm awake again myself now. I might play the piano for a while or something.'

'Are you sure? You're the one who has to get up in the morning.'

'I'm sure. It relaxes me.'

'OK then.'

Jin padded into the bathroom and then into the bedroom while Andie pottered round the flat clearing things up. After a few minutes she heard the sound of snores and smiled to herself. She'd forgotten that Jin snored, forgotten the impassioned plea she'd once made to Des to extend the house and slap on an extra bedroom so that she could have one of her own and get a bit of sleep. She walked over to the piano and sat down. She thought for a moment and then began to play Rachmaninov's Rhapsody on a Theme of Paganini. The famous piece was seriously romantic. Andie didn't know why

441

she was playing it when everyone but Cora had seen romance spit in their faces, but somehow the music, with its wonderful cadences and softly falling notes, seemed to match her mood.

She jumped as she heard the knock at the door, her heart thudding violently in her chest. Tom, she thought irrationally, for a heartbeat. Now?

She opened the door.

'That was lovely,' said Dominic.

'Oh God,' she said. 'Don't tell me I woke you?'

'How could you possibly wake me?' he said. 'When I was in a frenzy to know what the hell was going on down here! I could see that your sister was seriously upset earlier and then, of course, I heard loads of people arriving.' He looked at her, concern in his eyes. 'Is everything OK?'

'Yes.' She smiled faintly at him. 'Everything's fine.'

'And you?' he asked. 'You're OK?'

'I will be,' she said.

'In that case I suppose I'd better get back to bed,' he said. 'You planning to play any more?'

'Will it keep you awake if I do?' she asked.

'Not especially,' he said. 'But to be honest with you, Andie, if you're going to play I'd rather listen properly.'

'What do you mean?' she asked.

'I could sit down.'

'Here, d'you mean?'

'Why not?'

'Jin's asleep in the bedroom.'

'I wasn't planning on going into the bedroom.'

She paused for a moment and then shrugged gently. 'Suit yourself. But I'll ignore you while I'm playing. You can make yourself a cup of something if you like.'

'I'll just sit here and listen,' said Dominic easily. 'You're really very good.'

She was about to say no, she wasn't, because she'd never managed to tour with the orchestra. But she didn't. Instead she sat down at the piano and flexed her slender fingers.

'Thank you,' she said, and began to play.